ALEX THOMAS survived six winter
irresponsible adventures to bring you
inspired by the strange and wonderful world of season life: the high
heights of delicious fluffy powder fields, the low depths of crevasse
interiors and lots more in between.

She no longer lives and works in the mountains, which is probably the
only reason any of this ever got written down. Still, she can often be
spotted skulking around the Austrian Arlberg and the Swiss Alps, camera
in hand, smile on face.

Alex Thomas is not quite her real name. She is a writer and
photographer and currently divides her time between Dublin and
London, completing a PhD and plotting her escape.

Find out more at
www.warandpiste.com
and at
www.facebook.com/WarAndPiste

WAR
AND
PISTE

ALEX THOMAS

TRAUDL PUBLISHING

LONDON

This novel is entirely a work of fiction.
The names, characters and incidents portrayed in it are the work
of the author's imagination. Any resemblance to past events or to real
persons, living or dead, is purely coincidental.

TRAUDL PUBLISHING
An independently published novel

A Paperback Original 2011

First published in Great Britain by
TRAUDL PUBLISHING

Copyright © Alex Thomas 2011

Alex Thomas asserts the moral right to
be identified as the author of this work

A catalogue record for this book is
available from the British Library

ISBN: 9781849141796

Printed and bound in Great Britain

Dedicated most solemnly to the following:

Ms. A. "With a gun? Is he dead?" Aldridge
Ms. P. "Seriously, Mum, I did not do any of those things" Campbell
Ms. P. "Is there anything to be said for another spreadsheet?" Courtney
Ms. B. "Most elaborate ever ruse to go on a road trip" Martin

And to the Hedgehiger – a very rare species indeed.

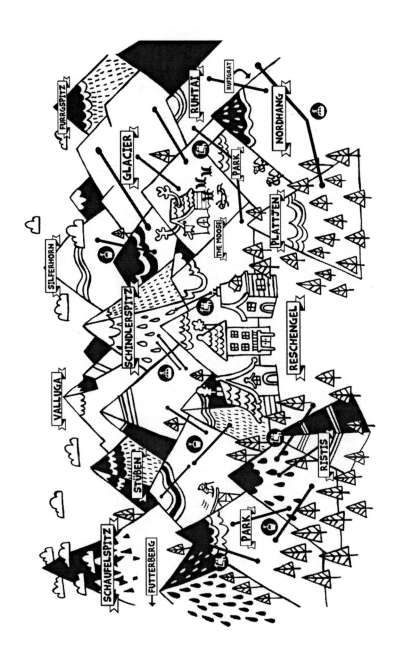

CAST OF CHARACTERS

Snowglobe Tour Ops
Poppy Connors
Rachel Scott
Gina Gibson – Resort manager
Tom, Karl, Temporary Simon – Reps
James Walker – Senior manager
Sarah Datchet – General manager
Liz – Hotels Coordinator

Snowglobe Club Hotel Staff
Suzanne
Carol
Mikey
Harry
Daniel
Tina
Eoghan
Arthur
Dylan
Dick the Chef
Odysseus

Staff for Chalets Elena, Tyrolerhof and Gerda
Antonia
Isadora
Mark
Tilly
Miranda
Joseph

Reschengel Seasonaires & Locals
Jon Berner
Nick Svedberg
Björn 'Head' Jenssen
Anderss – Extreme skier
Pieter – Happy Bar barman
Traudl – Mondschein Café owner
Marco – Rodeo Bar owner
Bella – SuperSki rep
Ed – SuperSki manager
Helen – SuperSki replacement chalet chef
Kat – Diamond Ski manager
Gav AKA Snowli – Ski school mascot
Chrigi – Gav/Snowli's girlfriend
Jan – Transfer company director
Andu – Snowboard clinic coach
Fritz Spitzer – Snowglobe Club Hotel owner
Maria Spitzer – Fritz's daughter
Alex Schneider – Local businessman
Karin, Charlotte, Kerstin, Aussie Ben – assorted seasonaires
and ski bums

Snowglobe staff in other resorts
Anna – Futterberg
Kim – St Anton
Emma – St Anton
Eleanor – Thurlech
Linda – Thurlech

Assorted Randoms
Lily and Kate – Poppy's sisters
Danny – James' friend
Hélène – Harry's girlfriend
Emilie Fournier – French extreme skier
Elisa – Futterberg ski instructor
Louisa and Karsten Bayer – Jon's colleagues at Element

DECEMBER
Mistletoe and Whine

Thursday 14 December

9.04pm. Reschengel Bus Terminal, somewhere in the Austrian Alps.

The first day of a new office job has a certain timeless predictability about it. You have no idea what to wear, and invariably you get it wrong. You then spend the entire day sweating and squirming in your inappropriately casual or formal clothes. Because you are busy focusing on that, the simple instructions given by your colleagues go completely over your head and you make all manner of stupid mistakes, but you can't ask anyone for help or advice because in your nervous state of anxiety you have instantly forgotten everybody's names. It takes about an hour of lip-gnawing indecision to drum up the courage to ask one of your new colleagues to reintroduce themselves, but by then, you have inevitably broken the photocopier and are so worked up by the stress of it all that you don't really listen to what they say and have to ask again fifteen minutes later.

In this way, it gets to lunchtime and your face aches with the tension of bewildered fear, but you still have not actually achieved anything more than the broken photocopier. You bolt off in the direction of the front door with no idea where the nearest café is but so very keen to put as much distance between yourself and that building as is physically possible in the space of one hour that you actually contemplate letting yourself get hit by a passing car just so that you have a good reason to never go back. By this point you're convinced that everybody hates you. Hates you twice over, in fact: first for looking like an idiot, and then for actually being an idiot. They probably do. You might as well embrace it – they've got nothing better to do.

It is infinitely worse to fight it by trying too hard. Of course you want to Make An Effort, of course you want to fit in as quickly and as seamlessly as possible. Some people try to achieve this by Being Funny. This is the absolute worst possible thing you can do. An office is a miniature society, a distinct civilisation in its own right, where interpersonal interactions are governed by highly complex, unspoken social rules. You need to steer well clear of attempted humour for at least the first week – for safety's sake, probably two (and in the communal audience of the coffee room, you need to give it at least a couple of months) – because invariably, even the most intelligent, vibrant and liberal-minded of people will come across as dull, slack-jawed, reactionary homophobic racists. No matter what you mean, however inoffensive, it will – as night follows day – just happen to be the exact worst possible thing to have said to that particular person, and everybody else in the room will make coughing noises and shuffle away, leaving you to your uncomprehending mortification.

If you're lucky, you'll just break the photocopier a few times. Even so, after twenty anguished minutes in the copy room fidgeting in a cold sweat, desperately trying to remember the name of your immediate superior – Jenny? Jilly? Julie? – so that you can call for help *again*, even you will wish you had just gone with your instincts and been hit by that car.

I lost my job in September. In another time and place, this mightn't have been a bad thing. My job – my hated job – was in IT design for the UK headquarters of a consultancy firm, a job I took in my first year out of university, thrilled at the excitement of London, and still have no idea how I spent four years doing. I always knew I'd leave before the eighty-hour weeks killed me (or worse, before they began to seem reasonable); I always knew there was something more interesting out there. Two years ago I would have considered redundancy a reasonably good break, but cardboard boxes on desks are all the rage in the City these days, and all the more so in Ireland where I had gone to university and had thought – naively it seems, for the Unemployed Eighties are upon us once again – that I could always go home some day. In desperation, I looked for work.

A month passed, then two. Rent and council tax, food and electricity began to dance an increasingly delicate waltz on my credit card and savings as I sat all day in my flat with the heating off, shivering over job applications. My boyfriend was already working ninety hours a week on half-pay; there was nothing he could do, even had he been inclined. For longer than I care now to admit to myself, I had been the one keeping afloat whatever it was that we had had, or that we remembered once having. I had been the one pouring energy into maintaining the illusion that work pressure could have done so much damage to us and that it could be undone. Our three years together weighed light against my mounting debt and cheerless uncertainty. We didn't last much into October.

And then came the call from my old employers. They were hiring new trainee associates, would I consider a new job role? Would I come for interview? *Gleeful dance around the living room, screaming silently into the phone.* 'Yes, great, thank you. I'll be there.' *Wearing a houseplant on my head and singing show tunes if you'd asked me to.*

It went well. It went surprisingly well, considering I have the business acumen of a spoon and had never, even in my darkest days in computer programming, ever contemplated selling one hundred and twenty hours a week of my life to the grim world of consultancy. Still, needs must. A job was a job, even corporate slave labour, and fortunately – in spite of my almost comical inability to lie – they mistook my desperation for passion and asked me to start at the beginning of December. A week later, they said January, possibly February. A couple of weeks after that, they confessed it would be September of next year, 'guaranteed' and sent me a cheque for four thousand pounds.

'Oh my freaking GOD,' said Rachel, 'it's a sign, Pops. *IT'S A SIGN.*'

I had thought it was a sign that I need to find a one-year IT contract somewhere in London, and that I'd more likely be stuck tripping from temp job to temp job. I had been glum at the prospect. *Same shit, different Tube stop.* And all those gut-twistingly awful first days…ghastly prospect.

Rachel however, leaping up and down on a sofa in her Snowglobe staff chalet in Austria, had different ideas. It is for this reason that I am standing where I am standing right now: at a deserted bus station, fourteen hundred metres up the side of an

Austrian Alp. It is just after eleven o'clock, and between the hulking dark silhouettes of mountain peaks, the sky is a dusty mass of light, more stars than darkness, the like of which I have never seen.

The coach that brought me from Salzburg has vanished once again into the bitter cold of the Alpine air, leaving me here with my suitcase on the slick ice of the asphalt coach park, empty but for the small, violently peroxide-bleached blonde woman pacing up and down in front of me barking instructions into a shiny pink mobile phone. The mass of bangles on her wrists jangles noisily as she gesticulates wildly with a cigarette, struggling to help the unknown caller locate a key-ring in, it appears, an Alp-sized mountain of similar key-rings.

'One minute,' she mouths at me yet again, her face twisted into a pained expression of long-suffering forbearance as she casts her eyes to heaven. *The trials of working with idiots, eh?* 'Yah, sweetie, yah,' she drawls, her voice an odd blend of throaty and raspy, with an English accent I can't quite work out – somehow posh and horsey, and yet also Essex. 'No, *under* it. The big one. No, that's the one for the Gerda. Does it say "Gerda" on it? Yah, that's for the Gerda then. It should say "Tyrolerhof". Yah, "Tyrolerhof." Mmm-hmm. Green, no blue, I think.'

She pauses and nods into the phone, muttering something incomprehensible as she lights a new cigarette from the stub of the old one. The temperature is about minus eighteen degrees and I am trying to be as subtle as possible about blowing into my hands to stop myself losing all circulation in my extremities. I can't help but stare – a little hypnotised, possibly – at the trailing light of the cigarette that she is twirling about with the grace of an Olympic rhythmic gymnast. I am very tempted to ask her for one just so that I can huddle around it for warmth, but I think this might not be the best first impression to make on my new boss. From the way she is sucking air through those Camel Extra Strengths, I sense she is not a person who would appreciate the casual wastage of a single one.

The lights of the village of Reschengel lie nestled up the valley to my left. I can hear the vague strains of dance music on the night air, though I can't quite make out what is playing. The mountains rise high above us, higher and more imposing than I had expected. Far away toward the end of the valley where the moonlight catches the glacier, I can just about make out the white glow of snow and ice.

So this place that I laid eyes upon for the first time eighteen minutes ago is to be my home for the next five months. And this extraordinarily tanned blonde woman pacing back and forth before me must be Gina, the resort manager and the person in charge of turning me from the blank canvas of recent recruit to super-efficient ski rep in the single day before I am unleashed on the guests. The man in Snowglobe Holidays' headquarters in London where I signed my contract on Wednesday told me to expect to be met by the resort manager, Gina, who would, I was promised with a strangely sympathetic pat on the shoulder, 'get you up to speed in no time, don't worry. Oh, and I won't bother sending you out with a uniform. The girl you're replacing is about the same size as you. You can use hers.'

'Why, if you don't mind me asking, did she quit?'

'Oh,' he said, waving vaguely, 'some sort of misunderstanding, no doubt. All I know is that she was moved to another programme in the French Alps. Maybe Recruitment got her placement wrong. Anyway,' his smile was slightly unnerving, 'her loss is your gain, eh?'

It sure is. Rachel couldn't believe her good fortune. She happened to phone me to moan about her colleague's departure about an hour after I got the news that the McIntyre job wouldn't start until next year. 'Oh, my days,' she squawked excitedly when I told her, 'I have the most *AMAZING* idea.'

How she engineered it all in the space of literally five days is beyond me, but one entirely token phone interview later, there it was in my email inbox: a job offer from Snowglobe and a boarding pass on a flight to Salzburg, leaving two days later. In return, it was the least I could do to pack up my flat, get rid of my car and take a pair of scissors to my Oyster card (prematurely, as it

17

happened – I forgot I still had to get to the Gatwick Express, curses). Remarkably, not one of my family members so much as raised a questioning eyebrow. My twin sister Lily practically shoved me through airport security. Her long, heartfelt speech about how proud she was that I had stopped letting my time slip by, waiting without any idea what for, that I was finally *doing* something, was I suspected more about her delight in the holiday-visiting opportunity of a sister in the Alps than my personal growth, but I hugged her tightly nonetheless and promised to love every moment.

Rachel, bless her suspicious mind, was on the phone to me every day. 'I can't believe you're *actually coming*,' she said last night. 'I can't believe I get to keep you for *five whole months*. My word, Poppy Connors: London escapee. How long has it been?'

'I think it was…'

'No, actually I take it back, shut up, say nothing. We'll catch up in person when you get here. For now, you just focus on getting here. And getting KEEN. Please don't forget my mini Dairy Milks and my cheddar. Especially my cheddar. I can't believe those security bastards at Heathrow. I mean, come on. Who would waste half a kilo of Seriously Strong on a bomb, for heaven's sake?'

'I'd pity the fool.'

'I know, right? I don't think much of their terrorist profiling. But it's all rectified now that you're coming out. I'm beside myself, Connors, *beside myself*. So don't you dare miss that flight or I will hunt you down and have you maimed.'

'Got it.'

'Good. Oh, and one other thing – get lots of sleep tonight. You'll need it. It's going to be an epic five months, lady friend. Just you wait.'

Just you wait. I turn my face to look back up the valley to where a black, rocky ridge snakes its way from the peak of one mountain right down to the tree line. A shiver runs down my spine at the sight and I can't help but hug my arms tightly to myself. It's partly the Arctic-like chill, admittedly, but mostly it's the delicious anticipation of the snow: the powder bowls, the tree runs and the deserted, immaculately groomed perfection of first-lifts corduroy piste. It's knowing that the mountains are within reach, that soon I will be back on my snowboard for the first time in what feels like a lifetime; and getting to stay for a *whole winter* in one of the best resorts in the Alps before going back to the grind. I say a silent thank you to McInytre for their recruitment screw-up; this is surely the best way imaginable of killing time. I just can't quite believe it, staring at the mountains around me in all the vastness of their potential. It is almost too wonderful to be true. I haven't even got first day fear. Tomorrow will be low-key, a world apart from first-day coffee room hell and mass introductions. And, with my orange, yellow and bright blue striped uniform and solid company-issue black boots, I don't even need to worry about what to wear. Bonus.

Provided I still have feet by then, of course, which is not guaranteed. My lungs hurt from the frozen air. I glance over at Gina. She is pacing further and faster now, listening intently to the unknown caller, frowning and saying very little, aside from intermittent bursts of 'yah?…mmm?…go on…yah, yah?' and then 'noooo? *NO. Really?*' interspersed with a strange noise that is half laugh, half hacking cough as she stamps her feet. 'No! Really? Noooo! In a bathrobe! Haw, haw, haw! Go on…'

I think she may have forgotten that I exist.

She glances over some considerable time later. By this point, I've given up on poise and patience and am outright hopping from frostnibbled foot to frostnibbled foot, wondering how many toes I have left and how many have already withered into gangrenous black stumps. I don't know if it is the gentle suggestive power of the hopping or the pain on my face, but either way, she nods sympathetically at me, motioning with her cigarette to indicate that she is winding things up.

'Yah, right, look, I'll be there in half an hour or so. Just picked up the new rep and I'm dropping her off to staff accomm first. Well, yes I know, but I won't be long. Keep looking and let me know if you… Oh, you've found it? You see it? "Tyrolerhof," yah.

T-Y-R-O-L-E-R-H… No, sweetie, that's for Tensinghof, and that's not ours. No. Try *under* it. Uh huh. Yah. Blue, or maybe green. Not sure. Well, no, not there.'

And so on. I tune out.

As of forty-three minutes ago, I am a seasonaire, whatever that means.

Later.

'Err, Poppy? A word, please?'

I had more or less just heaved my bags up the steps of our staff accommodation – about which divey hellhole more later – and been ambushed by Rachel.

'*POPPAAAY!*'

'Oof. Hello, Rachel.'

'Thank *God* you're here. I've been doing my nut the past few days. Gina is insane and Karl is a weirdo.'

'Who's Karl?'

'The other rep. He's around somewhere, I just finished hotel visits with him. Whatever. Here you are!' She gripped my shoulders, beaming at me, all porcelain skin, shiny copper hair and buzzing energy. 'Like, actually, literally here. It's unbelievable, Connors, genuinely unbelievable. Well done, McIntyre, you *douche-*faces. For once, I am unequivocally in their debt. Right, let's get you unpacked and over the road to Happy Bar. You look like you need a drink. All our other flatmates are still at work in the Club Hotel. They'll pop in and say hi when they're…oh. Hi, Gina.'

'Hello, sweeties. Err, Poppy?'

In retrospect, I can see that I should have been instantly suspicious of anything that would make Gina smile at me in that open, friendly and inviting way and beckon me back downstairs to her apartment like Gretel to the gingerbread house, saying 'I have a favour to ask, sweetie…' Gina does not use the word 'favour' to imply any element of choice, I have learned. I followed her in. In the living room, the other rep, Karl, was hunched over on the sofa watching *CSI: Miami*, a slightly odd-shaped lump of a man who refused to make eye contact. Gina patted his shoulder comfortingly and they both turned to look at me.

Still later.

Disbelief. Other Rep Karl can't ski. He forgot to tell anyone in Recruitment that he injured his knee two months ago playing rugby and isn't allowed to do any kind of sport until February. 'That's awful, you poor thing,' I said, wondering why on earth he had signed up for this job at all and feeling terribly sorry for him; terribly sorry, that is, until I realised why they were telling me this – they need me to ski guide tomorrow.

'Ski?'

'Yes, sweetie. No snowboarding. It's in the brochure.'

'Guide?'

'Uh huh.'

'Tomorrow?'

'*Yes*, Poppy.'

Where to begin with all the reasons this simply could not be? 'Err, Gina,' I smiled apologetically, 'I've never skied beyond the snowplough-turns stage.' I had tried skiing once before as a teenager, but since Rachel got her board-obsessed mittens on me in our first year of university I hadn't looked back. I wasn't even sure I could remember how to turn a pair of skis anymore.

Of course Gina was not interested in such details. 'Oh, well!' she beamed as she wandered into her kitchen.

I waited for the rest, but that was it – it was sorted as far as she was concerned. 'But Gina,' I followed her, trying to hold my voice in check, 'I can't *ski*.'

'No problem, you'll deal with it, yah?' She opened her handbag, fishing around in it, pulling out her cigarettes and lighter. 'You have a few days. You can pick up your skis from the shop tomorrow and go up the mountain to practice. Here's your pass, in fact,' she said chirpily, handing it to me before casually dropping the next bombshell. 'Yah, actually,' she tapped a cigarette against the carton once, twice, 'that's the other thing. Jan, the new regional director of the coach company Snowglobe uses for airport transfers is visiting Reschengel tomorrow and I've told him you'll show him around. He's very sweet. You two will have lots of fun. He's a great skier, too. Ooh, he might give you pointers!'

I blinked, horrified. 'Wait, wait. Do you mean I have to *guide* him around the resort ski area? On skis? Tomorrow morning? Gina, I've never even been up there.'

She regarded me disinterestedly through half-closed eyes while

22

she made smoke rings in the air and poked at them with her finger. 'Err, two words, yeah? "Piste map", haw haw.' Her laugh slid into another hacking cough. I waited.

She can't be serious.

I waited some more. She *was* serious. She couldn't be, but somehow she was.

There had to be another way. I made a desperate face. 'Hey, how about *you* take him skiing? I mean, you told me earlier that you've been here for eleven years. You know the place so well and you actually know this guy, Jan. Would you not maybe prefer to…? I mean, just for a couple of hours…? I could…'

I trailed away into silence as she exhaled sharply, ground her cigarette into a seashell of over-spilling ash and butts and turned to me, her eyes narrowed and her face flushed with irritation.

'I,' she said, drawing her clipboard to her chest and squaring her shoulders at me, 'have far too much paperwork to do. How on earth can *I* go skiing during resort set-up? We're only a week into the season, for God's sake. Don't you realise just how much work the chalets are? And how long it takes the hosts to get oriented and get their order systems sorted, maintenance problems fixed? Welcome packs? Departure arrangements? Inventories? Sales targets? Supplier confirmations? And that's before all the staffing work. I have personal development reports to file on each and every one of you, discipline monitoring checks…oh, the list goes on forever. You have no idea, Poppy, none, for heavens sake.'

True, I thought, but it couldn't all need to get done tomorrow morning, surely? *(Also, how much paperwork is it possible for one company to produce??)* 'Well, maybe I can help, Gina. There's got to be something I can do. You know, some paperwork I can take over for a few hours to give you a time to…'

'Hah! Pah! Hah!' She rhymed in this way for some time, then patted my shoulder with a smile of patient condescension and changed tack. 'Look, not being funny, yah? But I think you would be in a little over your head. I mean, what I do, it's…' she searched for words, her hand on her chest, 'it's a holistic responsibility, you know what I mean? I'm never just thinking about one task or another that just anyone can do. It's about the *system*.' She was really feeling this. 'I haven't taken a day off in years. Yes, Poppy – *years*. Do you know why? Because there are people out there who *depend on me*. They need me to be constantly there, understanding, knowing, sensing. They are my responsibility, yah? I mean, this job is not a science that comes with a set of instructions; it's all about feeling. It's...it's about...really knowing, you know?' I didn't, but I nodded, hypnotised. 'I *never* let myself get out of touch with even the smallest thing. Remember that, Poppy – I know *everything* that goes on in this resort. Every. Single. Thing.' Her eyes bulged, staring at me, and I nodded automatically, unsure of why. She smiled, satisfied, as she patted my back rather forcefully toward the front door. 'You young ones, I really envy you, truly. Go skiing. Learn! Grow!' She sighed a smile. 'You are just so lucky that you are not me.'

On that we agreed, though I suspect not about precisely why.

Friday 15 December

8.25am

This will totally be OK. Got skis. Got map. In lift queue. Feeling totally fine. Completely. Even – tentatively – a little excited. Snow! Snowy mountains!

And this Jan guy will be fun, I'm sure. We'll cruise about, have a relaxed time, grab a glühwein or two. Feeling good, feeling good.

9.05am

The signs are bad. We're on the gondola lift and Jan (who showed up to meet me wearing actual Spandex – *Spandex?*) casually lets slip that he is some sort of Austrian national champion of downhill racing or something, and that he has not yet been skiing this season so he's itching to get on the piste.

'Grr…you know the film *Top Gun, ja?* Ha, ha! *Ja, ja,* I will be Maverick, *ja?* You can be Goose. Come *onnnn!* Woo! "I feel the need for speed!" Woo! High five!'

By the way he keeps looking out the window, twitching, growling, clenching his fists and whispering 'need for speed,' I think he means it.

Doesn't Goose get killed? Yes – in a gruesome, bloody explosion of broken bones and guts and stuff, trying to eject.

I might in fact be in over my head.

10.16. Below Furggspitz, somewhere between humiliation and blind panic.

Blue slope? *Blue slope??* I think not.

Goddamn it, pockets full of snow. Now the piste map is now in three pieces. Where's the…? Right, yes, this *is* a blue squiggly line. Bollocks. But where does it go? Is that lift symbol up or down from here?

Three hypothermic minutes pass and I'm no closer to deciphering this soggy, disintegrating piece of incomprehensible fiction. I stuff it back into my pocket, infuriated. I wipe the snow from the inside of my goggle with a wet glove, fizzing with anger and frustration. I was fine for the first bit, making my way slowly down the piste, getting my legs together. Then we hit a windblown, nasty mogul field. Now I'm stranded about two hundred metres below the top station in the midst of a sea of dinosaur eggs made of rock and ice. A little outside my comfort zone, it pains me to admit.

Argh.

Spandex Jan is long gone. Utterly disgusted with me, he disappeared off down the piste about twenty minutes ago in a swish, swish of slick, impossibly bendy skiing and flying snow.

OK, *focus, Poppy*. You just need to get moving and turn around the bumps. Just need to get moving. And keep skis parallel, yes. Oh, this is very strange.

Right, need to get moving, speed is your friend, speed is your fr…Arrgh…*ohh, pain*…

Saturday 16 December

11.50am

It took me three attempts to heave myself up into a sitting position this morning. I spent rather too much of yesterday landing on my face, it seems. Everything hurts, to varying degrees and with almost no exceptions. Arms, from digging myself out of deep powder snowdrifts (who knew it was so much harder on skis?), stomach muscles (by God, this is a more physical sport than snowboarding), feet (bloody rental boots) but most of all, thighs, due to descending about fifteen hundred vertical metres in the snowplough position with only one ski pole.

Actually, I take that back. Pride is the most bruised of all. When I finally caught up with Jan again yesterday, it was hours later. He was having a cigarette with Gina outside her apartment.

'Poppy, Poppy, Poppy,' chided Gina, 'couldn't keep up, eh? Tut, tut, tut. Taking it easy! Really, Jan, I'm going to send through a recommendation to the General Manager today that in future, people who let themselves be hired as ski guides do at least basic physical fitness tests prior to coming out here.'

Jan nodded his firm agreement. '*Ja*, and I think you would benefit from some ski lessons too, Poppy! Ho, ho,' he chuckled, 'You know, I would think you should able to fucking parallel turn. It is quite basic, *ja*? I know skiing is more difficult for you women, especially you English girls. You come here as hockey players and rowers and dog walkers, *ja*? Obviously you can know nothing about the mountains and the altitude, but, hey, the Austrian ski school is very good and maybe...' he trailed off with a shrug.

There were so many objectionable clauses there, I couldn't pick one to react to and just stood there, sort of sputtering. Gina frowned at me.

'You should have called me, Poppy. If I had known you were struggling, I would have come up and taken over from you. Poor Jan got a bit lost! He nearly missed the last lift up from Stüben. That would have been an expensive taxi ride home. Really, I sent you with him for a reason. It's a big ski area, you know.'

'No, I don't know, actually,' I responded through gritted teeth, gripping my one remaining ski pole and thinking about running her through with it. *Jan* got a bit lost? I nearly broke myself careering down the mountain after the little tosspot. They were both due a large piece of my mind and they were going to get it.

Gina sensed that I was about to go on and suddenly lunged forward, grabbing my wrist and breathing dramatically, 'DID YOU HEAR about Karl?'

I hadn't. 'What about Karl?'

'He quit.'

I was stunned. Jan's smirking face was forgotten. 'How? When? *Why?*

'I know, I know. Mmm. Disaster.' She didn't actually look that concerned.

'But, when is he leaving? How much notice did he give?' By this I meant: who would the company find to replace him? And what if he only worked two weeks' notice? That only took us up to New Year's Eve, and Rachel and I would be stuck with hundreds of guests between the two of us. I couldn't even imagine how that would work.

'Oh, that's just it. He's left. Vanished last night and no-one noticed.'

'*What??* He's *gone?*'

How could he just be gone? It was Friday. How on earth could we replace him by Sunday??

'I know. He must have taken the last train out. He just upped and left, imagine that! He left his company phone wrapped up in a note under the pillow.'

'What did the note say?'

'Something like, "I'm sorry, I can't go on here, I hope you understand. It's nothing you did, it's me. This is all a bit too much. Goodbye."'

Crikey. That sounded a little dark, surely? I had to ask: 'Gina, are you absolutely sure that he's left resort and hasn't, you know, chucked himself off a bridge or something?'

Gina looked startled. 'Ooh, I didn't think of that.' She considered it a minute. 'Oh, wait, phew! No, can't have. He took his stuff with him. Ha, ha. Imagine.'

'But… but what are we going to do on Sunday?'

Gina gave a little wave that suggested she had it all in hand, lit another cigarette and got back to her far more interesting conversation with Jan about how, really, you just cannot get the staff these days.

Is this normal, I wondered, trudging up the steps to the staff accommodation, to lose two of three reps in the first two weeks? How does Snowglobe manage that kind of turnover? And how would we run airport transfers tomorrow?

Transfer day, I have been told (over and over and over and over again in the past two days) is 'like, no laughing matter, yah? I mean, you *will* crumble under the pressure, so it's OK to cry, but like, not in front of the guests. And if you let us all down on lift pass targets, it comes out of your pocket. Just, you know, FYI, honey,' she added, squeezing my arm and making a face that was more teeth than smile.

Even with Karl, transferring all those guests up and down to the airport would have been enough of a logistical challenge.

Without him, it'll be a nightmare. I really could not understand how Gina was so very relaxed. She just kept saying last night in a bafflingly calm and serene way, 'look, relax. It'll be fine, yah? It'll be sorted.'

Carol, the Club Hotel massage and beauty therapist, shed some light on this today when Rachel brought me around to her apartment to introduce us. 'Oh, that's simple, Poppy. She's waiting for James, God of the World, Lord of Austria, to descend from on high and save her.'

'Who?'

'James Walker. You'll meet him down at the airport tomorrow. He's the country manager for Austria and Gina's boss. He is *her hero*,' Carol whispered and mock-swooned, inhaled deeply from her cigarette and went on matter-of-factly. 'Actually, it's not so much a case of hero-worship as stalker-love. I think she has Glenn Close potential. James is a few years younger than her, about twenty nine or something, and she pretends to be big-sister protective of him but it's a lot creepier than that.'

I was intrigued. 'How so?'

'Too many ways to count. Probably the worst in recent times was the photograph incident last spring.'

'What happened?'

'Well, early in the season James got wind that Kev, one of the reps, had been a photographer back home. Football matches and weddings and all that. Of course, he became all matey with Kev and got him to bring his camera up the mountain. James fancies himself as a bit of a "backcountry shredder", you see. He even made a stab at going pro when he was younger.'

'Wow, cool. Did Kev photograph them?'

'Yeah, Kev went up with them quite a few times during the winter. He showed us a gallery of shots one day. They were wicked, to be fair – big airs, cliff-drops, glacier stuff, that sort of thing. James asked that Kev send them off to the skiers' sponsors, but Kev wasn't the most organised and he just didn't get around to it off for ages. At some point, Gina overheard a conversation between them about it. She said nothing to Kev – not a word –

but one day, she snuck into his room, broke into his computer and copied every picture he had ever taken of James. Then she put them on her laptop *and* on the desktop computer in her office as a continuous-run screensaver. James came over one evening, walked into her place and saw the screensaver running on both computers simultaneously. Of course he got arsey with Kev about it, but poor Kev didn't know what the hell was going on. In the end, Gina came up with this ridiculous story about how she had found a laptop, thought it was hers, plugged in her USB memory stick and somehow all the images on his hard drive "accidentally" copied themselves. It was about as believable as her CV – '

'Her CV?'

'Has she not told you about her degrees in Law and Economics, her years in the Peace Corps and the Qantas plane crash in Laos that she rescued two hundred passengers from? No? What about her stint in Kuwait during Desert Storm? Oh, you have a lot to look forward to. Anyway, aside from being massively creeped out, there wasn't really anything James or Kev could say.'

'Hmm. So she is actually, properly mental.'

'Of course.' Carol looked surprised that I might even ask. 'How do you think you got this job so easily?'

'I thought it was because I spoke German.'

Carol's smile was one of mild pity.

'Sorry, Poppy.' Rachel smiled apologetically. 'Look what I've got us both in for. I swear when I met her I genuinely thought she was just a bit over-zealous. But then she made me stay in for three hours the other day helping her inventory her Sylvanian Families collection and spent the whole time going on about James. I thought he was her ex-boyfriend or something. Seriously, how have you put up with her for four seasons, Carol?'

'I don't have to.' Carol stubbed out her cigarette with a smirk. 'She's terrified of me.'

I told her about my ski guiding experience with Jan. She made me feel a little better by telling me that Jan was not in fact a top Austrian downhill ski racer, but rather a former member of the under-16 synchronised ski team. And they never won anything.

Later.

A temporary rep has been sorted out to cover Karl this week. Enormous relief all round when Gina told us that snippet of news this evening. His name is Simon and he'll meet us at Salzburg airport tomorrow.

'How long do we have him for?' asked Rachel.

'Just the week, unfortunately. He's needed back in Söll after next Sunday so hopefully James will have got Recruitment to send us someone new by then. Ooh, right, that's the other thing I need to tell you about tomorrow…*James*,' she breathed, 'is the Country Manager for Austria. He'll be down at the airport tomorrow and every Sunday. No Rachel, you didn't meet him last week but you will definitely see him tomorrow. Sooo, I want you both to make sure,' – and she said this very sternly – 'that your uniform is absolutely spot-on and your hair is neat and tidy. No sunglasses, no hats, no gloves. He will check.' We nodded dutifully. 'When he calls you, go *quickly* to him and find out what he needs. Anything he asks you to do, anything at all, jump to it immediately and get it right first time. If he asks for coffee, it's black with one and a half sugars, and be super-quick about it, yah? He really hates inefficiency and he has no patience for idiots. Believe me, you do not want to get on the wrong side of his temper.'

'Ooh, he sounds like a deliciously strict schoolmaster…Mmm!' Rachel giggled. 'Does he, like, spank us if we're bad?'

Of course after what Carol said, we had spent a happy hour thinking of ways we could use this information to wind up Gina, beginning immediately.

Gina's face flushed a little and she said with quite convincing outrage, 'Rachel! James is your *area manager* and he is a *professional.*'

'Mmm, but is he fit?'

'Fit? Oh, well, really…I mean,' she flapped a little, trying to compose herself, 'I… well, *I* don't see it, but I don't really look at him that way. He's my friend, you see, as well as my boss. Well, actually,' her eyes opened wide, 'we're very close, James and I. He lives over in the next valley; you know the resort of Futterberg? Yah, he's based there but he comes over here quite a lot. To see

31

me, you know.'

Rachel gasped, hand to her mouth. 'Oh, Gina, you should get him to come over some evening soon. We would *love* to get to know him.'

'Oh yes!' I chimed in. 'What a great idea, Rachel! You have a spare sofa bed in your living room, Gina, maybe he'll stay over?'

'Girls! What has gotten into you two? You haven't even met him yet.' Gina shook her blonde head in baffled exasperation but we could see the wheels in her head turning slowly over this prospect. 'OK, look, we'll see,' she said after a moment with a great sigh of reluctance. 'He is a very serious sportsman and he isn't really into the partying side of things but I'll tell him how much you want to meet him properly and maybe he'll come over.'

Rachel clapped her hands excitedly. 'Oh, *do*, Gina. I never got to know any of the French area managers in any of my other seasons. They didn't have anything to do with chalet hosts. None of them were serious sportsmen either, mmm. Hey, Poppy, maybe he'll give us pointers? Wouldn't it be *so* much fun, hanging out with a real pro? What do you think, Gina? Us girls and your James!'

Gina blinked and gave out a high-pitched little laugh. 'He's hardly *my* James. Although,' she clutched my elbow and leaned in conspiratorially, 'we do have these nicknames for each other. Don't tell anyone, but I call him Lord Walker and he calls me Princess Angelina.'

She giggled. I thought I might be ill. Even Rachel was silenced by that. Gina's phone started to ring just then, mercifully, and she turned to head out the door. 'Anyway, early to bed, ladies, big day tomorrow. Remember, don't make me look bad!'

She said it with a breezy tone, but the undercurrent was *make me look bad and I will fucking have you.*

Sunday 17 December, Transfer Day.

3.15am

Our alarm clocks went off like air-raid sirens at twenty to three this morning. By 0300 hours we were lined up in Gina's apartment for a bizarre military-like uniform inspection. She tut-tutted as she tucked in our stray shirttails, straightened our jacket collars, combed back our hair from our faces and made us brush every speck of dirt from our boots, all of which was a trifle excessive, I thought, and rather pointless, since we were about to pull on beanie hats and wade through several feet of freshly fallen snow outside the door. Still, she was enjoying her role as Major General so we went along with it.

'Right, off we go then!' She handed us both a brown paper bag each as we walked out the door. 'Lunch and snacks, girls. Keep those energy levels up!'

It was rather sweet, actually. She had packed us a chicken salad sandwich, a chocolate bar, an apple and a carton of juice.

In fear that I might somehow have failed to absorb the Transfer Day enormity, Rachel was instructed by Gina to brief me last night yet again on the 'sales sequence': pick up allocated coach and put guests on it. Do headcount. Leave airport. Make a speech featuring the "Sales Sandwich." ("The Sales Sandwich," the explanatory leaflet informs in big, bold letters, "is the core theory behind your personal growth as a valued member of the Snowglobe team. Succeed! Develop! Shine!" 'Ha,' Rachel snorted derisively. 'Why don't they just say, "Sell, sell, sell, you miserable little drones, or we'll sack you?"')

Calculator? Quick check, yes, it is in my bag. Voucher pads, yes. Price list, got it. Exchange rate? £0.82 to the euro. Sorted.

Waiting now at the designated coach stop for the next load of guests to assemble for an 0330 departure. I have been told that as my coach leaves resort I will have to give the first of many coach speeches, informing guests in a pleasantly undulating tone about such things as the transfer time (two and a half hours) and the need to wear seatbelts. Rachel 'Method Acting' Scott has been in character since she woke up this morning.

'Nowww, ladies and gentlemen, please do take a moment to fasten your seatbelts and take note of the emergency exits located to the front and rear of the coach, and the toilet, located toward the centre of the vehicle. The air conditioning panels are to be found overhead, and can be adjusted hot or cold. Please do note that there is no smoking on board and that the transfer time is just under three hours.'

'Well done, Rach, you have it nailed.'

'Thank you, madam, your compliment is duly noted and will be dealt with in the soonest possible time. Please remain seated until the coach has come to a complete stop and the seatbelt sign has been switched off.'

'Do you want a cup of tea from the machine?'

'Teas and coffees will be served in due course, mine will be a double espresso, so please do feel free to walk the length of the cabin to get it for me, at all times being considerate of your fellow passengers.'

'Rachel, please stop.'

'I must advise that I no longer believe this is possible. Please brace for impact and attend to your own mask before dealing with that of a child or fellow passenger.'

'I am going to punch you.'

'Cabin crew, seats please. Seats for landing.'

I need tea.

6.51am. Salzburg Airport Charter Arrivals.

I got down to the airport just after six and dispatched my guests to the Departures area with a cheery goodbye. It was only then, standing vaguely in the coach park watching my coach drive off, that I realised that Gina had only told me about speeches and sales on the coach back to Reschengel – and how challenging the day would be generally – but she had never told me what I need to actually *do* when I got to the doors of the airport. Was this the Main or Charter Terminal? Where would I find my coach? And where, for that matter, were the other reps?

Rachel's phone was engaged and I was absolutely sure I didn't want to try Gina's. After much aimless wandering, I eventually spotted the large glass doors of Charter Arrivals, where inside, I was pleased to see, half a dozen unfamiliar Snowglobe reps were standing around a whiteboard. Rachel had promised to introduce me to everyone when she arrived, so in the meantime, I thought I might as well go about fulfilling my Important Task.

Last thing before my coach pulled out of Reschengel a few hours ago, Gina hurtled up the steps with a sealed folder of some mysterious but highly important resort paperwork.

'Now, Poppy,' she said, 'this is extremely important. Focus. I am trusting you to do this for me the second you get to the airport. Find James and give this directly to him. Only to James, OK? It is very, very important that you don't forget, yah?' She placed it carefully into my hands as one might a donor organ.

I found James' desk tucked in a row of tour operators' booths but there was no-one at it. That was almost twenty minutes ago. I'm still sort of hovering here, feeling like a spare tool, not really sure what to do. Do I wait? I suppose I haven't got much of a choice. I would have gone and chatted to the other reps but they skulked outside fifteen minutes ago with the distinct look about them of a group of people heading for a surreptitious cigarette.

Come back! I feel a bit pointless, standing here all alone in my brightly coloured uniform with my backpack, clipboard, mysteriously sealed folder and paper lunch bag.

Hmm…quite thirsty. Will I have my juice carton now? No, tea. Need to wake up. But there's no café in this part of the terminal.

Dum-da-dumm…

Maybe I'll go and get some tea, and come back. Would that be bad?

I have no idea how far away the nearest cup of tea is though. What if the famous James is expecting this highly important folder right now and I am nowhere to be found? Will this unleash the awful wrath? How scared should I be of this man?

But, really, how urgent is this folder likely to be? It's probably just a weekly report or something. Though it *is* sealed…

I examine it a bit more closely and hold it up to the light. The plastic cover is difficult to see through but it seems to be papers and…a USB memory stick? Ooh, maybe it's a confidential, top-secret report on Karl's disappearance. Maybe there's more to it all than we think and it's sealed because something happened to him that we can't know about. Yes…that went-home-in-the-dead-of-night story was pretty unconvincing. Perhaps Gina was somehow involved in something dodgy?

I think about this a little. But then I can't really imagine Gina having the wherewithal to mastermind some sort of illegal cover-up. She'd only leave a welcome pack, clipboard, fake nail or similar at the crime scene.

Maybe it is some sort of cipher, without which the mighty power of James is rendered useless. Maybe it's something like a set of detonation codes, only not codes for blowing up planes, obviously, but for landing them. Maybe without them all the guests would be left stranded in the air.

Or maybe it's full of photos. Maybe Gina's returning the stolen photos of James. Or maybe they're photos *of her*.

Why, brain, why would you think that? Ghastly mental images. No, no, they won't go away. What the…HeaaAAh!

Later.

Oh dear. Feel quite wobbly.

It was a voice very close behind me, low and deep but startling in the silence of the empty terminal.

'Are you quite all right?'

I nearly jumped out of my skin. 'Jesus! Oh, yes…hi.' He was tall, and standing just behind me, looking down at me like I was a strange curiosity or mysterious creature someone had left on his desk. I realised how odd I must have looked, holding the folder up to the light, moving it back and forth about five inches from my face and squinting crazily at the blurry shapes of text through the opaque purple plastic. 'Errm. Yes. Anyway, ahh. You must be James, I suppose.'

He was not wearing anything that suggested he had any association with Snowglobe, just a pale shirt and dark trousers.

36

But who else would be here at that hour, standing at this desk, accosting evidently confused and over-brightly attired reps and staring at them with silent intensity? And probably not a little judgement.

He said nothing, just raised his eyebrows a little and continued to stare at me. I stepped back a little and held out the folder to him.

'I'm Poppy, by the way. I don't know if you…' I swallowed nervously. He didn't react in any way. 'Well, anyway, I think this is for you, if you're James.'

He didn't take it from me, but stared at me for a few seconds more and then asked 'What is it?'

'I don't know.' The staring was making me nervous and blinky. 'Apparently it is very important and crucial and you must have it as soon as possible or else the universe will come to a swift and gruesome end.'

'It's from Gina, then, is it?'

I nodded. *Good, he must be James, and definitely not some random folder-thief.*

'And you don't know what it is? Really? I was watching you, you seemed to be pretty engrossed in it.'

Shit, how long was he standing there? Mildly mortified – nothing for it but to laugh. 'Err, yeah. I was bored. Gina was a bit,' I waved my hands in a way that suggested crazy manic obsessive, 'about getting it to you. I was trying to imagine what could be so critical to the continued survival of the company.'

'And what did you come up with?'

'Well, I have a couple of theories,' I heard myself say. *Stop talking, Poppy, stop, for the love of God. The man does not need to know.* But his eyes were on me in a very unnerving manner. It was weirdly like being undressed, though obviously as soon as my brain registered this comparison, it was impossible to banish it and so spent I the rest of the conversation trying desperately not to think about him *actually* undressing me. And undressing himself…*oh*. A most irritating reversal of the received wisdom, as imagining the other person naked in this tense work situation was making me talk more, and not less, utter shite.

I told him what my theories were (except the one about the Gina photos, as I am still trying to gouge that one out of my imagination). We both agreed that it was unlikely that Gina could mastermind a covert assassination, and James did not think a lot of the idea that she could have anything at all to do with landing planes.

'She'd get distracted by something shiny and we'd have an air disaster of monumental proportions on our hands.'

'So it *is* just something unspeakably dull like a weekly report. *"On Sunday, I made Rachel climb a twenty-foot flagpole to sort out a wrapped halyard and hoist the company flag. On Thursday, I made everyone do a brochure quiz fourteen times until they all got up to 50%..."*'

'She did not.'

'Oh, but she did. I'm sorry I missed it. It was most illuminating, apparently. *"On Friday, I narrowly escaped an assassination-by-toilet-brush attempt by a mutinous Club Hotel staff..."*'

He laughed. 'I wish resort managers' weekly reports were so honest. No, no, this isn't actually anything like that.' He paused, looked around the empty room to check that no-one was listening, leaned toward me and said very softly in a low, gravelly voice, 'The truth is far more sinister.'

I ignored the little shiver that went down my spine. 'Go on then.'

'I will have to kill you.'

'OK, Danger Mouse, let's hear it.'

'It's...uh...plans. Construction plans. Encoded within a fake resort report.'

I raised a sceptical eyebrow. 'Really...'

'Oh, yes. For my secret lair.'

'You're building a secret lair.' *Ha. Oh, good. Talking utter shite is evidently not a sackable offence here.*

'Yup. Under the Schaufelspitz peak, the mountain between Futterberg and Reschengel, you know it? The really high, pointy one? Always has a cloud hanging around its sides?'

I knew it. It was famously distinctive and towered over the

38

village. 'Good location, I'll give you that. Will you use it for good or evil?'

'Evil, of course.'

'Excellent, there's always far more fun to be had in an evil lair.'

'Indeed. And it's almost done. These plans are for...uh, an extension.'

'Ah, how lovely. One always needs a conservatory, even in a subterranean evil lair. So is it all set up with rocket launchers, nuclear warheads, Thunderbirds One, Two and Three...?'

'Exactly. And stockpiles of proper coffee, Cadburys chocolate, decent bacon, beer kegs, state of the art entertainment system... You know, the essentials.'

'And what will you do with this secret evil lair?'

'Wait until the time is right, like when the snow is rubbish and I'm bored out of my tree, and then set in motion my plan for world domination.'

'Starting with what?'

'Well, Reschengel, of course, and once I have that I'll take over all the other decent resorts in the Alps and cleanse them of terrible skiers and all the snowboarders...' – I kept my mouth shut – '...and then probably bomb the really pointless countries out of existence, bully the important ones, pay off some dodgy ex-generals to be dictators-by-proxy because I can't really be bothered with the details, and sort of see where we go from there. Are you in?'

'I'll think about it and let you know. The genocide troubles me a little, but the rest sounds like fun. So is Gina your partner in crime, then?'

He laughed and shuddered at the same time. 'No.'

'I don't know, James, she could be a convincing Bond villain. Or a Lady Penelope. She'd love that.'

He looked at me like I might be mad. 'Let her into *your* evil lair then. She's not coming anywhere near mine.'

'So how come she had the construction plans then?' I challenged him with a triumphant smile.

He thought about this for a split second. 'Karl was the courier, he made the drop. She knows nothing.'

Damn it, he's good.

Just then, my work phone beeped a text message alert and I came back to reality, back to the room and my senses. It was Rachel, asking where I was and telling me to come to the coffee shop over by the Departures drop-off. I looked up at James again and realised only then that we were standing very close to one another, our hands almost touching as we both leaned on his desk. I was suddenly very self-conscious. I blushed, rather annoyingly, then got annoyed, which always makes me blush even more. I stepped away from him.

'Right, well, eh. Yeah. Best of luck with that, then. I'll let you know my decision in due course. I should probably go now and do something, you know, productive.' He said nothing but nodded, watching me, a half-smile playing on his lips. 'OK, super,' I said and blushed some more – *damn it!* – turned and wandered off in no particular direction, feeling a bit vague.

'Err, Poppy?' I turned around. He was watching me with amusement. 'What are you doing?'

'You know, I have no idea actually. What am I doing? Trying to remember how to get back to Departures, but after that, no clue.'

'So Gina didn't talk you through…?'

'No, not exactly. She pretty much just warned me repeatedly not to do anything, *anything* to annoy you, and to, err, speak only when spoken to.'

He laughed again, the nervous laugh of the stalkee. 'Yes, yes, I am very scary, that's true. OK, head over to the coffee shop now with the others. Nothing really happens here until about nine-thirty, that's when the first big wave of flights land. You're scheduled to be at the airport…' he checked a list on his desk, 'most of the day, aren't you? Good. About nine-fifteen or so, come find me. We'll grab a quick coffee and I'll talk you through the coach allocations so you know who's taking who to the various resorts.'

I nodded. It all sounded pretty straightforward. Guests, flights, casual work meeting over coffee…can do.

'And you can pretty much ignore whatever Gina has told you about me,' he added with a wry smile, his gaze flicking ever so subtly over my face, my hair, back to my eyes as I blinked, trying not to blush any deeper. 'She tends to be…dramatic. Don't ever hesitate to ask if you need anything at all explained to you, OK? Just pop over to my desk for a chat whenever you want. I'll probably just be sitting here, pretending to be very busy and important.'

'While you're actually just planning the interior décor of the evil lair?'

'Exactly. And trying to work out what "ochre" might be.'

Still later.

All a blur of people and noise. Hundreds of people coming in waves through the arrivals doors, many of them looking for us, many for the reps of the eight or so other tour operators using this airport.

Feeling somewhat fuzzy. It's rather fortunate that a trained monkey could do what I am doing right now: holding a large Snowglobe sign over my head and dumbly waving people out the door. Every now and then I glance in his general direction and catch him watching me. It's all a bit teenage, what's going on in my head. Oh, my.

12.04am. Back in Reschengel.

Right. I understand a little better now what all the transfer day fuss and panic was about: it was a bloody pressurised trip back, a two and a half hour flurry of names, faces and numbers, tearing voucher pads, counting lift pass cards, stabbing numbers into my calculator, dropping my calculator, watching my calculator slide around the floor of the coach while I groped uselessly for it and the driver swung the coach violently up the winding mountain roads.

At least it's finished now. Gina and Rachel got back to Reschengel before me and Simon, the temporary rep from Söll, is

41

due to arrive in resort soon on the last coach.

Once we'd handed over all the day's cash and paperwork to Gina, Rachel and I wandered across the road to Happy Bar for a quiet drink to celebrate my first completed transfer. Pieter the barman was most pleased to see us.

'Beautiful English Rachel, a Jäger Bomb?'

'Ahhh, no, not this time, Beautiful Dutch Pieter. I need to sleep tonight.'

'Stroh 80?'

'Good God, no. Never making that mistake again. I nearly had to be resuscitated after the last one of those.'

'Absinthe?' he tried.

'How about a nice glass of wine?'

Pieter sighed – *how very dull* – and poured us two monstrous glasses of red.

Rachel turned to me with a leading 'so…'

I ignored her tone, raised eyebrows and general air of excitement. 'That wasn't so bad, was it?' I said brightly.

'Oh come on,' she said, poking me in the arm, 'you must have noticed! We were all whispering about it. How could you not notice?'

Oh, God, was I really obvious? Was everyone talking about me? Shame, mortal shame… 'Ehh…what?'

'Gina's James, you numpty! Did you see how fit he was? Phwooar. Mmmm, mmm.' She thought about this for a second and qualified it. 'Ok, Not *fit* exactly, I mean, not a face you would say was gorgeous, but there's definitely something about him, don't you think? It's the voice. Or those eyes, they're so clear. Or maybe it's just a *power* thing. Mmm, forbidden lust for the boss, no? Come on, didn't you think there was something sort of quiet, serious, commanding…' She drifted off.

'Shall I leave you two alone?'

'Oh, come on, you know what I mean. He *is* fit, just in a strange way. You definitely would.'

'Would I?'

'OK, *one* definitely would. No? Well *I* would.' She made a face

42

at my noncommittal shrug. 'Poppy, seriously, you must think there is something a little hot about him. You two spent half the day chatting. You were all leaning over his desk, looking deeply at each other...'

'He was explaining coach allocations, Rach, not whispering sweet nothings.'

'Yeah, well I thought Emma and Kim were going to claw your eyes out. Ha, ha, not to mention Gina! If she'd had a voodoo doll to hand, she would *not* have held back, girlfriend. I bet she's holed up in her bathroom right now, furiously slathering on more fake tan... if there is any left in the world, that is.'

'Oh, stop it. Look, I like him,' I said simply. 'He's funny, a nice guy, easy to chat to but, you know, not *that* good looking.' *Just scarily, sexily hypnotic, staring at me all afternoon with sex eyes and making me bubble and melt with desire... Oh God, my inner monologue is a Judith Krantz novel.* 'I just... I didn't really see him like that,' I finished lamely.

'Oh, burn. You're putting him in the Friend Zone. Poor James, he was probably flirting outrageously with you and you didn't even notice. Good thing, I suppose, he'd probably fall desperately in love with you, sack poor Orangina, give you her job and get himself sued for gross unprofessional conduct.' Rachel pondered the relative benefits of this. 'Actually that would be just fine with me, and rather entertaining. Win-win, surely? Are you sure you won't give him even a pity shag?'

I had stopped listening. Where had I heard that sort of expression recently, *I just don't see him like that*?

Christ. *Gina.*

Horrified moment of realisation that I have a massive crush – *massive* – on the same person as my psychotic resort manager.

Oh, crap.

1.32am

Text message. From *James.*

'Made it back to RSL in one piece I hope? Flights delayed, spent whole bloody evening at SZG pretending to be busy and

43

important. Still in car. Long, dull drive home. Lots of progress on lair however. Let me know what you decide and I'll keep you posted…'

Oops, should have had my phone on silent – it's woken the two hotel staff we share a room with. Suzanne in the other bottom bunk jumps up in the darkness, gasping at the sudden noise. Tina, in the bunk above mine, moans a bleary 'whatthefuck? Ugh…' and Rachel, who has just stumbled in from an extended Jägermeister-infused heart-to-heart with Pieter the barman which I had the good sense to escape from early, whisper-shrieks (with more shriek than whisper, although she did try) 'Who the hell is texting you at this hour? Gina? For fuck's sake, that woman needs to be stopped.'

'Eh, no, it's…my sister.'

'Who, Lily? Kate? Is everything OK? Has something happened?'

God, I am such a poor liar. My sister? I can do better than that, and now Rachel is concerned. She has known my sisters for years. 'No, no, everything's fine, Lily's just… out in Dublin with some people I know. I'll put my phone on silent.'

James and I exchange a few texts, mainly mutual sympathy about transfers and earnest discussion about the merits of evil lairs, before I tell him I have to go as I'm in my warm bed and very much looking forward to blissful unconsciousness ahead of another extremely early start.

James: 'Bitterly, bitterly jealous. Am only passing through Täsch now. Still hairpin bends to navigate. Your duty here is probably to keep me awake, you know. Very sleepy…'

Me: 'On balance probably wiser to not distract you with any more texts, surely? Am most concerned at this texting-while-driving thing. Would feel quite bad if you plummeted to your death.'

James: 'Quite bad?? Your compassion overwhelms me.'

Me: 'I'm practicing for world domination…'

James: 'Oh good, you're in then… Sweet dreams, Connors.'

Oh dear. How do I sleep after *that?*

Monday 18 December

10.30pm

No further text messages from James today…hmm. I would like to pretend I didn't spend all day surreptitiously checking my phone, but come on. Of course I did. Not before checking at least three (fifteen) times this morning that I hadn't somehow dreamt our text conversation last night – or infinitely worse, that my subconscious brain hadn't made me imagine a conversation and send him a series of sleep-texts, *cringe*. (Can this happen?? Don't know. It's my biggest secret fear: a more excruciating version of sleepwalking naked as it would involve exposing one's naked *thoughts* – an unquantifiably mortifying concept…)

Whatever. It is irrelevant anyway. I've decided that I was in some sort of altered mental state when I met him yesterday, potentially as a result of being very tired, semi-first day nerves and all that. Perhaps even still suffering from some sort of ski-related head trauma from Friday (evidence: my neck is still very stiff). Obviously, it didn't help that he kept staring at me, but he was probably just curious about what the newest rep was like. Or maybe he had trouble focusing at distant objects or people. It doesn't matter. Even leaving aside the spectacularly unprofessional doomed-to-tragedy-ness of it all (and the nigh-on certainty that the only possible outcome of the slightest hint of reciprocated interest from James would be a scenario in which Gina is standing over my bloodied, ski-pole-impaled corpse, baying at the moon), James lives on the other side of a rather large Alpine ridge, so there is no way I will ever get to know him outside of Sunday chaos in Salzburg. And he probably has an impossibly stunning pro-skier girlfriend who can launch herself off forty-foot cliffs and land effortlessly into three metres of powder, while I am still trying to grasp the basics of remaining upright. These are only the top four reasons why I must erase the entire strange fascination from my brain. There are more.

Fortunately, today was a busy day. Monday in Reschengel always is apparently, when all the recently arrived guests get set up for their first day's skiing. It is our job to make sure this goes as smoothly as possible. For Temporary Rep Simon, this meant taking the ski guiding group. He offered, (having heard about my last pitiful attempt) and I very gratefully took him up on it.

Rachel was sent to bring the Snowglobe Club Hotel guests to the ski school meeting point. Meanwhile I got the job of dashing madly around the chalets distributing the last remaining lift passes, ski school vouchers and equipment rental coupons before the lifts opened at 9am. I was just finishing this job when my phone rang.

'Help me,' gasped Rachel in a strangled voice. '*Help. Me.*'

I found her down by the ski school in the midst of an ocean of colour; bright reds and greens and pinks and oranges, colourful novelty hats and fluttering red and blue flags. Ski school was due to begin in sixteen minutes and Rachel was struggling to remain composed behind her sunglasses in the swelling crowd. I tried not to laugh, but she was as pale as the snow and looked like she was seriously regretting every drop of Jägermeister Pieter the barman had 'forced upon me, Poppy' last night.

'I am going to kill him, Pops. I am going to hunt him down and…oh, hold me.'

I patted her arm reassuringly as she mock-wept into my shoulder and covered her ears against the pounding roar of the particularly beetroot-coloured man behind us demanding that his tantrum-throwing four year-old '*SHUT BLOODY WELL UP OR I WILL GO THROUGH YOU FOR A FUCKING SHORTCUT.*'

And then there was the singing. Into my left peripheral vision swam a large white rabbit dancing his way through the crowd, singing something jolly and bouncy and hopping from foot to foot as toddlers grabbed at his tail, screaming 'SNOWLI! SNOWLI!!'

The bouncing of Snowli's foamy ears was too much for Rachel.

'Is everyone having FUN?' boomed Snowli over the loudspeaker. A hundred toddlers squealed. 'Is everyone feeling GOOD?' OKAAAY!' The music kicked in, high-pitched accordion and drum machine pop blaring from a nearby speaker. 'Let's DANCE!'

47

Rachel made a snorting noise, then instantly regretted it. 'I am going to vomit Poppy. Do something. *Quickly.*'

I fended off the last of the guests, pointing them in the direction of their various classes while Rachel slunk away to die quietly behind the nearest available building. After the crowd had dispersed I found her there, lying in the snow. She was talking to – of all people – Snowli the Rabbit, who was slumped against a railing, his big, white, fluffy head leaning despondently on one hand.

'Ugh, I feel your pain mate,' Snowli was saying in a strong Mancunian accent. 'I'm way too hungover for this shit. We're gettin' old, eh? Alright, Poppy,' he said, noticing me there. 'Got a cigarette? No? Ah, s'alright. How've you been?'

Snowli, it turns out, is called Gavin and apparently we met on Friday night. I say 'apparently' because Friday night is still a bit of a blur to me. After the pain – mental and physical – of my day out with Jan, Rachel thought I needed a pick me up. She brought me into the centre of town for the Bar Cuba season kick-off party where, to celebrate the first big snowfall of the winter, all shots were two euro, including – shudder at the memory – something unspeakably awful called 'Stroh 80'. My memories of the rest of the night spiral into a comfortable blur of names, faces, smiles, bobble hats and baggy trousers, the finer details of which I have no chance of remembering. And now, three days later, this large, talking rabbit was looking at me intently (I assumed, since he was still wearing his Snowli head) and, well, rabbitting on about all the people dancing on the bar that night and the stories people were telling, like the one Rachel told about that summer she got stranded for two weeks in a nudist hippie hostel in deepest, darkest Utah and had to spend the entire time scrubbing mildew out of shower tiles with a toothbrush to earn enough money for a Greyhound ride to anywhere else. I still had no recollection whatsoever of any Gavin in all this until I spotted Rachel mouthing over his shoulder 'The one with the bad facial hair,' gesturing at her upper lip and sideburns area.

Oh, *Gav.* Yes, of course. With the crazy Swiss girlfriend,

Chrigi, who was incredibly drunk and got thrown out of the bar for biting a girl on the cheek and drawing blood. How could I forget? As we stumbled out of the chip shop much later, Gav and Chrigi were having a blazing row on the street, over, as far as I could gather, a rock.

'Yeah, how's Chrigi? Everything OK after the other night?'

Gav was baffled. 'She's fine, why? What do you mean? What happened?'

Rachel was incredulous. 'Mate, you two were screaming at each other about a stone or something. She clawed your face when you called her a whorebag and she kicked you in the shins. You screamed after her that she stank of fish and her mother looks like a man.'

Recognition dawned, I think. His ears bounced as he nodded. 'Yeah, yeah. Mental, eh? Friday night with Chrigi.'

'What, like just-your-average?'

'Oh yeah, standard stuff that. She's a bit wired. Never a dull moment.'

I tried not to have an expression of 'you've got problems' written on my face. Probably unsuccessfully, since Gav looked from me to Rachel and back and tried to explain.

'No, it's just that she gets quite...angry when she's drunk, yeah? That night, she was trying to throw a rock through this guy's window because he owed her money. Thing is, he's her boss and owns, like, most of the resort so it was a pretty bad plan. I was just trying to talk her out of it.'

'Did you manage to?'

'Nah, she did it anyway, but she said I ruined the satisfaction for her, so we're walking past Spar and she chucks an empty gas canister through the display window. It was fucking stupid. They caught it all on CCTV, so Spar sent the police around and she's got to pay sixteen hundred euro for that. And Alex Schneider knows it was her who done his window too, and he's looking for eight hundred euro to replace it.'

'How much did he owe her in the first place?'

'Eighty.'

'Shit.'

'Yeah.'

We paused again, not really sure what to say.

Snowli seemed oblivious. 'Hey,' he said brightly, 'if you're thinking of coming out tonight, Chrigi's sister dropped in a bottle of tequila to commiserate. You two should come over to ours first.'

Rachel's face said 'eject, EJECT.' I just nodded vaguely. 'Yeah maybe, cheers. We've got our welcome meeting in the Club Hotel tonight so we'll have to play it by ear. I'm sure we'll see you out later though. Meanwhile, we should probably run.' I looked at my watch. 'Gina's told us to get back quickly once we're done here.'

Snowli gave a bunny shudder. 'Gina! Man, good luck. I dunno how you lot deal with *that* every day.' He sauntered off, chuckling. 'You poor bastards!'

Rachel and I headed back to the staff chalet, where we spent the rest of the day 'preparing' for our welcome meeting (i.e. Rachel had a nap and I caught up on emails).

Actually, the word 'chalet' is somewhat misleading, I think – it has all sorts of rustic Alpine charm connotations; open log fires, hearty stews and general good cheer – a world apart from the festering death trap we actually live in. The night I arrived in Reschengel, Gina spent most of the journey from the bus station going on and on about our '"ccomm," how old and picturesque it was, how much character and history it had attached to it. Call me cynical, but I thought this sounded ominously like an estate agent describing a three-walled sea of brambles in the middle reaches of nowhere as a 'splendidly isolated retreat from everyday cares and woes,' with 'old world charm' and 'opportunities for revival'.

Cynicism was vindicated when we arrived. We stood outside the dilapidated old pile, me in shocked silence, her in silent awe.

'Oldest building in Reschengel!' she informed me with some pride, as though she had built it herself.

Relax, I told myself. *Most likely wonderfully refurbished inside?*

Wrong – worse on the inside. Our 'chalet' is actually one floor of the building, a simple three-bedroom apartment with a

50

bathroom and a kitchen. By the look of the cheap lino and mouldy green and yellow curtains, it has never since the late Sixties been touched by the benevolent hand of modernity. The company rents it as accommodation for eleven of us: three reps and eight Club Hotel staff. In fact, at a closer look, the three bedrooms are actually sections of one large room partitioned with sheets of plywood and duct tape to separate the two rooms of boys from that of the girls. Our bedroom – the one Rachel and I share with Tina, a hotel host and Suzanne, the Club Hotel manager – is about twelve feet by fifteen, with smelly, disintegrating curtains and two sets of bunk beds.

At least the kitchen is large enough, though partly taken up by an ancient and very suspect-looking yellowish couch. The theme of 'original retro' is continued here too, with walls tiled green and black, and cracked and stained green and yellow flower-print linoleum lifting off at all corners, revealing little holes in the skirting boards which I have wild hope are not what they look like. French doors open out onto a creaky, sagging wooden balcony, which I suspect I will never use, not since I stepped out there on that first evening and the whole thing sort of hiccupped downwards in a most alarming way.

Our bathroom is scarcely better, with a showerhead in the bath and bulging walls where moisture has seeped in over the years and pushed out the tiles. The bath drain does not work either, and Rachel and I learned very quickly that it is well worth being the first out of bed in the morning, or the first to shower coming down off the mountain, since everyone else would be showering up to their ankles, knees or thighs in the progressively deeper, dirtier, soap-scummed water of the previous user.

All rather unpleasant, in short, and a little troubling from a sanitary point of view. Still, what is far and away most worrying is the high probability of death-by-fiery-inferno while we sleep. Two of the three electrical sockets in our bedroom hang out of the wall, with exposed wires and no insulating tape, and the rest of the chalet's electrics are no better. The kitchen light switch gives out little electric shocks about eighty percent of the time (you don't want to be the first to try it after it's stopped doing that for a while), and on that first grand tour, Gina also mentioned casually that it's 'best not to' touch the metal extractor fan when the oven is on because 'sometimes it can give you a small jolt.'

It would all be a lot less alarming if the place were not

1) built entirely of wood and

2) overheated and dried out like a tinderbox.

I've found myself standing in the various rooms of the chalet thinking about fire escape routes more often than could be considered normal in the past two days.

Still, it could be worse; it could be the Club Hotel. It's hard to believe guests are actually required to pay for that accommodation. I had my first encounter with this hideous monstrosity at the welcome meeting this evening. Previously, all I had seen of it was the spread in the Snowglobe brochure, which gives the impression (and the price) of a four-star palace, using candlelight, clever camera angles and roaring log fires to disguise the damp, grimy and generally oppressive air of the place, its windowless walls of poured concrete, buckled linoleum floors and 'muddy vomit' themed brown and orange decor. Eoghan, another of the hotel hosts, described it as 'a Cold War bunker, only dirtier' and Rachel told me that four out of every five guest complaints she had to deal with last week related to the hotel, its freezing bedrooms and the terrible, terrible food dished up by the obnoxious chef, Richard, AKA Dick the Chef.

Rachel, Temporary Rep Simon and I put on our stripy American-diner-style rep shirts and our bravest beaming smiles for the welcome meeting this evening, hoping to distract the roomful of guests with talk of fantastic snow conditions and thrilling après-ski possibilities. It went surprisingly well, all things considered, and so much the better once we drafted in Tina to help. It turns out that she has worked three summers as a beach rep in Ayia Napa and has the all-singing-all-dancing customer-facing enthusiasm nailed, striking the perfect balance between entertaining people, plying them with useful information and yet subtly seducing them with cunning sales pitches for things like ice-skating, paragliding and the bar crawl later that evening. I was quite in awe.

Still, away from the packed hotel bar, the rest of the place still looks rather grim, particularly the restaurant, bathed as it is in pretty unforgiving fluorescent light. From the look of the limp vegetables and colourless meat being served, I sense that we shouldn't hold out much hope that the cuisine will serve to distract our more discerning guests from their surroundings.

I kept my head down and out of sight as I made my way past the restaurant door, beelining for the exit and blissful distance. Just as I was reaching for the door handle, I heard an odd noise coming from the little hotel office. It was Suzanne, the manager. She was sitting in front of the computer, head in hands. She looked up and attempted a smile but gave up and let her lip tremble.

'Oh, Poppy,' she quivered, 'it's not good.'

'What's happened?'

'Oh, oh, it's Richard the Chef. He's just being impossible. He's not speaking to me since I told him last night that concentrate soup, a bowl of creamy pasta and a fruit salad of oranges and grapes just was not good enough for a paying guest's evening meal.'

'He *served* them that?'

She sighed, weak with relief. 'I'm *so* glad you agree that's not quite right. I was worried that maybe I was out of line in criticising him so early into our working relationship. You don't think I was out of line, do you?'

'Suzanne, you cannot be serious.'

'At first I thought it was first week jitters,' she carried on, wringing her hands, 'but I got so worried that I thought it best to have a little word. Now he's not speaking to me and he refuses to give me a menu plan. I just know it will be awful and the guests will complain, and I just can't bear it. I'm so scared to go out into the restaurant and see what he's serving tonight.' She slumped low in her seat, her eyes imploring.

'Why don't you just stick your head into the kitchen and see it for yourself?'

'Oh, no, Poppy, no. I can't. He's barred me from his kitchen.'

'Come on Suzanne, you're the manager, for Christ's sake. You're *his* manager. Just go in there.' *And stop being such a dishcloth.*

'I can't. Really, I just can't. He said he'll go on strike if he so much as sees me looking in the door. But I think the staff will go on strike if I *don't* do something.' She gave another shuddering sigh. 'It's the staff food too, you see. It's been soggy pasta and canned tomato sauce for five nights now. I mean, that's not really good enough, is it? Everyone's been complaining to me, Poppy. I don't know what to do. Daniel and Harry said they'll help themselves to whatever they find in the storeroom if Richard won't feed them properly. Oh, oh, but I can't bear to imagine what will happen then. Everyone knows the storeroom is sacred. I just don't know…'

Just then, Fritz Spitzer, the huge, bear-like hotel owner, marched in to the office to roar at Suzanne about towels on the floor in the leisure centre changing room and a smell 'like sweaty crotch' somewhere in the basement. I muttered something about having to go get ready for chalet visits and the bar crawl and fled before she started crying again.

I ran into Carol sharing a cigarette with Mikey, another of the hotel staff, on the back steps as I left.

'Don't stress it too much, Poppy,' said Carol with an enigmatic smile. 'These situations have a way of resolving themselves in a swift, brutal fashion.'

'Aye,' Mikey grinned, 'they sure do. Whatever about the guests, you definitely do not want to push a group of seasonaires about their staff food allowance.'

Carol nodded. 'Ten euro says drippy Suzanne does nothing at all, the whole thing blows up by Friday and Dick the Chef gets a kick in the head from George.'

'George?' I frowned, confused. I ran through my memorised list of hotel staff names – Dick the Chef and Scottish Arthur the Kitchen Porter in the kitchen; Mikey, Tina, Daniel, Harry and Eoghan on general host duties, and the slightly creepy Slick Dylan the barman with the pink ('magenta, actually') shirt who stares really inappropriately at Tina's breasts all the time and constantly appears to have just eaten some bad cheese. *Was there another one?* 'Who's George?'

'Oh, you know...' She waved her cigarette idly. 'Host. Tall one. Northern.'

'You mean Daniel? Or Harry?'

'Yeah, why not.'

Mikey threw his eyes to heaven. 'They're all "George," Poppy. Carol remembers one name a season, that's it.'

'But who's George?'

'Oh, he was here last year. She usually starts to tell the nameless, faceless masses apart by April. Last year they were all Fred.'

'And the girls?'

'Mandy.'

Carol waved away this unnecessary digression. 'Whatever. Anyway, watch this space. Let's see whose head rolls first and where it ends up. I bet you by next week we have either lost a manager or a chef.'

'I say both,' said Mikey.

'Ooh, big talk, Freddie. What'll we say? Ten? Twenty?' They shook on a bet of twenty euro. I couldn't believe they were so blasé.

'Am I missing something? Are you not worried? It's Christmas Week next week. What will we do if we lose them?'

Carol shrugged. 'We'll just deal with it. It's always like this.'

'Really?'

'Oh, yeah. The start of season is all about waiting and seeing what new disaster unfolds. Hirings, firings, incestuous shagging, massive blowouts, walks of shame... You can't take any of it too seriously.'

'Do the guests not notice?'

'Oh, of course they do, but they like to get stuck in here and there, given half the chance.'

'Get stuck in? In what way?'

Mikey grinned. 'Any way they can. Give Tina a week or two. My money's on her.'

'The "full service," yes, there's always one,' said Carol drily. 'But we're getting ahead of ourselves here,' she said, businesslike again. 'It's early days. First up, I reckon it is really only a matter of time before someone punches Arrogant Dick.'

They smiled at one another, eyebrows raised in anticipation. I couldn't believe that they knowingly came back for more than one season of this soap opera.

'It's simple,' Mikey explained. 'After a few months in this place, I knew I could never work a desk job with normal, well-adjusted people again. I'll bet you planned this as a kind of year out, huh? And you think you'll go back home to reality?' He and Carol exchanged a look and turned to smile at me. 'Don't count on it.'

It was most unsettlingly like being sized up for a top-secret mission I knew nothing about. 'Hmm,' I smiled, waving as I headed down the steps. 'I've got visits to do. See you both on the bar crawl later.'

Turning up the hill toward the Chalet Elena, my phone beeped a text message from Carol. 'You'll see.'

I smiled to myself. *Not likely.*

Tuesday 19 December
10.10am

Oh, my. I am an *awesome* rep. Oh yeah. What a night last night. Total success. First bar crawl of the season, got thirty-eight of our guests on it, took them round the best five bars in town, gave them some shots, showed them a good time, broke someone's nose…

It started so well. Loads of people showed up, many of whom turned out to be from Temporary Simon's guiding group earlier in the day, a large party of junior doctors from Manchester. They, it transpired, could drink for England.

We got them through Happy Bar, Keller Bar, Bar Cuba, and even Rodeo unscathed. It was only when we got to our final destination, Damage, that things came unstuck. Clearly, by this point there was some amount of drink taken. I suspect it was largely for this reason that the two pairs of skis screwed to the ceiling gained a certain irresistible allure. The idea is that the barman gives you two pairs of ski boots and a pitcher of beer and you and an opponent get your friends to turn you upside down and hoist you upwards. You clip into the bindings and the crowd counts you down to a beer-chugging race. The NHS doctors led the way with an impressive demonstration of spillage-minimising skill that paid homage to the training and dedication of their student years. After spectating a few such races, Rach and I were grabbed, ski boots shoved on us and we were hoisted up for a rep's drink-off with the whole place roaring beneath us.

I'm a little vague on the details of what happened next, but it seems that just as I was about to clip in, someone underneath me slipped on a slick of beer and went to ground taking several others with him, me included, flipping over as I fell and clocking someone full whack in the face with a flailing ski boot.

There was blood everywhere. The doctors stood around for a while arguing over specifically what they thought the injury was, ('fractured shheptum,' 'no, no s'ruptured, s'ruptured…uh…*cartilage*,' 'no, shattered, I'd say…') before someone finally thought to cart him off to the gents to get him cleaned up.

I felt extremely bad about it all, but he was back at the bar twenty minutes later, looking a little shaken but less bloody. He introduced himself from behind a wad of toilet paper as Stephen Keane, a dermatologist in the making.

'Ehh, sorry about your nose.'

'Not a problem.'

The doctors had lined up eight shooter glasses of whiskey at the bar. His mate Bob, the tall, gangly looking one, said it was time for some good old-fashioned anaesthesia, but Stephen couldn't tilt his head back far enough to drink without blood gushing down his throat. We all agreed that this was very serious. One can deal with a deformed face, but not with a compromised ability to undergo essential treatment. The doctors debated the merits of intravenous whiskey administration but, in the end, Rachel solved the problem with typical efficiency. She grabbed a tumbler, poured three shots into it, stuck a straw in his hand and, with a shout of 'Physician, heal thyself!' clapped him on the back and poured two shots of sambuca down her throat.

Everyone cheered.

I'm now trying desperately to suppress pangs of moderate-to-severe guilt at drunkenly smashing a guest's nose with my foot (see how much worse it sounds when put like that?). Gina went mental when she heard the story (it didn't help that Rachel told it in very abridged form: 'Hey, Gina! Guess what? Poppy kicked a guest in the face! Broke his nose, yeah. No, no, it's funny, really. Everyone thought it was funny.') Gina puffed herself up to full height and got very officious. Apparently we're not supposed to drink with the guests, even on the bar crawl (how? How would that ever work??). Now Gina will have to make an official incident report to James and to someone called Sarah Datchet. From the way Rachel and Gina say her name, I take it this is very, very bad.

Can only imagine what James will think of me. At best, hideous messy wreck. More likely, violent psychopath.

I'm trying to block it out. On a chairlift now with Rachel, Simon and Mikey, and the sun is ridiculously bright, reflecting crazily off the snow and making every eye movement a test of endurance. Still, we were determined to get an afternoon's riding in, and so my battered crock of a snowboard is making its first appearance of the season. This is largely Rachel's doing. She has not bothered to conceal her disgust that I have skied three days here already and not yet snowboarded. She simply cannot understand how I have so quickly and comprehensively lost my mind (this coming from a girl who keeps her Libtech snowboard beside her bed and kisses it goodnight) so I promised her I would board with her today.

It feels wrong though. It has felt wrong since my first run of the day, and I can't seem to shake that feeling. I don't know if it's the thumping hangover or the fact that after three days on skis I have oriented my head back to the idea of moving forwards and not sideways, but I'm just not enjoying my board today at all. I keep catching edges and whacking my head, wrists and tailbone; wrists, tailbone and head – the same extremely specific three spots over and over and over again in only mildly varying patterns. *At least when I'm skiing the parts I land on tend to vary*, I grumble to myself as another dart of pain shoots through my coccyx. *Sigh*. I need impact shorts and a helmet. No, sod it. I need my skis. Crappy as they are, my rental planks are what I want to be on right now. The skiing thing is a matter of pride now.

Wednesday 20 December

2.02pm

Drama. Suzanne is crying again. Hotel bar manager Dylan quit this morning.

'You're joking,' I said when I heard the news. 'He's been here, what? Two weeks? He hasn't even been up the mountain yet.'

Apparently it all came about because Suzanne asked him to pitch in and help her move something that was blocking a vent in the sauna area. He refused on the grounds that the leisure centre is outside his remit. She told him that it was a once-off request and that she was only asking because the bar and dining room were finished and everyone else was busy.

'I just asked him to "go that extra mile,"' she sniffed.

Dylan told her where to stick her extra mile. Rachel and I found her sobbing behind the bar an hour later and a rather bizarre post-break-up scene ensued as we tried to make her feel a bit better about the whole thing. Suzanne blamed herself, of course, felt she had been too demanding, should have backed off when he resisted and should have respected his boundaries. I told her it wasn't her, it was him and she's better off without him.

'I suppose you're right,' she sniffed after a good deal of analysis. 'He was never going to commit, I can see that now. If he was prepared to quit after so little time, I suppose it was inevitable. At least he did it sooner rather than later.'

'Exactly.'

'But what will I do without him? How will we cope?'

'Promote someone else to his job. How about Eoghan? He's managed a bar for a couple of years. He'll be good. And he's Irish, the guests will love it.'

'I don't know,' she worried, 'the bar manager has a lot of guest contact and I just don't know if Eoghan is... well...'

'What?'

Suzanne looked hopeless. 'He'd have to wear a name badge, wouldn't he? And no-one can read his name. It would cause a *lot* of problems.' She shook her head and frowned. 'Ohhh, I just can't see it working. But then Mikey... What do we *really* know about

Mikey? God, I don't know how to deal with this, really I just… I just…'

'Suzanne. Seriously. One of them will be able to change a barrel, do a stock-take and work a till. Pick someone.'

She twisted the Kleenex in her hands into a tight knot, blinking hard. 'But what if he is,' she looked around and hissed quietly 'dishonest? How do I know he won't be terrible? If he's terrible I will get in *so much* trouble.' She chewed her thumbnail and looked like she might cry again. 'Maybe I should call Liz.'

'Suzanne,' Rachel exhaled sharply, 'it's time to strap on a pair. This is not the kind of thing you refer to the Hotels Coordinator. This is your call. Go with your instincts. Flip a coin or something.'

Suzanne blinked, took a few wobbly deep breaths and eventually nodded. 'Right.'

'OK. Have you got a coin?'

'That's the spirit.'

Eoghan got the job, subject to wearing a name badge that says 'Owen.'

I saw Stephen-of-fractured-nose-fame this morning at hotel visits. He was looking very rough indeed, with two black eyes and a rigid plaster thing across his face. Massive guilt returned with a sickening wave, but he gave me a big grin (as big as possible, anyway) hugged me, told me he was having the *best holiday ever* and skipped out the door with his snowboard under his arm. His friend Bob explained just how many kinds of prescription drugs doctors tend to carry with them when they travel. After some experimentation, Stephen decided he liked Tramadol best and was sticking to that.

I found Carol skulking about her apartment and successfully dragged her out skiing. She was rather dismissive of my guilt at inadvertently being the cause of a doctor's slippery descent into prescription drug abuse and told me to quit my whining and steal his prescription pad. 'Then everyone's a winner.'

Carol, it turns out, is an excellent skier. I am utterly humbled by her skill and speed on skis. Most of all, though, I'm baffled by her patience. She seemed very happy (and Carol never seems happy) to potter about with me for the afternoon, running through drills to get me flexing up and down properly, get my upper body in the right position and my skis carving effectively. I would not have taken her for the patient type but she was incredibly encouraging. She even said something about powder snow. I suspect that the simplest explanation is the most likely one – i.e. that Carol is taking immense pleasure in how much it is annoying Rachel that I have gone to the dark side – but I don't care. I'm far too excited by how much progress I made today. Absolutely knackered now though.

It occurs to me that I haven't heard from James since Sunday night. Ha, ha, I say that very casually like I totally hadn't noticed, haven't been thinking about him at all, nooo, not me. No obsessing whatsoever. Am cool on the subject. Cucumber-like, almost.

Sigh. Still, on reflection, it is probably quite a good thing he has not been in touch. Quite possibly, this means he does not yet know about Monday's GBH incident. If he were to contact me, it could only be to yell at me or sack me for professional misconduct, assault and battery etc.

I am decidedly not thinking about him at all, in any sense. My latest theory is that when I met him, my brain was compromised by the constant presence in my peripheral vision of my bright blue and orange stripy uniform shirt and it subconsciously concluded it was a day for making Very Bad Choices. I'll be psychologically prepared for this effect by Sunday and will be capable of behaving like a rational adult.

Meanwhile, I'm focusing on a massive day of skiing tomorrow on our STAFF DAY OFF, ending with delightfully bad music and stomp-dancing in ski boots at the Moose, Reschengel's finest piste-side aprés-ski bar, all in celebration of the fact that Gina will not be phoning every forty minutes to delegate some tedious gruntwork. Hurrah!

Thursday 21 December

7.13am

Text message… James??

Fucking GINA! 'Sweeties, dnt 4get: day off dsnt mean PHONES off!! Must b contactble @ all times. Spk l8r, luv Gina.xoxox'

9.14pm

Txt msg frm Gna to say 'PANIC!! TWO CHLT HOSTS hve fckng quit!! Need u all 4 urgnt group hug @ mine ASAP!!'

Am rfsing to thnk abt ths ntl tmrrw. She cn go fck hrslf.

Saturday 23 December

6.18pm

Ugh. It's true – the two hosts from the Chalet Elena, Isadora and Antonia, have announced that they are leaving tomorrow for another job in the French Alps. Nobody was devastated to hear the news, admittedly – the girls have never made any secret of their feeling that a Snowglobe job was rather below them, and it was perhaps, as with Dylan, only a matter of time. Coming here to Reschengel had been a last minute change to their gap year plan after a job nannying for a Courchevel billionaire fell through. Although they were placed in the most beautiful chalet in the Snowglobe programme – one of the Egyptian-cotton-and-*fois-gras* 'Golden Globe' properties – it seems that this was still scraping the barrel to an unacceptable degree.

'Oh, the Courchevel thing was a *disaster,*' Isadora explained as she served dinner to the guests in the Elena on Monday evening. 'And we couldn't just *not* do the season. It's really the only thing one can *do* for the winter, you know, and moving up our summer plans was not really an option.'

'Good thing this job came up then, eh?' said one of the guests, smiling at me as I made my way around the table, topping up glasses of wine.

63

'Oh yes!' smiled Isadora, blinking a couple of times. Antonia said nothing but looked miserable, following her around, handing out sideplates.

'What are your summer plans then?' I asked.

'Well that's just it: the specifics are *sooo* up in the air at the moment,' Isadora sighed, adjusting her hairband, 'but basically we're thinking about doing Africa.'

'Doing what to Africa?'

'Oh,' she replied, loading that one word with more syllables than I had thought possible, 'build a well or a school or something, I suppose? My brother Jasper did that last year. He said it was awfully hard but terribly rewarding. And then of course one goes on safari. But until then,' she smiled bravely, 'here we are!'

'My company has a chalet in Courchevel,' another of the guests said suddenly, looking up from her BlackBerry. 'It hasn't been fully staffed yet, as far as I know. I could make a call…?'

I should have seen it coming I suppose, but I didn't know how serious they really were. Monday was the first time I had actually met Isadora and Antonia. They never came near our staff chalet and our local Happy Bar was less their scene than the bright lights of the Ice Bar in the centre of town, where they could sip champagne cocktails and twirl their studiously messy hair in the company of all the other bored-looking public schoolgirls.

I tried to see their departure as a good thing. They'd certainly be happier in Courchevel, I knew, but I still spent most of today worrying about how on earth we would manage short *four* staff members, what with Temporary Rep Simon due back to Söll tomorrow and still no news of permanent replacements for Karl or Dylan. And who would be the next to go? I fretted. The other two chalet hosts – Joseph in the Chalet Gerda and Mark in the Tyrolerhof? Or maybe Dick the Chef? I'm genuinely afraid to calculate what percentage of staff has quit within the first two weeks and extrapolate that against the remaining eighteen weeks of season. *Will there be anyone left by February??*

But then I heard the news that James has already found us

some replacements. In fact, I got a text message from him early this morning to that effect.

James: 'Connors, stop scaring away the staff. Am sending you a new rep AND a couple of new chalet hosts tomorrow. Please be careful with these ones. If you break them, you're not getting any more.'

Heart singing with glee. Glee! Yes, 'glee' is exactly the word. 'Glee' is such a good word, I think. Very…onomatopoeic.
Stop wittering, Poppy.

Sunday 24 December

4.40am

It's transfer day and I'm just leaving Reschengel for the airport. Feeling a little bit floaty, if the truth be told. Surely this is only because of the beautiful sight of snow falling heavily all the way down the valley...?

10.58pm. En route to Reschengel.

Ha. Obvious knock-on effect of heavy snow down into the valley is delayed flights. I probably should have anticipated this. The snow-clouds hit Salzburg in the late afternoon, after Gina, Rachel and the new replacement rep, Tom, had departed with their coaches. As I had drawn the short straw for the late coach, I got stranded in the airport with James and a handful of other reps to wait out the blizzard. *Unconvincing sigh of annoyance...*

Four hours passed without so much as a single flight, and in the quiet of the deserted Charter Terminal, and over enough caffeine to operate the New York Stock Exchange, I got rather a lot of mocking over the kicking-of-guest-in-face incident. It turned out James *had* heard; he just didn't care. He thought it was funny. Everyone else had heard too. Apparently the story grew legs around the Austrian programme and lots of people somehow got the impression I had a black belt in karate (and anger management issues, presumably). It didn't help that poor Temporary Simon had a going away party 'mishap' last night that left him with only one eyebrow (and the new nickname 'Juan Brow'...tequila was involved...) which most of the reps from other resorts seem to think is also somehow related to me. I struggled to convince them otherwise. James told me not to bother – a reputation for being dangerous to mess with can only be a good thing in this business.

'Especially with an Irish accent,' he added.

I'm not sure this makes me feel better. Still, I'm trying to forget about the whole sorry affair and just hoping that everyone else – especially the fractured-nose-guest, who is now at home in the cold light of litigation – does too.

James filled me in on our new rep, Tom. Tom has been repping in St. Anton for the past three seasons, is a skier and ski guide (hurrah!) and has worked a summer with Gina before so he knows what to expect from that quarter. He's also, from what James implied, something of a ladies' man.

At this, Anna, the resort manager from Futterberg and one of James' good friends, chimed in, 'Oh, yes, but Tom is sooo lovely! He's the polar opposite to Weird Karl. He's great fun. Such a charmer but so sincerely sweet too.' She smiled conspiratorially. 'And *very* cute, wait 'til you see him. Tall, sandy hair, rugby player's physique and just the naughtiest grin you've ever seen. Tell all the girls to be careful! You absolutely cannot *not* fall in love with him instantly.'

'Easy, there, Anna, you're not on commission,' said James, slightly grumpily. 'Let Poppy at least *try* to resist the little man-whore.'

'Oh, you know what I mean. Tom's adorable. They're very lucky to have got him and not some newbie. At least he will share the ski guiding with you, Pops.'

I had told them about the Jan experience. I had had to, as Jan was in the airport today and was rather nastily uncomplimentary about my skiing. James told me afterwards that I would be neither the first nor the last to punch the little git, and that he would be on hand with an ice pack if and when the time came. Love the management support this company provides. That, right there, is going the extra mile.

James also offered (and this is where the evening got a bit fizzy) to take me skiing. Because the resorts of Reschengel and Futterberg are linked by piste, it will be easy for us to meet up midway at Stüben and spend the day together. And since this week we launch our 'Futterberg Ski Away Day' (essentially a day's guided skiing over and back), James pointed out that it is about time someone showed *me* properly around the area. He also said he'd have a look at my technique and help me work on it, maybe teach me about powder skiing in a few weeks' time if I am up to it and we get the conditions.

Of course I said yes. We're going skiing together on Thursday. I'm resisting the urge to read any more into it all. Will not descend into multitude of exclamation marks.

OK, maybe one.

!

In other news, the replacement chalet hosts for the Elena came in with the last flight. My heart sank a little as I saw them come through the arrivals doors – two tall, slim girls of about nineteen or twenty in an almost identical uniform of fitted Jack Wills hoodies and blazers, miniskirts and striped knee-high socks over black leggings. I didn't have their names on my manifest but was not remotely surprised when one of them, the taller blonde girl with the most aggressively backcombed hair I have ever seen, held out her hand to me.

'Poppy, is it? Hello, I'm Tilly Bridgewater-Baker,' she said with the sort of clear and precise diction that always makes me think of earnest conversations about things to do with horses. 'And this is Mills. I mean, Miranda.' Miranda smiled shyly, saying nothing. 'We're from Paton's Cookery School. We're taking over the kitchen of the Chalet Elena in Reschengel, I believe?'

'Err, hello.' I shook their hands and helped them with their cases toward the coach bay. 'Yes,' I gulped, 'yes, yes, ha-ha it's lovely to meet you…'

Gina had evidently known in advance that Miranda and Tilly were the best of friends, and had therefore decided in her infinite wisdom that she would delegate to me the task of telling one of them that they would not in fact be taking over 'the kitchen' of the Elena. Rather, one of them would be placed in the Tyrolerhof, cooking and cleaning alone for eight guests. The other would be across the road with the former Tyrolerhof host, Mark, who Gina decided should move to the Elena to 'train in our new little Princess Arabella and make sure there were no big fuck-ups for our big-bucks guests. Imagine!'

How to impart such news? The Elena is a stunning creation of wood, glass and stone, with a sauna, swimming pool and games room, in a spectacular location with a panoramic view unparalleled anywhere else in the resort and the most luxurious imaginable staff accommodation. The Tyrolerhof, on the other hand, is no 'Golden Globe.' It is at the lino-and-plywood lowest rung of the chalet programme, advertised in the Globetrotter brochure and sold to young groups looking for cheap, cheerful and boozy breaks in the snow. For this, read: 'utter dive, stag parties, vomiting.' I sensed that this would not have gone down well with any two people who had been drawn out to Austria by the promise of working together, not to mind this pair who – short of sulking faces and ever present Marlboro Lights – were basically Isadora and Antonia all over again. *Why, Snowglobe, why??*

I put off telling them the unhappy truth until I had finished selling lift passes to all the guests on the coach, but at that point we were in Reschengel, pulling up outside the doors of the Elena and the girls had hopped off, giggling and hugging each other in excitement about the snow, the chalet, the absolute amaaaazingness of it all.

'Err, actually Miranda?' I scrambled out of the coach after them. She looked up from unloading her suitcase. 'Here's the thing…' I struggled with the words as they both stared at me, horrified. 'And so, err…' I said finally, 'your chalet is actually that one.' They followed the line of my finger to the creaky, mouldy eaves and slightly sagging roof of the chalet opposite, built down into the hill. They stood silent for a full two minutes, blinking. Miranda looked like she might cry. I patted her on the shoulder and told her it would be OK. The last part I approached with trepidation. 'And, ehhh, Gina picked up these for you from the hypermarket this afternoon.' I reached into the luggage compartment and pulled out a cardboard box. 'Just some cleaning products. Apparently the Tyrolerhof has been a bit short of disinfectant spray and toilet brushes and it needs a bit of a scrub.'

'Toilet brushes?' Miranda spoke at last, her voice wobbling slightly. 'How…often will I need to use those?'

'Every day.' Her face froze in horrified disgust. 'Well, not on your day off,' I added hurriedly.

It didn't help. She turned to Tilly with a dramatic swish of her hair and furrowed her pale brow in consternation. 'I really don't know about this, Tills. I mean, I took this to be a cook's job, yah?'

'I know, yah.'

'And they told us specifically that our chalet would be *five star*. That we were *cooking* in the *five star* chalet. Chalets have a cleaning staff, surely?'

'I would have thought so, absolutely.'

'It's not fair, Tills, how come *you* get the cook's job?'

'Oh, Tilly has to clean too,' I offered and instantly regretted it.

Tilly's eyebrows shot up. 'I was certainly *not* hired to clean an eighteen bed chalet.' She folded her arms. 'I'm sorry, but you simply cannot be serious.'

A quick call to Gina clarified things.

'What do they think this is, Eton? Haw, haw, haw! Windsor Castle? Bal-fucking-moral?' and laughed loudly for about five minutes, then said 'yeah, sort it,' and hung up.

'O.M.G., Mills.' Tilly chewed her thumbnail. 'Scrubbing toilets for the winter, can you imagine? My father will die.'

'I know, right? Can you picture his face?' They both laughed a little in spite of themselves. 'And Giles! Good Lord, you know what Giles will say. It will be like that time with Felix and the fishing trip.'

'Gosh, exactly, except at least he found someone to hire in the end.'

'Oh, this is vile. Why did no-one tell us about the cleaning until now?'

Tilly shook her head in bewilderment. 'I know, it's so wrong. It's like, entrapment or something. I cannot understand how no-one brought this to my attention before now.'

I could perfectly well understand, but I was not going to volunteer that just then.

Monday 25 December

1.20pm

Inhale…exhale…inhale…pause. Youuuu…cannot-be-fucking-serious. Text message from Mikey.

'Ehh…not sure if you're up the mountain or not…'

I wasn't, because, in lieu of Christmas card, Secret Santa gift or otherwise, Gina had handed me a twenty-three page printout this morning of ski hire packages sold to date to check against an over-spilling cardboard box of almost entirely illegible carbon copy duplicates – the intention, I suspect, being to ensure that I would have as lonely, pointless and dull a Christmas as possible, *quelle surprise*.

'…but you might want to drop everything and come rescue Suzanne. Is unresponsive in hotel kitchen, holding knife. Am worried might harm self or others??'

I found Suzanne standing alone in the empty kitchen, poking despondently at a baking tray encrusted with what looked like the charred remains of some sort of cake.

'A yule log, Poppy,' she sniffed. 'There's supposed to be a chocolate yule log for the guests when they come in from skiing. But I don't know how to make a yule log. I've never made one. I don't know what I did wrong…'

It transpired that she had another argument with Dick the Chef during breakfast clear-up this morning and the bastard threw a tantrum and quit on the spot. *On Christmas morning.* Eight hours before the Christmas gala dinner was to be served to sixty-three guests.

Oh, crap, I thought, scanning the kitchen surfaces in vain for evidence of even the slightest Christmas meal preparation. *This is not good.*

I wondered briefly if there was any hope of a reconciliation but Mikey explained that he ran down to Dick's room in the basement as soon as he heard what had happened, only to find that Dick – in his greatest show of efficiency since the season began – had already packed up and left. No-one has any idea where he has gone.

Suzanne blames herself. Apparently it all went wrong when she tried to discuss with Dick the vegetables he was planning to cook for Christmas dinner. 'Now what will we do?' she hiccuped. 'We have to find him. We need a yule log, and then a starter…and I don't know how to make pâté…and trifle and oh, Christmas crackers too, did I order the Christmas crackers? I don't think they ever arrived. Oh, Poppy, oh…'

I patted her shoulder consolingly. 'One thing at a time, OK? Firstly, forget the yule log. It doesn't matter. Why don't I pour you a big glass of red wine while you go outside for a calming little walk up and down in the fresh air for a few minutes?'

'Can't. Got to make another yule log. It's in the brochure.' She started to cry again. 'Why, Poppy, why did I insist on carrots and brussels sprouts? Cauliflower cheese is better than no food, ah haaaahaaaa…'

I'm not proud of it, but I really have no patience for tears in these situations. I grabbed the knife somewhat irritably out of her hand, took her by the shoulders and gave her a little shake. I told her to have a serious chat with herself and think positively or else just quit too, and go home. She said nothing, just froze and stared at me. I was suddenly afraid I might have broken her – literally. She was very thin and fragile under all those clothes; I couldn't help but wonder when she had last eaten.

It was by then apparent that the situation would require more than motivational guidance, Mr. T style, so Mikey and I sent her to the office and told her to write an email to someone. Meanwhile, Arthur had drafted in Carol, Tina, Eoghan and Harry to confer on what had to be done to produce Christmas dinner for sixty or so people. As it happened, of all of us, Mikey was the only one who appeared to have any clue about what was required (though not much) so he became the new chef for tonight. Tina offered to put on an impromptu tap-dance show in the hotel bar to create a diversion so we made her start washing vegetables in case she was serious.

2.50pm

We are still looking for the turkeys. No sign. Not in the walk-in fridge, nor the cellar. Very odd. Maybe they came frozen and are defrosting somewhere? But where??

4.00pm

There are no turkeys. There *are* no turkeys. There are *no turkeys*.

Wednesday 27 December
12.03pm

Things I have learned in the past forty-eight hours:

1. What vegetarians don't know can't hurt them.
2. Gravy is a food which comes from the same family as concrete, and is intended by nature to mask all evils. More is more.
3. Most people cannot tell the difference between natural yoghurt and a crafty natural-yoghurt-mayonnaise blend. Those that can think you have done something 'tangy.'
4. Cakes don't rise at altitude. Water doesn't boil at one hundred degrees and no matter how many you prepare, there are never, ever enough potatoes.
5. Allergies are more *guidelines* than strict life-and-death rules (surely the nut guy would be dead by now?)

Oh, and if a large roll of kitchen paper falls into, I don't know, say, a vat of leek and potato soup, and you only manage to fish out about half of it before dissolves into a greyish goopy mess, so long as it is undistinguishable from the soup, no-one will notice the difference.

It took us some time to quite believe that Dick the Chef had neglected to order the turkeys. It just didn't seem possible that anyone could be so unutterably dense, but then we reflected upon his record to date – a litany of watery pasta, tinned tuna and concentrated soup, after all – and decided that it was more surprising that he had actually bothered to order the vegetables.

This didn't leave us any closer to a solution, however. A quick phone around confirmed what we suspected: that there wasn't a fresh turkey to be had within a fifty-mile radius.

'We're screwed,' whispered Rachel, her eyes darting to the motionless figure of Suzanne sitting staring at the wall in the hotel office. 'If we can't even find one whole turkey, what on earth are we going to feed sixty-three guests? How many of them do you suppose might be open to the idea of sausages and eggs? Or perhaps a nice festive fondue?'

If we can't find one whole turkey…

'That's it, Rachel,' I gasped. 'You're a genius!' Everybody turned to look at me. 'We don't need *whole* turkeys, do we? And nor does anybody else.'

'Brilliant,' said Carol, nodding slowly. 'That's it.'

'What? I don't get it,' said Arthur the Kitchen Porter.

'Poultry pick 'n' mix, little man. Poultry pick 'n' mix.'

It was devastatingly simple in the end. All we had to do was beg, borrow and steal all the nasty, fiddly bits of turkeys from a variety of chalets and hotels around town then mask them with lashings of glue-like gravy (i.e. Lesson Two above). Most of the other tour operators were surprisingly accommodating with this plan, even reps and resort managers I had to phone up and introduce myself to for the first time. Bella, the rep from SuperSki, even managed to get us four whole breasts – generosity she has already lived to regret because Arthur and Eoghan have rewritten an ABBA classic in her honour and insist on serenading her with it at every possible opportunity. *Thank You For The Boobies* is already a hit with the seasonaire patrons of Happy Bar and Bar Cuba, although most people seem to be a bit confused on the subject of what exactly she did.

Some UK-run chalets were rather less enthusiastic about helping, however; specifically the new chef up at the Diamond Ski Finest chalet at the other end of town.

'I'm so sorry – err, Poppy, is it?' said Kat, the Diamond Ski resort manager, when she phoned me back. 'I know you're under pressure and I did communicate that to the chef, but he wouldn't even entertain the idea of making a contribution. He's quite stressed I think, and really just finding his feet in his new kitchen. We only hired him the other day, you see.'

'Oh, really?' My ears pricked up. 'He's new?'

'Yes. It's been one of those dramatic weeks – you know how it can be. His predecessor in that chalet gave a guest food poisoning a couple of days ago and I had to sack him on the spot. I thought we were totally screwed – I mean, we're talking about *Christmas*

Week in the most high-profile chalet in the Diamond Ski programme, for heaven's sake, but then this Rick fellow comes along. Turns out he's a highly qualified chef who had just arrived in resort and was looking for top-end chalet work. Of course I snapped him up on the spot. Amazing coincidence, eh?'

'Staggering,' I said.

'I know, right!' she gushed. 'Talk about *lucky*. Oh, sorry, I know you lot are having your own chef issues, but it was just such a *relief* to find him, you know?'

'No, no, I get it. Wow, you're really are,' *not very bright, Kat*, 'so lucky, Kat,' I said. 'Good for you. Glad it's going smoothly for someone, eh? I'd better go now. I'm afraid we still have our little drama to, err, *rectify*.'

'Of course, of course,' she squeaked. 'Good luck with it! I hope you get sorted soon. Tell Gina I said hi! Oh, and Merry Christmas!'

For three whole minutes after I hung up the phone I considered not using this new information to mess with Dick the Chef, which I was rather proud of. Then I told everyone. Somehow, two hours later, when 'Rick' opened up his state-of-the-art oven door to check on his two cranberry-and-honey-glazed turkeys, all he found was a somewhat battered and rather familiar old baking tray with a neat little pile of lukewarm turkey legs. Crime is a terrible thing, and people really ought to lock their patio doors, even in ski resorts. 'Who would come all the way up a steep hill to break into this chalet and steal a couple of turkeys?' one might ask, but if you are Dick the Chef, and the person asking is Kat the Manger, well – that's really not an easy question to answer. Last I heard Dick was spotted in the vicinity of the train station with a couple of suitcases. Good riddance.

Unfortunately, even with the bonus addition of Dick the Chef's two birds – which incidentally were tasty enough to prove what Carol and I suspected, that he had always been perfectly capable of cooking to the standard required but had been skimming the Club Hotel budget – we still didn't manage to scavenge quite enough other turkey bits to feed sixty-three people, particularly since guilt (mine, not Carol's) dictated that we leave something for the Diamond Ski guests' Christmas dinner. In desperation, we solved the problem finally by buying eight cooked chickens from the chip shop and concealing the pieces between genuine turkey parts. We were all absolutely exhausted by the time the guests sat down to dinner but the day's intrigues turned out to be a success – insofar as everybody got fed pieces of something that used to have wings and lay eggs – and more importantly, insofar as none of them appeared to notice anything amiss. Still, we spent an anxious two hours on Christmas Night wondering if we would get rumbled. "Poultrygate," as yet, remains under wraps.

Since that evening, and in the absence of anyone else with even the vaguest idea how to cater for a hotel full of guests, Mikey has remained in charge of the hotel kitchen. He has proven to be something of a rather natural intuitive chef, in fact (with some notable exceptions: the salmon and cheese soufflés with chocolate and balsamic vinegar reduction were a real low point) and certainly an improvement on Dick. But there is surely only so long a hotel kitchen can be kept afloat on adrenaline and improvisation (and really, it is only a matter of time before we actually do permanent damage to some poor unsuspecting guest) and so we've been praying to any deity that might listen that Snowglobe finds a replacement chef soon. I received a rather worrying phone call from James on this very subject at about six o'clock on Christmas Day. I couldn't really talk to him properly, as was at that moment skating up the treacherously icy main street with an enormous saucepan of steaming turkey legs, but I assumed that he was calling to say that the problem was being dealt with.

'Please tell me you're calling with good news, James.'

'Err… like what? The birth of our Lord? Or an update on the Santa situation? OK: this just in – he's real.'

James, it transpired, was actually only calling for a chat (!), to say 'Merry Christmas' and to see if I would be free to ski with him on Thursday. He was utterly baffled when I told him I would have to call him back, as I was at that moment part of a crack commando team infiltrating maximum-security kitchens all over the Reschengel area.

'Err, *why*, again, are you "acquiring" turkey bits from rival tour operators?'

That was how we discovered that no-one had told James what was going on with Dick the Chef. I think Suzanne had spent most of the evening paralysed by shock and fear, so I could understand her dropping the ball on this one. But surely Gina must have thought a hotel with a gaping hole where the chef should be qualified as that species of emergency one communicates to one's line manager? James got very arsey with me about it on the phone.

'So, this all happened, what, six hours ago? And I am hearing about it now, by sheer chance? Surely between all of you over there, there exists the combined brainpower to register that I can't fix this unless somebody thinks to actually tell me? Do you have any idea how long it can take to find a chef? What exactly was the plan there: wait for a week and then casually let it slip in conversation?'

It wasn't easy to articulate a good response to that, standing in the falling snow, weighed down by twenty kilos of turkey body parts. Still, I couldn't help but think that he was being very unfair in getting irritated with me of all people. I had not exactly spent a lot of the last six hours doing my nails and chatting on the phone, and anyway, surely it was not at all my place to presume to phone up my manager's manager to inform him about these things? Of course, I ended up just sort of muttering, 'ehh...I don't really...ehh...'

James just said, 'oh, fucking hell. Look, I've got to go,' and hung up.

Gina got a bit of a bollocking, by all accounts. Tom and Rachel were there when James phoned her and they heard most of what was said. Lots about big pictures, looking ahead, understanding her place, grasping basic logic, that sort of thing. Apparently Gina thought that as she had let me off my other rep duties to help cook in the hotel, the problem was solved. She had not really considered much beyond Christmas dinner.

I was pretty annoyed with James, once I got over the shock of being yelled at. I spent most of the walk back to the hotel thinking of excellent comebacks and winning arguments. He was quite out of order, I decided, and I was disappointed in him. It made me wonder if he was not in fact just an irritable bastard. But then a text message came in a while later with a rather sweet apology. 'Hey Poppy, I'm sorry about earlier. Absolutely not your fault, actually you're being a hero so ignore me completely. Can be v impatient idiot at times, you'll get used to it.'

I sent back: 'No problem, really.' And then felt a little cheeky, (and squiffy…mmm…Christmas) so I added: 'My forgiveness is easily bought with glühwein.'

He wrote back immediately: 'Excellent, then you'll have to come skiing with me on Thursday. In the meantime, if you get the chance to accidentally hit certain people in the face with a large saucepan, don't hold back. Just be sure to wipe the evidence of fake tan off the bottom.'

I replied: 'Would only be an improvement, let's face it.'

He phoned me then, just to agree with me on that. Oh, and to properly say Merry Christmas. And also to settle a time for Thursday…

Friday 29 December

4.40pm

Yesterday, yesterday…

Yesterday was staff and hotel day off, so I was free, *freeeee* at last of the hated hotel kitchen and I got to go skiing all day with James, followed by dinner and drinks in Futterberg, (or rather, drinks and then dinner) before he drove me home. Rachel nearly died when I walked in the door.

'YOU!' She pounced on me. 'I love you! Oh-my-actual-*GOD*, you should have been there to see Gina's face when James phoned to say that he was going to drive you home after dinner. It was like,' she twisted her face into a psychotic knot of shock, pain and fury, and trilled a slightly hysterical '"Super, yah! Course, no problem, sweetie. Just make sure to give her back to us!"'

Uh-oh. I hadn't really thought of that. Hadn't really – if I were to be totally honest with myself – been thinking of a whole lot more than *Ha-la-la-la-la-la-laaaa* for the past couple of hours.

'Oh-my-God-this-is-brilliant,' Rachel breathed. 'Epic! Love it! You two are totally going to get it on.'

'What an old romantic you are.'

'Ha! I knew it, you lurrrve him.' I strenuously denied this, but she was not to be stopped. 'Right, tell me everything. What was he wearing? How were you feeling? Did time go in slow motion? Was it,' she started humming and swaying, '*like the first time?*'

'Shut up.'

'I will not.'

James and I had arranged to meet that morning in the little hamlet of Stüben, midway between Reschengel and Futterberg. Unfortunately when I got there I found that about eleven hundred other people had also had the bright idea to make this their meeting place. It then dawned on me that I had absolutely no idea what colour ski jacket I should be looking for. I had obviously never seen James in his ski gear, only in trousers and a shirt, and I was pretty confident that that was the last thing he would be wearing. Likewise, under a helmet and a pair of goggles, my face was totally hidden and he would have no idea what I was wearing either. I thought of phoning him, but of course – as is the law of the universe in these situations – there was only very poor, wildly fluctuating reception.

Eventually, after some waiting and wondering if I might have been stood up – and, worse, wondering how I would ever know – a text message came through.

James: 'I'm here at the Albonalift. Are you here? Are you incognito, or are you the lady I can see in the gold fishscale-patterned one-piece?'

Me: 'She is a diversion. Am incognito, wearing red carnation, sitting under the clocktower with a green umbrella, reading an upside down copy of last week's *Pravda*.'

James: 'And really?'

Me: 'Standing by the *Kasse*. Green jacket, black salopettes, orange helmet.'

James: 'Is it St Patrick's Day??'

A familiar voice behind me then. 'I would have brought a bottle of something if I had known.'

'You haven't seen me ski. I already resemble a drunken giraffe. Trust me, the last thing I need is alcohol.'

'This, I am looking forward to.'

Me too, I thought. It wasn't until I was sitting on the chairlift that I registered what I had just committed to doing for the day. Aside from Carol, I have never skied with anyone who is actually any good. Wasn't James some sort of sponsored skier? A massive wave of panicked realisation hit me: even if I didn't seriously (like, embarrassingly-much) fancy this man, I would still ski like a total punter by comparison with him. Why, *oh why*, Poppy, did you think that skiing – a sport at which you are barely a step up from 'sheer liability' – with a man you are *so very into* could ever end well?

Actually it was a lot of fun in the end. He was patient, which I was not at all expecting, and funny, gently slagging off my odd need for speed in spite of wild lack of technique (I blame Jan), although not in an unkind way. He even took me off the piste a little (only into about a foot of soft snow mind you, though with predictable results) and he didn't even appear to mind every time he had to ski down, dig me out and locate my skis, goggles, dignity etc. Actually, he seemed to really enjoy himself. Meanwhile, I was just glad I'd bought a new helmet, orange as it was.

Just before three, we stopped on the Futterberg side of the ridge for a glühwein in a tiny, thumping little mountain-side aprés bar called the Muschhütte and had a long chat, mainly about work stuff. James then told me how, by a stroke of luck, he and Liz, Suzanne's line manager, had managed to find us a new chef for the Club Hotel. Not only that, but he was being driven over to Reschengel that very afternoon. I held myself back from diving across the table and hugging James. Back to my actual job! No more peeling potatoes! No more icing cakes with Nutella! No more hoping the vegetarians don't notice that the spinach ravioli tastes like bacon! I was so overwhelmed by relief I could hardly speak, and so confined myself to bouncing up and down and clapping my mittens.

James grinned. 'Do try not to scare this one away, Connors, if you could?'

It was getting close to a quarter to four and I was about to go and catch the connecting series of lifts back to Reschengel when Anna and two of her friends walked in to the Muschhütte. Of course then I ended up staying for one more 'quick' glühwein with them, but then someone (James) had the bright idea to get in a round of Jägermeisters and then another, and that was that – I had missed the last connection. James said not to worry, we'd all head down, grab a pizza and he would drive me back this evening once he was sure the Jägermeister had worn off, since he would feel quite bad if we were to plummet off the road to our deaths. Of course I felt slightly guilty that he would have to make almost a three-hour round trip to get me home but he didn't seem to mind; he said his whole job was driving around Austria visiting resorts, and one short hop over and back was not a big deal. Anyway, he argued, it was actually his fault that I missed the lift, which was true.

I got back at about nine-thirty to find our new chef had arrived. Aside from Rachel, he was the only one there in the staff chalet. Rachel and I stuck our heads in to the room where he was unpacking, and she began to introduce me.

'Poppy, this is our…'

'I'm JOHN,' he bellowed, then blinked and looked at the two of us as though daring us to disagree.

'Err…nice to meet you, JOHN.'

'Right, yeah, John.' He paused, and then remembered what he was supposed to do next. 'What's your name?'

'POPPY,' I said, very slowly and deliberately.

'Is that your real name?' he challenged me.

What an odd boy. 'Yes, it is indeed.' There was an awkward pause, which I filled by rambling. 'Yup, Poppy. That's it, yeah. Err, not short for anything, just Poppy. Like the flower.'

'Right, yeah, OK.' He nodded vigorously, his eyes darting in a slightly wired way from Rachel to me and back again.

'Where are you from, John? asked Rachel, purely to break the silence.

'Why? Where are *you* from?' he countered.

We gave up and hustled him out the door to join the others at Rodeo Bar where the music was loud and Marco the barman had been feeding the others his signature cocktail, the Flaming Lamborghini, to the extent that they were all utterly beyond repair by that point. I introduced John to a few people, and then naturally to the Lamborghini. *Aside from the twitchiness, he looks relatively normal, or at least healthy,* I caught myself thinking.

Good God, how long have I been here? I'm already dispassionately sizing up the life expectancy of the staff like beef cattle.

Saturday 30 December

9.08am

Ha, ha! *I knew* there was something odd about Chef John.

He has been very normal and fun at work, even actually quite good at his job, in a rather massive Snowglobe Recruitment success shocker. But there was definitely something strange going on with him. Every time he met someone new, he got all twitchy and starey while introducing himself, as though he were on the run from the law, in hiding from a Mafia vendetta or similar. I still couldn't quite decide what to make of it all, when James accidentally 'outed' him by text message.

James: 'What is Odysseus like?'
Me: 'Erm, dunno…beardy? Salty? Bit lost?'
James: 'Eh? Have you not met him yet?'
Me: 'No, James, last I heard he was still at sea…??'
James: 'The chef, Poppy. The chef.'

Chef John's real name is Odysseus. This is *brilliant*. Ha ha ha ha ha ha ha…what to do with this information. Must sit on it a while, like golden egg… must not tell everyone, however, as clearly is not his wish. Must respect that.

9.32am

It's too funny. Must tell someone. Must tell Rachel.

6.40pm

Rachel was totally inconsolable. She took Odysseus/John skiing today, and twisted the conversation on every chairlift to comparisons between the day they were having and Homeric episodes. When she described the clouds overhead as 'Zeus' shadow,' he thought she had a vivid way with words. When she described that magical first sip of the first glühwein of the day as 'akin to the first glimpse of Ithaca on the troubl'd and e'er darkening horizon,' he thought she was a little bit touched. By three o'clock, the terrifyingly blonde and stylishly coordinated girls who lounge about in the snowpark judging people were Sirens luring hapless park-monkeys toward their cruel demise upon the cold, sharp rails. Odysseus/John realised around then that Rachel really was not going to quit, so he cracked and told her the story.

His father was a French classicist who had died in a motorcycle accident two weeks before he was born. He had been returning home from a long sabbatical research trip around the universities of Europe, loaded up with notes and excited about a great discovery he had made which was going to change how the world saw Homer, but he never made it home. His wife was distraught, of course, and when the name 'Odysseus' came to her in a flash of inspiration during childbirth, she knew that it was a beyond-the-grave message from her husband. Odysseus is of the opinion that things would have looked a lot different if she had had time for an epidural, and tries as much as possible to go by the name of John. He had been sure that the anonymity of season life was the perfect opportunity.

Rachel swore that she and I would keep his secret. However by the time they got back to the chalet this afternoon, an oblivious Gina had read it on the staff payment forms and had let slip to Tina. It went around like wildfire and there is now a white bed-sheet shortage in resort due to an impromptu toga party tonight.

00.44am
Shhhit, safetyy pins, wheresit? Ooops…

Sunday 31 December
7.50am. Just outside Salzburg.
Ugh, cannot believe I went out last night. Of all the days in the week, transfer day is the one when you really do not want to wake up hungover. And of all the transfer days in the season, the one I pick to be absolutely dying is the one that General Manager Sarah Datchet (said in a tone of reverence) decides to be at the airport. Good job!

Sigh… I feel grey. Really not looking forward to this.

4.00pm

Managed to pull it together with enough tea and make-up to do a reasonably plausible impression of Normal Poppy. According to Rachel, only the well-trained eye could tell what a hungover beast was lurking below the surface.

James picked a bad moment (i.e., just then) to walk past, remarking, 'You're hanging, Connors. You look like shit.'

Rachel's eyes widened, but I was saved from an earful of her yapping glee by an impossibly small, immaculately dressed woman in a red suit with a clipboard, BlackBerry and very high heels.

She greeted Rachel with a smile and said to me, 'Hello. We haven't met. You're Poppy, I take it?'

Haaarrrgggh… 'Ehh, yes, hello. Lovely to meet you. You must be Sarah Datchet?'

She nodded and asked about the snow conditions in Reschengel. By this point, Gina had spotted that two of her reps were communicating with senior management, and she was bearing down upon us fast, her eyes bulging with alarm. Sarah Datchet smiled. Gina arrived just in time to hear her say, 'so, as I understand it, we have you to thank for holding the Reschengel Club Hotel together this week? Keeping them all well fed?'

I tried to ignore the murderous look in Gina's eyes. 'Oh, I can't take too much credit for that, Sarah,' I answered truthfully, thinking of the digestive tracts of the defenceless hotel guests.

'Don't be modest, Poppy,' she said. 'And you have been keeping the rowdy ones in check with your ski boot, too, by all accounts.'

Cringe. How long before they let that one go?

11.48pm

Back late on the last coach with seventy-two guests, of whom at least fifty-three fell under the category of Bloody Hard Work To Sell To. Absolutely shattered now. So much so that only now this moment, as I walk towards the town centre from the staff chalet and see the beginnings of a firework show starting to splash colour on the sky overhead, can I begin to register that it is New

Year's Eve.

So December is over already – how so quickly?? Only eighteen weeks or so left here before it's time to leave again. But equally, how has it been less than a month since I have been here? It seems impossible somehow – less than a month since I first laid eyes on Gina; less than a month since I clipped into a pair of skis; less than a month since I met James. James, who I just can't get out of my mind.

How odd now to think that this life has always existed, that had things happened differently last month, Rachel and everyone else would have been carrying on the season here without me and I would never have had the slightest idea what I was missing. For so long, I'd been irritably aware of how tightly wound life in London had made me, but I had no idea how quickly and easily I could get back to feeling like myself again. *This was exactly what I needed.*

Or what I need?

I shake my head to clear it. *Don't spoil it.* I have four whole months left to enjoy this place, followed by a summer of doing what I please. By then I'll be ready to get back to reality, even if that reality fills me with a moderate level of dread that rolls around in the pit of my stomach like a leaden plum every time I think about it. The McIntyre job is something I need. It can't possibly be as crap as I imagine. I know I will be ready to go back when the time goes. *Who could live like this forever?*

I make my way up the main street past crowds of people in various stages of drunkenness. Although it is not even midnight, people have already started letting off fireworks and it is something of a minefield here. Literally a minefield – there are more malfunctioning fireworks than normal ones, and they are shooting erratically up and down, in between legs of unsuspecting people.

I find the English-speaking seasonaire community grouped together in one massive throng just under the clocktower in the village square, drinking chalet-grade prosecco out of the bottles and (predictably – I might have known that our lot had something to do with it) setting off fireworks in a very drunken and distracted way.

The clock is counting down. We're almost at midnight and people are starting to pair up for their New Year's kisses. New Rep Tom is looking deeply into the eyes of Bella from SuperSki, while Gina and Tina prowl through the crowd, stalking wildebeest. I've pretty sure I have never actually seen Gina pull (and I am absolutely convinced I never want to), but I know from two weeks' solid experience that Tina is more than capable of bringing home the goods when she decides to gets the claws out. I can only imagine what random, greasy-haired, pimply eighteen year-old will end up rocking the bunk above mine tonight....*sigh*.

Meanwhile, Rachel is wrapped up in the arms of what looks like a ridiculously good-looking Scandinavian boy. They are totally engrossed in each other, laughing and joking like there is nobody else around. Intriguing – I'm not sure I've ever seen him before.

No sign of Carol, Odysseus, Eoghan, Mikey or the chalet hosts, and naturally no sign of Suzanne (I think she is still hiding under the hotel office desk, working through the emotional trauma of Poultrygate) but I think I spot Harry too, over in the corner entangled with a strikingly beautiful girl with long, curly dark hair. This must be his girlfriend, Hélène, the French girl. He has been talking incessantly for the past ten days about her coming to visit.

Who will be *my* first kiss of the New Year? I wonder idly, and James' face pops unbidden into my mind. *No chance of that*, I think sadly, and wonder who he is kissing tonight.

And then, with a minute to go, I look down at my phone and see that in all the noise and confusion, a text message has come through:

'Happy (almost) New Year, Connors... Try to stay out of trouble, won't you? x'

A million thoughts and images flash through my head, none of them sensible, as the clock strikes twelve and the new year arrives. A split second later I look up and, before I have time to register what is going on, a pigtailed blonde head with an implausibly tanned face and big puckered lips is descending upon me with a slobbery kiss and a squeal of 'Ooohey! Happy New Year, sweetie!'

JANUARY
The Best of Intentions
(or, Rex, Lies and the Cliff of Death)

Monday 1 January

9.20pm

Very sore head. Had the best part of a bottle of Jägermeister poured into me between the hours of twelve and two o'clock. If I ever hear the words 'catch up' again, my internal organs will weep tears of blood. It was a massive onslaught of highly potent alcohol into a person who was not only very sober, but exhausted and still residually hungover – all in all, a bad mix.

I am told that Rachel and Ridiculously Hot Swedish Guy (no-one appears to have any idea what his name is) spent a moony few hours together realising that they were soulmates before I started to become a danger to myself and others and Rachel felt obliged by the inconvenient ties of friendship to take me home. Ridiculously Hot Swedish Guy hadn't been drinking, so he drove us back to our chalet in his big green camper van. Apparently - and I only have Rachel's bitter, bitter word to go on here - as they were saying their fond farewells, I found a tube of superglue and a bag of plastic dinosaurs on the floor of the van, and could not be prevented from supergluing said dinosaur family to the dashboard and giving them all Swedish (ish) names. I narrowly avoided supergluing my own hand to my face, by all accounts, as I protested being hauled away from my new friends, Thor, Astrid, Mats and, predictably, Rex. In the struggle to get me up the stairs and out of harm's way, they didn't exchange phone numbers but agreed to meet in Happy Bar tonight at nine-thirty.

I can't believe Rachel has a date on bar crawl night, and in Happy Bar of all places. In fact, thinking about it, I wonder if there is some ethical reason why she ought not to have a date: we are not supposed to drink, after all; perhaps there are also Snowglobe regulations concerning fraternising? But then I realise that I am hardly the person to preach workplace ethics to anyone, thinking as I am right now about doing extremely unprofessional things with my area manager.

On that note, a text message from James has just reminded me that said bar crawl kicks off in ten minutes and I need to get dressed.

93

'Good luck tonight, Connors. Please refrain from assaulting any more guests if possible. Remember: deep, calming breath when the violent instinct kicks in. Go to your happy place.'

Ha-fricking-ha.

Later.

No sign of Ridiculously Hot Swedish Guy. Rachel is very edgy and keeps looking at the door.

Still later.

Still no sign. We have to move the guests on from Happy Bar, we're running very late now.

Rather annoyed by how many guests we have on this bar crawl, actually. We were not expecting anyone to show up this evening, it being New Year's Day. This ought to be a day for sore heads and mature reflection on the passage of time, the potential of the future and, most of all, the painful fruitlessness of immersing oneself in alcohol. This logic has not stopped Miranda's guests – a stag party of sweaty fat boys who all seem to be called Billy – from hitting the town and treating it like one large, snowy mosh-pit. I wish they would stop trying to hug me.

I think Rachel is quite upset about Ridiculously Hot Swedish Guy's no-show. I tried to broach the subject with her by suggesting that maybe something came up and he didn't mean to stand her up, that he just didn't have her number.

'You're damn right, Poppy, I don't *get* stood up. He must have died.'

She refused to talk about it after that, beyond wondering how he plausibly might have died. We agreed that it must have been some kind of tragic accident on the glacier today, though I think she secretly suspects that the dinosaurs were somehow involved. Damn it, Rex!

3.44am. Local police station.

Still up and about, and not by choice. Predictably, Miranda's stupid stag party guests are the reason. We never quite got them as far as Damage. We were leaving Keller Bar when one of them turned to run back downstairs into the underground bar, slipped on the icy steps and landed face-down on the ground. This all would have been fine – he was wasted after all – had he not had three shot glasses stuffed up each sleeve.

New Rep Tom went down the valley in the ambulance with him to make sure he actually made it to the hospital to get his arms stitched back together. From the way the guy was roaring 'partaay, partAAAY' out the back doors, chances seemed high that he might tackle the paramedics to the ground, raid the ambulance for morphine and get right back on it.

Meanwhile, Rachel and I soldiered on against our better sense, but by Bar Cuba, the bar crawl was getting all too literal. The last thing any of these guests needed was more alcohol, so the free shots magically became fruit juice, but it was too little too late. The final straw was when two of them were stopped by the bouncers while trying to sneak out the main entrance of the bar with toilet seats shoved up their T-shirts.

There is impaired judgement, and then there is a crusty toilet seat stuck under your clothes. I don't even want to think about the hygienic implications. I am still in the waiting room of the local *Polizei* headquarters with them, and they are not allowed to sit beside me.

Thursday 4 Jan

7.55pm

When my phone rang at nine this morning – nine o'clock on my day off, for the record – I didn't have the slightest doubt that it would be something to do with the stag party guests. It's been one thing after another all bloody week. Why would they give us a day off?

'Sorry to bother you, Poppy.' Miranda's voice sounded oddly tight. 'I'm afraid I need your help. Can you come up to the chalet? You'll want to see this for yourself, I expect.'

Cursing the day those men were born, I dragged myself out of bed and made to climb over the discarded pile of unfamiliar clothes on the floor when all of a sudden the clothes moved under my feet. I nearly jumped out of my skin leaping up onto the bunk bed ladder.

'*Jesuschrist!*' I shrieked. '*Mice, mice, mice, mice, mice!*'

A blonde head appeared from under a hoodie. '*Whosit?* Oh, hiya, Poppy,' said Tina, bleary-eyed, pushing her hair out of her face.

'What on earth are you...?'

The pile moved again, dislodging another hoodie and revealing a second naked body.

'Yeah, sorry,' whispered Tina. 'I've been thinking it's not right to wake you all the time climbing up the ladder, so I thought I'd try the floor last night 'stead of the bunk, yeah?'

It has never so much been her climbing up the ladder that has woken (and subsequently traumatised) me. Still, I appreciated the gesture, although only fully once I was sure none of the clothes in the pile were mine.

'Who is the boy?' I whispered back as I climbed over his comatose form. Tina looked at me as though to say *how in the hell should I know?*

I walked in the door of the Chalet Tyrolerhof twenty minutes later to find a pair of rubber chickens hanging from the ceiling in the hall, dressed as schoolgirls and arranged in a rather compromising position. Intriguing as that was, I followed

Miranda's voice into the kitchen, where the floor was a mess of smashed glass, mayonnaise, olives, pesto and the splintered remains of a shelf. Enormous holes had been kicked in the walls of the dining room, three light fittings had been ripped completely off the wall and the downstairs toilet was flooded and overflowing.

In an impressive display of self-sufficiency, Miranda had already phoned the maintenance man. She had had to call me over too, however, since Herr Zangerl didn't have a single word of English and her German was not quite up to the task of working out how we would go about making the necessary repairs. He arrived soon after I did. The three of us walked around the chalet making internationally recognised noises of disapproval, measuring holes in the plasterboard and gathering up the broken pieces of light fittings. Herr Zangerl didn't even seem particularly shocked, just annoyed, somewhat resigned and not a little fascinated by the rubber chickens.

I reminded Miranda that it was her day off and that she was well within her rights to leave the kitchen mess for the guests to clean up when they resurfaced. She decided that she would rather just do it herself than come back to find it still there tomorrow morning, so we blitzed it as quickly as possible and I made a shopping list to replace everything that was broken. As I left to go to the supermarket, Miranda and Herr Z were pulling the soggy remains of a baguette back up through the U-bend of the downstairs toilet and having a serious discussion through hand gestures and facial expressions about *who would do something like this* and just what exactly such people deserve. I stole a glance at Miranda's face, wondering if and when she would cry, but her face was like thunder. I almost felt a bit sorry for the stag party idiots. Almost, but not quite.

Saturday 6 January

8.22pm

Mystery solved on the Ridiculously Hot Swedish front! Actually, one exclamation mark will not suffice, surely two!!

Arthur the Kitchen Porter knocked on our bedroom door this morning, looking sheepish. 'Err, I'm really, really sorry, Rachel, but I just found this in my apron. A tall guy gave it to me really early on Monday morning just outside the chalet. I was absolutely dying on my way to work, and I was late and I just stuck it in my pocket and forgot, please don't kill me...'

It was a note from Ridiculously Hot Swedish Guy. Well, he obviously hadn't signed it that. It was signed 'Niklas,' but the content suggested that it was him (unless someone else 'fell for her like a stumbling mule' and was 'unearthed from loveless slumber' by her eyes. Good God). He apologised profusely that he would have to miss their date, but said that he was in town with his two friends, Jon and Björn, and that their plans had changed suddenly and that they had to fly back to Sweden urgently that evening. He left his number and asked her to call or text him to let him know she got the message. He added that he and his friends would be back in a month, and that he hoped to see her then?

Unfortunately, the bottom right hand corner of the page was caked with what looked like a congealed splodge of egg yolk, taking with it the last five digits of Niklas' number. I made a strangled noise of frustration and Arthur bolted, yelling behind him 'sorry, I know, *I know*, sorry, sorry, sorrryyy...'

I expected Rachel to be venting steam through her ears, but turned around to find her looking remarkably Zen about it all. Blasé, even. 'Oh well,' she said, shrugging and screwing up the note into a ball, 'no biggie.'

'No biggie?' I scrambled for the rubbish bin, fishing it out. 'Rach, you can't be serious. You've been depressed and moody ever since Monday. I've never seen you like this. I thought you were going to cry the other night when Tina asked about him.'

'Don't be ridiculous. I'm not bothered.'

'Shut *up*, you so are. Come on, let's try every permutation of those last five digits. It won't take us long. *You have to call him.*'

'No flippin' way. I'm not *calling* him, and I'm certainly not calling ten thousand other random Swedes. If he wants me, he knows where to find me – if he ever comes back, that is. Meanwhile,' she rubbed her hands together, 'I have a new man, Poppy. The coach from my snowboard clinic today. Three words for you: O. M. G.'

'Rachel…'

'Seriously. His name is Andu and he totally wants me. Fact. We hung out for the afternoon and he promised to train me for the Big Air competition in March. Imagine! And he has the MOST amazingly yellow Von Zipper goggles you'll ever see. They sponsor him and all…'

I let it go. Face-saving denial is not something I would normally let her get away with, but she is doing a remarkably good job of letting me off on the James front so I didn't push it. I know for sure that she is on to me. Every time my phone beeps with a text message so early in the morning or late at night that he must be texting me from his bed, I can see her react out of the corner of my eye. Considering this is Rachel, she is being incredibly restrained about it all.

The thing is, I am not even in denial about James anymore, not to myself at any rate. Although I will never confess a thing to anyone until something actually happens between us, I do accept that there is most definitely something going on. I have barely known him three weeks, yet he phones and texts me every single day, to the point where I wonder first, how on earth does he get any work done? And second, how I will ever explain it all to Gina, Sarah Datchet or whoever in head office reads our itemised phone bills? (Resolutely not thinking about this until I absolutely have to.)

Every time I hear my phone beep, I know that it is most likely him with some unexpected, random chat, e.g.:

'Need your guidance, Connors. As a style choice, is a big white puffa ski jacket:

a)   Gangsta and pimpin'?

b)   Acceptable nineties retro?

c)   Perhaps a little bit impractical?'

Me: 'I think the real question here is, 'who you gonna call?'

a)   Ghostbusters?

b)   Fiddy?'

I love it, this slow, flirtatious build-up. The longer this goes on, the more I realise that I have never been so unashamedly, unquestionably *pursued,* and in such a naughty, forbidden lust sort of context. Deliciously exciting all round.

Shit, shit, late for visits, stop mooning Poppy, you big loser.

8.35pm

I have just experienced the most surreal scene. Went around to visit Miranda's vile stag party guests at the Tyrolerhof to remind them that their transfer coach will leave at four in the morning with or without them. I had a whole speech worked out, cranky *don't mess with me* tone of voice and all, and had spent the walk up the road working myself up to righteous, impatient anger in case they were already too wasted to care. But as soon as I walked into the hallway of the Tyrolerhof, I knew that something was odd. It was alarmingly quiet for a stag party chalet – indeed any chalet in the midst of dinner service. In fact, it was silent but for the strains of some sort of relaxation music that seemed to be coming from the dining room. Puzzled, I headed straight for the kitchen, to find Miranda prepping a fruit salad for the morning's breakfast, the dinner pots and pans already washed and the surfaces polished and gleaming.

'Where are the guests?' I asked warily.

She smiled a triumphant smile and nodded in the direction of the dining room, so I peeped around the door. There they were, sitting quietly, eating plates of what looked like fish fingers, peas and mashed potato and listening to something that sounded for all the world like Enya. There was not so much as a wine glass on the table. When they saw me, one of them (the one who shredded his arms the other night, judging by the bandages) half-raised his hand and asked me if they could please, possibly have some more orange squash, if that's OK?

I was about to say yes, of course, no problem when Miranda shouted in, 'Have you finished your peas?'

He looked at his plate and ate another two spoonfuls before answering. 'Yes, Miranda!'

'Fine then, Billy. You can help yourselves to a glass each.'

I just stood there in amazement, watching the scene unfold. They finished up their meal, brought in their plates and glasses, washed and dried everything and put it away, thanked Miranda for dinner and asked her if it was OK if they went out for a drink.

'If you are not back here by eleven, there will be no packed breakfast bags in the morning, is that quite clear?'

They all nodded, thanked her again and left. I was speechless.

She wiped her hands on a cloth, poured us both a glass of wine and said, 'Here's to good old fashioned respect.'

Cannot believe that I have just witnessed this. I am still not sure that I did not simply imagine it.

Wednesday 10 January
11.15am

Ha-*aaaaaaa*-ah. Oh, oh. Right, OK. So much for long, slow flirtatious build-up. The cards, it would seem, are on the table now.

James phoned me not long ago, ostensibly to follow up on a piece of guest baggage that was mislaid at the airport on Sunday, but actually to ask if I would like to come out with a crowd of them in Futterberg tomorrow night and stay over. 'With Anna,' he added, after a fraction of a pause.

My heart skipped a little, and then sank. *Shit.* I had to tell him that I couldn't because, ironically, I was due to ski guide a group of guests from here over to Futterberg on the Ski Away Day on Friday. It was not something I could get out of doing. Tom has done it for the past three Fridays and his parents are visiting this week. There was no way I could ask him to cover this one for me so that I could go over the mountain for, let's face it, a booty call. (Obviously, I didn't say that. Can't quite believe I just thought it.)

'Oh, OK. Fair enough. Shame, that.' He sounded a little deflated, but then he phoned again a few minutes later with a watertight plan. 'Hey, I've just had a thought. I've checked the weather forecast and it looks like we're in for a big snowfall and some high winds in the next few days, which means there's quite a good chance the connecting lifts between the two resorts will be shut tomorrow and Friday. Why don't I drive over tomorrow evening and bring you back to Futterberg with me? We'll get someone to drive the guests over to Futterberg in the hotel van on Friday and meet them here. Provided you can still function at that point, of course,' he added. 'Tomorrow night looks set to be a big party. What do you say?'

What could I say? He had thought of everything.

Everything, that is, except how to ask Gina. Since my going over there is not something necessitated by work, James can't exactly *order* me to Futterberg. I bet to spite me, Gina will think of some reason why I can't go. The more I think about this, the more I am now absolutely convinced of it.

James laughed away this idea, and told me to just ask her, saying that she would be fine about it. He clearly then reflected a little upon this assumption and is now worried, however, as he has just texted me to ask what the verdict is.

Will ask her soon. Just need to think of a good way.

Later.

Still haven't asked. Nervous now.

Later again.

Another text from James: 'Well? What did she say?'

Me: 'Well…nothing as yet.'
James: 'Chicken…'

Grr… right, I'll ask her now.

Just then, Gina bursts into the room, 'super-stressed' about Tilly's and Mark's chalet budget for the Elena, and demands that I come join her for a calming cigarette on the balcony. Right, I'll ask her there.

Still later.

Chickened out completely. First, I couldn't think of a way to bring it up casually in conversation, and then I think I probably over-thought how best to coordinate my voice, facial expression and words so as to appear suitably disinterested, and so the end result was that I think I freaked her out slightly, opening and closing my mouth in manner of a drowning fish. (Do fish drown? Is that the word? Asphyxiate, probably.).

Argh.

The moment passed, and she buggered off again.

Right, I will go down there and ask her now. In five minutes.

Or ten.

I am a massive coward.

Eventually.

That did *not* go well.

I knocked on her door. She answered. I instantly lost my nerve and asked her something inane about lift pass prices in low season. She looked at me like I was on drugs. I hovered there for a minute, almost asked her and then lost my nerve again. I was about to bottle it completely when she cornered me with a devastatingly direct: 'Oh, come on, Poppy, spit it out. What?'

Then, of course, being under pressure to seem really nonchalant, I tried to pretend like the idea just popped into my head, but I realised midway through that this was stupid and… well, all in all, it was excruciating. A blind and deaf person in the next room could have worked out how scared I was that she would say no (or claw my eyes out).

She looked at me sideways, thought about it, thought about it a little more and then said, 'fine, no problem sweetie.' I waited for the catch. 'Just be careful, yeah?'

I am even more freaked out by her calmness than by her manifest psychosis, I have decided.

10.12pm

Text from James that made my breath catch in my throat:

'I see you finally found the nerve. V amusingly suspicious text message from Gina just now. I think she senses that something is up…'

So something *is* up…

Heart is singing. What a stupid expression that is, but so accurate.

Right. It's on, apparently. Absolutely, definitely not going to shag him, however.

12.41am

Might kiss him. Maybe, we'll see. Maybe if the opportunity arises. Must not get drunk though – must not get carried away.

2.22am

Definitely not going to shag him. Would send out totally the wrong signals. I am absolutely not that sort of girl, etc. etc.

Friday 12 January

7.57am. The left hand side of an unspecified bed with blue sheets.

Oh, dear. I shagged him.

7.59am

At least I think I did.

Oh no.

Where am I???

8.01am

Oh my *GOD*, I got very drunk last night. *Very drunk.* Blindsided by the vastly more alcohol tolerant. Ghastly, ghastly, awful, stupid Poppy, you idiot, you utter…

It's all James' fault. He came over to Reschengel and picked me up early. The first five minutes of the car journey were spent laughing at Gina and her muted, though unmistakable, hostility all day today (there was actual panting). Then for the next hour or so we talked utter rubbish to each other, I suspect to distract from the strange sort of charge in the air (at least that's my excuse). When we got over to Futterberg, I ditched my skis and bag in Anna's place and we all went for pizza – me, James, Anna and seven of their friends and Snowglobe colleagues. We entertained each other with the 'disasters' of the season so far, Reschengel's most recent one being the discovery that our new chef, Odysseus, has a phobia of eggs the like of which no one has ever seen. The hotel hosts have had to implement some bizarre arrangements in the kitchen to compensate, including the promotion of Arthur from lowly Kitchen Porter to exalted Egg Chef. His skill base has broadened from simple breaking, to beating, whipping, separating, poaching, boiling, frying and scrambling. You name it, Arthur can now do it to an egg.

I started off the evening with the absolute best of intentions, but then there was accidental knee-touching and flirting, and a lot of wine over dinner, and then James kept picking me up and throwing me in the snow all the way to the pub. The 'pub' was a little locals' bar where the spirit measures were basically pint glasses (no exaggeration. I cannot believe I finished a whole one but I think that explains a lot). By eleven, we were all utterly hammered, James and I holding hands as we tripped along happily in the direction of the nightclub.

I blame the fresh air on that walk for everything that happened next, because it all gets very vague indeed after that. I remember being introduced to lots of people. I remember being blown away that the club played an actual drum 'n' bass track and not the heady mix of Britney and Euro-trance I have come to know and love. Then I remember James' hand on my cheek as he kissed me unashamedly in front of about eight of the Snowglobe resort staff. I remember thinking, *I can't believe he is doing this. Does he not care if everyone sees?* After that, it is just flash images.

I don't remember leaving or how I got to where I am now. There was definitely some very frantic sex in a strange bed. After that, nothing at all until I drifted to consciousness a few minutes ago to feel an unfamiliar arm underneath me pulling me closer to a warm body at my back and a voice behind me murmuring sleepily, 'good morning, gorgeous.'

A moment of calm, and then I was hit by the crashing wave: *what-the-fuck-what-the-fuck-has-happened-what-have-I-done???* The arm – it must be James', right? I mean, oh God, what if it is *not James?* Can I put a face to the vague flashes of frantic sex? Argh, no. I can't even remember if it was any good, damn it.

I sense probably not.

But more seriously – what if it is not James? What if something went very, very wrong last night and this is some random friend of his? I take a moment to quantify the horror of that possibility: *oh, that would so not be good.*

Quick glance.

Massive relief. Thank God. It's James. A moment of peaceful joy washes over me, before sudden, sickening sense of horrible clarity.

Oh God, it's *James.*

8.07am. The left hand side of James Walker's bed.

I have just slept with my boss. This is such a painfully crap cliché. (Obviously I could have anticipated the crapness of the cliché when I began fancying the absolute pants off him – and actively encouraging the eventual removal of said pants – but naturally it only really hits me now that the deed is done.)

And actually, it's worse than sleeping with my boss. I have just had hideously drunken sex with my boss: hideously drunken, *stupidly public,* probable one-night-stand sex. Argh, aaaargh, everyone saw us, everyone knows. Imagine what the airport will be like from now on. Oh God, it is so embarrassing.

And *Gina.* Oh my GOD, Gina is going to kneecap me. When I get back to Reschengel later, she is going to…

Oh shit, *the guests.* They're on the way here right now. I suspect, since I have not yet been bludgeoned over the head with heavy, pointy pieces of machinery, that I am still quite drunk. How, how can I ski guide today? How?? On at least three distinct levels, I cannot contemplate anything so awful.

Where are my shoes? Where are my clothes?

No! My Snowglobe uniform is in my bag, which I so very faithfully and naively left in Anna's flat yesterday evening with my skis and boots. Is she even awake? Argh, how will I face her? How will I go outside?

Oh, this is all too much. I need water, I need…AAAaaaaRRRGHH he's waking up.

9.18am

It was lovely. He turned to me, said I looked far too awake and cuddled me for a bit as he slowly woke up. Then we sort of just lay there for a while, looking at each other and half-smiling. Then he kissed my shoulder, wrapped me up in his arms again and said that the only thing for it today would be to stay in bed for at least another hour or two, forage for breakfast when we absolutely had to and then promptly get straight back into bed for the rest of the afternoon.

I pointed out the unfortunate fact of my ski guiding group

arriving in, oh, twenty-five minutes.

He put on a very stern voice, rolled over, pinned me to the bed and growled, 'you're not guiding anyone today. Get down there and fake your best sore throat and send them off to fend for themselves with a piste map. Then get back to this bed within twenty minutes. Ideally with breakfast.'

'Hmm, I don't know, what if I get into trouble?'

'You're already in trouble. Insubordination. Come on, get to it.'

'But you're lying on top of me.'

'Rrr, so I am.'

Currently walking back up the hill from the lift station, where I've just done a remarkably good agonisingly painful raspy throat impression which the guests were totally convinced by, I am sure.

All sorts of pieces of jumbled, half-formed thoughts floating around my head now. James and me. Me and James. Moon, moon.

5.10pm

Sitting in the front seat of the minibus back to Reschengel with the guests now, painfully raspy voice back in place. They have totally bought the act and are even really sympathetic. Moderate-to-severe guilt pangs struck when the three middle-aged mummy-types started arguing over the best recipe for a hot lemon and ginger drink to make me feel better, but I beat my conscience down with one swift kick – there's no taking back what happened now and anyway, I wouldn't even if I could. I'm too busy fizzing with excitement about everything that has happened in the last twenty-four hours to regret a thing.

I tried to feel slightly guilty about ditching a whole day's work – specifically, abandoning guests to fend for themselves in a blizzard... for shame, Poppy – but it was rather difficult to sustain it, lying there in the arms of the one person whose responsibility it would have been to sack me for such bad behaviour. We had clearly just entered a whole other world of unprofessionalism but at least there was the reassurance that we were in it together, I thought, turning over to lay my head on his chest and drifting back to sleep.

Of course, there was still the question of how on earth we would contain the scandalised outrage on this one. The more I thought about it, the more horrible the visions of the Futterberg resort staff gossiping over breakfast about last night, texting and phoning their colleagues in all different resorts to fill them in and me arriving home to a whole world of drama and scandal, shocked faces and delighted whispers. I didn't know how to broach the subject with James however. I didn't want to give him the wrong impression, but one-night stands had never been my thing and I really hated the idea of what had happened between us being common knowledge. I wanted to keep this between ourselves until I knew for sure whether it would go somewhere, or if it was just last night.

'Errm, James?' I began eventually, once I had worked up the courage.

'Mmm?'

'About last night… You know, we weren't exactly subtle… And the reps and chalet staff…'

'Don't worry,' he reassured me, 'they know not to say anything. They won't all be talking about us down in Salzburg Airport…any more than they all already are, I suppose.'

Big sigh of relief. He was OK about keeping things with us very much under wraps for now; really quite keen on the idea actually.

'Are you suggesting an illicit little affair, Ms Connors?' he whispered, nuzzling at my neck and sending a shiver of excitement up my back. 'How very naughty.'

Mmm, mmm, mmm.

'Yes, I suppose I do like the sound of that, James. Our little secret…'

5.28pm. Still on the minibus.

Sigh…this road goes on forever. Still only halfway home. Really tired again now. Just going to have another little sleep.

110

5.58pm

RRRrring…right beside my ear…fffurgg…*where am I*…Aaahh, shit. It's Gina. Damn it. *Not asleep, not hungover, feeling good. Feeling good.* Ahem. Brightest and most awake voice ever, here we go:

'Hi Gina. Yup, in the bus. Just passing the Tensinghof. OK, ten minutes. See you then, byeee.'

6.03pm

Only as I hung up did I realise what I had done. Harry was looking over at me from the driver's seat, shaking his head and pointing at his throat.

Shiiit.

Afraid to turn around now.

Saturday 13 January
6.30pm. Staff chalet.

Amazingly, I think James was right – I'm in the clear here (well, as far as the Snowglobe staff is concerned. I think I have burned that bridge with the guests. They said nothing as they disembarked the minibus but each gave me a look of withering disapproval that made me feel about three inches tall).

But aside from Harry thinking I am an idiot for breaking my 'hangover cover,' nobody from Snowglobe appears to know or care what happened in Futterberg. All I got when I arrived in yesterday was Arthur's cursory, 'Yo, Pops, you look like shit. Good night then? Do anything stupid? No? Pity.' Everybody was a lot more interested in fighting over who got to tell me what had happened in Reschengel on Thursday night. Apparently Tom went home with a lesbian and then got in trouble when her girlfriend showed up. I'm still not all that clear on the details of what happened next and I sensed that Arthur and Eoghan were embellishing slightly when they started describing some sort of dildo swordfight, but Tom is remaining tight-lipped on the subject for now. Honestly, I'm not particularly bothered if I never find out. I'm just incredibly grateful for the deflection of everyone's attention and amazed (to the point of not quite believing it can possibly be true) that we got away with it.

I had expected a grilling from Gina at the very least, and felt every drop of blood drain out of my face when Tom, Rachel and I ran into her in the garden outside the staff chalet on our way to visits yesterday evening.

'Poppy, Jesus Christ,' she exclaimed, stopping us on the path, 'you look *awful*. What happened last night?'

'Yeah, yeah, err…went out,' I stammered, 'Anna and her mates…sambuca…err…yeah, yeah, big night. It was good. Yeah.'

I nodded quickly and smiled unconvincingly. Rachel threw her eyes to heaven.

Fortunately, even after more than a month of working with me, Gina remains totally oblivious to my complete inability to lie with conviction and she just shook her head in mock-disgust, trying not to look a little pleased, and wagged her finger in my face. 'I only hope you didn't let James see you like that this morning. And you didn't misbehave in front of him last night, did you? I don't want my reps giving this resort a bad reputation, yah? That Anna gets away with a lot because her and James are old friends but don't you let her drag you down in his eyes, sweetie. Don't lose his respect.'

Rachel snorted. 'I'm quite sure James still respected Poppy this morning,' she said, deadpan, with wide, innocent eyes. 'Don't worry, Gina, Poppy told me that James was out with them last night and he was the one buying the rounds of sambuca before they went clubbing.'

'Before he went home and we stayed out,' I added, stupidly. *Shh, Poppy. Why are you talking? Shhhh.*

Tom gave me a curious look. Rachel suppressed a grin. 'Anyway,' she went on, 'I don't think Poppy could damage the Reschengel team in James' eyes, Gina. Not when you're here.'

Gina's instinct was to take this as a compliment, but she wasn't sure. She hesitated and smiled a cautious half-smile but I could tell that her imagination was still in Futterberg, with James buying us all rounds of sambuca and her not invited. There was an awkward pause. I opened my mouth and closed it again.

It was enough to change the mood. Gina got into the resort van, ordering me to get a good night's sleep after visits. Then, as an afterthought, she called Tom to come with her to help her bring boxes of new crockery to the Tyrolerhof, where this week's stag party had apparently decided that the Jewish wedding ceremony of smashing plates was something that required advance practice.

Rachel shook her head in bewilderment as the van screeched off up the hill. 'Of all the people who could try to get away with an illicit affair, you, Poppy? Seriously? I think you have bitten off more than you can chew, lady friend.'

Of course I had had to tell her what happened with James in Futterberg, as it would have been physically impossible to keep a secret of any kind from her, let alone one of this magnitude. She was absolutely thrilled at the prospect of a little intrigue, of course, and swore she wouldn't breathe a word, although apparently Gina-baiting is exempt. She has also promised to help cover for me with Gina so that James and I can see each other in covert little rendezvouses. I am very glad to have her on my side. I think I will need all the help I can get.

Had to tell Carol too. Didn't feel that this was breaking the promise James and I made to one another, since Carol doesn't actually like anyone here, so therefore the chances of her gossiping about it are slim. Carol's reaction was less encouraging than Rachel's, however.

'Really?' She stared at me. 'You?'

I nodded.

'Right, OK.' She looked blank. 'Err, what do I say here? That's great?'

'Oh, come on, Carol,' Rachel nudged her, still grinning at me, 'I know you don't do enthusiasm, but it's wicked isn't it? Were we not saying just the other day how unbelievable it is that Poppy has never done a walk of shame in this resort? I mean, not even once! Imagine that! I'd say Eoghan and Mikey are in double digits by now, and Tina's broken the bloody counter. Well, the wait is over. Here it is! And in style, no?'

Carol was too busy lighting a cigarette to respond. Rachel stamped her foot in frustration. 'Carol, you are totally failing to acknowledge what an exciting turn of events this is. It's so *romantic!*'

'Romantic?' Carol raised an eyebrow. 'OK.'

'It *is*,' Rachel insisted. 'You should see the way he looks at her. It's like there's no one else around. He's totally besotted. It's like...oh, I don't know. Name some famous people in movies, I'm drawing a blank here.'

'Calm down, Rachel, you'll hurt yourself. It's not that romantic. It's just...' I struggled for words as Carol regarded me carefully, waiting, '...good to feel like I do about him. I don't know what it is about him, I can't say for sure, but I know I have to see where this takes me. Takes us, I suppose.'

Carol said nothing. She stared at me for long moment, then nodded and left the room to smoke outside on the balcony. Rachel turned to me, her face a picture of bafflement. I looked away, embarrassed though I wasn't sure why.

Sunday 14 January
7.43am

Argh. Not long until I arrive at the airport. Moment of truth – does everyone from – oh, my days – *every resort in Austria* know about Thursday night? How should I be around James? Like normal or distant and aloof? What if I am too friendly? And what if they all know? Will it show? Will Sarah Datchet take a hatchet to me? Argh, *argh.*

Gina is being very off with me. I am ninety-nine percent sure that she doesn't know anything specific (I can't see how I would still have an intact face if she did) but she has definitely decided that she doesn't like the friendship she sees growing between me and the Futterberg lot and she has grown positively frosty toward me in the past forty-eight hours. It's really not helping my nerves. Massive, untamed butterflies are beating each other to a violent death inside my stomach now as the coach slows down for the airport slip road.

8.44am. Salzburg Airport

Incredible. No-one seems to know a thing. Anna gave me a wink and left it at that. Cannot believe it, am so relieved.

9.57am

Actually a bit of an anti-climax.

10.42pm

In the end, I didn't really have to worry about how to act around James or Sarah Datchet or stress about my complete inability to lie. Bad weather and snowfall at Innsbruck this morning meant that all flights to and from that airport were diverted to Salzburg, bringing extra guests, coaches, panic, drama, missing luggage, wailing children, impatient grown-ups and all sorts of other fun besides. The airport was jam-packed and everybody was run off their feet for the whole day. I'm not complaining; the confusion and stress of it all made it very easy for me to avoid the departing Ski Away Day guests – who, to my immense relief and eternal gratitude, said nothing to Sarah Datchet about the Futterberg debacle on Friday. *Thank you, thank you, thank you, lovely people, I will never forget you* – and to keep busy thinking about other things than the delicious secret I am now hugging to my chest with the growing happiness of slowly fading disbelief.

James and I had no real reason or opportunity to talk all day, which was probably just as well. I'm not sure I could have handled normal interaction with him in front of the people who know us both. A few times during the day I caught him staring and felt my heart flip over in my chest at the sight of his eyes on me. Then he would give me a quick smile and look away, pretending to do something on his laptop or snapping at someone to run along quickly with some highly important piece of paper or other.

I left with my coachload of guests at four-thirty, glad to be away from the mayhem, and he sent me a text as I drove away:

'Good thing you're on the early coach. I might be able to get some bloody work done now. You're sacked.'

Mmm. Contented sigh. With the exception of Gina's ongoing silent hostility to me, all is right with the world (and even that, upon reflection, is somewhat comforting).

Wednesday 17 January

1.23pm. Ruhtai.

Skiing with Rachel, Carol, Mark, Arthur and Tom today. The boys found a 'sweet' little four-foot ledge drop yesterday over on the Ruhtai side of the ski area, so today we've all come along to have a play, bringing a video camera to record the carnage.

Chairlift chat on the way here was more or less confined to harassing Tom for the full story of what happened with the lesbians on Thursday. It's only the latest of what we now call 'Tom's accidental bedroom adventures': a list of romantic disasters that have been a remarkably consistent source of amusement since he has been here in Reschengel. Tom never seems to find stable, socially-adept single girls; rather he is a magnet for married women, attached women, highly-strung (i.e. insane) women, aesthetically unfortunate women and women so downright wrong they make Chrigi look well-adjusted and Tina look like Maria von Trapp. At first I thought that he was a deliberate player but soon discovered that quite the opposite is true. Tom's biggest problem is that he is such a genuinely nice boy, so eager to please and so interested in everyone he meets – particularly women – that he is an easy target for those looking for a little no-strings excitement. He never seems to recognise the signs. And when it all goes wrong, he feels obliged to take the blame and make things right, even when odds are that he will get his head kicked in by an angry boyfriend/husband/jealous best friend. Poor Tom has no 'run away' instinct whatsoever; no sense of impending doom. It's freakish.

Yet somehow – amazingly – he always seems to come out on top (often literally). It took a while, but he cracked after a couple of hours and told us the story of what happened on Thursday. Her name was Vicky. She approached him at the bar in Rodeo and he invited her to join in the Snowglobe drinking games at the bar. One thing led to another, as happens, and everything was great until about an hour after they got back to her place. That was when Vicky's girlfriend Cara walked in. Cara was less than pleased to find Tom in her bed, and the two girls broke into a

118

blazing row until Tom (dressed at this point) intervened. He's is not quite sure how, but somehow he managed to convince them both that things could only be resolved by all three of them hopping back into bed and 'sorting it out' there. They all lived happily ever after (although I think Tom was traumatised by something that happened afterwards involving a tongue piercing. He refused to elaborate beyond saying, 'I'm through with lesbians.')

'Yeah, yeah, but *two* lesbians?' Arthur was incredulous. 'Two lesbians invited you into their bed? That actually happens in real life?'

Tom shrugged.

'You're such a peacemaker,' said Carol.

At Ruhtai now, and this little drop is hilarious. The snow is just right for it – not too fluffy, not too crusty. And I'm totally getting the hang of being in the air; just got to sort out the landing part. The others keep yelling something about using my hands. I'm not clear on what they mean, though. Am I doing that too much, or not enough?…waaAAAAaahh…

Thursday 18 January

10.00am

Just saw the videos Mark made of us all on the cliff drop yesterday. The stars of the show were undoubtedly my comedy flailing windmill arms. OK, point taken about the hands now.

The others are heading back up to Ruhtai without me today. I just got a text from James to say that he's on his way over here and will meet me under Furggspitz at eleven.

3.08pm

Hee hee, a deliciously naughty plan is afoot. (In fact, for this very reason, James and I have just been discussing our shared love of the word, 'afoot.' It's a great word – conjures up all sorts of wildly secretive skulking, *Pink Panther* style – so we have decided that as we put our highly secret and very bold plan into action, we

119

will have to have the *Pink Panther* theme music on constant internal replay.) James has dreamt up the genius idea that I stay with him tonight by pretending to miss the last lift from Futterberg back to Reschengel. The only real problem with this is that I am supposed to do hotel visits first thing in the morning, which I will miss as a result, but James has said I can phone the hotels and tell them to put up a notice.

'Don't worry, you know they always call if anything interesting happens anyway. And I'll let Anna know to cover for you if Gina phones her.'

The really clever part is that I am going to tell Gina that the reason I can't get back tonight is that James is out of town visiting another resort and there is no-one else to drive me home, so I have to stay with Anna. It's foolproof. Provided we stay in, of course, and no-one sees us. We will not have much of a choice, actually, since I will have no clothes or shoes but my ski boots.

Hee hee, love the drama of conducting an illicit affair.

Da dum.

Da dum.

Da dum, da dum, da dum, da dum, da daaaaaaam…

9.40pm

Mmm, lovely times. James cooked me dinner and we sat outside on the balcony all evening under blankets, talking about everything and nothing until we both got cold. Now he has gone to dig out a DVD, which we both know we won't see much of.

Happy, happy. A proper night together, just us. And a night in bed with him that I will actually remember this time… hurrah!

Oh, my. I had totally forgotten what this feeling was like. It's wonderful to be single for a time and then do the whole falling in love thing again. You forget how bloody amazing a sensation it really is.

9.42pm

Not falling in love. I didn't mean love. I meant lust. Infatuation. Not love.

Friday 19 January

2.40pm

Gina was really *not* happy with me when I got back this morning. She came thundering up the stairs just after I got in, burst through the door and told me in no uncertain terms how unacceptable it is that I allowed myself to end up in this situation, and that I need not think for one minute that she was under any illusions about what was really going on. I felt my mouth go dry.

'Err, what? What do you mean?'

'Poppy, it is incredibly obvious that you planned this. I was not born yesterday.'

Oh, God, is it so obvious? Shit. She knows.

'I mean, look at the state you were in when you came back from Futterberg last week. Don't think I don't know what it's like over there, and what that girl Anna gets up to. I mean, as a manager, she does not work to quite the same, ahhh, *standards* that some of us insist upon, yah?'

Eh?

'It is quite clear to me,' she went on coldly, 'that you and Anna intentionally worked it so that you could stay over there last night and get drunk together. And if you think that James' being away means that he won't know, well, you're wrong. I'm calling him right now.' She started stabbing through her phone's contacts list with a triumphant smile, enjoying herself. 'I should warn you,' she said cattily, pressing her phone to her ear, 'he will *not* be so impressed with you now. Just because you think that you two are friends, you should not make the mistake of forgetting that he is your *manager*, and a *professional*. You might not take this seriously, but James does not forget his priorities.'

Oh my God, you have got to be kidding.

I then had to endure a ten-minute gut-wrenching struggle to hold it together as Gina paced the room, outlining the case for the prosecution. It didn't help that I could hear James' end of the conversation too, his suitably grave 'hmmms' and 'ahhhs' and occasional interjections. I nearly lost it when I heard him ask, 'do you think I should discipline her, Gina?'

'It's not funny,' she hissed at me before continuing with matching gravity, 'I think it is up to you James. You need to do whatever it takes to see that she shows both you and me the proper respect.'

In the end, James decided that he would deal with telling me off this time. He also had the bright idea that in the future if Anna and I wanted to organise nights over in Futterberg together, it would be no problem so long as I let everyone know in advance and rearranged visits to suit.

'That way no-one will be inconvenienced, and everyone is happy.'

Everyone but Gina, it would seem. She was not at all satisfied with this outcome, particularly since I seemed so pleased. She left the chalet under a preoccupied frown. I think she knew that she had been outsmarted, but was still trying to work out how.

Saturday 20 January

7.09pm

Out of nowhere, cryptic message from James: 'Start packing your bags, sunshine…' What? *Actually being sacked??*

7.52pm

Ah, all is now clear. Gina phoned me to say that James has just heard some unexpected news from another resort and, as a result, has had to change things around a little for next week. The rep in Thurlech has to go home for three days from Sunday to Tuesday and I am to be sent over there on the transfer coach tomorrow to cover her. It's quite exciting. I have never been to that part of Austria. The only thing that bothers me is that I will have to sell lift passes to one hundred and fifteen people on five separate transfer coaches tomorrow. Mildly concerned that such a thing is not humanly possible.

8.16pm

Sod the lift pass sales! Very excited now. James phoned just now to fill me in on the far more interesting details of the trip. He has sorted it so that I will have a hotel room to stay in during my time in Thurlech. Woo hoo! Two nights of luxury accommodation, presumably non-mouse-infested! Three days of no Gina! I can't quite believe my luck. And best of all, James is going to come over and stay with me on Monday night.

The official line is that he will have to drive over from Futterberg at some point on Tuesday to bring me back to Reschengel anyway, so, in the spirit of excellent senior management, he will drive over early that morning so that he can spend the day skiing with and 'getting to know' the combined resort staff of Thurlech and the nearby Müntzen. Nobody will know that he is actually going to drive over on Monday night under the cover of darkness, spend the night with me and then appear to meet us all totally innocently the following morning. So very covert, so very dramatic. Must start packing.

123

Monday 22 January
7.11pm. Thurlech.

Wow, there is really not a lot to do here in Thurlech. It's a fantastically pretty chocolate-box village, but I suspect I have exhausted the sights just walking between my hotel and the lift station. And apart from the bowling alley with a beer tap, there's no nightlife here to speak of. Hmm. I know I should be grateful that this is such a tobogganing-before-dinner, get-the-kids-to-bed-early kind of place because it means no bar crawl. Still, until James arrives, I am struggling to get through the mind-numbing dullness of this evening and really wishing I had brought a book or something, anything to pass the time.

I like the resort manager, Linda, and felt horribly guilty earlier this evening when she told me how she and the resort chalet staff wanted to take me out to dinner tonight. I had to feign tiredness to get out of it, knowing that if we all went out to eat at nine-thirty there would be no way I could be back at the hotel when James arrived.

Now I'm not only bored, but also quite hungry. Where does one find a takeaway pizza around here without being spotted out and about, I wonder? Without proper preparation and forethought, being covert can be a very hungry business, I have learned.

Just waiting in the hotel, lying on my bed, watching bad German TV, which, as far as I can see, is one small step away from outright pornography. Even the advertisements feature improbably svelte and alluring *Hausfraus* caressing themselves suggestively with detergent boxes and such. Delightful.

7.32pm

Oooh, text message.

Only Rachel. Says that not a lot is happening in Reschengel in my absence, that they are all missing me and that she is waiting by the phone for dramatic updates on my soap opera life.

'Make it good, Connors, Hot Andu is a LOT LESS FUN minus his snowboard. He's stuck to his Playstation – DULL! I'm living vicariously through you now. Don't you bore me rigid too.'

A dangerously likely outcome if I text back this evening, I think, just as I triumph over the remote control and finally work out how to change channels. Victory! Oh. There is only one other channel, and it is a current affairs panel discussing, as far as I can understand, the water table in Hamburg. Being covert can be an extraordinarily dull business too.

Sigh. I need something to do to distract my brain from talking to my conscience. I really can't stop the little twinge of guilt at the look on Linda's face earlier when I ducked out of the evening she had planned. All she wanted to do was welcome me to Thurlech and say thanks for helping them out, and in any other situation I would never have dreamed of throwing that kind of gesture back at someone. I felt awful, and the more I try to shake it, the worse it gets, thinking of her and all the chalet hosts cancelling the plans they made for me.

Erk, the longer I sit staring at the four walls of this tiny hotel room, the more I wonder about all of this: about James in his car on the way here now, about the various lies I have told and to whom, and what exactly all the various people concerned think I am doing right now. I think back yet again to the Futterberg Ski Away guests, who – let's face it, I ditched unceremoniously, lied to and got caught by. Yes, I got away with it, but what on earth did they think of me? And now here I am, hiding out in a hotel room to snatch a night with the man who has made all of this seem like not just a good idea, but totally essential – what am I doing?? Just how far will I go for this? More importantly, how far will I need to go?

I gulp down a glass of water and get to my feet, walking to the window. I know I need to stop over-thinking this, to stop freaking out mildly about something that really isn't hurting anyone. It's just a new and strange relationship whose beginnings in slightly weird circumstances make it all feel a bit off-balance; yes, we know each other, but there is so much that is just not there yet. The secrecy, the lying, the text messages and stolen time all sort of hide that fact, but I knew it last week – I felt it lying in bed as

James was falling asleep by my side on that first 'normal' night together. There's friendship between us, and attraction too, crackling sexual tension I don't think it would have been possible to ignore even if I had tried. But as for everything between friendship and sex, all the stuff that eventually turns a casual flirtation into a proper relationship – the trust, the feeling of being exactly what the other person wants, even the sex being, well, good…that's going to need more time.

I am going to stop thinking about this now. I can make things up to Linda. She probably thought nothing of it. And maybe the Ski Away Day guests had a good laugh at my expense.

James and I will be fine. We'll have to be, because I'm in this thing now and I have no idea how to be anything else with him.

Another text message comes in, and just at the exact moment I discover the existence of a room service menu – both excellent diversions. Who? I wonder, Rachel again?

No, James this time: 'The J crow has left the F nest.'

Me: 'ETA?'

James: 'All going to plan so far. See you at the X time in the Z place…'

Tuesday 23 January
5.20pm. Road home to Reschengel.

The plan Linda and James had made for today *had* been a rather simple one. James was to 'arrive' in Thurlech at about nine-thirty, park his car somewhere and meet us at the main lift station. But late last night, Linda was seized by the epiphany that we should all ski in the nearby resort of Müntzen rather than Thurlech today. This meant that I had to get up really early, meet her and the chalet hosts in the centre of town and catch the first train down the valley to Lautertal, the valley town between the two resorts where we would 'meet' James on his way over from Futterberg.

I was massively freaked out by this whole arrangement, particularly so once we boarded the train. The very straight train-line ran parallel to the very straight road down the valley, and of course Linda had picked a window seat looking back up the mountain. James would literally have to drive past her in his incredibly unsubtle company car to get down to Lautertal before the train. How were we going to get away with this??

He texted me just as his car was catching up with the rear carriages. 'Diversion! Quick, Connors! Hee hee.'

I thought fast and dived across the train. 'Oh, look, everyone, a deer!'

'A deer? No, it can't be a deer. Where?'

'No really, right there, look. Err, look *now*.'

I glanced back to see James pass by with a cheery wave. *Bastard.*

'Where, Poppy? I'm sure it's far too early in the season…'

'Oh, yeah, sorry. A house. My mistake.'

When we got to Lautertal, James and I said a very formal and stiff hello to each other. I deposited my bags in his car and we all headed up on the lift to Müntzen. Only much later did we manage to get on a two-person chairlift alone together and he slipped the heavy brass hotel room key into my hand in very theatrical spy-drop style. We realised then that we had totally gotten away with the whole covert adventure and couldn't believe it. Of course we got very giggly and stupid after that and spent the rest of the day acting like kids, chucking snowballs at each other and him throwing me repeatedly into the snow. It was only over lunch, when he started eating my ice cream out of my dish and I didn't even react, that I caught Linda giving me a very strange look. I suspect that we could have been a bit more subtle. If she doesn't think we are already sleeping together, she presumably thinks we soon will be.

James isn't particularly bothered by what Linda thinks however. 'She wouldn't dream of gossiping about me,' he laughed, patting my leg reassuringly as we drove out of Lautertal later that evening. 'She's afraid of her own shadow, for heaven's sake. Don't worry yourself on her account, Poppy.'

James has decided that it doesn't really matter how obvious we are so long as no-one knows for sure and no-one has any proof. The more obvious the better in some ways, he says – that way it looks like we have nothing to hide and we are just close friends after all. I have my doubts about the wisdom of this, but James seems convinced.

'Don't take it all so seriously,' he said with a finality that ended the conversation.

He's right, I realised when I thought about it. Who else in my position would be giving a second thought to whether they were doing the right thing? No-one would – they would be too busy enjoying themselves.

I can see James out of the corner of my eye, sitting back in the driver's seat, frowning with concentration as he steers the car with one hand, the other one scrolling through his iPod for a new tune. *Relax,* I tell myself, my eyes roaming over his broad shoulders and down the muscles of his bare forearm – at once so familiar and yet still in sudden moments almost shockingly unfamiliar – this is still really new. Feeling my eyes on him, he glances up at me and grins, and I know in that moment that I am right.

Much later.

Ah, Rachel. There was never any chance I was going to escape interrogation tonight. The moment she came in from hotel visits, she grabbed me by the arm and without a word, marched me out the door and across the road to Happy Bar where she sat me down and barked out, 'Pieter, a shaker, please. Make it dark rum and ginger.'

'Ah, like your hair,' sighed Pieter with a wistful smile.

'Err, yes.' Rachel made a face at me as he turned to find a cocktail shaker. 'Anyway, let's have it, Pops.'

She wanted to hear '*everything*. Leave out nothing, especially the really dirty bits.' So I told her about how great it was when James arrived last night, how we cuddled up in bed and talked, how James told me all about his family at home, the skiing in Müntzen today and the ice-cream and the clandestine key-drop and the drive home…

128

'Yes, yes, yes,' she said, 'that's all very...well, nauseating, frankly. But, anyway, come on, get to the point. Tell me about The Sex.'

'Well...'

Oh, the honesty unleashed by a rum shaker. Up to now I've been rather vague with Rachel on the subject of The Sex. I haven't known quite what to say. Everything else I feel about James is the giddy stuff of bullshit romance novels. I genuinely do get butterflies when I see him. I feel an actual tingle when he holds me in his arms. I bore myself rigid even thinking all this but it's true – I have it bad. So the one thing I really can't talk to Rachel about is the sex, because it is just *not that good.*

Argh.

So of course The Rum told her this. She gasped, hand to her mouth, and then, for added effect, rewound the scene and gasped again.

'Shut up, it's not funny.'

'Shut up, it is a bit funny. And you know it is totally karmic, because otherwise I might have had to hate you with jealousy. Oh!' She took a moment. 'It's too much. Dreamy James, our fearless leader. "Oh Captain, My Captain!" After all that, he's crap in bed.'

'I never said that. He's not crap in bed, it's just that...'

'Is it a size thing?'

'No. Well, a little bit...'

'How little?'

'Shut up. No, it's not so much that. I could handle that. It's more that he... well... he isn't the most...' I struggled.

'Spit it out. Or is that the problem?'

'Shut up. Err, *imaginative.*'

'Oh my God, he's crap in bed.'

'I didn't say that!'

'But you're not denying it?'

'I am, it's lovely, he's lovely.'

'"Lovely" is not even one full step up from "nice."'

The Rum couldn't argue with that. Sigh...

'What about the first night? Still no recollection?'

I shook my head. 'Not a thing. I somehow doubt the alcohol brought out an inner tiger I haven't seen since.'

'Well, let's think positively. So he's not a tiger. Give me some idea on the animal scale what we're talking about here.'

'One that hibernates in the winter months.'

'Oh dear.' She was trying very hard to be supportive and not laugh but, being Rachel, was losing the battle. 'Yeah, I did wonder why you kept banging on about how sweet it was that he cooked dinner for you the other night. Was the food even anything wildly interesting?'

'Pasta and pesto.'

Rachel snorted. I sighed into my glass, my heart sinking.

'But you've been so happy and excited since that first day, Pops,' she frowned. 'I don't understand.'

'Well, Rachel, sex isn't everything, you know,' I said, hating the defensive note in my voice; in fact, hating this whole conversation and wanting it to be over.

'True, but Bad Sex isn't anything.'

'It's not "Bad Sex." It's just New Sex. It'll get better.' Rachel raised a doubtful eyebrow. 'It will, Rachel,' I pressed. 'Think about it: it's a weird way to start a relationship. We've gone from barely knowing each other to concocting elaborate plans to sneak around Austria hiding from Snowglobe employees, for heaven's sake.'

'I hate to rain on your comforting theory but come on, you've got drama, you've got intrigue, you've got the delicious naughtiness of covert skulduggery. These are all ingredients for better sex, not worse.'

'That's just the thing – it still *is* deliciously exciting, all of it, even without being, you know…all that. I'm still loving it. And we'll work out the sex thing, I know we will.'

'What if the sex thing is already giving it all he's got?' Rachel made a face. 'Ugh, I crossed a mental-image line just there. What I mean is, surely it can't be enough?' She studied my face a little more closely. 'Crikey. You're blushing. You have proper feelings for him, ha!' She paused again and her eyes widened. 'Oh, my.

You *do*.'

'Shut up.' I stirred my rum and refused to catch her eye.

'This is something to you, isn't it?' she asked in a gentler tone than I'd expected.

I looked up. 'Don't be silly,' I frowned, sipping my drink. 'It's an illicit affair. It's fun, and...yeah, whatever.' I shrugged, noncommittal.

'Connors, Connors,' she smiled. 'Blinded by love into great sacrifice. I never thought I'd see the day.'

'What sacrifice? Stop putting words in my mouth. *I* never said it was Bad Sex. You decided that. I said it was perfectly adequate.'

'Rein in the passion!' Rachel held her hands up and sat back. 'OK, OK, you don't need to convince me of James Walker's earth-shattering adequacy. And anyway, you couldn't. From now on, every time I see him in Salzburg airport, I will have the words "Bad Sex" emblazoned across my brain. I will never, ever get the image of a small, burrowing, hibernating marmotte out of...'

'Yes, as time goes by, I increasingly understand the received wisdom about not sleeping with your boss and sharing with your workmates. Why do I share with you, Rachel?'

'Because you'd explode and die otherwise. And anyway, you know what they say: "a problem shared is a problem halved." Mind you, by the sounds of it, if you halved this problem there wouldn't be much left.'

I made to strangle her.

Much later.

I went to bed feeling infinitely more conflicted for having shared my minor doubts with Rachel. But then I got this message:

'Really, really missing you tonight. My bed is crap without you in it. Quite tempted to come over there, kidnap you in the dead of night and return you unharmed in the morning...'

131

Thursday 25 January

11.32am

My God, Rachel's Andu is boring. She can't tell because they communicate solely by hand gestures, sign language and a surprisingly effective series of grunting noises, but the man has literally got one dimension, if even that. And because I very foolishly mentioned to Rachel that James would be away today visiting staff in the resort of Alpbach, I was left without any plausible escape from her kind invitation to join the two of them for the day. Now I'm stuck making conversation with him, or rather feigning silent interest, since Andu has been directing an unbroken German monologue at me for *hours* now, first about why I am the spawn of Satan for abandoning snowboarding as a sport, and then about the kind of snowboard school he will set up someday. It sounds basically identical to every other ski and snowboard school in the Alps as far as I can tell, though I dare not ask questions.

My God, I cannot take any more. How long has it been? At least two hours. No, forty minutes!

Help me, someone.

4.20pm

I was unbelievably relieved when we ran into Harry, Arthur and Tina in a lift queue. From then on it became a comedy afternoon. I've never skied with Tina before today and I almost didn't recognise her in her enormous white puffa jacket but for the blond fringe peeping out from under her pink headband. She is hilarious on a snowboard; all high-pitched screeches of terror and wild flailing limbs, though actually pretty good underneath all the drama.

She is also the queen of controversial chairlift chat. I really hope that none of the people who shared lifts with us were Snowglobe guests, because Tina spent a good deal of the afternoon regaling us with the inventory of her guest conquests so far this winter, a worrying number of them in the leisure centre pool and hot tub.

'So *that's* why leisure centre duty always takes you so long,' said Rachel.

Tina let out a low, husky laugh. 'What, did you think I was scrubbing mildew in the showers? Ha, ha, as if! Ooh, wait 'til I tell you about yesterday.' She looked around and lowered her voice. We all leaned in. 'Right, hands down the best one I've had, no joke. Don't tell Suzanne, yeah? But you know those families in rooms five and eighteen? They've both got sixteen year-old boys and fit dads?' I had a horrible feeling I knew where she was going with this. 'Right, so last night I shagged the two boys in the hot tub. One after the other! Like, ten minutes apart! And they didn't even realise! Ha, ha. God, one of them was hung like a donkey. Like his dad, actually.'

'How do you know that?' asked Harry, dumbly.

'I gave him a blowjob in the shower on Tuesday morning. What a fittie.'

There was a loaded silence on the chairlift as everyone struggled to think of something to follow that.

'Wow,' I managed eventually, 'the leisure centre is where the action happens, eh?'

'Yeah,' said Tina, nodding enthusiastically at me, 'it's brilliant. Let me know if you ever need it, mate. If I'm on the rota, I'll sort you out any time. Just ask.'

It was sweet of her, really, though disturbing.

Tuesday 30 January

9.34am

Text on my phone from James this morning at some bizarre pre-dawn o'clock: 'Just heard rather an alarming fact: apparently marmottes, and not rats, were responsible for spreading the bubonic plague and killing about a billion people. Suddenly v aware that these mountains are riddled with ghastly death...could evil lair perhaps be relocated, I wonder?'

Me: 'James, what are you doing up at this hour?'

James: 'Ugh, three words...Mid-Season Blues.'

Me: 'I think that's technically two words.'

James: 'Poppy, what are you doing being pedantic at this hour? Feel sorry for me please.'

Me: 'I do. You poor thing. I'd much rather you were here with me and we were having this conversation in person.'

James: 'Me too – although, if we're being pedantic (and apparently we are), logically speaking, if I were actually there in person, we couldn't possibly be having this conversation.'

Me: 'Do you want sympathy or not? Can happily turn over and go back to sleep...'

James: 'No, no, sympathy now, please. I'm very cold and tired and it's still snowing down here and I can't find one of my snowchains so the car is doing all sorts of crazy shit and I really just want to be in bed with you. Moan, moan, moan.'

He was on the road to Saalbach-Hinterglemm at the time, just the latest in a series of resorts he has had to visit in the past week. It's that time of the season, apparently, when senior management is called upon to hold people's hands and diffuse the odd blend of post-Christmas-traumatic-shock and homesickness that seems to strike even experienced reps and management about seven or eight weeks into the winter, making them flirt with the idea of quitting and going home. Personally, I find the very idea of homesickness in a place like this totally baffling. I mean, I love my family and all that, but there's a mountain up there and we have still barely put a scratch on it even two months into the season. Why, oh why would anyone want to leave before exploring every single corner?

Speaking of which, I'm standing in the staff kitchen with Mikey, who is strapping strange electronic devices to me and talking me through the proper usage of an avalanche transceiver, shovel and probe. It all sounds rather complicated, but more worryingly, appears to imply that I will soon be in a place where being buried by two hundred tonnes of snow is a distinct possibility. Oh, joy.

The reason for this is that three feet of powder fell yesterday and now everyone is scrambling to finish work quickly, get up the mountain and find fresh tracks. Carol grabbed me in the staff chalet before work this morning and informed me that I was hers today.

'Get keen. Today's the day you ski some proper powder.'

'Carol, I don't know. I'm not ready for that yet. I'm still...'

'Don't be ridiculous. You're more than ready. You have skied obsessively since you've been here...'

'Amen,' Rachel called out pointedly from the bedroom. She still likes to express her disapproval from time to time.

'...and it shows in your technique,' continued Carol. 'You've taken the piste skiing thing as far as you need to for now. What you have left to learn only unpisted snow can start to teach you. It's the next step.'

I tried to tell her that she would probably have a lot more fun in today's conditions with people who know what they are doing, but she was hearing none of it. She told me that any further resistance on my part would be punishable with Stroh 80, which I would not only be forced to drink but would also have to buy. Then Mikey piped up that he had spare avalanche kit, which basically left me with no excuses.

Get to it, Poppy. Try not to die today. Or embarrass yourself.

10.40pm

Ooof. Creaking arms, creaking legs. Utterly knackered now. This powder thing is hard work. It's great when upright and floating, flying along and bouncing through the turns. It's the falling over that kills. Or more specifically, the digging/swimming back up to the surface. Basically, it would be easier to just attach twenty-pound weights to both feet and go for a swim in hardening concrete, fully clothed in every single item that I own.

As the day went on, I gradually began to get the hang of it though. I've definitely started to get the feel for flexing and extending my feet together as a single platform (mostly because I have come to appreciate what happens when I don't do this) and I think I am getting there with the arms position stuff. I even managed to ski an entire powder face without falling over, though naturally then fell over in spectacular style in a compression at the bottom.

Still, small victories. I'm at the Chalet Elena kitchen now, helping Mark and Tilly with the wash-up, having just had dinner with the guests. This is something I get to do whenever the occupancy is one or more below capacity and Tilly has some extra food. I cherish these nights. They are the few times I deviate from my now-staple diet of bread, cheese and cereal from the box. (I still haven't had the courage to cook in the staff kitchen. There are so many ways to get killed in this world-famous skiing destination that it would be terribly disappointing to be finished off by a dodgy light switch.)

It's also an opportunity to meet and chat to some of the guests. Rachel finds it highly amusing that I enjoy this extra, unnecessary guest contact, but it's true: I do. It's one of the rare times I get to meet them outside the context of being yelled at for either things that have already gone wrong, or during ski guiding, where I live on a knife edge that they are about to do so at any moment. Dinner is a far more relaxed and friendly environment – a chance to remind myself that our guests are not just scary people who shout about Snowglobe being substandard, but interesting people on holidays.

The Elena guest is not your average ski punter, it must be said. The chalet caters for the very, very rich: from families to young millionaire couples and high-flying corporate groups, and this week's guests are no exception. We were amazed to see when the manifest for this week came through that we had genuine aristocracy on the list: Viscount Hugh, his wife and thirteen of their friends.

Tilly wasn't the slightest bit fazed. She just scanned the list to see if there was anyone she knew. 'Oh, the Radleighs,' she said, and went back to her brandysnap basket mix. Mark and I suppressed a grin. The guests would love Tilly.

Sure enough, before the soup plates had even been cleared, 'the question' arose: the same question the guests always want to ask but which they feel obliged to think of imaginative ways to phrase – who 'that delightful cook' is and how on earth young Tilly ended up here in Reschengel, running a ski chalet with a boy from Coventry.

I should point out that we repeat our life stories *ad nauseam* in this job. I mean really. Between coach trips, visits, meetings, bar crawls, chalet dinners and quiz nights, I must have told some version of my personal history at least twenty-four times a week every week. And since I am responsible for repping the Elena, I have heard about Tilly's and Mark's childhoods and life aspirations so often I think I could ghostwrite their autobiographies.

And so when the Viscountess enquired, I was ready to explain that Tilly is of the Bridgewater-Bakers of Hertfordshire and to outline her ambitions in the high-end catering market once she is finished at Durham. I didn't get that far, however. Mark, who was clearing the table at that moment, interrupted with a dramatic 'Well!' and everybody at the table turned to look at him. He cast a sidelong glance at the kitchen door.

'Tilly would kill me for telling you this,' he whispered loudly enough for the whole table to hear, 'but her real name is actually Thalea. She comes from a Greek shipping family based in the Ionian Islands.'

The Viscountess gasped. 'No! Really?'

'Mark,' I began, raising an eyebrow.

He patted my hand reassuringly. 'Yeah, I know, Poppy, but I think we can trust them. Where was I? Oh, yes. Greek. Very rich. Related to the Onassises? Um, yes, I think so. But it's a very sad story. She's had a very stifled life, you see. And then a few months ago, her parents announced an arranged marriage for her. That was the final straw. She persuaded them to let her go on a school exchange to the UK and then one day in London, she gave her bodyguard the slip and ran away. I met her that same day in King's Cross Station, crying her poor heart out in the gap betweens platforms nine and ten. She had nothing: no money, no plan, no-one to turn to that wouldn't send her right back to the shuttered world of the multi-billion dollar heiress. I took pity on her of course and gave her a roof over her head until she figured something out. It turned out she was pretty useful in the kitchen. I guess growing up with a Michelin star personal chef will do that, eh? So I hooked her up with a job here. Really, I don't think she has ever been happier. She has come to life, blossomed almost. Would we say blossomed, Poppy?'

I nodded, thinking grave thoughts about things like the Ebola virus, the Congo and my student debt – anything to keep a straight face. They could not possibly be taking him seriously.

The guests were breathless.

'That's *amazing*. Does anyone at Snowglobe even know her real identity?'

Mark shook his head. 'No. So obviously you cannot breathe a word of this to anyone. There is a low-profile but very intense manhunt underway as we speak.' His voice was low and fast. 'They think she has been kidnapped. If and when they find me, I have no idea what they will do to me.'

'No!'

'Yes, it's true.' Mark's voice cracked slightly and my cheeks flared. 'But you know, every time I look at her,' he whispered, 'I think of how far she has come from that tear-streaked, ragamuffin little girl in the train station. It's worth it, all the risk, just to see

138

her smile,' he finished as Tilly breezed in through the door.

'Right, main courses are ready, tonight we will be having fillet of…why are you all looking at me like that?'

Tilly was really pissed off when we told her later. 'Oh, for fuck's sake, Mark. Poppy, stop laughing, it's not funny.'

'Ah, come now Thalea, it is really rather funny.'

'No, it's awful. I'm quite sure that Mr. Radleigh knows some friends of my parents. And they'll be walking on eggshells with me all week now. Or, worse – speaking to me in ancient bloody Greek. I guarantee you at least one of them is classically educated. How on earth am I going to keep it up? I am a horrible liar.'

'Relax,' said Mark, squeezing her arm affectionately. 'You don't need to lie. They don't know that you know they know, do they? Anyway, think of the tips. They think you're Grade-A wealth rendered tragically destitute. You're basically their fantasy pity project. Poor, but not smelly. The right sort, *yah*?'

'Oh shut up, Mark. I will think of something really vile to do to you, just you wait.'

'Bring it on, Lady O, bring it on.'

Wednesday 31 January
11.08am. Ruhtai chairlift.

My phone beeped another early-morning on-the-road text message from James this morning, this one even grumpier than yesterday's because today he was not alone; Gina was his road-trip partner to Innsbruck for the mid-season managers' meeting.

James: 'Kill me now. I don't care how.'
Me: 'With a ninja cow?'
James: 'What?'
Me: 'Oh. I thought we were rhyming.'

Naturally, I tried to feel sympathetic, but his morning with Gina was our morning without, and that is just what the doctor ordered for all of us.

'Thanks,' replied James when I told him that. 'How very selfless of you. There are what, fifteen of you there in RSL? There's ONE of me, Poppy. And she has brought her iPod.'

'Ooh, you should get her to play her Dolly Parton karaoke mix. Just the thing. You love a nice little singalong, don't deny it.'

Actually I genuinely think a morning with James may be just what Gina needs. I've noticed a dramatic decrease in her 'Me-and-James' tales of friendship and flirty banter in the past few weeks – since I have been conspicuously spending time with him, actually. What she needs is some proper time with him when I'm not around or I fear that she might soon succeed in turning me to stone with her jealous imaginary-ex-girlfriend death-stare.

He replied asking me to list three reasons why he should not just end it all right then by driving the car off the road into the ravine below.

Me: 'Cos I'd probably miss you?'
James: 'That's one...'

Sitting on a chairlift now with Mark. My phone beeps – James again, something about penguins and fridges; wow, it must be a

140

properly boring meeting. Mark gives me a curious look as I type out a quick reply but he doesn't ask and I don't tell. We're on our way back over towards the little cliff drop in the Ruhtai bowl, where I am going to nail that jump if it kills me (and it might – the landing is chopped up deep snow now, AKA: death-trap).

1.55pm

Hurray! I have totally nailed the cliff drop. OK, by that I mean I have learned to land it upright most of the time and am even sort of slightly tucking up and springing off the kicker we built on top of it. Mark has been taking video evidence, so I am sure my illusions will be crushed on the big screen, but for now am feeling very positive, stylish and skilful.

The piste down from here to the valley is a little windy track, how dull, so we're going to go for a little explore on the way home instead. Mark reckons we can go straight down the steep bit from the Ruhtai bowl through the trees toward Plattjen and pick up the piste again down there. Yes, looks like fun, let's do it.

2.35pm

Who told me it's not possible to ski the Plattjen trees? This is fun. And totally doable.

3.04pm

A little lost now. Hmm. That windy piste pathway definitely cuts into these trees somewhere near here, am sure of it. Over somewhere to the left, I think. Let's stay left.

3.22pm

Still no sign of the piste. Surely ought to have reached it by now? Puzzling...

3.38pm

Where are we?? Shit, where is Mark?
What was that noise?

3.39pm

Mark???

6.42pm

Noise, it transpires, was Mark falling off a two hundred-foot cliff.

Specifically, it was the noise of him coming to an abrupt halt at the lip of said two hundred-foot cliff, wobbling and tipping himself over it with a yelp of surprise and horror. I found him (by yelling MARK! MAAAARK!! over and over again until a whimper of winded pain led me to where he was) perched on a small ledge, wrapped bodily around a tree, clinging to it with one arm while using the other to unstrap his feet from his snowboard bindings.

Fortunately, it was not a sheer vertical cliff, but rather an extremely steep drop which rolled off at the top in a series of narrow ledges, one of which had caught Mark as he fell. He was remarkably calm about the fact that he would still have to climb about twenty vertical feet with no rope and nothing to catch him if he lost his grip.

'Yup, no worries, it's cool, there are plenty of trees.'

He turned himself around and, wedging his snowboard in a groove between the rock face and a tree above his head, he began to pull himself up from tree to tree. I thought I might vomit with terror watching this scene unfold, but Mark was bizarrely quite cheery, which made me have to stop repeatedly to reassess the situation: *AM I crazy? Is he not one sweaty mitten away from certain death?? Aaah, yes, he actually IS. Why is he so calm, why, does he not realise??? Shut up, Poppy, don't freak him out, he'll fall. Oh, GOD what if he falls? What should I do? Should I call someone? Argh, what is the number for mountain rescue?? How can I not know it?? Shit, he's looking up. Stop freaking out, Poppy, he'll notice and you'll scare him and then, Oh my God, what if…*

He did very well for about five minutes. He was taking it nice and slowly and was about halfway up when he said, 'Hey! Pops! You see that?' It was what looked like a black snowboard, wedged in the trees off to his right, a few feet below where he was perched. 'It's a Nidecker!' he shouted up happily to me. 'What are the odds of that?! A bloody Nidecker, sitting in the trees. Free board! Woo, hoo!'

Maybe I was seduced into calmness by his total lack of fear, maybe I was blinded by relief that he was almost back up to safety, maybe I was bewitched by some forest spirit. Who knows? But for some reason, him climbing across and down to get the abandoned board seemed like a totally normal thing to do. Sensible, even. Nothing about an abandoned black snowboard left to rust in the trees over a two hundred-foot cliff screamed 'imminent death' to me just then, not even when the Grim Reaper wandered past and gave us both a friendly wave.

In a slow-motion-movie sort of way, he reached for the Nidecker board, grasped it with one hand and turned to grin up at me. It was right about then that he lost his footing and slid, face down, feet-first through the trees.

I probably screamed. Mark just managed to grab the branch of a tree as his legs dropped over a little overhang and disappeared from sight. The black snowboard vanished from his hands. There was a long pause as it freefell, and then a rather too-long series of loud noises as it crashed through the trees below.

We looked at each other. He was far too far below me for me to reach him, and my hard plastic ski boots would not stand a chance of being able to climb down over the wet, mossy rocks to get to where he was. He would have to climb up himself. His own snowboard was – ironically – blocking his way back up however. He struggled for about five minutes to haul himself up and around it, before giving up, reaching up, dislodging the board and throwing it over the edge. There was another horribly extended pause before we heard it smash down the cliff.

Only then, watching him listen to his precious board hurtle into the oblivion of an immense Alpine forest, did I realise that Mark was losing it. His cheery, against-the-odds sort of calm had shattered into a million pieces and he was properly, properly freaked out now. He kept trying to swing his legs up onto the overhang, but he was starting to sweat and slide in his gloves and

143

the fatigue in his arms was beginning to show. He pulled off his gloves and threw them backwards over his head. He pulled off his goggles and helmet and tossed them down after his gloves.

'Stop it, Mark!' I shrieked. 'Stop throwing away your stuff, you'll get cold. I'm going to call for help. Just stay still. Hold on tight.'

I started going through my phone contacts. Ha! I *did* have the mountain rescue number. It was one of the several hundred local numbers Gina made us input at the beginning of season. *Thank you Gina, thank you, thank you, thank you.*

Wait, what? Low battery? *Fuck it, fuck it, fuck it, you cannot be serious.* But before I even had time to register what a problem this was going to be, there was a short yelp and Mark disappeared from view.

Holy shit. Oh my God, he's dead, he's dead, Mark is dead, Mark has just fallen and died. Oh, oh, oh...

Half a minute or so of blinding, startlingly horror passed before I heard it, a voice, suddenly, very faint and far away, shouting 'Poppy! Poppy!'

'Mark! You're OK?' I yelled back.

'Erm. Not exactly. That fucking *hurt,* man. But yeah, I'm stuck on another tree. There's definitely no way I can get back up from here. But I think I might be able to climb down if I sort of slide from tree to tree.'

'Are you insane? Stay where you are. Phone mountain rescue!'

'Err, I think I threw away my phone with the other stuff. I can't find it.'

Every instinct was telling me we had to stick together or one of us would get lost and die alone on the side of the mountain, but there was no way we could get to one another and I knew that we had to get down soon or Mark would start to get hypothermic. Fuck, fuck, *fuck.*

There was nothing for it but to move. We agreed a meeting place at the bottom, at the nearest lift station. I was to switch on my phone every fifteen minutes to check for a text message from Mark to say that he had made it down safely (as soon as he could find a random stranger to accost and beg for the use of a mobile phone). I knew that I had at least an hour-long climb back up a very steep mountainside, through increasingly deep snow, and only the vaguest idea of where I might logically find a piste that would get me to safety. I knew where it *wasn't*. For some reason, none of this frightened me as much as thinking about Mark's predicament, although in retrospect I can see that he only had to go down (admittedly, down a cliff), whereas I was wandering back up the mountain, in falling dusk, searching for a way down through unfamiliar terrain with no mobile phone, map or navigational assistance of any kind.

I got a text message from him a numb, terrified hour and fifteen minutes later to say that he had made it down, was at Plattjen lift station, shoulders just about still in place and scared beyond all rational sense but otherwise unscathed. Was I OK? Or should he send a search party up for me?

I had found the piste only minutes before by the miraculous coincidence that two piste patrollers happened to have stopped for a smoke at the hairpin bend where the piste wrapped back on itself and down the valley, away from where I was. I heard them laughing at a joke, thought I had imagined it, heard another laugh and realised that I was standing only about a hundred metres from where they were (though was about to walk straight past them and on up the mountain – curse the suicidal leanings of my internal compass).

I called out to them, trudged over through the snow and collapsed in an exhausted heap at their feet in a way that I think was suitably dramatic. Of course, they just shouted at me for being off-piste in a dangerous place (in fact, apparently a nature reserve; there was even talk of a two thousand euro fine until I cried).

Mark and I had a very stiff drink in Happy Bar before heading back to the staff chalet, where, naturally, no-one had any idea what we had just been through and Tilly was only interested in yelling at Mark for missing dinner prep. He said nothing but shocked them both by giving her a big hug. Then I went to lie

145

down.

10.43pm. Deepest slumber.
Whatthe? Ugh, phone ringing, shutup… Oh, good, it's James. Mmm, must have heard about near-death experience, calling to see if I'm OK in a lovely considerate way…Sleepyhello?

11.18pm
Hrrumph. Total lack of sympathy or interest. He hadn't heard anything about what happened. He was actually only calling to moan about the dullness of his day, reiterate how passionately he loathed Gina and tell me how he had entertained himself throughout today's managers' meeting by planning another highly clandestine road trip for us to go on next week.

Road trip? How could I think about a road trip at a time like this? I told him the whole story of what happened to us today, even all the bits about how utterly lost we were, Mark plummeting to his (almost) untimely death and my gnawing fear of wandering off in the wrong direction and having my half-eaten, semi-defrosted corpse found by passing hikers months from now, still clinging to a tree.

All he said was, 'that was pretty stupid, wasn't it? That'll teach you to go randomly exploring off-piste with some idiot chalet host who has no clue what he's doing. I mean, come on, Plattjen trees, for fuck's sake. Would have served him right if he'd eaten it there.'

'James!' I was shocked at his tone. He sounded odd – grumpy or preoccupied, like I'd caught him at a bad time in the airport. 'Are you even listening? Did you understand what I just told you? The cliff? The falling? The sheer, unmitigated terror of it all?'

'Yes, Poppy, all very extreme indeed. Well, you've learned your lesson – don't play in the woods with strange boys. Now listen, the reason I'm calling you is that…'

I shook my head, wondering if I was still half-asleep. And wondering – with a degree of surprise – why, when I'd heard him use that dismissive tone with other people, I had never noticed just how irritating it was. 'I'm sorry,' I cut in, 'are we finished talking about how unbelievably terrified I was today that my friend might have died? Or would you care to react a little more before we move on to your day?'

'Look,' James' voice was soft again, 'I'm sorry, I'm not expressing myself properly. Obviously I'm really glad you're not hurt; you know that. But it winds me up no end to see people taking unnecessary risks on the mountain, yeah? I know this guy Mark is your mate, but I'm struggling to feel much sympathy for him and his bloody snowboard. He had no right to drag you out there with him. You could have been really hurt, and for nothing.'

'Well, it wasn't totally his fault,' I said, suddenly feeling a bit foolish. 'I didn't know where we were going either. But you're right. Of course you're right – it was stupid. We should have known better.'

'Yes, you should. But you will in the future,' said James. 'Anyway, there's absolutely no need to take risks with people who don't know the mountain. If you really wanted to learn to ski off-piste, why didn't you just say so? I'll teach you. In fact, that's sort of indirectly the reason I phoned.'

'Oh? How so?'

'Big news, Connors. Somehow in the endless tedium of today, I've come up with a great idea. Genius really. Wait 'til you hear this…'

'OK, hit me.'

He took an excited breath. 'Your arrivals next week are too low to need three reps and an RM. Sooo…' I could tell he was really proud of himself, so I got ready to summon up the appropriate enthusiasm, 'I have told Gina I am going to move you to Thurlech for the week.'

Oh. Thurlech. Alone. For a week. How dull.

'Errm, OK,' I said. 'Sounds really boring, but fine.'

'No, no, no, no, I haven't got to the best part. So Gina thinks you'll be in Thurlech for the whole week, but I've told Linda that I'm only sending you over there to help with transfers from Salzburg on Sunday, and that I need you back in Reschengel on Monday night. I've told her you'll come back to Thurlech on

147

Saturday to do the outgoing transfer.'

'Where will I actually be for the rest of the week?'

'We. Where will *we* be.' He took a deep breath. 'Anderau!'

Anderau? I have heard a *lot* (from James) about the world-class terrain in that resort. The biggest unbroken off-piste vertical descent in Europe, apparently, and James' favourite place on earth. My first thought was *yikes, am I up to it?*

My second thought was *how in the bloody hell are we going to get away with this one?* Our Thurlech adventures were simple by comparison; this Anderau plan would involve a lot of variables – a lot of variables not talking to one another, specifically.

I vocalised Reservation Number Two to James, but he dismissed it and said it would be absolutely fine. Linda and Gina hardly even know each other. Linda always goes to Innsbruck Airport to pick up that half of the Thurlech arrivals, and is never down in Salzburg, so they won't ever see each other to discuss it. And if Gina needs to get in touch with me, she'll phone me directly, not Linda.

'It'll be fine. How will anyone ever know? And just think, pretty much a whole week together, just us. Don't you like the sound of that?'

Of course I did. But how on earth would James be able to take almost a whole week off? Whatever about me, his job involved real responsibility, surely?

'Yeah, but there's not a lot about my job that can't be done over the phone on a chairlift pretty much anywhere. It's cool, so long as you stay really quiet.'

Hmm. I told James I would need to think on this more, you know, when I am finished reeling from post-traumatic stress. He laughed and informed me that it was going ahead regardless: 'no thinking necessary, Sunshine.'

'Hmmphf. You're not the boss of me.'

'Well, actually,' he said with a tone of surprised pleasure, 'I am. In every possible way. Ha!'

'*Excuse* me?'

'I'm kidding. But come on, what's there to think about? You

don't have to do anything at all. Just leave it all to me and follow my lead when the time comes. Simple!'

'I'm not sure…'

'Not sure about what?' asked James, slightly impatiently. 'Relax! It's not a big deal. I'll look after everything. Just act like a girl who is preparing to spend a week in Thurlech.'

'What, morose and depressed? Searching desperately for anything vaguely fun to take with her? Wrenching half-finished Sudoku books out of the hands of unsuspecting passers-by?'

'Exactly,' he said cheerfully. 'It's going to be wonderful. Just you wait. So, in other news, what are you doing tomorrow? Fancy staying over here?'

Mmm. I would haven given anything to be wrapped up with him just then. 'That sounds great, James. But I really can't. It is definitely my turn to take the guiding group. Tom is a total hero about it but I don't want to absolutely take the piss, especially if I'm going off on a naughty road trip with you for the whole of next week.'

'Oh, come on. You know Tom will say yes if you ask him. And we haven't spent a night together in over a week, you know.'

'I know,' I said, deflated but feeling worse for having to disappoint him too, 'but I can't just do whatever I want. I have that pesky job thing to think about, remember? You should, being the boss of me and all.'

He didn't laugh. 'Oh, for God's sake, Poppy, listen to yourself. You are taking all this way too seriously. It's one night. He'll get it. He's a mate. And anyway, he's the one who's actually supposed to be the ski guide now, remember? If you think about it, the fact that you ever take the guiding groups is actually doing *him* a favour.'

'Hmm.'

'And it's not like you've never covered for him, is it?'

'True,' I said slowly, thinking about how grateful Tom was that I was there on Tuesday night when that Diamond Ski rep, Sally, showed up randomly at our chalet to surprise him.

'So just ask him, yeah? And call me when it's done?'

He waited for me to reply.

'OK,' I said eventually, struggling to want to agree with him, and to swallow the feeling that I had no choice. 'You're right. Of all people, Tom would understand if he knew.'

'Exactly. No need whatsoever to feel bad. I can't wait to see you, Connors. It has been way, way too long.'

11.56pm

There really is no such thing as keeping everyone happy. I told Rachel about tomorrow and about the road trip next week. I thought she would hit the roof with the audacity of it all, but she just gave a tired shrug. She was disappointed, but said nothing.

'What, Rach?'

'Nothing.'

'Oh, come on, I would have thought you of all people would have been more excited about the intrigue.'

'Yeah, no, it's wicked, mate, very naughty. I'm just disappointed you're not going to be around tomorrow. I was hoping you would come up to the park with Andu and me and his boys.'

'What, are you stuck for a translator?'

She didn't laugh. 'No, well, OK, yes in a way, but mainly no. Would have been nice to spend some time with you on our day off, that's all. And then you're heading off on a random road trip next week. It just seems like every spare minute you have, you rush off to spend it with him.'

'That's not true.'

'It is, Pops. If you're not in Thurlech, you're over in Futterberg for the night, or skiing with him all day. It's OK, I understand. I just miss you, mate.'

'Rachel, I skied with you last Thursday.'

'Only because he went away.'

She had me there. Point taken.

FEBRUARY

Friendly Fires
(or, I could tell that you wanted to...)

Monday 5 February

4.45pm. Nervous in Thurlech.

James will be here soon to take me away. I'm sitting in the lobby of my hotel with Linda and I am very on edge right now. *How to get through the next few hours without exploding and dying of terrified suspense?*

Since the idea came up last week, I have tried to come around to The Audacious Plan, but yesterday in Salzburg airport threw cold water over the first brave sparks of my enthusiasm. Rachel was still rather distant and lukewarm on the subject of James, Gina was still barely speaking to me and James was far too busy yelling at Kim and Emma about St Anton's voucher pad allocation to be any use as a distraction. And then on my coffee break I got chatting to a Snowglobe rep called Eleanor in the queue at the Main Terminal café and realised that James had forgotten to mention one rather significant detail of the puzzle – that Eleanor, the girl standing right beside me, was the Thurlech-Müntzen rep for whom I had stood in last week. Needless to say, I nearly died a panicked death when she started talking about how she wished I were staying for the whole week this week and not just a couple of days. Fortunately, we were the only two Snowglobe staff in the café at the time, and Eleanor went on to leave the airport with her coachload of guests half an hour later without, it would appear, letting anything slip to anyone else. Still, her words continued to ring in my ears long after she was gone. She explained that they are due to have almost one hundred and fifty percent of normal guest numbers, and without me she'll have to singlehandedly cover everything – all the hotel and chalet visits, ski school bookings and tobogganing excursions, not to mention whatever dramas unfold during the course of the week.

I tried to stamp it down, telling myself it was not my problem, but I've been feeling massively guilty since that conversation. I tried to corner James in the airport yesterday to discuss whether we really ought to go ahead with the plan under the circumstances, but he just stared at me with absolute incredulity and hissed, '*not here,* Poppy,' glancing pointedly at the fifteen or so reps huddled around the noticeboard about twenty feet away from his desk.

'What the hell is wrong with you?' he snapped at me an hour or so later when we managed to snatch a quiet moment. 'If you are trying to draw attention to us, you couldn't be doing a better job of it.'

'I'm sorry,' I said, blinking unhappily. 'I don't mean to. It's just that Eleanor seemed so stressed and I couldn't help feeling that maybe we should...' I sighed and twisted my hands. 'Look, I should have explained before we got into this whole "illicit affair" thing that I am the world's worst liar. I just can't do it. I feel like they can all tell what's going on just by looking at me.'

James' glacial expression cracked. He smiled and pulled gently at my hair. 'Poor Poppy. You're funny when you're freaked out.'

'Shut up.'

'No, really, it's adorable. But, seriously, relax. It's OK. I told you I was dealing with all this, didn't I?' I nodded and he smiled and squeezed my arm, drawing me into a hug. 'Trust me, then. You have nothing to feel guilty about anyway. It's not like I've given you a choice, is it?' he grinned and kissed me quickly on the lips before turning to head back to his desk.

He was right and I knew it. It *is* more James' responsibility to worry about all this than it is mine. I promise I will do that literally the moment we leave Thurlech this evening. Because until then, I can't help being very nervous and twitchy and I'm doing a bad job of looking Linda in the eye. The woman must think I am an extremely odd case by now.

I just really want James to get here so that this day can be over soon. I hate being tense and weird with people, afraid to relax in normal conversation in case I accidentally mention something I shouldn't. Here in Thurlech, it's been a constant struggle to remember what I am supposed to be doing as far as Linda and Eleanor are concerned, where I am supposed to be and when, all the while knowing that if I open myself up to even the slightest probing question, I will blush and crumble under the pressure of telling a direct lie. And that, as they say, will be that.

Later.

Relief.

James was very businesslike when he came to collect me. He and Linda had a long chat about how best to manage things in Thurlech this week. The upshot was that he basically halved Eleanor's workload, told Linda to reduce the timetabled hotel visits and communicate to the guests in outlying resorts that the rep service is done by phone, because, in fairness, they won't know the difference from week to week.

'A simpler life,' sighed Linda with a wobbly smile as she thanked him. She was visibly relieved. So was I.

James acted very cool with me in front of her, as though the primary point of his visit was to sort out her problems, and that now he was tired and bored and was only driving me back across Austria because he absolutely had to. But as soon as we got on the road, he was happy and wonderful, telling me all about what he had planned for the week, about the lush apartment in Anderau he had borrowed from a mate and about how excited he had been on the drive over, thinking about all the time we would have together this week, just the two of us. I was mildly concerned that he was going to crash the car, driving and changing gears with one hand because he wouldn't let go of mine with the other and leaning over to kiss me every few minutes all the way down the valley road.

When we got to the apartment in Anderau two hours later, he threw our bags on the floor, took me in his arms and that was that. I forgot everything – all my concerns and doubts, my guilt, my fear, everything but the intense grey eyes and strong arms of the man before me.

'Hello, beautiful,' he growled softly in my ear.

'Hello,' I whispered back, holding him tight.

His body was warm, and I ran my hands over the hard, smooth muscles of his back as he held me close against his chest.

'It's so good to have you all to myself at last,' he murmured into the nape of my neck and trailed gentle kisses along my collarbone.

'Mmm. Likewise,' I said, scratching my fingers through his hair and down his neck. 'I've missed you.'

He kissed me softly and stroked my hair with one hand, his other hand running across my cheek, over my shoulder, my neck and slowly down my back.

'I've missed you too,' he whispered, pulling back to look at my face. 'We don't ever seem to get enough time for this, do we?'

I returned his gaze, looking up at him and in that moment was overwhelmed by the strongest surge of something like adrenaline, a shock of an emotion I couldn't name, something so strong it surprised me, so powerful that it constricted my chest. *I really don't know him. But I just don't ever want to be without this man.*

Saturday 10 February

7.32am

In the car on the road back to Thurlech, driving slowly in heavy falling snow. It's not particularly early but it feels like dawn with the twilight-grey of the morning light and the overhanging tiredness of a poor night's sleep. It has been a very silent trip so far; me lost in vague, patternless thought, watching the swirling trajectories of the flakes that pass the side-window while James concentrates on driving. Every so often, there is the muted buzz of an incoming text message on his phone and the unmistakable click-click of his replies.

'Problem somewhere?' I say eventually as his phone vibrates yet again in its stand.

He turns sharply to look at me. 'Oh, you're awake. I thought you'd drifted off.'

'Mmm. Everything OK?' I nod at his phone.

'Yeah, yeah. It's just my mate Pete in Chamonix.' He shrugs and squeezes my leg. 'Nothing important. How're you?'

'I'm OK. This Pete guy's up early.'

'Yeah, yeah, he is. Wants to know what the snow's like over here.'

'Mmm. Tell him about the week we've had,' I smile, thinking of all the soft, untracked snow we have skied since Monday, the spectacular scenery and the deserted slopes. 'That ought to make him jealous.'

'Undoubtedly,' replies James with a quick smile, 'but that's perhaps an unwise move. Pete works for Sarah Datchet too. He's an area manager over there.'

'Ah,' I say, with a half-smile. *Of course, reality.* 'Perhaps best not to mention me then.'

'Indeed.'

It's been easy for me to forget about the world of Snowglobe this week. Aside from Rachel, nobody has called or texted my work phone. Admittedly it took me a day or two to adjust to the silence – we reps are programmed to feel that no news is rapidly compounding bad news – but after a couple of days' powder skiing in incredible terrain and several nights hanging out with James' friends, I managed to switch off from it completely.

James' week has carried on as normal, however, with calls and texts at all hours of the day and night – weepy resort managers, anxious suppliers, even Sarah Datchet from time to time. At times I wanted to snatch his phone from his hand and throw it off a chairlift. Still, during the times when James' phone was silent and his attention was one hundred percent here, it was like there was nothing else in the world but him and me, the mountain and our adopted flat. At last, we had what I had been craving – days spent together to get to know each other properly, with no deadlines or appointments or pressure of any kind. At last, I felt us in a kind of rhythm with each other, finally able to be who we would be around each other anywhere else in the world. I am trying not to hate that it is over now.

James pulls the car to a stop behind a row of vans in a strange sort of dead-end laneway that seems to come to an abrupt end at a rock face that soars upwards into an enormous cliff. I look at him, confused. He explains that the snowfall that began early this morning has meant that the road over the mountain pass we needed to take back is closed. Instead we have to wait here and take the road-train through the Furrital tunnel.

The empty train arrives moments later. It is a kind of train/barge hybrid, which the queue of cars drives up onto, parks and gets carried through the long tunnel.

We wait in line, drive into place and switch off the engine.

9.55am
Still waiting. Zzz, this is dull. We put our seats back and James leans over to lay his head on my chest, his fingers stroking the soft skin on the underside of my wrist. Feels nice. I kiss his forehead and run my fingers through his hair.

9.59am
At last. The train is finally moving.

10.10am

James sits up suddenly and pulls me into a surprisingly passionate kiss, tugging at my hair and pressing his lips hard against mine. Mmm, mmm, we're getting a little carried away now. It's very dark however. I can't see a thing, but I do know that we are bumper to bumper with other cars.

How long will we be in this tunnel? I wonder. Twenty minutes more, he thinks, but is not sure.

'Mmm... Poppy?'

Later.

Cannot believe what we have just done. Sex in a road tunnel. Worse, sex in the driver's seat of a car in a line of parked cars on a road train. Now that's a first. *Ouch*...and I think the seatbelt lock has done permanent damage to my knee.

Hmm. I'm pretty sure it was a *lot* darker at the start of the tunnel than it is here. In fact, I'm only now realising just how very visible the occupants of the cars ahead and behind are (as in, I can see the whites of their shocked and horrified eyes).

Oh, God.

Oh, *God.*

Still later.

Really cannot believe we just did that. Still, it improved our mood. We have been very giggly ever since, especially when we came out of the tunnel into broad daylight and spent the next three miles crawling through traffic on a winding road, horribly unable to overtake and get away from the cars in front and behind. I shrank low in my seat with the shame of it all but James just grinned away happily to himself, very amused that his car, like all the Snowglobe company cars, has French license plates. It's the sort of thing one expects from a Frenchman, to be overcome with le passion, *non?*

Oh, dear. My mother would be shocked to the core of her being.

Sunday 11 February
1.40am. Reschengel.

It still took me a full hour after arriving at the airport today to quite believe that we had got away with The Audacious Plan. Not until I had seen and spoken to both Gina and Sarah Datchet and neither of them had seized me by the throat did I entirely accept that James had judged it absolutely right.

'Told you so, Connors,' he smirked, pinching me lightly on the arm after the arrivals briefing. 'Simple, daring genius. May you never doubt me again.'

'I never shall,' I promised him with a smile, snatching a quick kiss behind the enormous Snowglobe advertising screen.

Nonetheless, I skulked around Charter Terminal like a wide-eyed fugitive for about another hour until James, who was struggling to keep a straight face by that point, said my guilty face was far too like my hungover face and he sent me off on a break before Sarah Datchet started to suspect that Linda had committed the cardinal sin of taking me boozing on the night before transfer day.

Anna was the only person aside from Rachel who knew what we had been up to, and she, for her part, left me in no doubt as to what she thought of it all. I found her outside having a cigarette behind the fire station with the reps from St Anton. She caught sight of me walking toward the group, made her excuses and vanished back indoors. It was obvious that she did not approve. I could understand that – this week hardly showed James or me at our professional best – but I wished James would give her the same lecture he gave me about not taking it all so seriously.

Kim and Emma were oblivious, of course. They were entirely occupied with the scandal of the week in their resort: a couple of chalet hosts were sacked after guests came back to the chalet one evening to find them having sex on the kitchen worktop during dinner prep. That cheered me up immensely. I would definitely never do *that*, I felt like shouting after Anna.

Thankfully Rachel, on the other hand, was back to her usual self. Far from being off with me, she was dying to hear all the sordid details about my Anderau trip. We only overlapped at the airport for about twenty minutes, so I promised her a full debrief back in Reschengel. I warned her in advance that the story would feature at least one frightfully scandalous public sexual encounter, the like of which had never before scarred the innocent population of central Austria. She was very excited at the prospect although slightly disbelieving that it could really be that shocking, given previous history with James.

'No, no, really, I think the long winter might be over.'

'Was it…you know, "grrRRR!!"?'

'Well, there was some pouncing. And a little devouring.'

'Oh, my. I can't wait to hear about this. I shall polish my shocked face for the occasion.'

I brought the last coach back to resort so it was almost midnight when I called to Gina's door to drop off cash, credit card slips and sales vouchers. I braced myself for a deluge of squeezy-tight hugs and entreaties to tell her *every detail* of the week I had survived away from her watchful eye, but she didn't seem particularly interested in an emotional reunion. She opened the door just enough to snatch the envelopes out of my hand with a quick 'yah, thanks. Good week? OK. Night, night, sweetie,' but not before I noticed the white sort of nightgown she was wearing and the multitude of tealight candles arranged around her room. If I didn't know better, I would have thought she had been in the midst of a full-on seduction. *Or maybe she has found God?*

Rachel was waiting for me at Happy Bar. She insisted on hearing everything, '*everything*, Pops, you understand?' about my trip before she disclosed one word of the 'epic' events of the past week here in Reschengel.

I told her all the best bits. She fell off her barstool, literally, when I told her about the Furrital tunnel incident.

'You *slut*,' she said approvingly. 'And James! Who knew?'

'Not me,' I answered truthfully.

'So things there are all good?' she asked.

'Yeah,' I said. 'Things are good.'

'Excellent. In that case, you're ready to hear the scandal of the week. Nay, the *season*. It's Gina. She has her hands full with a *new man*.'

'You're kidding me. Who?'

'Oh, that's the best bit. *Oh-my-God, oh-my-God, oh-my-God,* WAIT until you hear who it is!' Rachel bounced. 'Eeeeep!!'

'Who? Who?'

'None other than your nemesis. Remember Spandex Boy?'

It was my turn to choke on my drink. Rachel filled me in on the details. Eyebrows were raised early in the week when it was noticed that Gina was distinctly absent from the lives of her long-suffering staff. There was no lurking in the chalets, badgering Tilly, Joseph and Miranda to use cheaper cuts of meat; no haunting the Club Hotel to inflict supercilious management technique lectures on a stammering, trembling Suzanne, nor random phone and text message demands that Tom and Rachel come off the slopes in the middle of the afternoon to do something totally outside their job description like auditing the resort accounts for January or translating Japanese washing machine assembly instructions. Rachel described the silence as 'unnerving.'

And then, on Thursday, the reason became clear when Jan was spotted leaving her apartment at about eleven in the morning. Gina made no attempt to be subtle or pretend that it was anything other than what it was, but stood in her doorway in a short pink and blue satin dressing gown with wild just-got-out-of-bed-hair, cup of coffee in hand, cigarette in the other, calling bawdy remarks after him, laughing her guttural laugh and generally impersonating a heavy-smoking prostitute. This, it would seem, is Jan's type, since Spandex Boy has taken to staying over about every other night since.

Ah, I see. The candles in Gina's apartment tonight. And the heavier-than-usual fake tan.

'Oh, rats. He's there now?' Rachel sighed. 'I was really hoping for a night's sleep.'

'Oh, no.'

'Oh, yes. Or rather, "oh, yes, yes, yes, NO, NO, yes, YES,

YEEESSS…'" Rachel looked weary. 'He's a shouter.'

Wonderful.

Just then, Gav (AKA Snowli the Rabbit) and his girlfriend Chrigi walked into the bar and sat down at our table for a chat. There was something very odd about them. I couldn't put my finger on what it was until Gav got up to buy their drinks at the bar and came back with a couple of Diet Cokes. I looked at Rachel. She widened her eyes and nodded, as though to say *I know. Believe me, I know.*

The last time I saw Chrigi in Happy Bar was messy. She had the best part of a bottle of Jack Daniel's in her and, by the way she was scrubbing at her nose, at least a little something else. Pieter was trying to throw her out of the bar, literally kicking and screaming, for trying to bottle an unsuspecting Arthur, who had committed no graver an offence against her than that he and Mikey happened to be playing pool at the unfortunate moment that she suddenly decided it was her turn.

And now she was sitting peacefully, holding Gav's hand and drinking Diet Coke? Has *she* found God? No, it transpires. But she is pregnant.

'Shut *up*,' I exhaled in horrified disbelief.

'I know,' hissed Rachel. 'It's not even funny.'

Oh, it's all too much. I must not leave Reschengel again. I cannot believe how much I missed.

We left Happy Bar after an hour of shaker-bliss. It was time to get to Rodeo. The Snowglobe boys had challenged the Diamond Ski staff to a test of which side could stomach the greater consecutive number of Flaming Lamborghinis. I skipped down the hill, arm in arm with Rachel and Tom while Mikey ran ahead to knock on Carol's door. Arthur, Daniel and Eoghan were chasing Tina down the street, trying to throw her into the snow. Odysseus and Harry were walking slowly, deep in serious conversation, which we presumed to be heavy academic stuff, though as we approached them we realised that they were talking 'Lambo strategy' and the best way to sneak a crafty vomit under the table and 'power on through to the next round.'

163

Tom gave me a hug. 'Glad to be back, Pops?'

I was so squiffy and overcome with emotion I thought I might cry. 'So glad.'

My knee is still bloody sore though.

Thursday 15 February

8.15am

Day off, hurrah! I leap out of bed with unprecedented energy and jump up and down on Rachel until she wakes up.

'Day off, day off, day off!'

'Murrrghalll…a…what?'

'Come on, lazy wench. Move it, we have a date. Or *have you forgotten?*'

With one hand, I poke the duvet around where I think her ribs probably are, while wrenching open the curtains with the other. Piercing beams of sunlight pour into the room and Rachel swears blearily into her pillow, but I don't care because outside is the most beautiful sight. *A metre of snow!* Powder day! And one I wager we will actually get to enjoy, *sans* interference by Gina! Unprecedented!

It is truly unnerving, but Gina has been little more than an orange blur in our peripheral vision since her brief reappearance for transfer day on Sunday. My phone has been eerily silent. So much so that even if I wanted to know what was going on with her (an unlikely state of affairs), it would be difficult to find out.

I tried to explain this to Fritz Spitzer when he stopped me unexpectedly on the street yesterday to 'enquire' (i.e. interrogate me) about how things were progressing with Gina and Jan. I was stunned by the question and couldn't for the life of me work out what Gina's relationship had to do with Fritz. He is one of the two patriarchs of this resort, a scowling, tank-like man who owns about half of Reschengel, including all of our chalets, the Club Hotel, several of the other hotels and, most importantly, the Moose bar. Everyone is terrified of him, particularly his staff. Of course I feigned total ignorance, (getting implicated in gossip in this small town is a very, very bad idea) but Fritz was not to be dissuaded and pressed me on the subject for a good ten minutes. I eventually realised why. He explained that the relationship between Gina and Jan actually started about eight months ago, while Gina was managing Snowglobe's summer 'Activity Mountain' programme in Reschengel. Jan would come to town to go mountain biking at the weekends. One thing clearly led to another (ugh, horrendous mental image) and they have remained involved with each other on and off ever since. However, Jan has thus far neglected to mention one rather key detail to Gina – that he has a wife and two children in Innsbruck.

Stupid Spandex-wearing philandering bastard. I hadn't realised I could loathe him more, but this new information proved that there were new depths. But what did Fritz want me to do about it?

Nothing, he told me. Underneath the terrifying exterior, Fritz is very fond of Gina and very concerned that she might get hurt. Apparently she still knows nothing about the wife and kids (although she does know about the Spandex, and yet is still sleeping with Jan, so my sympathy has its limits) and Fritz says he wants to pick his moment to tell her. For now, he has asked me to simply 'keep an ear to the ground' and to keep him posted on any developments. I was too scared to say no.

I'll start tomorrow. Right now, there is *pulverschnee* to be had and I am impatient to get going. If it requires breaking several of Rachel's ribs to get her out of bed, so be it. I sit on her be-duveted shape and lift up the pillow hiding her face. She makes a pitiful moaning noise but I refuse to quit.

'Come on! Day of Fun, Day of Fun!'

3.25pm. Moose Bar.

Ahhh. Contented glühwein sigh. True to our plan, today Rachel and I skied together, just the two of us. No Andu, no James, not even Tom. We agreed on the lift this morning that not being hungover meant that we were invincible, so we spent the whole day trying do things we have seen done on the Extreme Sports Channel and by other people but have no clue how to do ourselves. Was there any reason why we could not 'slash the lip' with the same effortless grace and elegance as the pros, whipping big arcing turns on the lip of a gully, with snow flying high and our legs breaking through the snow crust at shoulder height? Of course not.

There is now so, so much melted snow down the back of my

salopettes, the only truly reliable test of how silly one has been on the mountain on a given day.

Ooh, *The Final Countdown* is playing. Must dance right now. This instant. On a table.

'Da da *daaaaaahh* da, da da da da *daaaaaah...*'

7.12pm

Rats. Phone ringing. And it's a UK number I don't recognise, so it is therefore almost undoubtedly a guest. Sigh...so much for day off.

7.22pm

It was a guest from the Davidson party in the Chalet Elena. We like them. They gave Tilly and Mark two mornings off this week so that they could go out and 'have a good night, let off some steam,' as Mr. Davidson put it, pressing a hundred euro note into Tilly's hand, and then invited the three of us to join them some evening in Reschengel's finest fondue restaurant. They are, in other words, the textbook ideal chalet guests.

Mrs. Davidson was very apologetic and said that she was phoning because she was rather concerned about going out and leaving the Swedish boys alone in the chalet pool. I thought about this for a second, realised that no, I had no idea what she was talking about.

'I beg your pardon?'

'I don't want to get anyone into trouble because we told them to go right ahead and it was great fun to watch actually. I am just a little worried now because we have dinner reservations, you see, and Tilly and Mark are off tonight so there's no-one here to check up on them later. Call me a silly old worrier, but I really felt I had to let you know because I am so afraid that they might lose track of time while we're out and, well, die of hypothermia.'

What??

Apparently, three 'very nice Swedish boys' showed up at their chalet this afternoon and asked politely if there was any way the guests would not mind their building a little ski jump into the

167

outdoor pool. Mr. and Mrs. Davidson thought that they were charming, had a long chat with them about the physics of the ski kicker (the Davidsons are both engineers) and even made them toast and tea. The Swedish boys finished construction an hour or so ago and have been entertaining the guests since with backflips, multiple rotations and all manner of other things besides.

I am walking quite fast now, in spite of the steep hill. There is no way this can *not* be worth seeing.

Much, much later, lying in bed.

Finding it very difficult to get to sleep now. Thoughts and images are racing through my brain and my body is tingling with excitement (and returning blood flow). What an evening.

The Elena was deserted when I arrived; the high windows of the downstairs floors dark but for the occasional flickers from the embers of a log fire. I let myself in the side gate and walked quietly down the passageway toward the pool area, where the chalet's fifteen-metre swimming pool dominates the outdoor terrace, positioned in the centre of a wide stone patio cut back into the hill. It is wrapped around on two sides by the floor-to-ceiling glass windows of the living area and gym, and on the other two sides, the snowy, tree-lined bank falls steeply onto the stone tiles. I knew what I had come there to see, but I suppose I hadn't quite believed Mrs. Davidson's description of what bizarreness was going on until I saw the scene with my own eyes.

Two tall, dark figures stood beside the pool, silhouetted eerily against the low lighting of the recessed outdoor lamps and the steam rising from the heated water into the crisp night-time air. They were deep in conversation, pausing every now and then to shout instructions in Swedish to a third figure, also dressed head-to-toe in black, who was positioned at the top of the bank. His skis were pointing downhill as he held tight to a couple of sapling trees on either side like a racer poised at a start gate. I waited in the shadows, skis still slung over my shoulder, afraid to blink. This was madness.

Minutes passed and he still did nothing. There seemed to be

some problem. The other two seemed pretty impatient. I noticed that one of them had taken off his ski boots and was hopping from foot to foot. They were both soaked to the skin. Eventually, the skier on the bank yelled back down to them. The pair beside the pool exchanged a few hushed words and the smaller of the two burst out laughing. Then (and this is where I really started to question the hallucinogenic properties of Birne Schnapps) they both turned back up the hill and launched into a vigorous, though tuneless, rendition of *Every Little Thing She Does Is Magic*. He laughed as he shouted down at them to fuck off (I'm guessing. Some expressions transcend the language barrier). Five lines into the song, he dropped.

He held his skis unflinchingly steady as he gathered speed very rapidly on the steep incline, then flexed low and sprung off the kicker, whipping himself through a double backflip as he soared over the patio and landed perfectly in the pool. I didn't see his skis pop off and I wondered for one horrified moment if it is possible to swim weighed down by boots and skis. He came to the surface a few seconds later, however, and I saw that he was wearing a wetsuit and something like a wakeboarding impact vest. The other two helped him out of the pool, clapping him on the back and laughing. The taller one of the pair by the pool took the impact vest, picked up his skis and began to make his way up the bank.

My heart was thumping hard. What would he do? What would he do?? This was so much more exciting than anything I had ever seen done off the kickers in the park. This was insane.

And then, just then, at the exact worst possible moment, my phone beeped a text message alert, shattering the whispered quiet of the air. The three skiers whipped around to see who or what had made the noise. They froze when they spotted me lurking in the shadows. *Great*, I thought, *now I look like some sort of unhinged voyeuristic stalker weirdo*. There was nothing for it but to step forward into the light and explain myself. I told them my name, that I work for Snowglobe and that the chalet guests had been a little anxious about them and had phoned to tell me that they were here. They said nothing in response, just exchanged glances, and

169

in the silence I wondered if they could understand my English. The two beside the pool whispered to each other and turned to look up at the skier on the bank.

He bounded down the slope, dropped his skis in the snow and strode over to me in squelching ski boots. He was very tall, at least a head taller than me, and very dark, with broad shoulders, a short, dark beard and wild hair sticking up at funny angles.

He stood in front of me, his eyes darting searchingly behind me and down the passageway then frowning intently at my face from under his black brows. Was he nervous or angry? I felt a little scared, or shy, or something. I wouldn't have thought that it was possible to look intimidating while sporting the unlikely ensemble of wetsuit, windsheeter and sodden ski boots, but he somehow managed it with a serious frown. Even in the low light, he had the most piercingly clear ice-blue eyes and a stare from which I could not break.

My thumping heart must have given me a very serious expression, because he stepped back a little and asked tentatively, 'Are you here to give us a bollock?'

'A what?!'

'A bollock.' He looked confused as I tried to swallow a smile. 'You know, are we in trouble?'

His face creased into a broad grin as I laughed and told him that it's 'give a bollock*ing*' and that, no, I was there because it sounded like a hell of a lot of fun and I wanted to see it for myself.

'You're all mad, by the way.'

'What have you seen?'

'Just the last skier. The double backflip. Very cool.'

He nodded vigorously, still staring at me for a long moment, although now his eyes were warm and crinkled and his smile was infectious.

'Well, come join us then! You're very welcome, Poppy. I'm Jon,' he said, clapping me on the back with a soggy mittened hand and steering me toward the others. 'This is Head and this is Nick. We live in the next chalet.' He gestured vaguely up the bank.

'*Tjena*, Poppy,' said Head, shaking my hand vigorously. 'Good to meet you. Hey, what did you think of our inspirational song?' He elbowed Nick, grinning. 'Did we get the words right?'

'Yeah, you did, and it was very…' I searched for the word, '…*melodic* too. But what was that about exactly?'

Head cast his eyes to heaven in mock despair. 'Nick needs to listen to his iPod to get psyched up and he can't use it in the water.'

'OK, that I can understand, but serenading him with The Police?'

'Don't ask,' muttered Nick darkly.

Jon clapped his hands together. 'Right, now, come on everyone, got to keep moving, cannot get cold. We only have about another two jumps left in us before we have to stop playing or we lose fingers and toes. Get ready, Poppy. You're up next.'

I felt myself go slightly pale, but he didn't hang around to see it. He marched up the hill, clipped into his skis and got into position.

Head called up to him in English, 'what will it be, Mr. Berner?'

Jon scratched his beard as though at a loss. 'I think I need inspiration, Mr. Jenssen. Poppy, tell me, what is your favourite trick?'

'To do or to watch?'

'To do.'

Stay upright, I thought. 'I'm not much of a…umm….freestyle expert. The best trick I have ever seen was a cork seven. I can't do it, mind you.'

'Cork seven! The lady is not easily pleased!' Jon exhaled sharply and shook his head. Then without any warning whatsoever, just as I was about to suggest something a little less stupidly dangerous in the context of stone patio tiles and water, he leapt from the gate and dropped down the slope. The words died in my throat as he flexed low and hit the kicker at a very high speed, sprung up, threw his shoulder back into a perfect off-axis seven hundred and twenty degree rotation and landed perfectly into the water.

Holy *shit*.

Nick turned to me with a questioning eye while Head helped to fish out Jon's skis. 'Happy?'

'That was incredible.'

'Ready?'

'Are you mad?'

'Yes. Are you ready?'

'I'm only here to watch.'

Nick shook his head and informed me very seriously, 'there is no spectating at this pool, Poppy.'

'I can't do that kicker.'

'Have you ever hit a kicker?'

'Yes, of course – little ones. That looks really fast and high.'

'You can drop in lower and slower.'

'Yes, but the landing…'

'…is in water. Believe me, it does not hurt. You can do whatever you like. That's why we use it today. To practice without consequences.'

'Yes, but it looks suicidal and…' I was losing this argument. My smile was giving away how much I really, really, really wanted to give it a go. '…I'm not wearing a wetsuit.'

'Not a problem,' Head chimed in. 'We have a nice warm chalet there next door. You can hit the kicker two or three times and afterwards go indoors. We only wear wetsuits so we can stay out here for hours. You'll be fine in your ski gear.'

'Yes, but my ski boots…'

'…will get wet but will be dry by tomorrow morning. We have a drying room.' Jon was out of the pool and shaking the water from his hair as he spoke. He walked over to me, taking off the flotation vest and handing it to me. 'I'll come up with you and we'll have a little look at it from there and you can decide. If you don't like it, don't do it.'

A little look. No obligation. I handed Nick my jacket and the contents of my pockets and, with a deep, steadying breath, trudged up the snow bank behind Jon.

We stopped about two thirds of the way up the slope, well below the tree gate the boys had been using, and looked at the kicker. Strangely from there, it did not look quite so high. I decided to hit it from the top. At least if I had too much speed, I decided, I would just land further down the pool. Too little, and I was terrified that I might hit the patio. We pushed on up to the two trees. *Oh, God,* I thought when we got there, and I dropped my skis to the snow, looking down at the water. *What am I doing?*

Jon looked at me and smiled encouragingly. 'What do you think?'

'It looks…a little sketchy.'

'Sketchy?'

'Dodgy. Scary. Potentially lethal. "Doomy," as my roommate would say.'

He laughed. 'No, no. You're not going to die. We won't let that happen. Then we would really be in trouble, eh?' He saw my face and went on hurriedly. 'It's straightforward, really. It's a small kicker, like a training kicker in the park. Think of all the kickers you have done of the same size.'

Not a lot, I had to confess. Did little miniature drops of about four feet count?

'Of course,' he said, with great confidence and respect, very disproportionate to that due to a four-foot cliff dropper. Perhaps he thought I meant four metres. *Oh, God.* I didn't have time to dwell on this possible misconception. He was full of instructions and advice and I had to pay attention. 'Right. For your first drop, you will do a straight air, OK? You will just jump, hold your skis straight and land solidly in the good position.'

I nodded dumbly. *What the hell did he think I was going to do for my second?*

'So you just need to spring and land. Spring and land. You don't even need that much speed. In fact, even if you take off almost all your speed before you hit the kicker, you are still certain to clear the patio. It is very narrow, you see?'

I had noticed with some relief how much narrower it was at this end, with the kicker built right out over the concrete.

'So you're going to ski down at a speed you are comfortable with, then you will crouch low with the ankles and knees as you

173

approach the edge, make fists with the hands and put them out far in front of you for good balance, then spring and land. Simple!'

Uh huh. Just like that. Spring and land. Spring and land. *Spring off the little kicker and splash into the water.* Easy. I dropped my skis into the snow and bent down to do up the clips on my ski boots. My heart thudded.

Spring off the ski jump at, oh, only about ninety-eight miles per hour, try to remain in the air as you fly over the rock-hard patio and land into two metres of water in your clothes and skis. Simple!

I slipped into the floatation vest and tightened the straps. Jon was still talking. 'You see Nick and Head? They will jump into the pool when you land and help you out of the water. They will make sure you are OK. There is nothing to worry about; you have a helmet and a vest and we have done this kind of thing a hundred times with trainees. You can trust us, I promise.'

I nodded. My hands shook a little as we swapped gloves, his wet ones for my dry ones and I clipped into my skis. Jon ducked his head to look up under my helmet at my face.

'Hey, Poppy, tell me, are you happy to be doing this?'

'"Happy?"' I laughed a little shakily. 'That's a strange word to use in this situation, Jon.'

'Yes, but if I told you now that I would not allow this and that you had to walk away, would you be relieved or disappointed? What I mean to ask is, are you "good" scared, or "bad" scared?'

I thought about this. 'Good scared,' I decided. 'Yes, good scared. I'm just, you know, bricking it right now.'

He nodded and his eyes crinkled as he smiled with satisfaction. 'Excellent,' he said. 'Then you'll be fine.'

I've heard it said that in these sorts of imminent-death-through-dangerous-sporting-activity situations it is best to have one good look at what you are about to do, and when you are sure you understand it, close your eyes. When you open them, it is time to go. No more hesitation. Hesitation is the mother of all injuries. I closed my eyes as I hung onto the trees and emptied my head of distractions. I pushed my skis back up the hill slightly until I felt the position was right. Then I opened my eyes and went for it.

It was a good, fast line into a well-built jump but I hit it slower than I had meant to. The Fear kicked in halfway down and I took off a little too much speed. The kicker had a sharp upward lip, sharper than I had expected, which threw my weight backwards. Mid-air I was seized by inevitable panic about smashing my head off the patio, but I cleared it by metres and splashed harmlessly into the pool on my back. Seconds later, I felt hands pulling me upwards and I broke the surface to the cheers of the boys.

'Well?' yelled Jon from the top of the bank.

I coughed out half a lungful of pool water and shouted 'Again! Again!'

Head jumped out of the pool, scampered up the hill and landed a brilliant triple scissors split before we even had time to blink.

'Go on then,' said Nick, pushing me back up the hill. 'And keep those hands forward and down. This keeps your weight forward. Stops you rolling back, OK?'

I hit it twice more, faster each time, but I still couldn't stop myself drifting backwards in the air and landing on my back.

Curses!

I refused to stop until I was happy with it, and marched back up the hill with Jon for a fourth run.

'It's a tricky kicker,' he explained. 'We built it mainly to practice flips and corks. Of course it is possible to go straight air off it, but you just have to really, really get yourself forward.'

I growled in frustration. 'I'm *trying*. I'm getting so far forward that I feel like I'm going to hit my head on my ski tips but it keeps throwing me back. So annoying!'

'That's because you're getting a lot of spring off the very end of the lip.'

'Is that bad?'

'No, no, not at all. That's a good thing usually, that's really good. Just on this kicker, it's actually easier to do a backflip than a straight air.'

Easier to do a backflip, eh...

Maybe it was a residual effect of the Birne Schnapps, maybe it was something to do with the moonlight, or maybe it was the rapt attention of three very damp but attractive Swedish boys, but something made me go big, well beyond the limits of what I know I can do, well beyond the boundaries of common sense and my trusty survival instincts. I felt myself drop low and fast, barely edging off any speed, flexing, springing and throwing my head and arms back into a flip. I felt my skis come over my head, heard a roar of delight and looked down to see my feet appearing underneath me as I splashed into the water on my knees. Not quite a landing, but close...

The boys were ecstatic, cheering wildly as I pulled myself out.

'A backflip!' Jon shook his head, grinning. 'Your first?'

I nodded. Head threw his arm around my shoulder. 'Well, Poppy, what a girl. We have to celebrate. That was just...'

'Mental,' and 'Epic,' chimed two voices simultaneously from the shadows near the chalet kitchen door.

The sceptic was Tilly. 'You're actually mental. Have you lost your mind?' She stepped into the light, looking shocked, while Mark stood behind her, grinning from ear to ear. 'You're dripping wet and it's below freezing. You're actually going to die now, you do realise that?'

Her matter-of-factness was touching. Mark ignored her. 'Poppy, marry me,' he said.

Tilly elbowed him in the ribs. 'Poppy, you're turning blue.'

'Am I?' I suddenly began to feel the frozen night air on the wet skin of my face. A violent shiver ran through me. 'Shit, I *am* cold.'

'Come on, come on.' Jon picked up my jacket and put it around my shoulders, then grabbed his skis and shooed us all toward the passageway. 'Let's all go back to ours. I need a good cup of tea. Come on, you as well, of course.' He stopped by Tilly and Mark and shook their hands. 'We haven't met. I'm Jon. You live here? We are neighbours.'

A hot shower, change of clothes and a cup of tea and I was a new person. Then one cup became three cups, followed by a couple of beers and a couple of hours of banter-fuelled poker across the road in the Flying Hirsch bar; me in Jon's tracksuit pants and hoodie with seven or eight rolls at the ankles and wrists.

At closing time, Jon and I went back to their chalet to collect my dry things, but my boot linings were still wet, as were my salopettes.

'No problem, hang on to the tracksuit bottoms and trainers for now. I'll drop your things down to you in the morning.'

It was very kind of him, I knew, but I had no idea how I would get down the hill in his trainers. The recent snow on the road had been worn down to a slick by passing traffic and it had been enough of a struggle just to get across the road without falling on my arse. Sure enough, I skated out the door and promptly fell over, skis and poles flying. Jon laughed at me for a full half-minute, but then picked up my skis, slid them back together and hoisted them up onto his shoulder.

'Come on,' he said with exaggerated patience, 'give me your arm, Miss Poppy-flower. I'll walk you home.'

We made it down the hill eventually. 'Thanks, Jon,' I smiled, taking my skis from him at the staff chalet's steps. 'And thank you for a wonderful evening. It's been great to meet you all.'

'Thank *you*,' he exclaimed. 'What an adventure, hey! Your first backflip! I'm very glad you shared it with us.'

'First and last, I suspect,' I confided in him. 'My instinct is telling me to retire at the height of my reputation.'

'So you won't be trying your new trick on the black kicker in Ruhtai park tomorrow then, no?' Jon smiled at me as I shook my head, laughing.

'Not likely.'

'What *will* you be doing tomorrow?'

'Oh, the usual,' I replied. 'Work in the morning, then skiing until visit-time. Tom's taking the guiding group to Futterberg, thankfully.'

'Come ski with me,' he said suddenly. 'Head and Nick are working in the morning. I'll be alone anyway and the snow is far too good at the moment not to share. Will you come with me?'

I couldn't quite believe that someone who could land a cork seven into a pool could possibly want to ski with me. 'Are you sure?'

'Of course,' he said. 'If you would like to, that is.'

'Absolutely, I'd love to. Where do you want to go?'

He smiled mysteriously. 'Oh, oh, Poppy,' he shook his head, 'just wait 'til you see.'

'Will I die?'

'No. Probably not. So long as you don't fall over in certain places, I guess.'

'Are you serious?' I asked, alarmed.

'No. Well, maybe. Ha, ha.'

I started mentally writing my will. Who would I leave my poor neglected snowboard to? Rachel, probably.

'OK, sorry, I'm kidding,' he said. 'I don't know where we're going yet. It depends on the conditions and avalanche risk. We'll find fresh stuff, and nothing you can't handle, so don't worry at all, OK?'

I nodded with a smile that matched his crinkled eyes. 'Just for the morning though, if that's OK? I'm meeting a friend for a quick ski in Futterberg in the afternoon.'

'No problem. I'll get you to Stüben in time to meet your Futterberg friend.'

Ha. My "Futterberg friend," I thought. James would love that – very mysterious. I should have got him to sign his Valentine's card with that yesterday. (OK, Valentine's bar napkin. I'd like to say that it's the thought that counts, but I think that particular wisdom goes against him on this occasion.)

'Great,' I nodded enthusiastically. 'I'll be free at nine-thirty. I can meet you here any time after that.'

'I'll be here at nine-thirty-five.' Jon turned to walk back home. I was almost at the top of the steps when he called back to me. 'Hey, what is the DIN setting on your skis?'

I told him, and then asked, 'why?'

'Because where we're going tomorrow, you're going to need a real pair of skis. Leave it with me.'

He gave me a wave and sauntered off.

Friday 16 February

11.24am. The Precipice of Probable Death.

'Are you fully mad? Have you *actually lost your mind*?'

I'm not sure he can hear me. Jon and I are standing on a perilously narrow ridge, barely as wide as my skis are long, with an icy, wind-blown crust underfoot that offers very little purchase to prevent my skis skating forwards or backwards toward the edges (which as far as I can tell is not a survivable option, but I don't even want to look.) I'm less grateful now for the amazing wax finish on these skis than I was first thing this morning. I'm also wondering how best to murder Jon. A crafty push should do it, but he is just out of earshot of my raspy, oxygen-deprived whisper and out of flailing distance of my ski pole.

We have just trudged up about six hundred vertical metres (OK, two hundred) through soft, soft powder on a steep gradient, carrying our skis over our shoulders to get over the ridge we are now standing on. There is no oxygen. None. I think I am going to die. I am quite sure that at the very least, I am going to vomit up both of my lungs. It is only a matter of time.

Gasp, gasp.

Of course Sweden is barely even puffed. I hate him.

'Check that out,' says Jon, pointing over the edge at something. I shuffle over to have a look.

Holy crap. The Couloir of *Certain* Death. It can't be more than four metres wide, with steep, rocky spines on either side. The skiable slope is about seventy degrees' gradient, with a large, solid overhanging cornice at the top. He cannot possibly be serious.

Can he? He is examining it very closely.

Oh, God, he is serious. My heart starts to beat very fast, as though trying to burst out of my ribcage. *Abandon ship!*

The idea with this couloir, as far as I can see, would be to leap off the cornice, drop about five feet and land on a slope almost steep enough to qualify as a cliff but so narrow that turning is not possible, making it necessary to ride it out on the fall line at Mach Three until we get past the rocky walls and have enough room to put in a turn and take off a little speed. By this point we will be

179

moving so fast that our skis will be able to smell our fear (OK, mine), and even the slightest hesitation or loss of balance will be terminal.

Jon is sizing it up, looking calm and collected. *Gulp. Trust him, Poppy, or you are on your own here.*

'Right,' I say with a little wobble, nodding at the couloir. 'What's the plan then? Ha, ha, I thought you said you didn't want to kill me?'

'You're up for this?'

'I…I'm not going first.'

He looks impressed, I think, or bewildered. Bewildered, actually. Yes, definitely bewildered.

'Are you mad?' he asks. 'I don't want to die. Look at that cornice. "Doomy," as you say. No, no, we're not going to drop in here. We'd get buried. I'm just having a look.'

Oh, thank God. Thank you, thank you, thank you.

'But it is a nice little couloir, eh? I think we'll save this one for later in the season. It's really cool in the right conditions.'

'Err, yeah.' *For sure, you bleeding head-case, you.*

'For now, let's keep walking around the ridge. You see there, where it drops down lower beyond that rocky outcrop? The slope opens out there into a nice, wide powder bowl, then drops into another one, and another. All good and steep stuff, perfect for balance and speed.'

I follow him, feeling massively relieved and happy. Relieved and happy, that is, until Jon calls back over his shoulder, 'but, hey, there *is* a way into this couloir about two thirds of the way down. How about we traverse over to it and have a look at it from down there, see what we think?'

'See what we think' is, in my experience, the skier's cheerfully misleading euphemism for 'we're going to do it regardless of what *you* think, but you don't need to know that just yet.' *Gulp.* Mental slap about the face. Good scared, good scared…

I *am* good scared, actually. I have been on that edge between fear and excitement all day, from the moment I got home from work this morning to find Jon sitting in the kitchen with Mikey –

who, it turned out, knows him from last season.

'Poppy!' Mikey yelled as I walked in. 'Look who's here! It's Jon! I hear you two have met.'

'We have,' I said with a smile. 'Hi Jon.'

Jon beamed back at me. Mikey shook his head. 'Jon says you jumped into a pool last night, you mentalist.'

'True.'

'Nutter. Oh, and he's brought your sock.'

Jon held up a familiar-looking ski sock. 'You left it in the dryer, Cinderella.'

Mikey tackled me onto the stinky couch and forced the ski sock onto my foot. 'It fits!'

'Now I just hope the rest fits too.' Jon vanished into the hall and reappeared holding my freshly dried salopettes, my ski boot inners and to my delight, an enormous, unfamiliar pair of skis. 'What do you think?'

'Amazing! Where did you get them? Whose are they?'

'They're yours. I have a few spare pairs hanging around the van, getting in the way. You'd be doing me a favour if you skied them, please. Stand up.' He held them up against me. 'Yes, that's a good length for you. I thought it would be.'

They were enormous: practically a hand span underfoot and about fifteen centimetres longer than my usual ski length. Each ski was about as wide as both of my rental skis stuck together.

'Jon, they're like *snowboards*.'

'Yes. For floating in powder. Cool, hey?' Jon grinned at me. 'It's OK, they do carve on the piste. You've just got to roll them a little harder.'

'Wow.' I admired the graphics and the funky orange and blue bindings. 'These are seriously cool skis.'

'Yes, they are,' he said with a hint of pride, 'and look,' he flexed one of the skis at tail and tip. 'Stiff, hey? You're going to have some fun with these today, I promise you that. You will not believe the difference between these and your rentals.'

'I can't wait, Jon. You're so kind to let me borrow... *Whoa.* Wait a sec.' I glimpsed a manufacturer's sticker on the base of one ski. I looked up at him. 'Are these *brand new?*'

He nodded. 'Yes, I just drilled them this morning. The bindings are a couple of seasons old but the skis are fresh.'

'Are you serious?' I blinked, alarmed. 'I can't use them, Jon. What if I damage them on a rock or something?'

He shrugged. 'Doesn't matter. I don't even know why I was sent them. They're a bit too short for my height.'

'A bit?' Mikey snorted. 'They're snowblades on you, Jon mate. Don't worry Pops. He gets them free. Sponsorship deal. He gets paid to ride powder – sweet, eh? And hey, if you think these ones are fat, wait until you see the skis *he's* taking up today.'

'Right, right, that's enough talk,' said Jon, clapping his hands suddenly and turning me around by the shoulders toward the kitchen door. 'It's getting on. We must get going.' I went to get changed. 'Hey, Mikey,' Jon's voice drifted in from the kitchen, 'you want to come with us? I'm taking Poppy to the Rufigrat ridge.'

'That sounds wicked but I would be an utter liability to you today, matey. I am absolutely hanging out my arse right now.'

'"Hanging out my arse!"' Jon exclaimed, delighted. 'I have never heard that before. What a great expression. I am going to use it. "I am hanging out my arse." Or would it be "hanging out *of* my arse?"'

They both thought about it and decided that 'hanging out *of* my arse' made more sense. Jon was very pleased with this acquisition.

'Thanks, buddy.'

On the way up in the lift, Jon and I agreed certain rules for the day. No mogul fields for me – I despise them. (And I can't do them, more importantly.) And no glacier-skiing for Jon. He had an 'incident' with a crevasse here last season.

'An "incident"?' I was horrified. The shadowy chasms of the glacial crevasses are clearly visible from the village and nothing has ever scared the b'jesus out of me like they do. 'Did it involve *falling?*'

Jon didn't want to talk about it. 'I'm a bit superstitious about the mountain hearing me. Anyway, I'm not saying never, but we don't have ice axes or ropes with us, so not today, OK?'

I couldn't even pretend to be disappointed. We settled on a plan to play about in trees and look for big powder lines. He said we would start with a 'little walk' up from the Nordhangbahn to the Rufigrat ridge, and then maybe head over the other side of the valley toward Ristis for some trees. I felt I ought to warn him not to expect too much though. Something about the way he said, 'pillows, Poppy! Pillows on Ristis, imagine!' and grinned like a lunatic made me wonder just exactly who he thought he was skiing with.

'Err, Jon?' I ventured. 'I don't want to disappoint you, but I am quite rubbish. If it's going to be really deep today, I mightn't be…'

He shook his head, smiling. 'Did you not backflip into a swimming pool last night?'

Unfounded optimism is not my friend. I tried again. 'I really do not want you labouring under any false illusions here. Number one, I was possibly a little drunk last night. Number two, it was a pool of water – there were no consequences. And number three, I didn't even land it.'

He scrunched up his nose and shook his head again. 'You went for it. That's the important thing; far more important than how long you have been skiing or what rules you have been taught. Far more important than anything else is attitude, hey? And anyway, it will be more or less the same thing today. In powder, nothing hurts much.'

Much?

That was when we started the climb up to the ridge, me with some trepidation…

1.20pm

Text message. Oh, it's James:

'Just saw Tom with the RSL guiding group. What's happened? Where are you? What's the story with lunch?'

I look at my watch. Surely it's a bit early to be… *Shit!* It's

183

almost half past one! *Where did the time go?*

I think about it for a minute. What can I do? Nothing really. We're miles from anywhere useful. It's a long traverse back to the Reschengel side of the Rufigrat back-bowls and then at least an hour to Stüben between lifts and skiing. I swear under my breath.

'What's up?' Jon has stopped. 'Damn, is it really that late? Oh, man, I am so sorry. I said I would get us back by one, didn't I?'

It's not his fault. I am by far the slower skier and I was the one who wanted to climb back up the ridge and do the back-bowls again. I should have kept an eye on the time.

Oh, well. It's not the end of the world. James will live. I'm not going to feel too guilty about letting him down this once. I skied with him all day Monday and Tuesday and anyway, he has plenty of people to ski with over in Futterberg. I reply:

'Sorry, James. Got delayed and am still really far away from Stüben. Won't make lunch I'm afraid.'

'Oh, oh, that sounds like the sort of thing that Gina might be responsible for. Poor you, how dull! I'll just enjoy the powder twice as much on your behalf, shall I? Heh, heh.'

Well, he's not totally wrong there, in an indirect way. I'll go with that.

Me: 'Bah, humbug. Go on then, if you must. I'll call you later.'
James: 'OK, sexy. Looking forward to hearing your voice. Good luck with the orange one.'

Feeling a bit guilty now, it has to be said. I hope he's not skiing alone off-piste. No, he would never be so stupid, would he?

7.14pm

Of course I spent the next hour worrying about leaving James to ski alone, which cast a bit of a downer on things. Then, karma being what it is, I got a call from Tom about an urgent guest issue that put a swift end to my day of skiing.

It seems that Gina forgot to inform Tom at the start of the week that two of his guests booked to travel on to another ski resort by train this evening and that their tickets were supposed to be delivered to them at their hotel. When their tickets still had not materialised by midday today, they phoned the resort office in a mild panic. They were told by a very apologetic Gina that 'the rep' had evidently 'dropped the ball' and that she would deal with it immediately. Gina then called a very confused Tom to yell at him for his inefficiency. She demanded that he come back to resort and 'sort it' and slammed down the phone. He tried to call her back to remind her that he was in Futterberg with fifteen guests, but she refused to answer every time.

Jon skied with me as far as Furggspitz and the main pistes down to the village.

'Will you be long?' he asked.

'No, it should be a very quick thing to sort out. Just a simple drop-off,' I told him.

In fact there was no reason aside from pure stubborn childishness that Gina could not hop into the resort van parked thirty paces from her door and deal with the problem in less than ten minutes, but I decided not to think about that because I was determined to stay in the excellent mood I was in.

'Come back up as soon as you can then,' said Jon. 'There'll be a crowd of us in the Moose and a Birne Schnapps with your name on it. We have lots to celebrate! It's not every day a person conquers Rufigrat for the first time!'

I smiled and skied off with a wave.

It was just a matter of picking up the tickets from Gina (with a look that left her in no doubt as to where she could stick her demand that I go home and change into uniform), then walking to the hotel, handing them over to the guests and wishing them a good trip. Nevertheless, between getting from the hotel to the lift station and negotiating a few pistes, it was four-fifteen by the time I rounded the last bend and found myself at the entrance of the Moose. As always by that time, it was heaving.

The Moose bar is legendary amongst skiers and snowboarders. This is because every day at three-thirty, the DJ comes on. The blinds drop. The disco lights are lowered. And, with the push of a button, enormous speakers begin to pump out the opening bars of *The Final Countdown*. From that moment on, the bar and its outdoor terrace are transformed from a relatively normal lunch spot to a heaving mass of people cheering, roaring and stamping their ski boots to the bizarre blend of 1980s stadium rock songs and cheesy Euro-pop known as aprés-ski music. From '*Heeeeyyyy, heeeeyyyy baby, oooh, aahh*' to *Highway to Hell* and back to '*Cowboys und Indianen,*' aprés-ski music has a logic only Jägermeister can explain.

Most days, season workers leave the Moose to the tourists and their much larger wallets, instead flocking to the nearby and somewhat lower-key Taps Bar. Today, however, everybody was here and most of them in fancy dress. Of course! Bella's birthday! How could I have forgotten? The SuperSki reps had planned a "B" party in the park followed by an afterparty here in the Moose, where Bella's boyfriend, the bar manager, was laying on a special free-Birne-Schnapps-with-every-drink Happy Hour for everyone in costume. I fought my way to the bar through swaying crowds of bees, bushes, brothel madams, biscuits, Mister Bumps, ballistic missiles and all manner of other things besides until I spotted Arthur and Eoghan propping up the bar dressed as Barney and Betty Rubble, and had the dubious pleasure of being shown Arthur's newly acquired friction burns.

'S'fine. Doesn't hurt yet,' he slurred, poking his buttocks to prove it.

I ran into Jon moments later and quite by accident, both of us crossing the crowded terrace to tackle the same passing waiter. Jon brought me over to introduce me to some of his friends.

'Boys and girls,' he announced, clapping me enthusiastically on the back, 'this is Poppy.'

One of the group, a broad, sandy-haired and very serious-looking man, stepped forward to shake my hand. I recognised his face from various times I'd spotted him prowling around resort over the past few months. Although I had never spoken to him, I knew his name and knew that he had a reputation for being at the black-belt end of extreme-skiing: fearless, technically flawless and hard as nails.

'Poppy, like the flower?' he asked, gripping my hand like an ice-axe. I nodded. 'Hello,' he growled. 'I am Anderss.'

'But you can call him "Thor, God of War,"' interjected a blonde girl with a mock-serious frown. She introduced herself as Karin. Another girl, small and dark-haired, appeared beside me with a smile.

'*Hej, hej.* I am Charlotte. How are you, Poppy? I hear you have been skiing today with Jon, yes? In all that powder! What a day it was, eh? The best so far this season I think. By the way, this is Kerstin and here also is Aussie Ben.'

We all shook hands and kissed cheeks. Karin explained that she, Charlotte and Ben were all ski and snowboard instructors, while Kerstin, who is Ben's girlfriend, worked in the ski school office in the village centre. We chatted for a while over a couple of glühweins, exchanging stories of the season so far and competing as to who had the most unhinged manager. Kerstin won with her story of being knocked unconscious when her boss threw a wastepaper basket at her head, but only because I held back from giving the by-now legendary chronicle of Gina's declared life's achievements (the most recent one being that she secretly publishes chick-lit novels under the pseudonym Cecilia Ahern. Going along with this is a new low for me.)

By then, Jon had disappeared again in the direction of the bar (with the promise that he had just had 'the best idea') and Karin and Charlotte got to telling me stories about things he, Head and Nick have got up to during their several winter seasons together in Reschengel.

'Lotte, do you remember the year they tried to live the whole winter in that freezing little tin-can camper van?' Karin shivered. 'That was the first season I knew Nick. I thought he naturally had a sort of bluish skintone.'

'Yes,' Charlotte chuckled, 'that was the year they nearly got deported, remember? Must have been, what, five or six years ago? Really, Poppy, it was crazy. The police could not understand how the three of them could be living and working here with no fixed address. The boys had to bring them around to the van. And then the police did not believe that all of them slept in one big sleeping bag for warmth, so they had to climb in to demonstrate it. In the end, they were allowed to stay, but they had to pay four and a half thousand euro in parking fines. They decided it made more sense to just rent a place next time.' She shook her head. 'Just as well, I suppose. The next year, Jon met Emilie.'

Karin made a face. 'And, here we are, as they say.' In silence, they both reflected upon this. 'Hmm,' said Karin finally. Charlotte nodded and they both took a long drink.

'Is Emilie Jon's girlfriend?' I asked.

'Ehh...' Charlotte swirled her glühwein slowly. Karin said nothing. 'Well,' began Charlotte eventually, 'you see, it...'

At that moment, Jon wandered back over with – *oh, no* – a round of Birne Schnapps. Karin grabbed his arm.

'Hey, Jon, wasn't it two years ago that you and Head and Nick went on that road-trip to St Anton and had the Jägermeister shot contest with Hannes from Tom Dooley's bar? And you woke up two days later in Liechtenstein? Remember that?'

'Honestly, no,' said Jon, grinning. 'Although I think Hannes has the photo evidence, so I really should pay him a return visit sometime soon. Here, Poppy – your favourite.'

He handed me a shot glass. We toasted to the powder, and many more days like it.

Unfortunately, it was a work evening and visits time was creeping up quite fast. I made my apologies.

'That's fine,' said Jon. 'We are not staying much longer anyway. Head and Nick are also working from six o'clock. Actually, Head is driving down the hill from here if you would like a lift?'

'Yes, please,' I said, delighted. 'That'll save me the twenty-minute walk from the bottom. Cheers, Jon.'

'OK, Poppy-flower, go grab your skis and I will find the other two boys. We will meet you at the exit in a minute.'

'Is there room for one more in your car?' I had just spotted Rachel dancing the robot dance on a table with Tina. 'My mate Rachel could probably use a lift too. We both start work together.'

He gave me a strange look and then a big, beaming grin.

'Rachel? Yes!' he exclaimed, looking from me over to her and back again. 'Ha, ha! Not a problem! Tell her she is very, very, very welcome!'

He clapped me on the back and meandered off through the crowd. *What a delightfully odd boy*, I thought as I rounded up Rachel and we made our way through to the exit.

'It's that one over there,' said Jon, pointing to an oddly familiar-looking camper van on the edge of the car park. It was a funny shade of green. Where had I seen it before? I wondered. Or one like it? I couldn't place it and decided it probably reminded me of a scene from a film or something. I climbed in the side door and set my skis and poles on the floor of the van and was just reaching out to grab Rachel's board from her when I spotted them through the driver's cab window.

Dinosaurs.

Dinosaurs on the dashboard.

Dinosaurs *glued to the dashboard.*

Niklas.

Niklas… Nick?? Nick! NICK!

Holy crap!

I looked back and forth from Rex and friends to Nick and Head, to Rachel, climbing into the van, utterly oblivious. Head burst out laughing. Nick looked pale. Rachel glanced up and saw him. There was a long moment's silence, punctuated only by the universal language of furious blushing and darting of eyes.

In these sorts of situations, as a spectator, what does one do? The British Way requires one to studiously ignore the tension in the air with a great deal of 'Ahemming' and offering of tea. Clearly that's not the Swedish Way. Or maybe it was just that Jon was a little drunk and Head was…well, himself. The two boys caught each other's eye, sat down either side of Nick, threw an arm around him and burst into a swaying first verse and chorus of *Every Little Thing She Does Is Magic* until Rachel smiled, shooed Jon out of the way and sat down in his place. She looked at her hands for an awkward moment, and then at Nick.

'Hi,' she said quietly.

189

'Hi.'

Head got into the front cab to drive the van, and Jon and I joined him. It was time to catch up with my dino buddies. It had been too long.

Saturday 17 February

10.10pm

By the time I got home from visits this evening, Rachel and Tom had already been and gone. Tom was out on the prowl. As of four days ago, he has been besotted with Reschengel's new girl ('my eyes have been opened, Poppy. She is the one'). Her name is Helen and she is tiny, raven-haired and spectacularly beautiful. She came out earlier this week to replace one of the SuperSki chalet chefs and has been the talk of the town (or at least the single male population) ever since. So enchanted is Tom that he has recruited Eoghan, Arthur and Mikey as his wingmen and they have gone to Scotty's, a bar we normally never darken the door of, to track her down tonight. Rachel and I spent a futile twenty minutes this morning trying to talk him out of Plan A (serenading her in the bar) and the even worse Plan B (following her home and serenading her bedroom window) but Tom was not to be dissuaded. I can only hope Helen has a decent sense of humour.

Rachel, meanwhile, had already left to meet Nick in the village somewhere. I still cannot quite believe that my Nick from the Elena pool has turned out to be her Niklas, largely because I could never, ever, in my wildest imagination visualise the Nick I met being the same person who wrote that note to Rachel last month. Nothing about Nick screams 'stumbling mule': not his tall, broad-shouldered, blonde good looks, not his dry sense of humour and calm sort of self-confidence, not the fascinating way he talks about his offshore engineering work back home nor his quietly precise, focused skill on skis.

Rachel explained it to me on a chairlift this morning as we made our way up to meet Jon, Nick and Head to ski the Kuhtälli. On New Year's Eve, the night they met, the whole Snowglobe crew had been walking into the centre of town when they passed Nick and Jon hiding behind a nearby row of wheelie bins, hurling snowball missiles at innocent passers-by and wrestling people they knew into the snow. Nick was aiming for Mikey and only got a good look at Rachel about half a second after he had already launched a snowball at her head. He broke cover to go and

191

apologise and to offer to let her hit him with some retributive snow missiles, but as he wiped the snow from her hair, face and eyes, he stepped back, gasped with awe-stuck amazement and professed to be utterly blown away by the beauty of her 'dazzling azure eyes' and 'the rippling flames of her fiery, crimson mane.'

'"Fiery crimson mane?"'

'I know. Head and Jon joined in for a while too before they buggered off to that Swedish party and left Nick with me. It was quite funny being followed around by my Swedish fanbase. I could get used to that kind of adoration.'

'First he wooed you with poetry, and then he actually fell in love with you,' I sighed. 'Oh, how *romantic*.'

'I just assumed that their English teacher spent longer on Shakespeare than on basic conversational skills.'

What a relief. Since I read that note, I had quietly wondered what sort of a weirdo she had snared that night and had sort of hoped he might not reappear.

Our whole floor seemed to be in darkness as I walked up the pathway to the staff chalet; all but a flickering blue light barely visible through the kitchen curtains. Someone watching a DVD, I thought, wondering who it was and whether they might be persuaded to come with me to Happy Bar for a quiet after-work drink. I was disappointed to find it was only Daniel. Of all my housemates, Daniel is by far the least fun. Since about mid-January, he has stopped bothering to make an effort of any kind – not in the Club Hotel, not on the mountain and certainly not with any of us. He never goes skiing anymore, just drags himself listlessly from bed to work and back to bed again, where he lounges about all afternoon snoozing, eating takeaway pizza and watching his extensive collection of downloaded movies. At first I thought it might be man-flu. It took me ages to realise that this was what people meant when they talked about 'mid-season blues': a simple loss of interest. Now I don't know why he stays – it's certainly not out of politeness to his colleagues or a sense of commitment to his job, and I can't help thinking he'd be better off at home in the UK.

He nodded at me as I walked in the door. He was stretched out on the stinky couch, can of beer in hand and his laptop balanced on his chest with the sound blaring out of his enormous Skullcandy headphones.

'Hey,' I mouthed at him, motioning at the screen, 'what's this?'

He lifted a headphone and I repeated the question.

'Oh, uhh… *Spiderman 3*. It's shit.'

'Yeah,' I said as a truck or bus or something exploded across the screen. 'Yeah, it looks it.' He grunted. I hesitated, debating whether to ask, knowing what the answer would be but deciding to try anyway. 'You want to come across the road for a beer?'

'Nah. Can't be arsed. I'm tired.'

'Oh, come on,' I said, without a lot of conviction. 'It'll be good to get out of the house for a bit.'

'Ugh,' he grumbled, 'you sound like Hélène. And she was only trying to get rid of me so that she could violate Harry.'

'What?' I frowned. 'Is Hélène here now?'

'In the bedroom. Can you not hear her?' he grimaced, nodding at the hallway. 'She arrived this afternoon.'

Oh, scheisse, I thought, realising that the noises I was hearing were not all headphone-leakage but the all-too-familiar soundtrack of Harry and his girlfriend getting reacquainted. I stepped into the hallway and suddenly there was no mistaking the creaking bedsprings and moans of '*alors! Mon dieu! Oof! 'Arrie! 'Arrie!*' No wonder Daniel had the subwoofers on.

'Yeah, I'm going out,' I told Daniel hurriedly. He nodded silently and turned back to *Spiderman 3*.

Sigh… I stood outside the chalet door, watching the first flakes of a recently arrived snowcloud float downwards and settle on the wooden railing. There was definitely one person who could be prevailed upon to come to the pub for a quiet one, even on a deserted Saturday evening.

'Carol? It's me. You busy?'

'Not really. Mondschein?'

'OK, see you in five.'

The Mondschein Café is my favourite little corner of

Reschengel village. Tucked away a street back from the main thoroughfare, the Mondschein displays almost no outward markings to indicate that it is a café. Nor indeed is anything about the interior even remotely warm or welcoming: not the faded grey and brown décor, nor Traudl, the terrifying old lady behind the bar who greets newcomers with an extended silent stare and an eventual, accusatory *'Ja?'* and certainly not the agonised expressions on the faces of the fifteen or so stuffed rat-like animals decorating the walls between the four enormous, blood-soaked crucifixes that stare down from every corner of the room. What it lacks in obvious charm, however, it more than makes up for by being a blissfully secluded little haven from all things related to Snowglobe and the seasonaire world. It is the absolute last place you would find a novelty cocktail, piste map or whistling-marmotte keyring, and so most definitely the last place for say, a psychotic resort manager to come looking for us at any given moment. Carol, Rachel and I have been coming here at least twice a week since early December, generally in search of either a stiff drink or a restorative *Schinken-Käse Toast* and always for a bit of peace and quiet. Of course our loyalty to the place doesn't mean that we have quite come to be welcomed with open arms just yet – the local patrons still stare at us for an unashamed ten minutes every time we walk in. Still, I think we might have their grudging acceptance by now since Traudl has taken to greeting us with a nod of recognition and even smiling as she brings us our usual drinks without asking for an order. (Also, we haven't been run through with a pitchfork yet, which is encouraging.)

It felt like ages since I'd last had a good chat and catch-up with Carol. She was most pleased to hear that Rachel's mysterious 'Niklas' and Nick are one and the same, and that he is a friend of Head and Jon, whom she also knows from last season.

'Why do they call him Head?' I had been wondering this for some time. 'Is it a Swedish name?'

'No,' replied Carol. 'It's because his name is Björn. Björn Jenssen.'

I still didn't get it.

'They started off calling him "Bee Jorn",' she explained, 'then "Bee Gee." Then that became "BJ." And then "Head." You can see the logical progression.'

I told Carol about our adventures skiing the Kuhtälli today, a route that she told me that she has never yet got round to doing. It was epic, beautiful skiing that she would have loved, including a fantastically long, narrow little gully with steep sides where I cackled with delight when Nick showed us how to properly 'slash the lip' at last. To get there and back involved a long hike in and a long flat run-out, admittedly, which caused some grumbling among the snowboarding contingent (Rachel), but it was worth it for the untracked, shaded little paradise we found. I made Carol promise that she would come the next time I go skiing with the Swedish boys and Rachel.

'They're really good skiers,' I told her.

'So I believe,' she said, smiling into her vodka.

'And Nick has said that he will take over Andu's job of coaching Rachel for the Big Air contest next month,' I went on. 'He is meant to be pretty handy with a snowboard too, right?'

Carol was amused by this. 'Pretty handy,' she snorted. 'That's one way of putting it.' She opened her box of Marlboros and regarded me through the flickering light of a flame. 'Poppy, do you even know who you've been skiing with?'

I sensed a mountain-responsibility lecture coming, one about not putting your life in the hands of someone you have only just met, *et cetera, et cetera.* 'Give me a break,' I said. 'OK, fine, no, I don't really know these guys. I've only just met them, but I do trust them. Jon was absolutely fantastic the first day we went up. He watched my technique and advised me every few runs about simple, small things I could change about my position and movement to improve my bounce and turning. It was amazing – I could actually feel the difference with every little change he told me to try. I felt like a better skier at the end of the day.'

Carol's eyes widened with glee. 'So he's a better teacher than James, God of the World?'

I stuck out my tongue at her and said nothing. He is, actually,

195

but I wasn't going to give her the satisfaction of admitting as much. Jon's job out here (on the few days he seems to actually work) is in off-piste and freestyle ski clinic coaching, so he is well practiced in the art of talking people through descents they have the ability for but not the confidence. His voice is very calming. Skiing in front of him somehow does not make me tense up and lose concentration the way I do when I ski with James. I wish that wasn't the case but it is; I can't help it. James has an odd and not always particularly welcome sort of magnetic effect on me. I feel it across the crowded arrivals hall at Salzburg airport just as strongly as I feel it across the table in Muschhütte, making it hard to focus entirely on what I am doing and whomever else I might be speaking to. I try to push it to the peripheries, but when we are skiing together, that magnetism has an unfortunate way of pulling me into the snow, repeatedly, at speed. Worst of all is when we ski with his friends; they're a silent lot who aren't used to waiting around. The pressure to not screw up means I invariably spend the day digging myself out while they watch, wait and pretend not to look at their watches. It's no wonder James still thinks I am such a punter on skis; I just can't relax, no matter how hard I try – or perhaps because I am trying so hard.

But with Jon, I can relax. Since that night in the pool, I suppose my fear of the unknown is diminished when he is around. After I trusted him enough to ski into a swimming pool on his say-so, I can't help but ask myself how badly wrong can something go if he promises me it will be OK.

'Jon Berner, teaching you to ski couloirs up on Rufigrat. Heh, heh. I love it.' Carol shook her head and muttered something that sounded suspiciously like 'poor, poor James,' but she would say nothing more on the subject, just continued to look enormously amused.

I thought about this as she went to the bar for another round. *Would* James be jealous? I'd never even considered that possibility. James knows I ski with other people most days, male and female. There's no reason for him to even care. Maybe he would be annoyed if I told him that someone else had been teaching me stuff about off-piste though, since he did offer to teach me himself. And he would definitely be irked if he knew I missed lunch the other day because of losing track of the time up on Rufigrat with Jon.

Hmm, I thought then, *speaking of James – my phone has been very quiet this evening.* That's odd – it's transfer day tomorrow. Normally there is at least a text message from Gina, reminding me of this fact, (as though I could forget). And it's almost time for bed, so where's my message from James?

Or, more pertinently, where's my phone?

10.14pm

Oh, shit. *Where is my phone??* Not on the table, not on the bar, not in my bag, not in my pockets, not in my jacket. Oh, *crap.*

10.18pm

Trapped in an ascending state of panic. A lost phone is what our fearless leader calls a 'Rep Disaster Grade FIVE. It's a Code... like, SERIOUS, yah?'

And on *transfer day.* No, that is just not possible. It has to be somewhere. It has to be somewhere or else Sarah Datchet is going to wring my neck, rip out my small intestine and use it to tie up my body bag.

Calm. I will find it. It must be somewhere.

I dial my number from Carol's phone. No answer. *Argh, argh, argh.*

Poppy! Come on, think calmly. It must be in the staff chalet, where else can it be?

10.54pm

Shit fuck shit fuck shit fuck shit fuck shit fuck shit fuck shit fuck shit fuck shit fuck shit fuck shit fuck shit fuck shit fuck shit fuck. It's not in the staff chalet. It's not on the road between the chalet and the Mondschein. It's not anywhere. I have lost it somewhere in the vast snowy wastes and someone has found it and stolen it. I will never see it again.

197

Oh, *God*, and that's only if I am lucky. *What if Gina has found it?? She'll have read all my text messages to and from James.*

I feel ill.

11.09pm

Still no sign. A sense of calm descends on me, not unlike a condemned criminal awaiting lethal injection.

11.23pm

Ohthankgod. I found it just at the moment I had abandoned all hope and decided that there was still time to smoke myself into metastatic cancer between now and tomorrow morning. It must have fallen out of my pocket after I phoned Carol earlier because there it was on the steps just outside the front door of the chalet, sitting in a pile of cigarette butts. Mmm. Fragrant.

Predictably, there were three text messages from Gina and a missed call.

'Sweetieees, hope ur all set 4 "T-Day" 2mrrw!!! All guns blazing! xxx haw, haw, haw.'

(OK, the 'haw, haw, haw' was implied.)

And then two hours later:

'Poppy? I hope u r in bed asleep nd thats why u hvnt confrmd A-OK 4 2mrrw???'

And then:

'Poppy, this is nt funny. Answr ur phone, like, now???'

There were also four increasingly alarmed messages and missed calls from James. Rather odd, actually.

8.55pm: 'Poppy! Entertain me please. Currently writing weekly report – monumentally boring. I need some inspiration to explain our rubbish lift pass pick-up. So far, this is all I've got: "This week, a guest spontaneously combusted on a transfer coach, taking 53% of sales vouchers with him. The rep escaped unharmed and compensation had been offered to the affected parties in the form of a complimentary Snowglobe T-shirt."'

9.25pm: 'What I need, actually, is for you to steal a car and come over here to really ruin my concentration. What are you doing at the moment…?'

11.08pm: 'Poppy, why are you ignoring me? What is going on? What has happened? Call me as soon as you can.'

11.20pm: 'I'm actually worried now that something has happened to you since you're not even answering your phone. I'm even thinking of contacting Gina. So if you are just not talking to me for some reason because of something you think I have done, at least tell me that so I'll know nothing else has happened to you. Otherwise I will call her. Please. x'

Oh, dear. Sent him back a calming message. 'I'm alive, just lost my phone for a few hours. Relax!'

James' relief was palpable. 'You lost your phone?' he wrote back. 'You numpty. Thought you might have passed out under a snow-cannon and died of exposure. Or joined a cult and sacrificed yourself.'

Me: 'Tell me, what would Gina have been able to do about that, exactly?'
James: 'I don't know actually. She would probably have been responsible for initiating you.'
Me: 'Into the cult of "Walker is the Antichrist?" Why would I decide randomly to just start ignoring you? Have you been smoking crack? Had funny mushroom pasta for dinner??'
James: 'Shut up. Let's get back to the fact that you lost your phone six hours before transfers begin. I bet you're drunk too. Tut, tut.'
Me: 'Not guilty.'
James: 'Hmm. I am deeply sceptical.'

Me: 'It's true! Sober as a judge.'

James: 'Hmm. Hmm. I don't believe it for a second. People with funny accents and midgets. Never trust either.'

Me: 'And midgets with funny accents?'

James: 'Poppy! They are called Little People. Have some respect. This is all just too much. Drunk and abusive, and to your area manager, no less. Disciplinary meeting tomorrow.'

Me: 'Oh, dear. How humiliating, in front of all the reps, guests and Gina. I might cry.'

James: 'Can't have that. Bad for staff morale. Fortunately, it looks like we will have a break in the flights from around 1 until 4. I'll be taking you aside then.'

Me: 'Right, you can buy me lunch so. Then I'll totally listen to whatever you're banging on about, I promise.'

James: 'Insubordination. You're sacked. See you in the morning, beautiful.'

Sunday 18 February

11.56pm

The less said about 'lunch' the better. Suffice to say I am very glad I met Rachel on the way back in to the Charter Terminal. She stopped me, gave me a curious look and pulled a couple of leaves from my hair.

'I walked into a tree.'

'Uh huh.'

'Shut up.'

'You are un…'

'Shut up.'

Anyway. Charter Terminal was cleared of passengers by about four o'clock and was almost deserted for the remainder of the evening but for a handful of us waiting for a couple of Innsbruck Airport diverts to arrive. Bloody Innsbruck! Still, bad weather in the Innsbruck region often means that we in Central Austria are in for a bit of snowfall if the system tracks east. Hopeful that this was the case, Rachel and I got James to check the online long-range forecast for the week. Disappointingly however, nothing significant was forecast in the next three days. Instead we found out that we are in for some rather high temperatures – as high as seventeen degrees Celsius in Reschengel village. *Damn it.*

James nudged me with his elbow as we leaned over his computer. 'Glad I'm not you, Connors. To think, you missed skiing on Friday! It was probably the best day of the season so far. Certainly the best for quite some considerable time to come…bet you're regretting that now!' He grinned wickedly and turned to Rachel. 'Did Gina nab you for paperwork too?'

Rachel gave me an amused and incredulous look. I'd forgotten to tell her about my little white lie. Fortunately, she is a much better 'truth-omitter' than I am. She simply smiled conspiratorially at James and said, 'oh, no, no, no, I had a cunning plan. I managed to escape Gina by completely avoiding Poppy on Friday. I'm actually avoiding Poppy generally these days. Her pool adventures on Thursday have made me think she has become dangerously unhinged.'

201

'Yes, actually, about that,' James turned back to me, 'I was driving when you sent me that message. I thought afterwards that I must have imagined it. Did you say you skied into a *swimming* pool on Thursday? Or did you mean pool table?'

'The watery kind.'

'Intentionally?'

'Well…mostly.'

James shook his head, bewildered. 'You skied into water in your clothes and ski boots? Have you not noticed that it gets rather cold here sometimes, what with being a vertical mile up a snowy mountain and all that?'

'Yes,' I nodded ponderously, 'I did notice a chill in the air after a while.'

'You utter liability. I can't believe you didn't kill yourself. That might be the stupidest thing I have ever heard.'

'It wasn't my idea,' I protested, 'it was the guys in the chalet next door: Nick and Jon and…'

'Whatever,' James interrupted. 'Did you not think it was a bit stupid to get your ski boots wet? Or that you might sink and drown, maybe?'

'Nope. Jon lent me a buoyancy thingy. They were very prepared. And anyway, I think I am more likely to drown in powder than water, to be fair.'

'Hmm. True,' he conceded, 'your powder technique does rather resemble a retarded fish on roller skates. Perhaps water is your natural environment.'

I stuck out my tongue at him, not totally convinced that he was wrong, but Rachel wagged her finger at him and told him to be careful. 'You should have seen her on Kuhtälli yesterday, James. The girl was on fire. You sure you can still keep up, old man?'

I smiled at her for her very convincing loyalty. James just laughed. 'What, has she learned the mysteries of pole planting?' he asked, patting my arm condescendingly. 'Or has she just discovered how to dig herself out in super-quick time?'

'No,' said Rachel bristling slightly, 'just, like, backflipping,

202

couloir skiing up on Rufigrat and hitting the Ristis trees.' She beamed triumphantly and folded her arms with a look of *put that in your pipe and smoke it, you sarky git.*

James snorted derisively. 'Yeah, "hitting" being the operative word.' He saw my face and Rachel's and said quickly, 'Joking! You're learning very fast, it's good. It's great. But come on, you're not going to run before you can walk. Let's save Rufigrat and Ristis for when you have a bit more experience, OK?' Rachel gave me a sideways look as he went on, smirking as he patted my arm. 'No shame in being a sunglasses-skier for a while. I'll still be seen in public with you. At a distance obviously.'

Hrrmph. 'Screw you, James, I don't even wear sunglasses.'

'But you do wear an orange helmet.'

'It's progressive. Just you wait, the world will catch up with that one.'

'You mean it was the only one you could find in the special shop,' he laughed.

'Shut up. Rachel, do you mind being seen skiing with me?'

'On the contrary,' she whispered, 'it is *an honour.*'

'OK, OK,' said James with exaggerated patience. 'Look, I'll take you skiing during the week, we'll go up to Ruhtai and have a look at the bowls, how about that?'

I shrugged nonchalantly just as Sarah Datchet walked through the doors, striding purposefully toward James' desk. Suddenly, he was all business again.

'Right, I need to do some work now. Sod off, girls.'

'Charmer,' muttered Rachel as we drifted off to the coffee shop.

Tuesday 20 February
1.45pm. Reschengel.

It was the loud crashing noise downstairs followed by the piercing shriek that first alerted us to the fact that something was amiss.

Rachel, Tom and I had come home from guest visits about forty minutes previously and were sitting in the kitchen procrastinating heavily about getting out of our uniforms and going skiing. The shriek held its note for an improbably long period of time and then descended into a high-pitched wail with a peculiarly mesmeric, undulating banshee-like quality. We exchanged a puzzled look. We've heard many unwelcome sounds coming from that apartment over the past few weeks, but nothing like this. Moments later, we heard the sound of small feet thundering up the stairs and Gina burst into the room.

'Right,' she barked, but there was something very odd about her face. She was almost...*pale*. 'You're very funny, very funny, I'm laughing, yah?' she said, wide-eyed and intent. 'Now I really need to get going, so give it back.' We looked at her blankly. 'Come on,' she said, clapping her hands and darting around the kitchen table, looking underneath the plastic tablecloth and pulling us off our chairs to look at the chairs where we had been sitting.

Whatever she was looking for was not in the kitchen, so she dashed out and started rummaging in the hall cupboard. She banged the door shut after a moment and headed for the larger of the boys' bedrooms.

We followed her. 'Gina, what are you looking for?'

She turned and stared at me. 'One of you has it,' she said matter-of-factly. We looked at one another and back at her, utterly bewildered. 'One of you *has got* to have it,' she repeated, a strangled note of desperation creeping into her voice.

'Have what?'

'Is this a joke? Because it's very funny, it's very funny, all right? You got me. But I really need it back now.'

'Gina, we really haven't taken anything of yours, and no-one has come in or gone out of this chalet while we have been here.

They're all at work. Just tell us what you have lost and we will help you look for it.'

She blinked rapidly and swallowed hard, her eyes brimming with tears. 'If it's gone, I'm dead,' she whispered.

'What??'

'The money.'

'What mon… Oh, *Christ.*'

Every weekend we take in anything between two and twenty-two thousand euro in cash from our lift pass sales, depending on how many people choose to pay in cash on the transfer coaches. Gina totals the sales and finalises the accounts on Monday night while we run the bar crawl, and the money sits in the resort safe in her apartment until the following morning. Then every Tuesday morning before eleven, she is responsible for depositing it in the bank. A simple system.

But not a foolproof one, it would seem. This morning, Gina took the money from the safe at nine-thirty, as she always does. She checked that the brown envelope was still sealed, with the total amount it contained written across the back flap and sellotaped shut. She put the brown envelope into her bag and put her handbag down beside the bed while she put on her makeup and got her coat.

Just then, a horn blared outside on the street. She stuck her head out the door. A delivery man in a white van waved to her and called out that he had a delivery of plumbing parts for Chalet Elena and that Fritz Spitzer had sent him to talk to her. She walked the thirty or so paces to the roadway to talk to the driver about access to the Elena and where the hot tub was located. She was there for no more than two minutes…

('Two?'

'Well, I had a cigarette with him. He was from Interlaken originally and I have a mate there and…OK, so maybe not two minutes, but no more than five or six, yah?')

…six minutes. Then the delivery man drove off and Gina walked back into her apartment, grabbed her bag and went to leave for the bank. Only when she went to check that her keys were in her bag did she realise that the envelope was gone.

'Gone? Just vanished?'

'Gone.'

'And you definitely put it in the bag? Are you absolutely sure it's not still in the safe, or on the desk? Did you check that it didn't accidentally fall into the bin or something?'

'It's gone.'

She was whispering again, tears streaming down her face as she lifted a shaky hand to light a new cigarette from the stub of the old one.

'How much are we talking about?'

'Seventeen thousand, three hundred and seventy eight euro and sixty-six cent.'

Rachel exhaled sharply.

'Shit,' I said.

'That's a lot of money,' offered Tom.

Gina nodded, her eyes searching us desperately, as though still clinging to the hope that it was a joke after all, that we were holding really good poker faces and that someone was going to make this go away with a smile and a laugh. She shivered slightly as I took her elbow as we walked down the stairs to her apartment to help her search it once again, though none of us expected to find any trace of the money, and indeed we did not.

'Did they take anything else from your bag? Your wallet or anything?'

She shook her head. 'Just the money envelope.'

'Shit, Gina,' said Tom, running his hands through his hair in genuine distress. 'I don't know what to say. What unbelievable bad luck, mate.'

'Luck?' said Rachel, frowning as she looked around Gina's small bedroom. 'I don't think so' Her eyes narrowed slightly as she stared through the net-curtained window into the middle distance. 'There was so little time involved. Whoever it was must have known exactly where the money was. They would have had to see you put it there. But how?'

'What do you mean?' frowned Gina.

'Did you see anyone hovering about outside your window, Gina?'

'No. What, like a pervert? No, of course not. I would have said.'

'Hmmm.' Rachel stroked her chin, frowning. 'It's those net curtains, you see,' she explained in the gravelly voice of the *CSI* investigator (she later confessed that this was the effect she was going for). 'It would take a lot more that a quick glance through those things to see what was going on inside.'

A strange feeling came over me at the thought of anyone watching the building so closely without being noticed. There is always so much coming and going amongst our housemates that we rarely even lock our door. Reschengel never seemed like the sort of place where you'd need to.

Rachel blinked as another thought came to her. 'Actually, you know if you think about it, if somebody *was* hanging about outside the flat, the delivery man might have seen something. Which way was he facing when you were talking to him, Gina?'

'Ohmygod,' breathed Gina. 'He was facing the door. He *must* have seen whoever it was. I'll get his number from Fritz.' She wrenched her phone from her pocket and starting punching her way through her contacts list. 'And then the police can work out who it was and we'll get the money back,' she said happily. 'Oh, Rachel! You're a genius.'

'True.'

'Oh, I hope he saw something, I hope, I hope, I hope,' chanted Gina as she held the phone to her ear, waiting. 'Fuck it, if only Jan had stayed inside. The fool chose that exact moment to go and put out the recycling...'

'Wait, wait, wait. *Jan* was here the whole time?' A horrible sick knot twisted at my stomach.

'No,' explained Gina with exasperation. 'The useless little twat popped outside just after I went to talk to the delivery man. He says he had no idea that the envelope was worth so much. To be fair, I've never told him what was in it. By the time he came back inside, it was gone and he hadn't seen anything.'

I could feel Rachel's eyes on me. I looked at Tom. He was staring at Gina in disbelief. We were all thinking the same thing. Surely the obvious must hit her in the face?

No-one said anything for a long moment. Gina jumped as Fritz answered his phone and she explained what she needed from him. He gave her the delivery van driver's mobile number and she phoned it immediately. We held our breath as she outlined in a breathless voice what had happened and asked if he had seen anything.

There was a silence as the slightly manic hope on her face faded and slid away.

'Oh. OK. Thanks.' Gina literally deflated in front of our eyes. 'He swears that no-one went in,' she told us, flipping her phone shut with a sad little click. 'The only person he saw was Jan walking out with the recycling bag.'

We looked at one another. Someone had to ask.

'Is there any way,' I volunteered hesitantly, 'that maybe, that errm…Jan could have taken it?'

She dismissed this suggestion with a quick wave. 'No, no, no, he hasn't got that sort of sense of humour. And even if he did, he wouldn't have taken it quite this far.'

Tom tried a different tack. 'Where is Jan now?'

'Oh, something came up and he had to go down the valley to his office.' She sighed and sat down heavily on the floor, her hands shaking as she opened her box of cigarettes. Tears brimmed in her eyes again. 'The stupid bastard, leaving me alone to deal with this. I could really use a hug.'

Tom sat down beside her and put his arm around her shoulder. 'We won't leave you alone.'

She clung to him and cried quietly.

'Let's go to the police and make a report,' said Rachel kindly but firmly. 'The sooner the better, eh?'

Gina nodded dumbly as we led her out the door.

The *Polizei* were predictably efficient. They took the details of the story, quizzing Gina about Rachel, Tom and me, and particularly closely about Jan. They took the delivery man's phone number and promised to look further into the case, but as the theft involved unmarked currency in all denominations, they did not offer much encouragement that the money would ever be recovered. We were cheered a little, however, when they explained that many large companies have insurance against these things, and, if a claim is successful, that Gina may not be personally liable for the whole amount.

Some of the colour returned to her cheeks at that news, but she was still hugely afraid of phoning James to let him know what had happened, and put it off by dragging us to Café Häferl for a hot chocolate and another eight or ten cigarettes.

'You've got to do it, Gina,' Tom told her eventually. 'He has got to know about this soon. He's your line manager. There are protocols to be followed now.'

She nodded, sinking into her seat and inhaling deeply to steady herself. She stared hard at her phone and did not move. 'But what am I going to say? How am I going to tell him? He is going to be so disappointed in me.'

Her words were more to herself than to us. We left her in the peace of the quiet booth and went to pay the bill.

Later.

Gina didn't say anything about the conversation with James but she didn't cry any more after that. She didn't say anything at all, in fact, until we brought her home. She told us then in a quiet voice that she needed some time alone so we left her there and promised to look in on her later.

I phoned James soon after. 'How are you doing?'

'Great. Everything's just great,' he replied drily. 'Aside, of course, from now being accountable for a missing envelope containing thousands of the company's money. Not only that, but I had to listen to Gina talk about it for fifteen minutes. Can this morning get any better? I can't wait until Datchet picks up her voicemail on this one.'

'Will it come down on you?'

'Yes.' He sounded grim. '*She*,' he spat with a certain level of bitterness, 'is my responsibility. And I always knew that she was enough of a fucking liability to pull something like this and yet I still left her in the job, so I suppose I am mostly to blame, when you th...'

'Wait, wait. Do you think that she did this intentionally?'

'Do you *not* think she did this intentionally?'

I thought about it, but it just didn't fit with her body language and everything about this morning. She was genuinely terrified. And she was devastated, most of all by the knowledge of what James would think and say about her now. That, to her, was worse than the financial liability.

'You're so naïve, Poppy,' James snorted. 'Who do you think took it, her imaginary stalker?'

'I think it is pretty obvious who took it,' I said quietly, though even talking about him made me feel sick.

'Who?'

I told him. There was a silence at the other end of the phone. 'Be careful with that opinion,' he said eventually. 'Remember that he is the regional director of one of our supplier companies.'

'And she is innocent until pr...'

'Whatever. At the very least, she has certainly been grossly negligent with company property, and that is a sackable offence in its own right.'

'So what happens next?'

'I'm sure you can work that out, genius.'

'You're going to sack her, aren't you? Just like that.' I felt cold at the idea. It didn't seem right.

'Well, no,' he admitted, a hint of irritation creeping into his voice. 'It's Datchet's call. We'll have to wait and see what she thinks. But as far as I can see, it's textbook. There is a clear company protocol for gross negligence. The only question is how fast we can get rid of her and find a replacement.'

I said nothing. Something about this whole conversation was making me very uncomfortable. I decided then that James and I discussing this before Sarah Datchet had made a decision was an example of crossing one of those professional lines that I try to stay away from in keeping my James separate from Snowglobe's James.

'I've got to go,' I said suddenly.

'Are you OK, Poppy?'

I muttered something.

'Look,' James said, suddenly firm. 'Gina is incompetent. You and I both know that. How many times have you and the others had to sort out her fuck-ups, complete the basic tasks she has neglected to do and deal with complaining guests because she refuses to see them? Don't think we don't all realise what really goes on in Reschengel. We do. This is just one further example of the disorganisation and mismanagement that has plagued that resort since she has been there, and the sooner she gets the boot, the better for all concerned.'

'I don't know, James. It's a senior management call, and I think it is best if I don't influence you either way. You know what you want to do. I guess we'll soon find out what Sarah Datchet thinks.'

This irritated him and he told me so. 'Poppy, she lost seventeen grand of the company's money. Lost or stole. What would you do in Datchet's position? It's a no-brainer.'

Lost or stole. I couldn't shake the image of her earlier, sleeves rolled up, eyes wide with fear and adrenaline, two lit cigarettes pressed between white lips as we searched her apartment frantically, uprooting everything from its careful tidiness, ripping the place apart.

'We'll see,' was all I said.

'Yes, Poppy, we shall,' said James firmly. 'And you'll see that what has happened gives us a hell of an opportunity to do what should have been done long ago. Anyway, enough about that; what time shall I meet you tomorrow night?'

'Seriously?' I frowned into the phone. 'We're still going to go ahead with that? Even after what's happened?'

James and I had planned yet another dastardly plot this week – that he would drive over to Reschengel late on Wednesday and, under the cover of darkness, kidnap me (well, collect me from the car park) and return me early in the morning before anyone noticed my empty bed. It's a trick we've managed to get away with more times in the past month than I have kept track of, but is nonetheless quite a gamble and this week, given everything that has happened, seems a bit foolish.

'Of course.' James sounded surprised that I might ask such a thing. 'What's changed?'

'Well, I would have thought now that there's a question of Gina being... I mean, are you sure it's a good idea, all things considered?'

'Of course it is, Poppy,' said James gently. 'It's a fantastic idea. I get to see you. We get to wake up together. Gina was never going to know about it anyway, was she? Nothing has changed. Gina has nothing to do with *us*.'

He was right, I realised after a pause. It was as wrong for me to get involved in discussing Gina's future with her boss as it was for me to let Gina's work dramas affect my personal relationship with my boyfriend. *Gina has nothing to do with us.* It was none of my business.

'Ten-thirty then?'

Friday 23 February
10.55am

Again, for the fifth time this week, I woke this morning rather earlier than the season average and with most uncharacteristic morning pep hopped straight out of bed. I wandered into the kitchen, found it empty and, to kill time, decided to try my luck at making a cup of tea. The electric kettle was obviously in a good mood this morning – it only gave me a slight jolt as I switched it on. I stepped out onto the perilous balcony, where the crisp, cold air was a wonderful relief from the stifling, stale smell of the chalet and I looked up to the sharp white and black outlines of the mountain peaks against the blue sky. *Mmm. Another beautiful day.*

And then he was there. 'Hello, Poppy-flower!' came Jon's voice from the bottom of the steps, breaking the silence. 'Just the person I was coming to see.'

Somehow, although it has been literally a week since I first met him, it's become entirely the norm these days to find Jon in our kitchen in the mornings looking for accomplices for the day's adventures. Head and Nick work early mornings and so until this week, Jon has been skiing mostly alone. He beamed at me as he bounded up the chalet steps toward me in his ski boots and propped his skis against the other side of the balcony railing. 'May I come in?'

'Of course,' I smiled, blinking at the brightness of his electric blue Norønna jacket and acid yellow salopettes.

He grinned and hopped over the balcony railing. It shuddered slightly under the weight of both of us and we retreated to the safety of the kitchen.

'Man, that is so not safe,' said Jon shaking his head.

I eyed him slightly warily, wondering if he was here for the reason I thought he was. *Would he remember? Would he have brought it?* My heart thudded hard as I saw him reach into his rucksack, but he only pulled out a bakery bag.

'Excellent,' he said lightly, handing me a pastry on a plate and reaching for the teapot. 'Today will be a special day. I have a good feeling about it. Is Rachel awake yet?'

213

'Not quite. I have to warn you, when I left her in Rodeo at two o'clock, she had had three Jäger-bombs and was talking about a fourth. The evidence would suggest she may not be feeling the joys of spring today.'

'I hope she can shake it off quickly. You know how much snow fell last night? Sixty centimetres!'

'Really?' I clapped my hands. 'Brilliant. I can't wait to get up there.'

'Great,' Jon beamed from ear to ear, 'so you're all set for our photo shoot today then!'

Oh, *crap*. He remembered.

Rewind to Wednesday, when Carol, Jon and I went skiing together. The snow was still nothing particularly amazing – the predicted high pressure had arrived and stayed – but there was still some fresh stuff in the shade between the trees in the Ristis forest, so that was where we headed for a play. Carol and Jon took to racing each other, the third run of which I watched from below. It looked amazing, their bodies tearing impossibly fast between the trees, split-second reactions and faces registering only furious, precision focus, as shafts of sunlight pierced the shadows and illuminated the flying explosions of snow.

'Damn, I wish I had brought a camera,' I said when they stopped below me, panting and firing snowballs at each other as they argued over who had won overall. 'I wish you could see what that looked like. It would have made for some awesome photos.'

'Do you own a camera?' Jon asked, suddenly interested. 'You should bring it up the mountain in future.'

'My camera wouldn't be any good for taking pictures of skiers.'

'Why not?'

'Well, it's only a little automatic one. It doesn't have a fast enough shutter speed or autofocus to capture fast movement without making it blur. You need quite a good camera for that.'

'Hey, do you know how to work a good camera?' he asked, leaning on his ski pole and watching me closely.

'Well, sort of. I'm no expert but my father is a photographer so I have a basic grasp. Why?'

Jon explained that he bought a digital SLR camera last year but still has no idea how it works. I offered to talk him through it and so he brought it over to our place yesterday morning. It was an excellent camera from one of the top brands on the market, and not unlike one of the cameras my dad has at home, so I told him everything I knew, especially all the stuff he would need for taking ski shots.

'OK. So remind me: which one is the polariser?' he asked some time later, looking a bit confused.

I held up a filter. 'This one. And that one there,' I pointed to another transparent disc, 'is for UV light.'

'OK. And so the fast shutter speed, that will catch the snow flying in the air when the skier turns?'

'Exactly.'

'OK. That's pretty straightforward.'

'Although actually,' I added, 'you'll need a fill-in flash if the light isn't great or the fast shutter will make the picture really dark. And sometimes it looks cool to have a motion blur, so it depends on what you want your picture to look like in the end.'

He looked from the camera to me and back again. 'Poppy, you're hired.'

'Eh?'

'I have an idea. How big is your rucksack?'

Now, somehow, twenty-four hours later, I was standing in my kitchen in my panda-print pyjamas, packing a heavily padded camera case into my rucksack on top of my avalanche equipment.

'It fits,' I said, closing the zip. 'Terrific.' *I get to ski with about two thousand pounds worth of camera equipment. Off-piste. In crust. On moguls. Over rocks. With more rocks. And falling over.* 'Fantastic.'

'It fits!' Jon was very pleased with himself.

Our bedroom door opened and Rachel tramped into the kitchen looking bleary-eyed and murderous. 'Connors, you did it again. You gave me your hangover. Ugh. Hi, Jon.'

'Lovely Rachel, you look like you are hanging out of your arse,' said Jon, looking even more pleased with himself.

'Cheers, mate.'

215

'All set for today?' I asked her.

'Shut up, Perky, I'm suffering for two right now. Make me a fresh pot.' She lay her head down on the table and moaned. 'Go on then, tell me. Where are we going this morning? Who's coming? What are we snapping? What should I wear?'

'Don't worry,' I said, handing her a glass of water, 'it'll just be you, me, Jon and Carol playing in the powder somewhere.'

'Yes, about that,' said Jon slowly, looking a little guilty. 'I… hmmm… well, it won't just be the four of us this morning. I've sort of invited some other people along also.'

'Oh?' I said uncertainly. 'Err…OK.'

'And…' he twisted his hands, looking sheepish, 'and I might have mentioned to them that there would be a photographer.'

'You did *what?*' I exploded.

He gave me a cheeky and only slightly apologetic grin. 'You like to start at the deep end, though, hey? That was the first thing I learned about you.' He dodged as I threw a cereal box at him.

'I am going to kill you. Who have you invited exactly?'

'Well… Karin, who you know, yes? And, ummm,' he looked up at me from under his brow, trying not to smile, 'someone else you have met once or twice, I think.'

'Who?'

Jon paused, then said with some trepidation, 'Anderss.'

'Anderss? *ANDERSS?* You invited *Anderss* to come and be photographed by me?'

'Yes, it sort of just happened. He was in the circle of conversation and, you know how it goes…'

Jon was still grinning. Rachel and I had both gone pale. Jon stood up to fill the kettle again while I gesticulated uselessly in speechless silence. *Dear God above.* Anderss is not the sort of person you just go for a harmless ski with. He is a Serious Skier. He does Serious things. He's the sort of person who'll go and ice-climb a perilous serac, skin up a mountain peak for five hours and then drop a fifty-foot cliff into a right-angled couloir. You know, just for fun. He is one of those fearless, unbreakable, extreme folk who seem to be constructed of steel and totally lacking any kind of survival instinct. Last season, he nearly died here in Reschengel after he dropped off a twelve-foot cornice into a couloir off the back of Schindler. He caught his ski on a rock in the landing and hit eighteen trees on the way down. He woke up in hospital a week later with four titanium bars in his leg, both wrists in casts, twenty-nine stitches in his face and an artificial cheekbone. Three weeks later, he was spotted dropping off the back of Valluga down to Zürs. Switch. (Well, so the story goes anyway.)

'Oh, dear, Pops.' Rachel shook her head in disbelief. 'And you thought skiing with James' mates was stressful.'

Jon looked up sharply at Rachel as he filled the kettle.

'It bloody well is,' I replied, 'and they've probably got nothing on Jon's Swedish crew.'

'What do you mean, Poppy?' asked Jon, frowning slightly.

'Oh,' I sighed, 'James' friends always make it quite obvious that they're wondering who the hell I am and why on earth he has brought me along. It's fair enough really; I do spend most of the time trying desperately to stay upright and to not make a complete tool of myself. Unsuccessfully, of course. I really don't want to inflict that on your friends.'

'Don't be silly.'

'Look,' I tried again, 'here's the thing. Even on a good day, I would struggle to keep up with skiers like that, let alone with a heavy camera-pack on my back. I don't think this is a good idea. I doubt that your friends will be keen on dragging my dead weight. Maybe you should call them and let them know I...'

'My friends are not like that, Poppy,' said Jon quietly. 'It was their idea to join *us*. And anyway, why would anybody be judging you unless you are clearly miserable, in which case they are wondering why the hell you are not just enjoying yourself and getting on with it like everybody else?'

I thought about that.

'And besides,' he continued, holding the rucksack up to me, 'you're the one behind the camera. They're there to impress *you*.'

'Yeah, Pops,' Rachel cut in, nodding enthusiastically, 'and since the camera is: 1. worth about a grand and a half, and 2. not yours, you have a pretty good excuse to take it easy up there, wherever we go, eh?'

I decided I liked their logic. 'So that rules out Valluga to Zürs switch then? *Dayymm*,'

'Sadly yes,' she said. 'We'll save that for some other day with James and his lot, eh?'

Jon gave me a long, thoughtful look. He opened his mouth to say something, but just at that moment Tom thumped into the room in a pair of boxers and Mister Men socks. He was carrying an armful of clothes and all of his hair was sticking out of one side of his head. He had about him the bewildered look of someone who had just been hit over the head with a giant foam mallet.

'Oh, cool camera. Can I come too?'

8.16pm. The Swedish boys' chalet.

Fuzzy warm open-fire-and-red-wine feeling and the smell of roasting vegetables and frying fish… Mmm. What a day.

Poor Nick rather gallantly offered to cook a romantic dinner for his lady Rachel this evening – such a lovely gesture, until Jon, Carol, Tom, Head and I crashed it. Now, in trying to feed five extra people, the entire contents of the cupboards and freezer are being cooked up in a random blend of dishes, the eventual contents of which nobody including the chefs (Jon is assisting) can predict. Nick is calling it tapas, though I'm sure the Spanish as a nation would collectively weep at the idea of that name being applied to – amongst other inventions – a mixture of pasta, tinned tuna, broccoli, fondue cheese and sweet chilli sauce. I'll hold off on judgement until I taste it however; after my brief stint in the hotel kitchens at Christmas, I'm hardly one to criticise culinary experimentation.

We superfluous non-cooks are keeping well clear of the kitchen and are instead looking through today's pictures on Jon's laptop. Our photo shoot, if you could call it that, went surprisingly well. Most amazingly, this was more or less all down to Anderss. After some initial terror, he turned out to have a somewhat calming effect on me on the mountain, rather like Jon. He had some brilliant ideas for spots, never far from the pistes and lifts, where we found all kinds of wind lips, rock drops, tree routes and natural kickers that made for wonderfully spontaneous-looking shots. He showed us nooks and crannies of the Reschengel ski area I never imagined existed, even after almost three months.

Anderss stayed with me to help set up every picture, making clever suggestions about what angle to shoot from and how to use the sunlight to best effect. Then he acted as spotter while the others dropped down toward the kicker, lip or powder line we had set up, calling out to let me know how far away the skier was and when I would need to open the shutter for that split-second moment. And then, when it came to his turn to hit something, he was the picture of über-focused single-mindedness, doing exactly what he had told me he would do every single time with clockwork precision.

Some of the shots came out really well. I am surprised and very pleased with them, although I do realise that with Anderss there, a trained monkey could probably have captured good pictures today. Karin could only stay with us for an hour or so, but in that time she nailed three big air shots, one with an incredible double rotation and cross-grab and another with an even more incredible front-flip. Her photos came out all the more impressive for the hot pink one-piece ski outfit she was wearing. I've often wondered who could get away with wearing something like that; now I know.

Carol's shots also came out fantastically well. She's not a fan of big airs (I'm not sure anyone who has seen as many back injuries as she has could be) and says she prefers to ski trees because they're 'safer.' *Safer?* I thought as I snapped the third sequence shot of her bursting through a two-foot gap and dropping from pillow to pillow down a slope of about a seventy-five degree gradient. *That depends on your definition of danger, I suppose.*

Of course we got some predictably amazing pictures of Anderss, including one where he is spinning a triple rotation off a blue ice wall at the edge of the glacier. Still, for all the size and impressiveness of that, I still think my favourite shot of the day is the one of Jon in the Ristis trees, where he hit a compression and launched himself sideways off a small lip, hand-planting on a tree stump as he looked straight at the camera. I didn't think the shot would work because it was too late in the afternoon for decent light in the trees, but a shaft of sunlight caught him just as he lined up his skis in a perfect horizontal parallel and looked straight at me, the spray of snow gleaming in a perfect arc of white light against the moody gloom of the forest backdrop.

For sheer comedy value, my other favourite shot from today has got to be the one with Rachel and the tree. After a few hours of following the suggestions of Anderss and occasionally Jon, Rachel ventured an idea of her own. She knew of a tree on Ristis, she explained, which grew in a U-shape, the trunk branching out into one other thick branch, with a good clearing below it.

'Maybe we could build a little kicker running into it,' she suggested, 'and jump through the gap?'

We found the tree and built a ramp in less than twenty minutes. Rachel had the honour of going first. She hit it confidently and with a lot of speed, soared between the trunk and the branch with ease, grabbed the tail of her board and smiled straight at the camera. Unfortunately, when she came to land, she found that she had slightly overshot the clearing. We found her wrapped around a silver birch fifty metres down the slope. It took her about twenty minutes to get her breath back enough to say '*Mother*fucker,' and stomp back up to hit it again.

Looking at the picture, though, you wouldn't guess that it had ended badly. That's the beauty of ski and snowboard photography, I now realise. As far as the shot is concerned, it is a frozen moment of perfection with no consequences. And when it ends with the rider wrapped around a tree, it will always, always until the end of time give the photographer a laugh. That picture of Rachel has made me snort tea through my nose twice already today.

Later in the day, sitting on the last chairlift with Jon and me, Anderss produced a hipflask of something unspeakably horrid and a tub of *snuss* tobacco and the boys began to discuss potential photo set-ups for another day. I didn't catch a lot of what was being debated, largely because Jon and Anderss both know Reschengel's terrain in more detail than I could ever hope to (and I suspect, have their own very strange-sounding Swedish names for a lot of it) but I did pick up on some talk of cliffs, with alarming concepts such as 'not more than eighteen metres' featuring strongly. I just nodded a lot whenever they asked my opinion on any particular spot, wondering privately whether ski photographers ever live to draw a pension.

After a time, I gathered that they had me in mind to rope up and trek with them across the Rote Wand glacier to photograph a skier on an ice-bridge. This, they reckoned, could make the most epic ski shot ever to come out of Reschengel.

'An ice-bridge?' I asked. They nodded. 'Doesn't that imply that it is a bridge over something?' They nodded, more slowly. 'So you mean a crevasse. A big, scary, potentially bottomless crevasse.' It wasn't a question. Just a toneless acknowledgement of their lunacy. They both smiled.

'You're keen then,' said Jon, rubbing his mittens together. 'Excellent.'

Saturday 24 February

1.15pm. Muschhütte.

'Hey, Poppy,' said James as I put my phone back in my pocket, 'what was it that posh old gent called you at a welcome meeting in the Chalet Elena? I can't quite remember. Was it "incomprehensible"?'

'Ha ha.'

'But he did say that you "have a certain rustic charm," didn't he?'

'Yes, James, he did. And I only didn't punch him because he was elderly.'

I had just got off the phone with my twin sister, Lily. She and our younger sister, Kate, are due to arrive in Salzburg airport tomorrow and we were making some last minute arrangements, including confirming the exact quantities of cheese, trashy magazines and cigarettes that various staff members had asked them to bring out from home. James spent the entire time I was on the phone making ear-horn gestures in the background and looking totally lost.

'I mean, my God, that was like a foreign language,' he exclaimed. 'You Irish talk *fast* to each other. I take it your sisters are incomprehensible provincials too,' I raised a warning eyebrow, 'but are they hot?'

I elbowed him in the ribs and he fell off his bar stool in mock agony. 'My sisters are *dangerous*. I dare you to mess with them.'

'Dangerous how?'

'Usually inadvertently,' I replied with a smile. 'I have Reschengel on high alert.'

'I think Reschengel will cope,' said James, reaching for his beer. 'They can't be any worse than your average seasonaire.'

'You'd think that, but Kate and Lily together are a phenomenon that has to be seen to be believed. Why don't you come over this week and see for yourself?'

'Ha, yeah right.' James placed his empty glass on the table. 'Much as I would love to, I don't really think that us getting drunk together in front of all the Reschengel staff is a good idea, do you?'

'Probably not. But you could organise a staff bonding evening, take us all out to dinner or something, you know, like an area manager might?'

'Not likely, given the current climate over there. Maybe on Tuesday, after Datchet sacks the Orange One.'

'What, to celebrate?'

He laughed again. 'I hadn't thought of that. Good idea.'

'That's harsh.'

'But fair.' His smile faded a little and his eyes hardened. 'Don't think for one minute that her getting sacked is unfair. It's not. You wouldn't avoid a sacking if you managed to lose seventeen grand. It's protocol. But hey,' he patted my knee, 'I probably wouldn't drink champagne if it was you. And I might give you a lift to the airport.'

'Charming. I'm blushing, James.'

'Amazing to think our lives could soon be Gina-free, eh? Two days from now, imagine!'

James grinned happily and tapped out a jolly little drum rhythm on the table with his hands as we stood up to leave. I hesitated, less sure. I wondered what I could say to make him realise how much Gina genuinely respected and valued his opinion of her. I wanted to say something that might make him consider her feelings at least a little, because however pleased he might be that all this is happening, she is devastated, and while she may be a pain in the arse of galactic proportions, she's not actually a bad person. I knew that he was the only one whose words could make this easier on her, but I couldn't think of how to put it so that he would understand.

'She won't feel the same about you, you know,' I said eventually.

'Believe me, I know.' James shuddered. 'Well, you never know, I might even miss her, in time. Give me a decade or so. Anyway, come on, you. Let's go skiing.'

James' enthusiasm for the slopes was very misplaced. The fresh, light snow from yesterday was already gone – melted and baked into a nasty, sticky sort of crust by the overnight return of abnormally high temperatures for this time of year. Horrible conditions, in other words. I had never seen snow change so fast. It was depressing.

James clapped his mittens. 'Time to learn moguls, fool.'

'No.'

'Yes.'

'No. Anything else. I hate them.'

'Precisely.'

'Why? Why? They're one thing I despise. Why would you make me do them?'

'Because you're rubbish at them.'

'And you think that's funny to watch?'

'No, because I can teach you better technique,' he smiled, pulling me into his arms in the doorway and kissing me lightly on the forehead. 'You're the one who is always saying that you want to improve. If you can manage moguls, you can manage anything.'

'True...I suppose.' I knew I should just man up and focus on my biggest failing, but it sounded painful on both levels – to body and pride. *It is sweet, though*, I thought, *that he has my best interests at heart.*

'And it will be hugely entertaining for me to watch you ski like an epileptic spider,' he added, throwing his head around and flailing his arms and legs for effect.

'I hate you.'

He smirked. 'Come on, Connors. Spit, spot.'

He clicked his tongue at me, as one might at a dog, then saw my dark look and ambled off, chuckling.

Sunday 25 February

4.35am

Transfer day dawned as it always does: long before dawn. We got up at three, complained about the hour, put on our uniforms and headed for the central coach meeting point to meet the first coachload of guests as their hotel taxis dropped them off. Gina was very quiet as she handed out sales voucher pads and manifests. She didn't make a big show of checking uniforms or shoes, just handed us our packed lunches as always and gave us a small smile as she got on board the first coach. We watched in silence as the doors closed and the coach pulled off, rounded the first bend and disappeared from sight.

'You reckon that was the last time she'll ever do that?' asked Tom.

None of us had an answer to that.

'I hope not,' said Rachel after a minute.

12.34pm. Salzburg Airport.

I escorted my guests to Departures when we arrived. There was no sign of Sarah Datchet so I signed the check-in sheet on her desk and fought my way through the drizzle over to Main Terminal to bring an injured guest to the special assistance check-in.

I ran into James between two empty coaches in the coach park on the way back. He was in excellent form despite the rainy greyness of the day. He took a quick look around, pulled me into a spin and kissed me hard, squeezed my bum, then without even a word carried on toward Main Terminal, presumably to get his breakfast.

'What was that for?' I called after him.

He shrugged and grinned as he sauntered off, hands in pockets.

Sarah Datchet came marching through the doors in a foul mood about an hour later. Gina, who was standing on the opposite side of the arrivals hall at the time, winced as she heard the unmistakable clack of tiny heels and buried her face in her clipboard, trying to appear as busy and efficient as possible. James sat up slightly in his chair, but Sarah Datchet walked right past him and straight over to me.

'Poppy, a word please?' she said in her low, calm voice, regarding me with level, steely eyes.

She didn't wait for an answer, but spun on her heel and stalked out the main door. I glanced at James as I followed her. I had never before seen that look on his face. I instantly thought of how he had kissed me in the coach park earlier this morning and was gripped with horrified fear. *What had she seen?* I wondered. *Stupid James*, I thought as we walked under the rain canopy to the outdoor sitting area, *stupid thing to do at the bloody airport where anyone could see, including his boss. That is beyond reckless; that is just plain arrogant.*

Sarah Datchet motioned for me to take a seat on the stone bench beside her. I prayed that she would light a cigarette and tell me that she just wanted company for five minutes. Unsurprisingly, she didn't. What she did want, however, was even more unexpected.

'Tell me what happened last Tuesday,' she said, hands folded in her lap and a serious expression on her face although not an angry one. 'I have heard the story from Gina and I have heard James' thoughts on it too, but you were there with her just after it happened, so I think you might have some useful insight to add.'

I was too relieved (and too residually on edge) to even think about measuring my words, so I just told her everything, exactly as I saw it.

'So you think it was Jan,' she concluded.

I nodded. I hadn't said as much, but I had related the story of the day's events from my point of view and Sarah Datchet is far from stupid.

'Honestly, I can't see who else would have had the opportunity,' I said.

Sarah Datchet nodded and fell silent, thinking for a couple of minutes. I tried to sit still like she did but I didn't know what to do with my hands. Eventually she broke the silence with a sigh of resignation.

'This is coming at a very bad time,' she said, shaking her head. 'You'd think the mid-season blues would have passed by now wouldn't you? But for some reason this past few weeks has brought a second wave of quitters across the board. It's ridiculous. Normally the hotel and chalet hosts who don't like the idea of chalet shutdown wait until mid-April to disappear, but they're all taking fright now. It's putting huge pressure on us to fill places. So obviously, you can imagine that a massive upset at management level in a resort the size of Reschengel is the last thing we need at the moment. I already have Thurlech and Müntzen to worry about. Did you know that Linda has left?'

I didn't. 'What happened?'

'It's an odd one, actually.' Sarah Datchet frowned. 'As far as I can tell it was some kind of falling-out over her workload but I find that strange actually because she's always been such a trooper about that job. But then you would know that, wouldn't you, having spent two weeks with her?' She glanced at me and I nodded rather too quickly, hoping that she wouldn't ask me to elaborate in any way. 'Yes, I need to contact her in the UK to get the details straight on that one. Eleanor has been great and has taken up a lot of the slack, but it's a lot to ask of her, especially now that a couple of chalet hosts in Müntzen have both handed in their notice.' Sarah Datchet shook her head, exasperated. 'And then there's Alpbach and Obertauern and... well, it never ends. Still, hopefully you'll be spared it all with your Club Hotel and chalet hosts. You seem to have quite a cohesive team there, as far as I can see.'

'Yes. Yes, we do. We have had our ups and downs,' I said, realising how true this was with every word that came out of my mouth, 'but the last thing we want or need is for anything to change.'

'Really?' Sarah Datchet leaned forward slightly. 'You think it is still possible to carry on regardless?'

Clearly we were back to talking about Gina.

'Yes, I think so. I mean, obviously I don't know what you have in mind and I wouldn't presume to tell you what I think you should do,' I realised that I was flapping as I backpedalled, 'nor tell you how to apply the company's rules and protocols…'

Sarah Datchet interrupted, 'Rules and protocols are two different things, Poppy. Protocols are not absolute. Nor are rules, in certain circumstances,' she added quietly, staring across the tarmac at the distant mountains. Another heavy pause and she turned to me. 'So what do you think I should do?' Her voice was soft but when she looked up at me her eyes were hard. 'Off the record, naturally.'

I blinked, thrown off balance yet again by this conversation and so, unable to even begin to second-guess what she wanted to hear – whether it was something to justify sacking Gina or to justify not sacking her – I just told her what I honestly thought.

'Frankly, Gina has her problems as a manager, and that is no secret,' I said. 'She and I do not always see eye to eye on things but I can tell you this: I'm sure she did not plan this. Nothing about her body language or reaction that day or afterwards has made me even consider it. And I don't think that she deserves to be held fully responsible for the loss of the money. Yes, she left it unattended, but Jan was there in the apartment. He is after all a company associate, and could reasonably be expected to have only the company's best interests at heart.' I was bullshitting now, and had no idea if any of this was a useful argument but I went on. 'So I think she could be defended for having left the money accessible to him since he is, if not technically an employee of equal status, the closest thing to it.'

'So you think that a charge of gross negligence is questionable,' she concluded.

'At the least.'

She looked hard at me for a long moment before she spoke again. 'I gather that the only people in the chalet upstairs were you, Rachel and Tom. And you were all sitting together in the kitchen, drinking tea?'

'That's right.'

'Gina did mention that when I asked her if it was at all feasible that another staff member could have had access to the apartment and might have had time to get in and out while Jan was out of the building.'

I was stunned at the implication, but Sarah Datchet wasn't finished.

'When I asked her if she thought that any of you would have done such a thing, she swore on her life that she did not believe it possible that any one of you had it in you personally. She was adamant about that.'

And we were the only other reasonable suspects she could point to, aside from her boyfriend. It took me another moment to let this sink in. Sarah Datchet watched me, waiting for me to speak.

'You don't necessarily have to like a person,' I said eventually, 'nor even particularly respect their methods to defend them when they are being dealt an unfair hand.' She nodded, but said nothing. 'I can't tell you what to do, but I can tell you this: if I ever find a way to get that money back from that slimy little git, I will. I should warn you, if that time comes, you may have to sack me for it. After you call the ambulance.'

She laughed and stood up to walk inside.

'Call me if you need someone to hold your handbag.'

Sarah Datchet and I were walking back through the main door into Arrivals when Kim spotted me and came over, looking perplexed. 'Poppy, there was someone here looking for you a short while ago.'

'Who?'

'Err, *you*. With short, dark hair.'

'POPP*AAAA*YYY*!!*' came a shriek from the direction of the side entrance near James' desk and my sister, Kate, came bounding over and threw her arms around me.

I hadn't seen her in over eighteen months, not since she left with a one-way ticket to New Zealand. I was amazed to see that all her limbs seemed intact. Lily was right behind her.

Kate was unstoppable. 'Ohmygod-it's-so-amazing-to-see-you-ohmygod-though-that-uniform-is-vile-you-look-like-a-spanner-

but-your-hair-looks-amazing-how-have-you-been-ohmygod-the-
pictures-on-Facebook-are-unreal…wait-til-I-tell-you-about-what-
Martha-did-in-Christchurch-one-night-it-is-the-funniest-thing-
you-have-ever-heard…and-then-he-looked-at-the-hole-in-the-
bucket-and-said-"has-anyone-seen-my-hat?"…and-I-was-like-
"Seriously,-who-would-buy-a-three-thousand-pound-henhouse?"'

Lily looked at me and raised an eyebrow. 'Just like Delphine,
you know, with the eggs, remember?'

I laughed. 'Yeah, but that was a lot more…you know, with
the…' I waved my hand in a circular motion.

'Yeah.' She nodded her head imperceptibly to the right. 'Is that
the?'

'Yes, and it's…'

'Right. I thought so.'

'What language are they speaking?' I heard James ask.

Monday 26 February

9.06am. En route to the ski school meeting point.

My hip joints are aching. I feel about ninety-seven years old.
Kate.

Kate is of course responsible. I only ever feel this horrendous
when she has had something to do with the quantity of alcohol
involved, and today more so than usual because Kate was seized
with 'the best idea *ever*' on the way home last night. 'Wheelie-bin
bobsleigh!' Ohmygod,-this-is-going-to-be-amaaaazing!'

Cut to flashbacks of Mark's head peering out of the wheelie
bin as it bounced off the brick wall at the bottom of the slope,
saying 'Dude! This totally does not hurt!' and Tilly shaking her
head in silent disapproving resignation right before Mark talked
her into having a go.

Why, I ask myself in the cold light of day. *Why?*

'Shit,' says Rachel, slowing down and lifting her sunglasses
slowly.

I follow her gaze to the wheelie bin sitting where we left it last
night at the top of the hill.

'Oh, crap.' In daylight, I can see two enormous cracks running up the sides of the bin. I look down the 'hill' and realise it is actually a driveway, and not only that, but the driveway of none other than Fritz Spitzer's house. 'Did you know it was…?'

'No, of course not. Do you think I'm mad?'

'What'll we do?'

We share a worried look.

'We'll have to replace it,' says Rachel.

'Yeah, but we can't do it now, and what if he sees it? He'll go mental.'

I do not much relish that prospect. Rachel has a wild look of panic in her eye as she glances at her watch and back at the wheelie bin.

'We have time to hide the evidence.'

9.58am. Ski school meeting point.

Ha! And I thought *I* felt bad this morning. Just saw Gav, AKA Snowli the rabbit. There was a decided lack of bounce in his foamy ears this morning.

'I have come so close to yakking all over the inside of my rabbit suit this morning, I can't tell you. Fake You is evil, Poppy,' he moaned.

'You mean Lily?' I frowned. 'When did you meet her?'

'On the way home from Scotty's. You sent them back to their accommodation with Bella, didn't you? Yeah, she brought us all to a houseparty in the SuperSki staff flat instead.'

'Oh, no.'

'Yeah, it weren't pretty. Your sisters know a *lot* of drinking games. I couldn't keep track of what was going on. I just kept banging the table and shouting "five." I thought that was what everyone else was doing.'

Rachel tried not to laugh.

'I don't remember much after that. I woke up on the couch covered in some sort of foam, with Ed their manager roaring about the fire extinguisher. Everyone was running around, looking green. I don't think any of them made it in to their chalets this morning. One of 'em was lying on the floor of the bathroom unable to move. I got the fuck out of there.'

'Oh dear. Poor SuperSki Ed. Some days being in charge of season workers must really suck.'

For some reason I found myself looking at Rachel as I said that. *Resort manager...job...sucks...who in their right mind would...* Yes, it *did* happen, it wasn't a dream. A fragment of a memory from last night: Rachel pulling me aside as we walked home and asking me why Sarah Datchet had wanted to talk to me in private in the airport yesterday. Me telling her what had been said.

'And you told her that you think Gina should be allowed to stay? Thank fuck for that.' Rachel's face registered huge relief.

'Why?' I asked.

'Because Sarah Datchet is a smart lady, Pops.' I didn't understand. 'Who do you think James will have put forward to take over Gina's job?' asked Rachel, her eyebrows raised. 'Imagine how that must have looked.'

I felt horribly cold all of a sudden, for the second time in as many days.

2.32pm. Ruhtai Park.

Gina's disciplinary meeting with James and Sarah Datchet must have started already. I wonder how it is going. I've had no text from James, but I wasn't expecting him to keep me briefed. I guess we'll find out when we get back from skiing.

True to form, my sisters were looking bright and sprightly and ready to go skiing, so off we went. Today is their introduction to Reschengel (and first day on skis in over a year) so we're having a cruisy day. We started with a tour of some of the pistes of Reschengel and Stüben, followed by a trip to the park to check out Rachel, who is training with Nick for the fast-approaching Big Air competition. The amateur event is on Saturday and she is nervous.

Jon won the undying gratitude of my sisters within seconds of meeting them this morning by arriving at the chalet with breakfast baguettes (egg, pickle and Bratwurst – an unexpectedly heroic blend) and asking if he may join us skiing today.

'Jon, for this,' Kate said through a bite of baguette the size of her head, 'I would give you a kidney. Not mine – you wouldn't want mine. Poppy's probably.'

One chairlift-ride into the day, he was hearing their life stories. Two chairlifts later, he was hearing the proverbial family album of my lifetime of embarrassments. Three chairlifts later, even Lily was in love.

For some reason, Jon has spent a good deal of the day trying to learn something that it had 'just never occurred to me to try before,' skiing backwards, and on one ski. He says it is crucial for balance to be able to ski on one ski, and a useful skill if you lose a ski forever in deep powder (I tried it, facing forwards, and gave up after one piste, sixty-seven falls later). Trying to do it switch has no practical use, I suspect, but he has been gripped with the idea and will not let it go.

I have never met anyone like Jon for single-minded focus and determination to master the task at hand. So far, it's not been going well for him however. Just when he starts to get the hang of it, he loses concentration and lets his idle leg drop, upsetting his balance and sending him cursing and swearing into a backwards somersault down the piste. My sisters think he is probably terminally unhinged, but amusingly so. I am just finding it refreshingly different to be the one picking up *his* skis and poles and bringing them down to him.

At the park now, stretched out in the sun beside the kickers, watching people practicing their jumps, rails and pipe tricks, while surreptitiously spying on Rachel as Nick coaches her on her barrel roll 540.

'Do you do jumps like these, Jon?' asked Kate.

'Sometimes, but I prefer off-piste skiing to freestyle.'

'But you can jump?'

'Some things, yes.'

'Do one. Show us,' piped up Lily.

'Lily, he's not a performing monkey.'

'Ah, go on. Be a performing monkey. There's a beer in it for you.'

Jon shrugged and smiled. 'OK. You're on. Which kicker?'

'Your choice.'

'And what trick would you like me to do, Miss Connors?'

'I get to choose the trick?' Lily asked and he nodded. Lily didn't have the first clue what any of the tricks were called, so she pointed uphill to a skier lining up on the second biggest kicker. 'Whatever he does.'

We watched the skier psych himself up, drop in, gather speed and throw himself into a ten-eighty.

'Oh,' I said, impressed.

'Oh,' Jon said, alarmed, as the skier didn't quite make it through the three full rotations, came down at ninety degrees to the fall line and whipped over into a spine-crunching fall, with his skis, poles and goggles flying everywhere.

'He's not wearing a helmet,' I heard Jon say as he clipped into his skis and dropped down to where the skier had stopped and was lying very still.

Is he twitching? I hoped I was imagining that. A few anxious minutes passed, but then the unlucky skier stood up rather shakily, dusted himself off and popped back into his skis, apparently unharmed. He wobbled off down to the sun deck of the park's outdoor bar to take a break. Jon gave us two thumbs up and jumped onto the drag lift up to the kickers' drop-in zone.

'Here goes,' I said. 'Hey, Lily, if he breaks himself on this, will you feel bad?'

She didn't respond. She was watching him on the lift, looking very worried. 'Do you think he's really going to try that ten-eighty thing?' she asked eventually.

'After that? No, don't be daft,' I reassured her.

We watched as he lined up for the kicker, then seemed to change his mind and took off his skis.

'Phew,' said Kate, before she realised that he was walking up to the run-in for the bigger one beside it. 'Oh, no.' She closed her eyes, then opened one as Jon turned his skis down the fall line and dropped in. He disappeared into the dip of the kicker and out of our view for a moment, then reappeared with a sudden burst, whipped through three very fast spins, realigned his skis parallel and landed easily. 'Holy crap!' she yelled. 'He nailed it! Did you see that, Lily? *Ohmygod*, did you see the height of that?'

'Bloody *hell*.' Lily blinked a couple of times in disbelief. 'I suppose I'd better get him that beer.'

6.34pm

Gina's apartment has been in darkness since we got back from skiing. How odd. I wonder where she had the meeting, and what happened. The suspense is killing us all, but so far no word.

10.18pm

Amazing. Unprecedented. Stunning (in a shocked sense).

Rachel, Tom and I were just leaving the staff chalet for the Club Hotel when we were joined by none other than Gina *in full Snowglobe uniform*.

'Hello sweeties!' She gave us a big toothy grin. 'I'm coming to help you with the welcome meeting!'

The grin could only mean one thing, surely? It did. The verdict from her meeting with Sarah Datchet was that Gina was responsible for the money envelope not being literally attached to her body at all times that it was not in the safe, but that gross negligence was too extreme a charge, all things considered. Sarah Datchet told her that the company's solicitors have confirmed with the insurance company that the police report supports a claim that will cover eighty percent of the loss. Gina will have to cover the remaining twenty percent: a total of about three and a half thousand euro, but the company will let her do this through taking a wage cut and paying it off in instalments over a long time.

'All sorted!' She clasped my hand and Tom's, smiling a warm smile at all three of us. 'Thank you,' she said. 'Thank you for helping me that day and for supporting me.'

We nodded, unsure of this new manifestation of Gina. It was as much the gentle sincerity as the sight of her in uniform. Very unnerving indeed.

She rummaged in her bag for a cigarette. 'Oh, it reminds me of the time I got cleared of those libel charges. When I was a journalist for the *Daily Mail*, you know. Big relief, eh?' She smiled, satisfied and content, pushing open the door to the Club Hotel, where a throng of guests were already waiting outside the bar. 'Oh, Poppy,' she whispered happily to me, 'I just *knew* James would stand by me.'

No wonder I haven't heard from James, I thought, smiling at guests and distributing information leaflets as Rachel began to talk on the microphone. I decided to hold off on texting him until later. *Or maybe tomorrow.*

Tonight's welcome meeting was like no other. Gina was in her element. I don't know why she never usually does the welcome meetings; she was born for it. She took over the microphone for all the sales pitches while Tom, Rachel and I went around the room, signing people up for excursions.

'Well, it depends,' she said in response to a question from the audience about whether the traditional sleds rented out on Sledding Night can take two people. 'Are you a big lad?' The man stood up and turned around slowly. 'Ooh, ooh, you are!' she giggled. 'You can ride with me! Haw, haw,' she guffawed into the microphone as the crowd cheered.

'That woman puts the "ass" in "crass,"' muttered Lily to me, a little too loudly.

I heard a snort of laughter behind me and I turned around. Sarah Datchet and James were there, sitting in the shadows, watching the meeting. James said nothing. Sarah Datchet smiled apologetically and leaned toward me.

'Sorry,' she whispered, 'I would have warned you that we'd be here but I didn't want to throw you off your usual standard.'

I smiled and nodded a little insanely and said nothing, walking on, very glad that I had turned down the sneaky vodka cocktail Eoghan had offered me a moment ago.

'So what did you think of the welcome meeting?' I texted James a couple of hours later from Keller Bar, the second bar crawl stop.

'That old gent a few weeks back was spot on,' he replied. 'You are incomprehensible, but you do exude a certain rustic charm.'

Me: 'Ha, ha. You're very amusing. Home now?'
James: 'Yes.'
Me: 'You OK?'
James: 'Fine.'
Me: 'You sure? x'

He didn't reply for an hour or so. Eventually:
'Not really in the mood to chat tonight. Enjoy the bar crawl. See you tomorrow.'

'Hey, Pops,' Kate calls me to the bar, where Tom has lined up some shots of something very pink indeed. It's still early enough in the evening that the guests are hovering politely, waiting to be offered drinks and generally feeling awkward. Rachel is in the midst of the group, taking the situation by the throat and telling some wildly funny story about accidentally letting pigeons into a bakery while backpacking in Azerbaijan. 'Here,' says Kate, handing me a shot. A chorus of *prost!* goes around and eighteen measures disappear down eighteen throats. Kate makes a face – at once a grimace and a nod of appreciation. 'Ugh, that's good stuff.'

'Hey, where's Jon?' asks Lily, semi-casually. Kate's ears prick up.

'Don't know,' I reply. 'Not here. Why? Were you hoping to see him?'

'Yeah, he's great, Pops,' chimes in Kate, nodding enthusiastically. 'Really lovely. And funny and kind too.'

'Yes, he is.'

'I hope he'll be out tonight.'

'Oh? You're interested in him?'

My skin prickles slightly with irritation at this idea, but I know I am being stupid. *Why shouldn't Kate fancy Jon?*

'No, I'm not,' she replies with a half-laugh. 'Don't be daft. He's pretty obviously taken.'

Emilie. Of course.

237

'Oh, really? Did he tell you that?'

Lily and Kate exchange a glance.

'Not in so many words,' says Lily.

Tuesday 27 February

10.14am. Stüben, en route to Futterberg.

I woke up this morning to the sight of Arthur's blinking eyes about three inches from mine, their whiteness all the more startling in his black-painted face. I nearly jumped out of my skin.

'Oh, good,' he said. 'You're awake. Whatdoyouthink, *whatdoyouthink?*'

He stood back and twirled. I sat up. 'Let me guess,' I croaked. 'You're a spider.' He had painted his arms black too, and was wearing a black leotard and black tights with orange stripes spray-painted on. He had attached what looked like three pairs of stuffed tights to an elaborately designed contraption on his back that made all the legs move together as he raised and lowered his arms. And when he smiled I saw that he had painted his teeth black and stuck on hairy fangs made out of a couple of black fuzzy pipe cleaners. 'It's brilliant, Arthur. How long did it take to make?'

'Don't ask. And don't respond if Suzanne asks any questions about her tights. You know nothing.'

'Arthur!'

'I'll put them back, honest. She has about three hundred pairs, come on.'

'Don't you have to be in the kitchen in,' I checked my watch, 'fifteen minutes?'

'Yup. It's *Fasching* though. I'm going like this.'

'Mate, take off the extra legs at least. You'll burn the hotel down.'

Fasching (or, variously, *Faschingsdienstag, Karneval* and *Fastnacht*) is the festival we have all been waiting for. Traditionally, it's meant to be some kind of pre-Lent blowout street party. For seasonaires and ski bums, it is simply a fantastic reason to get dressed up in the most elaborate and bizarre costumes we can think of and party all day and all night. As such, it is taken very seriously. My costume took me three days to make and is top secret. (It was inspired by a large, battery-powered rotating light we found in the Club Hotel cellar and also features chicken wire and wallpaper

239

glue. That's all I'm saying.)

My sisters have taken to the idea of Fasching with great enthusiasm. Kate has brought her Princess Jasmine costume with her and I believe that Lily has made an enormous lily pad out of green felt, complete with frog, flowers and bugs, though I have yet to see it. We're on our way to Stüben now to meet James and, although we three decided not to ski in costume today, every lift queue we have come across so far has been peopled with all manner of superheroes, aerobics instructors, giant bunnies, monoskiers in retro fluorescent one-piece ski outfits and the like. Lily and Kate are loving it, but my mind is elsewhere. I don't know why, but I'm a little nervous about them meeting James.

Fortunately, he disappeared from the Club Hotel last night before the issue of introducing him to my sisters in front of Sarah Datchet arose, which was something of a relief. Now I'm just hoping his mood has improved. I tried to explain to Lily and Kate that it has been a tough week with all the Gina drama and such, and that sometimes the best of James doesn't quite make it to the surface on first impressions.

I hope they like him.

10.10pm

OK, that last statement was supposed to be rhetorical. It could have gone better. It could have gone at least a *little* bit well.

James was already at the top of the Egginerjoch chairlift when we got there. He was in a foul temper, barking instructions down the phone. He half-waved as we arrived.

'No. Listen.' He paused. '*Listen* to me. Listen, yeah? I'm not interested in hearing you say it can't be done. It can. Go back down there and just insist.' Another pause, and he rolled his eyes at me exaggeratedly. 'Tell them that's not acceptable. That is not how we deal with them and you will not accept that price. They're taking advantage. Just put your foot down.' Another pause. 'Eleanor, I don't care. I'm not driving all the way over there to tell them what you should be able to tell them yourself. Sort it out.' Pause. 'I know you're not, but that's life.' Pause. 'Well, who the

240

fuck signed off on that?' Pause. 'No, that's not possible. It must have been Linda. What was she at?' He sighed. 'Right. OK. I'll get someone in head office to look at it. In the meantime, don't agree to anything.' Pause, followed by a slightly sarcastic 'yes. It will be,' and he hung up.

'Fucking Thurlech,' he grumbled, zipping his phone back into his shoulder pocket. 'Seriously, someone should put that place out of its misery.' He nodded at Lily and Kate. 'Hi, sorry about that. Quite a week we're having. How are you?' He smiled as he reached out to shake their hands and I introduced them. 'Good to meet you. How has Reschengel been so far?'

'Great, really great,' said Lily brightly and I began to relax. 'It's a world apart from Poppy's last job, I'll tell you that.'

'Yes, she's got the right idea now, working in Europe's best ski resort,' grinned Kate.

'Second best,' James smiled back. 'Come on, I'll show you Futterberg. You can decide then which you prefer. Should be no contest, really,' he said, chucking a snowball at me and vanishing down the first piste at lightening speed before I had a chance to respond.

'Amazing,' Kate breathed some time later, looking down from the chairlift at a group of blue Smurfs skiing on tandem skis. 'I'm am *so* up for this Fasching thing tonight.' She turned to James. 'What's your costume going to be?'

He shook his head slightly. 'Not for me. It gets old after a few seasons.'

'Where have you worked seasons before, James?' asked Lily.

'Futterberg for the past few years and St Anton for a while when I was a resort manager. Before that, I did a couple of seasons in Verbier as a rep.'

'Verbier is in French-speaking Switzerland, isn't it?'

'Yes.'

Kate turned to Lily. 'Isn't that where Head said Jon did that competition last year? The big off-piste race, was that Verbier?'

'Yes,' said Lily. 'The Verbier Xtreme. It's the final of the Freeride World Tour. Head told me later that Jon actually won it,

241

you know, the whole tour. He said that's quite a big deal in the skiing world.'

'Jon *won it?*' I was stunned. *How had I not known this?* How had Jon never said anything?

James sat forward, suddenly interested. 'Who, Jon Berner?'

'Yes,' I said. 'You know him?'

'*You* know him?'

'He's a mate. We were skiing with him yesterday. I told you that.'

'You're hanging out with Jon Berner? You're skiing with Jon Berner?' James turned his whole body around on the chairlift to look at me. His expression was more incredulous than anything.

'Yes, James,' I said patiently. 'I have told you that before, you know.'

'When?'

'Do you listen when I talk? Remember the night with the pool? That was Jon. And he's the guy I skied Rufigrat with, and Ristis, Kuhtälli, Schindlerspitz, Maienvasen and the Hinteres Ruhtai bowls, remember? And the photos? Or did you think that was all a figment of my imagination?'

'Frankly, yes.'

I gave him a look.

'OK, I'm kidding,' he laughed, patting my leg. 'But you just mentioned some guy called "John." I didn't realise it was Jon-bloody-*Berner*. I assumed you meant some British chalet host punter. Jon Berner is a world-class extreme skier. What on earth are you doing skiing with him?' He laughed again. 'I mean, no offence, but how did *that* happen?'

'They met in a pool,' Lily said with a winning smile. 'Now he is her powder-skiing buddy. He's taking her around all the really cool "doom-ridden" places in Reschengel, isn't that what you say?'

James just seemed amused by the very idea. He shook his head in bewilderment. 'Jon Berner,' he said, almost to himself. 'Ha! He must be a patient man.'

I caught Kate's eye over James' shoulder. Lily was staring hard at James. She opened her mouth to say something but his phone rang just then. It was Anna, with a query about a replacement hotel kitchen porter who had been due to arrive that morning from Innsbruck. We got off the lift and carried on.

We didn't hear a lot from James for the next hour beyond a few more questions about Jon Berner. His phone was going off even more than usual; text messages every few minutes and phone calls that came in pretty much every time we decided to set off down a piste. Then he would hang up and, presumably to try to make up for all the stoppages, would zoom off at a pace about three times faster than my sisters could manage. Eventually, after an hour or so of this, he made his apologies and said that he should probably leave us to it.

'It's no use,' he said, glaring at his phone as it started to ring again. 'Have a good ski,' he kissed me quickly on the lips. 'Sorry I can't be more fun today. I'll call you tomorrow – maybe we can go up Ristis or something, eh? Good to meet you, Lily, Kate,' he called out to my sisters and skied off, clicking open his phone to answer the call as he did.

Just before he disappeared from sight, he popped off a little ridge to the side of the piste, spun a 360 and vanished over the horizon of the piste, all while talking on the phone. It was like he sensed that we were still watching him, though I doubt he understood why.

None of us said anything for a long moment.

'It's been a pretty stressful week,' I said eventually.

Lily said nothing.

My phone beeped a text message alert late in the afternoon as we skied back down towards the village. It was Nick.

'*Hej, hej!* Special Faschingsdienstag dinner tonight cooked by us at our chalet for the Connors ladies and Miss Scott. Hope you can make it! Fillet steaks. Fresh. (The fewer questions asked the better…)'

We walked in the door promptly at nine o'clock armed with two bottles of wine each, kicking off our shoes and sidestepping a large polystyrene crate marked 'Property of Schlosserfhof Hotel.'

No questions. Not a one.

'Jon!' Kate threw her arms around him by way of a greeting. 'We have been reliably informed today that you are a world-class ski celebrity. Will you sign my ski boot?'

Jon scratched his cheek, looking embarrassed. 'Who told you that?'

'Poppy's, errm, boss,' said Kate. 'James.'

'James Walker?' Jon looked at me. 'From Futterberg, right?'

I nodded. He held my eye and neither of us said anything, both waiting for the other to elaborate. Lily watched the wrestle of wills with some amusement.

'I have an idea,' she said. 'Wine anyone?'

A couple of hours and one astonishingly good dinner later, Kate was explaining to the Swedish boys how, since she is due to begin an internship with a legal firm in September, this summer will be all about having one final student-style blowout somewhere in South America.

'In fact,' she beamed at me, 'I've been thinking of recruiting a certain sister of mine, and heading off on the greatest adventure of our lives, the like of which...'

'No, Kate,' I said, laughing. 'I'm sorry, but there's no way I can afford it.'

'Pah, money is just money. Imagine it! Patagonia! The plains! The lakes and mountains! It'd be like nothing you have every seen or done before!'

'Kate, I am sorry to burst your bubble, but you know that Patagonia will be under about five metres of snow during July and August?' interrupted Nick with an apologetic smile. 'It's not really the time of year for trekking there, I'm afraid.'

'Shit.' Kate frowned and thought about this. 'Guess I need a new plan. Maybe Mexico. I've never been to Mexico. Hey, Pops, we could get a Cadillac and drive down to Guatemala! Or travel the South Sea islands on a post boat! Or, hey, maybe we could go skiing in Chile. Wow, imagine: skiing the *Andes*.'

'Rachel,' I said, desperately changing the subject, 'what's your summer plan?'

She glanced at Nick. 'I'm not sure yet.'

I looked at him. 'Nick?'

He shrugged. 'Going north in the camper van, I think. But ask me in a month.'

'I'm going logging,' said Head proudly. 'Family business. I show my face every April and stay until October.'

'You're a lumberjack?'

He nodded.

'Do you sleep all night and work all day?' asked Kate.

Head looked confused. 'Of course.'

'Anyone ever been summer-skiing on a glacier?' I cut in.

'Like in Saas Fee or Zermatt?' asked Jon. 'I've done that for a few summers. It's OK, but pretty limited stuff. Only any good if you're really committed to your freestyle. Or to working on your bikini tan.'

Head muttered a response to that in Swedish. All I caught was one word 'Emilie.' Nick laughed and Jon scowled.

'So what do *you* want to do in the summer, Poppy?' asked Jon, changing the subject before I could ask. 'I can't believe it's only about seven weeks to the end of season, hey? Where does the time go?'

Seven weeks? 'I don't know,' I replied, blinking, half-numb. I hadn't been counting. *Is it really only seven weeks to the end?* I remembered with a sudden bolt of guilt the forty-seven McIntyre practice case studies still sitting unopened in my email account. I had absolutely no idea what I was doing between now and when I would be needing them. Summer – the bit between the end of this and the start of that.

The end...of everything? James and I had never discussed summer at all, I realised. He had mentioned how he works for himself in France in the summers, but it had never occurred to me to check whether that plan might this year somehow include me. 'Summer has always seemed quite far away since I've been here,' I said eventually, 'but I guess it's not anymore.' I tried to smile. 'I'd better make a plan soon, eh? I'm due back to work in London in September, so whatever I do for the summer, it'll have to be a hell

245

of a swan song for my year of freedom.'

Kate beamed at me, taking that as an encouraging sign. She was mentally packing her bags for Guatemala, I could tell. Lily frowned a little.

'Yes, Poppy, I've been meaning to ask you about that. What is this new job about anyway? You've been really vague on the subject. You're moving to a different company or something, are you?'

'No, I'm staying at McIntyre. Actually moving up the ranks a bit!' I said brightly. 'Somehow managed to turn redundancy to a promotion. Although not in IT,' I added.

Kate smiled encouragingly. 'Something new! Cool!'

'Oh,' said Lily, frowning a little more. 'Not consultancy?'

'Yes, actually,' I said brightly, hoping that she wouldn't hear the slight tightness in my voice, but being Lily, of course she did. 'I'm going to be an associate, apparently.'

Lily shook her head in disbelief. 'I don't understand, Poppy. Consultancy? You pitied those people for four years. You used to say that the only people in the McIntyre building more miserable than the IT lot was everybody else.'

I shook my head, feeling the heat rise in my cheeks and wanting the conversation to move onto something else. 'It's a job, Lily. It's the best I could get.'

'Yeah, in the Square Mile maybe, but it's not like you don't have other...'

'*I* got the impression you jacked in McIntyre so that you could get back to design,' said Kate loudly. 'That's what Dad seemed to...'

'No, that's what Dad *wishes* I'd said,' I interrupted a little crossly, 'it's not what I told him.' Jon, Nick and Head looked a bit lost, so I turned to them. 'I used to be quite into art stuff when I was in school,' I explained, 'and I got into graphic design and websites and stuff as a part time job when I was an undergrad. My dad really wanted me to go on from there to become some kind of hotshot designer but it was unrealistic. There was no work in that area when I graduated, and anyway, it wasn't even my degree

246

subject. So I got a job in London like everybody else. My dad has been hoping and praying ever since that I'll see the light and do what he told me to do from the start.'

'Poppy, be fair,' Lily cut in gently. 'He was never trying to make you something you were not. He just wanted to see you do something you cared about. And not...'

'Working for McIntyre?'

'Well... yes.'

'Forgive me,' interrupted Nick, 'but what is McIntyre?'

'It was Poppy's Mc-Entire life, that's what,' muttered Kate. 'What? That's funny!' she protested when I banged my water glass down on the table somewhat sharply.

Lily gave her a warning look. 'It's one of the original management consultancy companies,' she explained to Jon. 'They tell other kinds of companies how to function better, make more money, that sort of thing. Poppy worked on their computer systems. In September, she'll be going back to a different kind of job.'

'Something you'll enjoy more?' asked Jon. 'Something you'll feel a bit more passionate about, yes?'

'Ha,' I laughed mirthlessly. 'We'll see. Rach, could you pass the water jug please?'

'And still you want to go back to that life again, after the experience of the winter here?' Jon pressed. 'Are your priorities still the same as they were in November?'

I struggled to think of a reply.

'Yeah, Pops,' Kate chimed in, 'is that still what you want? I mean, have you ever thought of doing something else?'

'Like what?'

'I don't know, something you...' she struggled to measure her words but Kate has never known how to be anything but direct '...something you can talk about without making that face? Something you're actually *proud* of?'

I looked around the table. They were all watching me, waiting. Rachel and Lily exchanged a look. I felt my blood start to simmer and I clenched my fists.

'Look, it's a job,' I snapped irritably. 'What's the problem? Everyone has to grow up sometime. Everyone has to build a secure foundation. It may not seem like the most exciting thing in the world to you lot, but I'm not going to turn thirty with 27p in my current account and nothing more than a suitcase and a map of the world to my name.'

'There's a middle ground, Poppy,' said Jon in a mild but firm tone, 'and you know it. You don't have to do something you hate.'

'Who says I hate it?'

'Your face,' he said simply.

I wheeled around on him. 'Yes, well, it's pretty easy for you to judge, isn't it? Shame we can't all amuse ourselves by swanning around ski resorts, slapping on our sponsored skis and entering the occasional competition when we can be bothered. That *is* all you do, isn't it?'

Lily was shocked. 'Poppy!'

Jon seemed slightly taken aback but said quickly, 'No, Poppy has a point, actually. I'm not doing much at the moment. My professional career ended quite suddenly earlier this year and I guess I have been drifting a bit as I decide what comes next.'

'Oh, really?' asked Kate in a slightly desperate tone, trying to diffuse the awkwardness of my rudeness. I could feel myself blushing already. 'What do you think that will be?'

'I'm still not sure,' he confessed, scratching his beard thoughtfully. 'It's stupid, I know, but it gives me a bit of a headache to think of April. That's when I will have to choose between all my ideas and decide which one or two of them to turn into something concrete.' He looked at me with his intense stare. 'I'm sorry,' he said in the same voice that makes me follow him over ridges and down couloirs. 'I didn't mean to sound judgemental. I was just surprised, that's all.'

I nodded wordlessly and smiled at him. He smiled back and I felt my annoyance melt away because I understood exactly what he was trying to say and how he had felt it. I wondered yet again how a person I have known for such a short time could feel like one of my oldest friends.

'So what are these ideas you're considering, Jon?' Lily cut in.

'This and that,' he smiled mysteriously, 'I know for sure that I want to stay in the mountains, so I have been considering an exciting new business idea. But I can't tell you what it is yet.'

'Come on, give us a clue.'

'No chance.' Nick shook his head. 'He won't even discuss it with us.'

Jon smiled apologetically. 'Sorry, I'm a bit superstitious about discussing it until I'm sure that it will work and I have to investigate all of the many, many different aspects about it before I will know.'

'Sounds like a lot to take on by yourself,' I said quietly and Jon looked at me, his eyes thoughtful.

'You know, this all reminds me of a very ancient and wise story my old grandmother, Mamma Frida, used to tell,' said Head in a very serious voice. 'It's about the lone bear, who would roam the wilds of the great forests of the north. One day, he met a three-legged moose...'

Everybody laughed, but Jon's eyes were still on me and his face was serious. 'Actually, Poppy,' he said quietly, out of earshot of the others, 'I think there is something you could help me with.'

'What do you need?'

'A new website. Can you build one?'

'Of course. What kind?'

'I will fill you in on the details another time,' he said, smiling mysteriously. 'But first, I would like to upload some of those pictures you took the other day to my old website. Do you know how to do that?'

'Yes. I'll show you how. Which pictures?'

He opened up his laptop and showed me a selection he had made of the of shots I had taken of him.

'Do you give your permission for me to use them?' he asked.

'Do I need to?'

'Of course,' he said. 'They're your work.' He showed me the tagline of each of the shots: "Photographer: Poppy Connors." 'Your dad would be proud.'

'Actually he would tell me not to overexpose those two hundred pixels in the left foreground,' I chuckled, 'and he'd be right. Don't get me wrong; they're not bad shots for our first attempt, but I'd do better with a bit more practice at it.'

'Well, you'll get your chance. Anderss is still pretty keen to go up to the glacier next week for that ice-bridge shot.'

We shared a look of some misgiving and both laughed.

'You bring the ice axes,' I said. 'I'll bring the Dutch courage.'

Rachel spotted the open laptop and jumped up. 'Hey, Lily, Kate, come here, check out these pictures. There's a great one of me about to twat myself on a tree. I totally punctured a lung that day and your sister just bloody laughed.'

12.20am

On the street in the centre of Reschengel now, where there has been an explosion of colour and noise, streamers and fire. At the more respectable end of the spectrum, people of all ages are lining the walkways to cheer along the late-night parade as it passes through the main street carrying torches of fire and throwing sweets into the crowd. Locals and tourists alike stand around glugging steaming mugs of glühwein, eating warm pretzels from street stalls and dancing to the fast-paced music of the groups of old men in lederhosen playing the accordion, guitar and clarinet. Toward the central square where the nightlife is based, the tone drops slightly. It seems that most seasonaires have taken their inspiration for their Fasching costumes from Rodeo Bar's 'Heroes and Villains' theme; one would be forgiven for thinking that the resort has been colonised by superheroes and their arch-enemies on their way to Ibiza.

Out of the corner of my eye I spot a wheelie bin in an alleyway (it's hard to miss, with Batman and Cruella deVil being led off it by the Polizei and cautioned for an overzealous public display of affection) and make a note to self: I *really* must remember to do something about Fritz Spitzer's wheelie bin first thing tomorrow. *First thing.*

Suddenly four pitchers of something blue and toxic-looking

appear over the heads of the crowd, bearing down upon us. The pitchers turn out to be Bar Cuba's signature "Cuban Cocaine" and the bearers, Rachel and Nick. She grins as she hands me a straw.

'See you tomorrow!'

Oh, dear.

Hee, hee, hee. *Ich liebe Österreich.*

Wednesday 28 February

11.14am

Oh, merciful death. Come to me swiftly.

Uggghghghaaaarrrrrrrrrrrr...*shuddup, phone.*

I haul myself into one-eyed blinking consciousness. How is it already after eleven o'clock? Have only been asleep for about twenty minutes, surely?

Text message. Carol. Oh, crap. She met Fritz on the street. (WHAT is she doing awake? She had three Flaming Lamborghinis last night. I would need immediate hospitalisation after that, but Carol's gone skiing. Is ethanol her fuel source??)

But Fritz, that was the point. He's on the warpath about a missing wheelie bin. Fuck, fuck, fuck. Should have known he'd be looking for it by now.

I'm going to have to deal with this now, aren't I?

11.18am

Could ignore it. Wasn't my sole responsibility. Could let one of the others sort it. Could go back to sleep. Could claim complete ignorance. Amnesia, if necessary.

11.28am

Bloody guilt. Damn it all to hell. Right. I will do this now while I am feeling motivated.

11.29am

In three minutes. I'll get up in three minutes.

11.32am

Cannot. Face. Being. Vertical. Right. Now.

11.33am

Shit! Lily! Kate!! Their flight home!

3.20pm. Täsch.

Cannot believe that between us all, no one had the sense to set an alarm of any kind. Of course by the time I managed to locate and wake Lily and Kate, they had missed the only transport connection out of Reschengel that would meet their flight. I ended up having to wheedle and beg Gina for the resort van to drive them down the valley to Täsch to catch one of the more frequent trains from there.

It was a very rushed and hungover goodbye in the end. Very nostalgic too, with blown kisses as the train pulled away from the platform. It might have even been filmic, had Lily's face not still been mostly painted green and had Kate not only been leaning out the window to stop herself projectile vomiting inside the carriage. Bless. I will really miss them.

It was a great night last night, although I think, in retrospect, that I possibly should not have introduced my sisters to the Flaming Lamborghini – Kate burned off a chunk of her thumb trying to light her second one (but interestingly, felt no pain), and then spent most of the rest of the night dancing on the bar – well, until the vigorous-flailing-limbs dance-off got a little out of hand.

Anyway. Task at hand, Poppy. I'm currently driving around Täsch, looking for the agency that sells the special wheelie bins for public refuse collection. (The Austrians have a very particular and specifically codified waste disposal system which I could explain, but won't. It is amazing the things you learn in more detail than you would ever think possible while doing a ski season. Possible or desirable.)

Aha, found it. Brilliant, I think as I park it in the back of the van. Now all we'll have to do is think of a way to secret it back to Fritz's place without him spotting us. Surely once it is replaced he will stop asking questions?

4.10pm. En route back to Reschengel.

Text from Rachel: 'Pops. Massive guilt. You'll never guess what.'

She says that she ran into Marco the barman, who told her that three people fell off the crowded bar in Rodeo last night dancing to *Push the Button*. One broke an ankle, one dislocated a shoulder and the other one landed on the barmaid and gave her a concussion.

Rachel: 'Think it might have been my "running man" moves that did it...'

Me: 'Or Lily's "butterfly stroke," possibly?'

Rachel: 'You're right, could be that. Marco is v confused. Asked me what your costume was and if you cut your hair midway through the night...??!'

Me: 'Deny all knowledge!!'

4.18pm

It could definitely have gone worse.

5.12pm

Another brief flash of a memory has just come to me. The street party at two am. Fireworks going off in all directions. Jon's face behind me was lit up by flashes and explosions of green and yellow.

His voice then, low in my ear, saying, 'if you keep your eyes open, you'll make good choices.'

I tried to tell him that the choice was already made, but the drums were too loud, so we just smiled at each other as the party surged around us.

MARCH

All Good Things

Sunday 4 March

2.34pm. Salzburg airport, lunchtime break.

Rachel and I have been engaged for some time in a serious wheelie bin replacement scheme discussion. This situation with Fritz Spitzer is getting ridiculous. We have tried three times in the past four days to drop the new bin anonymously into his garage or garden, but *Operation Cuckoo* Marks I to III have all been thwarted. We tried the simple fly-by, but lost our nerve when we saw his car pulling into his driveway. Twice, then, we tried a moderately complex two-pronged intervention, with Arthur and Mikey positioned in the bushes across from his driveway, acting as mobile phone-linked surveillance but there doesn't appear to be a time during the day when Fritz, his wife and his nosey neighbours are all out of visual range of the driveway entrance. At night-time, it's the damned security sensor light outside that causes the problem.

Over lunch today, we have agreed that more radical measures are needed to resolve this situation. The first idea (Rachel's, naturally) was to find a way to somehow disable the security sensor and use the cover of darkness to 'make the drop.' I vetoed this pretty hastily, not being particularly keen on either the complexity or the criminal damage implications. Nor could I see how it could ever succeed, since however much Rachel would like to believe she has some innate Special Forces instinct, between us all we haven't found the wherewithal to break into a garden and deposit a bin, not to mind locate and disarm anything. The second and far more appealing option was to make the drop while creating some sort of diversion in front of Fritz's. For this, Tina was the first person who sprang to mind. Although still very vague on the details of what she would have to do, we both somehow sensed that she was the woman for the job.

Rachel and I were still mid-debate when James came over to join us in the café, accompanied – to my immense surprise – by Anna. It had been about a month since she had last spoken to me in any way other than what work made strictly necessary. Today, it seems, she suddenly decided to stop steering clear. I still have absolutely no idea what I did to offend her in the first place and nor does James, (or rather, he thinks I was imagining things) but I'm too relieved to wonder what it was all about. I'll find a way to talk to her about it sometime; for now, I'm just glad the Anna I knew is back.

They were both most helpful on the wheelie bin dilemma - Anna more than James, unsurprisingly (he was with Rachel on the 'covert ops' side of the fence).

'You know what they say about hiding in plain sight,' said Anna, matter-of-factly. 'Just bring the bin to his front door. Say you found it somewhere and you thought it might be his. Just be sure to paint on his house number on the new one exactly as it is on the old one.'

'You're a genius.' I couldn't believe how simple and brilliant it was. She smiled. 'We can do that first thing tomorrow.'

There was definitely a mutual awkwardness, but it passed quickly. Before long we were catching up on everything from Anna's staffing woes in Futterberg to my sisters' visit and the 'amazing' rumour she had heard about me training with Jon Berner.

'I'm not *training* with him. He's a friend.'

'She takes pictures of him,' Rachel explained to Anna. 'Ski photos. Mate, you should see the pictures from last week. I was too busy impaling myself on trees to fully appreciate it, but Jon and Nick have got some gnarly-ass skier friends.'

'Mmm.' Anna gave us a wink. 'Lucky, lucky, both of you. If the ski magazines do him justice, Jon Berner is sexy as all hell and as for Niklas Svedberg! I've met him. Wow, Rach, nice one. He is ridiculously hot.'

Rachel nodded. 'I can't tell a lie. There's something in the water up in the snowy wastes of Scandinavia to be sure.' Her phone rang just then and she jumped, moaning with the effort. 'Ooh, insurance company! Wish me luck.' She creaked upright and waddled over to another table to take the call.

Poor Rachel is in bits. The Big Air competition was yesterday. It was the culmination of six weeks of training and about five years of accumulated ambition and Rachel was really gunning to win the amateur ladies' division. She breezed through to the final, but that was when her drive and determination got the better of her common sense and she hit the biggest kicker in the park about fifty percent harder than she should have. She overshot the landing and came down very, very hard on the flat. The crowd winced collectively as we watched her crumple, her back bending in a rather unnatural way. The event organisers did not take any chances and had her airlifted by helicopter to the nearest hospital, where the doctor's verdict was that she had had a lucky escape, with only a severe back strain requiring ice, heat and gentle stretch-like exercise. She is under orders to wear an extremely odd-looking ice-and-heat pack velcro-strapped to her back that makes her look like Quasimodo's more attractive sister.

'Poor Rachel, what a dose.' Anna watched her shuffle away, then grasped my elbow lightly as an idea came to her. 'Hey, you know what would cheer her up? You two should come over to Futterberg some night. It's been ages since that first legendary session. Remember the dancing on the barrels in Fracas?'

'Frankly, no.'

'I'm not surprised. What a blur. Good times though, let's do it again.'

'Yes, let's, except for the barrel dancing, maybe. I'm not sure Rachel will manage that in her state.'

James, who had stayed silent and stock-still throughout this conversation, looked suddenly thoughtful, as though he were trying to work something out. 'How about Wednesday night?' he said eventually. 'Or Friday?'

'Whenever you'd like, Poppy,' Anna said firmly, although she was looking at James throughout. 'Come over whenever, even if James is out of town. You can always stay at mine and you're always welcome. I'll take you out and introduce you to everyone.'

'Hey, I have an even better idea,' James cut in before I had the chance to answer her. 'Why don't we see if we can move Poppy to Futterberg for a whole week?' He stared hard at Anna. 'Do you think that your arrivals over the next few weeks will justify an extra rep, Anna?'

I glanced at her. She was holding his stare, her eyebrows raised. 'What a good idea,' she said brightly. 'I'll have a look at the numbers, shall I?'

'Do that.'

I looked from one to the other, with no idea what was going on.

James turned to me as though that little exchange hadn't just happened. 'You free on Wednesday? Let's go skiing. Looks like more snow tomorrow and Tuesday. We could be in for some freshies.'

'Sure,' I said, still a little bemused. 'You up for it too, Anna?'

'Yes, absolutely. I'd love to come. Do you mind if I bring a mate or two? I know a couple of freelance ski instructors who are at a bit of a loose end these days.'

'Not at all,' I said, although I don't know if she heard me, because at that moment, James stood up sharply, the metal of his chair scraping off the tiled floor, and he muttered 'Gotta go. Planes down in fifteen. Finish up here, girls.'

I watched him go, half-aware that I was blinking away that familiar sense of mild irritation I get when he is like that at the airport. I turned to smile at Anna.

'Moody git, isn't he?' she said. 'You must be used to it by now.'

'Not really, honestly.'

She gave me a strange look then, half a smile and a frown at the same time. 'Good,' was all she said, and we walked slowly back toward the bustling arrivals hall.

Monday 5 March

9.58am

Another Monday, another ski school orientation done and dusted. What a nice feeling that is. It is definitely one thing I won't miss when I go home next month, although Monday mornings just won't quite be the same without Snowli's weekly updates on impending fatherhood and the alcohol-fuelled carnival that was his weekend (not always in that order).

Right, time to go over to Fritz Spitzer's to drop off the wheelie bin and be done with the whole ridiculous saga. Can't wait to get it off my hands.

12.12pm

Thwarted *again*. Why, *why??*

I was totally psyched up for strolling innocently down the street with Fritz's bin. *This strategy is foolproof.* Then, just as I was about to pick up the new bin from its hiding place amongst our recycling, I was accosted outside the chalet by none other than Fritz Spitzer himself.

'Let me see your gloves.'

'I beg your pardon?'

'*Deine Handschuhe,*' he barked and pulled one of my hands out of my pocket.

He examined it closely then let it drop to my side.

'Hmm.'

'*Was ist los, Herr Spitzer? Ich verstehe nicht.*'

'*Was ist los? Hier.*'

He thrust a piece of paper into my hand.

Oh for fuck's sake.

It was a ransom note, with a grainy black and white photo of a wheelie bin being wheeled through the snow by two mystery hands. Underneath was a message made up of colourful words glued onto the paper. I'm no detective, but I could have sworn I recognised the print as being from the copy of *Cosmopolitan* Kate left in the staff chalet that I walked in on Arthur and Eoghan 'reading' yesterday.

The note read:

WE have *your* **RUBBISH** bin. It *will* be returned
TO you in **exchange** for one pair of lederhoseN (
SIZE *Medium*) to be deposited at a place of
our designation. *Further* Instructions will
follow.'

'Do you know who is responsible?' he demanded.

I shook my head. (It was true, in a manner of speaking.)

'When I find out who has done this, there will be kicked ass, do you understand?'

I nodded.

'Snowglobe,' he said thoughtfully, looking up at our chalet. 'Snowglobe or Diamond Ski. It must be one of you two. The cretins from SuperSki wouldn't know how to work a pair of scissors.' He turned and looked hard at me again. 'I'm watching you all, you understand? And if I find out you had anything to do with this,' he stabbed the note hard with his finger, 'well, by God, there will be war.'

He marched off up the hill, fuming. I turned toward our chalet steps. There was a scuffling noise on the perilous balcony and the grinning faces of Arthur and Mikey appeared over the solid wooden railing.

'I'm going to kill you.'

They ran.

12.04am

It was decided after much consideration that the only way to resolve this mess was to send Odysseus to Fritz's place this evening with the new bin. Odysseus actually volunteered for this, despite not having had anything to do with either the initial bin destruction nor the ill-advised ransom note ('In English, Arthur?

What were you thinking?'

'Erm, that I don't speak German?'

'But Lederhosen? Really? Seriously?'

Arthur shrugged. 'What can I say, Poppy? A man's got needs.')

The reasoning behind Odysseus' spearheading the new plan, *Operation Cuckoo* Mark V, was that Odysseus is unique in Reschengel for being a season worker that Fritz Spitzer actually likes. No-one could have predicted it, least of all Odysseus, but the two bonded over a bottle of whiskey one afternoon in the Club Hotel while waiting for an electrician to come and fix the broken oven. Now they meet for a weekly pint in the Mondschein. Of all of us, Odysseus was therefore deemed the least likely to get chased out of town with a sawn-off shotgun if something went wrong.

The strategy was this: Odysseus would show up at Fritz's place, present him with a new wheelie bin and announce that he had heard about the ransom note and was appalled at the lack of respect being shown to one of the patriarchs of this fine village, so he decided to take matters into his own hands and teach the punks involved a lesson. If Fritz asks who was involved, Odysseus will simply say, 'Ask no questions, man, just enjoy the bin. The less you know the better.'

'Brilliant,' said Rachel. 'That will totally appeal to his Godfather side. Genius.'

We waved him off enthusiastically an hour ago and sat in the kitchen, waiting for him to get back. Still waiting though, and slightly apprehensive now.

12.45am

He's still not back.

1.14am

He's *still* not back. We've opened up the chalet wine to while away the time. We're all quite squiffy now and starting to discuss rescue strategies (which, to be fair, we might have considered before we waved him off).

1.38am

He's alive! And intact!

And *hammered.*

1.43am

Fritz, it transpired, embraced him like a son when he heard of Odysseus' defence of his honour. He cracked out the good whiskey and his finest Cuban cigars and welcomed Odysseus into the fold. Two hours and half a bottle later, Fritz was offering him next season's head chef's job in his finest restaurant (which elicited from the boys a chorus of 'Dude!' Score!' 'Nice one!') and his daughter Maria's hand in marriage (which didn't).

'Actually, "offering" is the wrong word,' Odysseus slurred. 'He sort of hasn't given me a choice. I think we might be engaged now.'

'Err…what did Maria have to say about it?'

'She wasn't there. I've never met her. Dunno what she's like. She's studying in Vienna. Has any of you ever met her?' He looked around the room, slightly desperately. 'Mikey?'

We shook our heads. Arthur was wide-eyed. 'Dude, did Fritz even show you a picture?'

'Nope. I've never seen her. But I have seen Fritz's wife.'

He looked very alarmed and the boys made sympathetic noises.

'That bad?' I asked.

'I thought she was his brother.'

Oh.

Tuesday 6 March

11.32am

There is a lot to be said for being a deep sleeper. Within minutes of being vertical this morning, I gathered from the traumatised, sleep-deprived faces of my housemates that something very troubling indeed happened last night.

'Tina,' whispered Rachel between Nurofens, 'shagged Eoghan.'

'Eoghan?' I asked incredulously through a mouthful of toothpaste. The mental image was ghastly of course, but also seemed rather implausible. 'Eoghan? Are you sure?'

She gave me a very dark look. 'Oh, yes. It is beyond question. I have the psychological scars to prove it.'

No wonder Tina was up and gone to work so early. She has always been a wham, bam, get-the-fuck-out-of-there kind of girl.

'It wasn't in our room, though, was it?'

'No, in the kitchen.'

'Not on the table, I hope?' I made a face but Rachel shook her head. 'The work surfaces?' I cringed at the idea.

'Ugh, no. Although probably just as vile, actually. The stinky couch.'

'Oh, Christ. Is that what the smell is?' Something very stale and malodorous had permeated the whole chalet overnight.

'Yup. I think they unleashed something. That couch was not made for lovin'.'

Just at that moment, Eoghan staggered past the bathroom and into the kitchen. He re-emerged a minute or two later looking shaky and stood at the bathroom door, staring at us as though transfixed.

'Morning, Eoghan!' said Rachel brightly.

'Ehh. Yeah.' He looked like he wanted to say something, but couldn't remember the first word of the sentence.

We both smiled at him, and waited.

His eyes widened in horror. 'I did, didn't I?'

We nodded.

'Oh, fuck *me*.'

'Good,' said Rachel cheerily, 'you even remember the

265

dialogue.'

Eoghan went from strangely blotchy to very, very pale all of a sudden. We cleared the way to the toilet and, with a commiserating pat on the shoulder, left him to it.

I was delighted to find when I left the chalet for this morning's visits that there was a good half-metre of fresh snow to stumble through. And it's still snowing, even now. All morning it has been impossible to see more than about twenty feet ahead. If it is like this down here at village level, I can only imagine what it is like up on the mountain. Zero visibility day! *Schnee! Neige!* Powder! Hurrah!

8.32pm

Oof. Skiing in zero visibility is bloody hard work. It never hits you until you have sat down for a couple of hours in the evening. Then everything seizes up in protest. I'm creaking slowly back to the staff accommodation from evening chalet visits and every single muscle hurts.

Happy sigh. There is no better feeling. With more of the same to look forward to tomorrow, and with James!

I can't wait. I wonder if Anna will come along too after all? I must text her to remind her, and of course to say that her ski instructor friends are more than welcome too. I will stay over at James' place tomorrow night after skiing, I think. I'll cover Rachel's morning visits and ask her to do my evening ones. *Mmm.* The prospect of a night together, just the two of us. The more I think about it the more I really, really can't wait. These past few weeks we seem to have been conducting a relationship more by text message and snatched moments here and there than solid time. I miss him. At times like this, I just want him to be a part of my normal life, although I know that would mean wishing away the season, which I don't. I just want him here.

So I'll call him and make a plan for tomorrow. No word from him as yet about it, which is odd.

8.38pm

No answer. Will call later.

9.30pm

Straight to voicemail this time, but he called me back minutes later.

'Hey, did I miss a call from you earlier? Sorry, I'm in and out of tunnels here. What's up?'

'Are you driving?'

'Yes, clearly. Hence the tunnels. I'm on the way to Innsbruck.'

'At this hour? What for?'

'Tomorrow is the senior management season review meeting. I have to wear a suit and do a PowerPoint presentation,' he said bitterly. 'Imagine that dullness while you're skiing freshies tomorrow.'

'Oh. I see.' I felt a bubble of disappointment and annoyance rise in my throat but I swallowed it fast, before it had time to wash through and sour the delicious anticipation that had been holding me up. 'What about what you said at the airport on Sunday, James? The plan to ski together tomorrow?' I asked in a neutral tone. 'I presume you won't be back for that.'

There was a silence at the end of the line.

'Oh,' he said eventually, 'sorry, yeah.' He thought about it. 'I must have been having a special moment when I suggested that the other day. This meeting has been on the cards for weeks.'

'Right.'

'Sorry.'

'It's OK.'

'Maybe Thursday instead? Oh, no, actually, Friday would be better.'

'I don't know, I'll see,' I said tonelessly. 'I might be guiding on Friday.'

'Well, then maybe you could come over Friday night? I could pick you up late and get you back nice and early on Saturday morning?'

'I'll think about it.' My jaw hurt from the effort to keep my

267

voice steady. I really, really didn't want to be annoyed, or hurt, or…whatever that feeling was that made me feel very far away from him all of a sudden in every possible way. I knew it wasn't logical, I knew that he was on his way to a meeting that Gina would know about, that Sarah Datchet would be at, but every instinct told me that his voice sounded odd, that there was something wrong. I tried to visualise his face and I found that I couldn't. 'We'll talk about it again,' I said, shocked at myself. 'I have to go now. Rachel needs me to stretch her.'

'I hope that is as kinky as it sounds.'

'Hardly.'

'OK.' He hesitated. 'Are you all right?'

'Yes,' I said, forcing a cheerful wave through me, aware that I was being grouchy and completely irrational. *He's driving. He is on speakerphone.* I pressed my disappointment into a manageable ball. This was just a small miscommunication, an irritant that seemed worse than it was simply because I missed him so much. Like everyone, he has his annoying habits. These only really bother me at those times when I need him most, like when he spends whole chairlift rides texting his mates in Chamonix and Val d'Isère, patting my leg absentmindedly when all I want is a hug and a chat. His life goes on the majority of the time without me, and mine without him; I can almost always understand and handle that reality. I don't know why it was so hard to at that moment. 'It would have been nice to see you.' I said finally.

I hung up soon after, feeling a bit glum, though when I tried to think about why, it was difficult to articulate, even to myself, and so it was a hard feeling to shake. I went to bed early.

Wednesday 7 March
1.15pm

Fortunately, I didn't have much opportunity to sulk this morning. I looked out the window and saw that the cloud had cleared and given way to the bluest skies. And when I walked into the kitchen, I found that Carol cleared her diary completely of appointments last night and was sitting fully geared up and ready to go skiing. She handed me a cup of tea and tapped her watch.

Oddly, Jon didn't appear in our kitchen this morning. I called and left him a message, asking first if he was alive, and if so, was he free to come skiing with Carol and me? He was alive, thankfully, but wasn't free for skiing because he had to work. 'Be careful today, please,' he said in his text message. 'The avalanche warning is very high. I don't think many lifts will be open. See you in the Flying Hirsch later? I'll be there from nine with some friends. Pop in if you can.'

He was right about the lifts. Ristis forest was the best of what was open, and by ten, the lift queue was packed full of seasonaires. We found Mikey, Eoghan and Arthur within minutes and we have spent the day so far playing 'chicken' with trees.

It has been a long morning for Eoghan. There are a lot of chairlifts on the Ristis side of the resort, and the only entertainment we have needed to get through them all has been the sight of his face every time we mention Tina's name.

'Do you think Gina and Tina could actually be sisters?' asked Arthur ponderously.

'Shut up,' growled Eoghan as Mikey launched into what I'm told is an astonishingly good impression of Tina's reaction to discovering the rhyming names phenomenon back in December: '"Oohey! Tina and Gina! Gina and Tina! Lol! Like G&T! G&T, the drink, imagine!! Watch out boys, ha, ha, ha…double trouble!"'

'You know,' said Carol, 'that exact thought has crossed my mind more than once. What if they are long-lost sisters, separated by cruel fate and reunited by Snowglobe?'

Eoghan took a deep breath and said nothing. We all considered this.

'What if Gina is Tina's *mother?*' offered Mikey eventually.

'Oh my God, that is actually biologically possible,' groaned Eoghan while we all fell about the place laughing.

'Didn't Gina try to shag you back in January, Eoghan?'

'Yeah. She was tipsy and she pinned me behind the bar during clean-up one night when no-one else was around.' He shuddered. 'I told her I fancied Arthur.'

'Dude, you never told me that part.'

'Sorry.'

'Ach, it's understandable. I am a sex god.'

'And now,' said Carol, enjoying herself, 'not only does she know that you lied about being gay, but she knows that you've shagged her daughter. And she probably heard the whole thing.'

'God knows everyone else did,' said Mikey, darkly.

'Shit, Eoghan, I bet you're regretting turning her down now though,' I said. 'You could have had the whole "Double Trouble" package.'

'You probably still could, mate,' said Carol, 'they're very open-minded girls.'

And so on.

10.25pm. The Hirsch bar.

I tried to call James to say hi this afternoon (OK, put myself in a better mood with him by gloating about the powder) but his phone rang out and I didn't feel like leaving a voicemail.

I got to the Hirsch just before ten, where I found Jon sitting with two people I didn't recognise. He introduced them as Louisa and Karsten Bayer. I realised quickly that I had come in the middle of a serious conversation when Louisa reached over and squeezed Jon's forearm, saying, 'anyway, look, we'll discuss it further another time but we are definitely interested. I'll have a chat with Matthias and Leon and get back to you, OK?'

'If I'm interrupting something,' I said quietly to Jon, 'I can go and...'

He shook his head and murmured, 'no, perfect timing.'

Jon explained to me that Karsten and Louisa are the

270

administrative directors of the Alpine branch of Element, the adventure sports company for whom he runs ski clinics, and that they were staying in Reschengel for three days.

'You timed it well, with all this snow,' I said. 'You must be pleased.'

'We are, of course. We live in Luzern normally, so we are spoiled to have Engelberg at our doorstep, but every now and then it is great to go a little further afield. The beauty of the job,' Louisa winked, 'is that when we take three days to go ski new off-piste routes, we can chalk it down to product research for the company.'

'Yes, it is a tough life,' agreed Jon. 'I had a really hard day's work that time last season when they forced me to go to Grindelwald to try out the Eiger ski-gliding. I'm dreading the day the company sends me on a biplane tour of the Okovango or horse-riding in Kashmir.' He sighed dramatically. 'But when the time comes, I will of course oblige.'

'You're such a giver, Jon.'

'Ah, but I am. Tell her about the wonderful, exciting, extreme-adventure-skiing day I took you on today, Karsten,' said Jon with a wry smile.

Karsten shook his head. 'We couldn't get much further than Furggspitz, Poppy. There was great powder, but nothing out of sight of the piste that was stable enough to ski. You can imagine how tracked it was by lunchtime.'

'Tomorrow will be better,' said Jon. 'There should be more options when they can get the lifts open, and I think many will open tomorrow.' As though to confirm this, we heard the muffled thud of yet another faraway avalanche blast.

'Where do you plan to ski tomorrow?' I asked Louisa.

'One of our other guides, Fabien, is taking us off the back of Valluga if the lifts open,' she told me. 'And I believe you are getting the guiding expertise of Jon for a...'

'No, no, no, Louisa,' Jon interrupted, 'say nothing. She doesn't know a thing about it and it is a surprise.'

My eyes widened. 'What is?'

'You have a day off tomorrow, don't you?' he said, turning to me. 'We are going on an adventure. You need to be ready at eight-thirty.'

'What for?'

'A surprise, Poppy, is something that remains a mystery until it happens. You'll find out tomorrow.'

No amount of persuasion would make him budge any further. All he would say on the subject was that I should bring a couple of chocolate bars.

Thursday 8 March

8.42am

A large heap of ski gear appeared at my doorstep at precisely eight twenty-five this morning and rang the bell.

'What on earth?'

I had counted two pairs of odd-looking skis, a couple of rucksacks, three lengths of rope, ice-axes, a shovel-handle, camera case, miscellaneous toolbox-type things and a large brown paper bag when the heap shuffled, held out the brown paper bag to me and spoke: 'Breakfast is served. We are going touring, Poppy!'

11.55am

Touring…is…bloody…*bastarding*…hard…work…*gasp*.

1.18pm

Touring rocks! We are literally in the middle of nowhere, not a track in sight, but perfect, open powder in every direction. It's *amazing* (all the more so for the effort it took to get here, *pant, gasp, pant*).

After a long (long, long, long) climb, we have just reached the most western of the Hinteres Ruhtai bowl ridges. Here, we get to pack away our skins and reset our bindings to normal ski settings to begin the descent. My toes curl as I look down at the terrain that stretches out below us, a long series of interconnecting bowls that are inaccessible from the resort lifts and so will be completely untracked. The anticipation is almost as good as the experience.

For the moment, we lie back in the snow to relax, have a bite of lunch and savour the view. So quiet. So peaceful. *Bliss*. There is not a soul in sight nor a sound to be heard. There isn't even phone reception.

I let this worry me for a moment (what if there is an emergency? What if Gina needs me? What if James is trying to get hold of me?) before I laugh a little morbidly to myself and think that I should be far more worried about the issue of an accident or avalanche hitting one of us out here; Jon, specifically, since he actually knows where we are and I haven't got a clue.

273

James may or may not be trying to reach me, and I can't quite decide if I would rather hear from him right now or not. He didn't return my missed call yesterday. In fact, I still haven't heard from him at all since Tuesday night. I don't know if he will remember that he had wanted to pick me up on the way back to Futterberg from Innsbruck tonight, or that he wanted to ski with me tomorrow, but it doesn't matter anyway: I have told Tom I will guide the Ski Away Day group in the morning. I don't have to, strictly speaking, since I did it last week but I quite enjoy guiding these days and in any case, I owe Tom for the many times he has covered me. More than anything, though, I'm feeling rather disinclined to bend over backwards to see James tomorrow. I'm not keeping my day free on the off-chance that he will want to spend it with me. I miss him, but he has got to miss me too.

'What's the frown for, Poppy-flower? Are you worried about this?'

'About skiing down?' I smile at Jon and shake my head. 'No, I haven't got around to worrying about that yet. And it looks just fine.'

'It will be. What is it that you are thinking about so seriously?'

I can feel his eyes on me and I know that I could tell him anything, nothing, something inane, or even just make a joke of it, but the stillness of this place is very welcoming. Before I have time to measure my words or consider what I am doing, I am telling Jon about James and the odd sensation of waiting, always waiting, and not having any control. Before I know it, I am telling him about Sarah Datchet, Linda, Anna and how much I hate the position I have put myself in relative to everybody else, and how I don't know how to get out of it without losing something, or everything.

He says nothing throughout, just watches me with an inscrutable expression, even as I fall silent. I am suddenly embarrassed.

'But you know,' I continue after a long, mortified pause, 'it's hard when something that means so much to you has to grow in difficult circumstances, isn't it? I suppose the more you care, the more you sacrifice. You have to adapt, eh?'

Jon sits back against his rucksack, kicking the heel of his right boot into the soft snow and pulling absently at the thumb of his left mitten. 'I think I know what you mean,' he says eventually. 'But I cannot agree.'

'Oh?'

He appears to struggle a little to find the right words. 'I once thought that was true,' he says, 'but five years later, I finally understood those sacrifices for what they were.'

'What do you mean?'

'Just that it's never worth doing things you hate – in work or in love. Emilie taught me that.'

Emilie.

'She was my girlfriend. We broke up last year.'

'Oh. I'm so sorry.'

'So was I,' he says with a small smile, 'but for unexpected reasons. It was because of Emilie that my life became what it did, and in spite of her that it is what it is now. We met here in Reschengel,' Jon explains. 'She was then and still is one of the biggest names on the international circuit. You have probably heard of her – Emilie Fournier?'

'Yes, I have.' Emilie *Fournier*, of course. Her face is on billboards for all the biggest snow and surfwear brands. 'Of course. She is an icon. And beautiful.'

'Yes. Hard like nails too. It was she who pushed me from being an enthusiastic amateur to the professional competition circuit soon after we began to be together. Then everything sort of took off. We both hit the top of the rankings around the same time and the media called us a "golden couple." Before I knew it I was being photographed and interviewed and videoed every time I clipped into my skis. Every brand on the market was competing for our endorsement and it was just a shower of constant free stuff, lots of crap we didn't need in return for photos of us using it. Not my proudest moments, really,' Jon's smile is sheepish, 'but it was like being on a fast train and it was hard to imagine how or where to jump off.'

275

'But you wanted out?'

'I did. Emilie lived for it, of course, but after two years, I knew I had had enough. But by then, her ski sponsor was paying a full-time photographer to travel with her all over the world, winter and summer. I knew I had to choose that life or find some other, so I chose to be with her and I held out for two years more. By then, Emilie was being tipped for the French Olympic ski team. I was still at the top of the rankings, but I had totally lost my focus and found it hard to even pretend anymore. At every event we went to, I would feel so guilty seeing these kids that were so driven. They had the look in their eyes of a winner; the burning competitive drive, you know, like they would rather break themselves than quit. Does that make sense?'

Rather too much, I feel like saying. *It sounds like half of the associates at McIntyre.*

'Anyway, all that stuff was spinning round my head when I got to the Verbier Xtreme last year. That turned out to be my last competition.'

'How come?'

'Well, I hadn't actually planned it that way, but I had a fateful beer with a new friend I met on the night of the prize-giving.' Jon smiles. 'He was twenty-eight years old and he had been an Olympic moguls skier. He showed me the scars from his sixteen knee operations. It was messy.'

'Bloody hell.'

'And he still had very little movement on the right knee, so he told me he was about to have his seventeenth. We drank to his good health, but he said, "I think that ship has sailed, brother, but that's what you give to win gold twice." And then he said something that I have thought about many, many times since. He said, "Once would have been enough."

'He said that he would give back the second medal, and even the first, for one more backcountry powder day like this. Just one. Of course that's not how everyone should feel,' Jon hurries to add. 'I mean, there would be no sporting heroes if so. But what I am saying is that that day I came to understand how the role of the "sporting hero" is for people who feel in their blood only complete when they are striving for that goal and who cannot imagine feeling so fulfilled by anything else, no matter what the sacrifice. It was not for me, and afterwards, when he counted the cost, it was not for my mogul-skier friend either.'

'So you retired from the international circuit after that?'

'Yes. There and then,' he says with a happy grin. 'It was the most liberating decision I ever made. Unfortunately Emilie didn't see it quite the same way.'

'What happened?'

'She was shooting a DVD at the time so I flew over to Jackson Hole to tell her the news. I thought that she would be happy that I would be available to spend more time with her and support her career. I had bought a camera on the way over and I joked that I would learn photography and take over as her full-time photographer.'

'What did she say?'

'She was disgusted. She said that I was being weak, and that I didn't have the backbone to see it through. I thought perhaps that was just a knee-jerk reaction, so I gave her a bit of space to get used to the idea. But she came back to me the following day and told me that she would have no further use for me in her life. She said she didn't need an "accessory." I think what she meant was "dead weight."'

'Just like that, she ended five years together? In one day?'

'Well, that's what I thought until she explained things more clearly. She had been sleeping with Sebastian, her photographer, for the past two or three years and she had been deferring making a proper decision between us until it was absolutely necessary. Which, obviously, it then suddenly was.' Frowning, he turns his goggles over and over in his hands, his voice low and steady. 'He had a skill that put her ahead of the competition, you see. She told me that in such a matter-of-fact voice.' Jon catches a glimpse of my expression and laughs. 'I know. Cold, hey?'

'To say the least.'

He begins to sweep snow together and pack it into a snowball, methodically squeezing and shaping it into a perfect sphere. '"No friends on a powder day": that was her motto. I probably always knew deep down that she would live her whole life by that way of thinking.'

'So you left her in Jackson Hole.'

'Yes. And I haven't seen her since.'

'It must have been...' I search for a word that fits, 'devastating.'

'Devastating. Yes,' he nods, turning his snowball around and around in his hands, 'but in an odd way. It was like hurt pride, and certainly anger, and a strong feeling of wasted time. I think more than anything I was disappointed in her.'

'Did you love her?' I blurt out before I think what I am saying, and he stops moving.

'No, I didn't,' he says eventually. 'I know this because soon as she was gone, I didn't miss her. I missed caring about her, but I missed the feelings more than who I had felt them for, does that make sense?' I nod, saying nothing. 'I always remember what an American journalist at Niseko once called her: "a brilliant blend of magnetic and elusive." I knew even then that he was exactly right. She was always playing a clever game; it was her instinct. One day, she'd be close and wonderful, the next day distant again. It was the most frustrating thing, trying to win her completely. In the end, far too late, I realised that this challenge was all that there was. Underneath the exterior she was a rock of selfishness that you could break yourself on, trying to hold on to. With a person like that, you only realise when you are finally close enough to see them clearly that they just aren't worth it at all.'

I nod, thinking that he is finished, but after a pause, he adds quietly, 'which, Poppy, unfortunately I am afraid you will find is not unlike your James.'

It takes a moment for this to travel from my ears to my brain, and around my brain from the bit that controls disbelief, to the bit that does shock and then confusion. My heart thuds once, suddenly, hard against my ribs and I swallow, staring at the snow. *Did he just say that?* I glance over at him and his eyes are still on me. I turn back to the snow and wonder what to say, or think, or do next.

Seconds tick by. About seventeen different responses are competing in my mind, none of them articulate enough to make it as far as my mouth, and the net result is that I am frozen in stony silence with his eyes on me.

How *dare* he?

Well, maybe it's not his fault. It's mine. I should not have said anything to him about James. It always seems like such a good idea to unload your relationship concerns to your friends, but then they form a negative, one-dimensional view, and this is all they ever see again. I should have explained myself better, not blurted out ill-considered frustrations. I should explain it to him properly now.

No, I should leave it. Let it pass. Say nothing.

Eventually, I stand up.

'All set?' I say cheerily, as though the past half hour never happened.

Friday 9 March

10.02am

Daniel the hotel host quit last night. I took the news when I heard it this morning with devastating apathy. So, I believe, did everyone else. It's the best thing for him and it has just been a matter of time.

For once, the loss of a staff member and their refusal to work a notice period has not been the slightest bit traumatic. Well, Suzanne the hotel manager is weeping but that is standard form and nobody takes the slightest notice of that anymore. Carol, on the other hand, had the foresight to phone the hotels area manager two weeks ago to warn him that a resignation was coming, so he had already lined up a replacement to fly out from the UK at short notice. I am told that the new host's name is Robert, and he will arrive on Sunday. Mikey suggested throwing a leaving party tonight for Daniel but it was a pretty half-hearted suggestion and I don't think anyone will be dressing up for the occasion.

I won't be there in any case. I told him that I have some friends in resort and I am going for dinner in their chalet. Which of course is not strictly accurate, but close-ish to the truth – James will be waiting for me in the car park at nine.

Until then, another joy-filled day of guiding awaits. Just getting on the lift now. Looks like it is going to be a rather easy-going day, actually. My guiding group consists of only three people and, as they all seem to be over sixty, I doubt that they will be up for trying to cover all three hundred and twenty-seven kilometres of available piste. Cruisy day, I think, punctuated by a hot chocolate or two and a nice long lunch on the Berghaus terrace in the sun.

10.32am

Oh, dear Lord. I take it all back.

We got chatting on the lift as I always do with my groups. They asked me where I'm from and how the season has been so far. I told them the standard few things about myself and, in turn, asked them the usual questions about themselves: where they are from, how they know one another etc. I was *not* expecting the response I got.

'Well, Judith and I are married, of course,' said Henry, the taller of the two men, 'and Graham and I were in the same regiment during the war, that was how we met.'

It took me a moment to work out which war he might mean. The Gulf seemed a bit recent.

'The War, my dear. The biggie.'

'Vietnam?' I said, doubtfully.

'Ha, ha, ha,' laughed Henry. 'Youngsters! Vietnam, imagine.'

'The Falklands?'

'No, no, Poppy dear,' Judith patted my arm. 'The *War*. You know, the one against the,' she glanced furtively around the cable car full of German-speakers and finished in a whisper, '*Nazis.*'

'No way. There is no way you are all…' I paused, acutely aware that mental maths has never been my strong point and that the pressure was on, 'over eighty. Come on. You're having a laugh.'

'Oh, *I'm* not over eighty,' said Judith. 'I'm seventy-seven. I married Henry in 'forty-nine. These old geese are another story though.'

'Eighty-four,' said Graham.

'Eighty-five and a half,' said Henry proudly, 'and still able to qualify for a downhill.'

'Stop it.' Judith poked him lightly. 'He is not, although if you challenge him he will certainly try, so don't, please.'

I had no intention of it. *Eighty-five??* We impose a lower age limit of sixteen for unaccompanied minors on our ski guiding days, but no-one ever considered an upper age limit. *What if they keel over and die??*

'Don't be alarmed if Henry tries to lead the way, Poppy,' added Graham with a deep chuckle. 'You can take the Major out of troop command, eh, Henry?'

'Precisely.'

'You should have seen him in his day, Poppy, leading the ski patrols in Norway,' said Judith. 'He was the CO to Graham, and I was training on the same base. He used to reprimand us severely if our skis weren't tuned properly.'

'Hrrumph,' said Henry, frowning conspiratorially at me, 'those were the days.'

'By gum, they were,' Graham nodded. 'The USSR with Khrushchev at the helm. We never let our guard down for one minute. What went on up north, out of the way of journalists and cameras…oh, interesting times.'

'Aye, but they were,' Judith smiled wistfully.

'Not a patch on Normandy for outright drama, of course.' They all nodded. 'But there was no rationing,' said Graham.

'And we got to hunt down dirty Communists,' growled Henry.

The conversation continued along this vein for some time. I gathered that this trip is their annual regimental reunion (they keep talking about 'Checkpoint Charlie' being down in the hotel, resting his hip). I am normally gripped by exciting army stories, but am struggling this morning to think anything other than 'please don't die today, any of you. Please don't die.'

Later.

'Tell me one of them died,' said James, pouring sauce over the pasta, 'and this is your idea of an incident report.'

'James! How awful. No, they didn't die. I think they will probably outlive me, frankly. They had the stamina of eighteen year-old marathon runners on steroids. Those old school two-and-a-half-metre skis can really *move*.'

'It's not the length,' smirked James, 'it's what you do with it.'

'Well, the oldest codger knew exactly what to do with it: point it straight down the hill and turn only for trees and people. I was absolutely shattered by lunchtime,' I sighed at a forkful of penne. 'And I think I lost a year of my life today through worry. Every snowboarder I saw, I thought "head injury." Every patch of ice was a broken pelvis. I was bloody glad when Graham produced a hipflask on the Egginerjoch chairlift. Steadied the nerves.'

'They must have had some interesting stories to tell.'

'Oh, yeah, Judith especially. She was a teenager in London during the Blitz, and I'd say a damn good skier in her day. She has fifty-one years on me, but I think the only reason she didn't utterly whip my ass today was that she was too polite. She commanded a unit up in the Arctic for years. You name it, she's trekked it: Greenland, Alaska, even staged some covert ops across the polar ice-cap into Siberia, apparently.'

'I want to meet them. They sound awesome.'

'They are. My Granddad would have loved them.'

'Was he army too?'

'Have you not heard of my Granddad? He won the war for the Allies.'

'Really?'

'No. But you'd think he had if you'd spoken to him on the subject. He worked in Army Intelligence.'

'Sounds like a legend. Tell me about him.'

Some time later.

'...and not long after that, the whole African front collapsed. I have to say, I'm sceptical about the part with the masking tape, not to mention the go-go dancer in Berlin. Also, I really don't think Rommel would have committed so much to paper, but Granddad was adamant so we all went along with it. I'm not totally convinced that he didn't lose the finger in a tragic stapler accident in an office somewhere, but he always insisted that the nickname, "Farmboy," came from his deadly knowledge of homemade explosives.'

'That's hardly a stand-alone trait among you Irish though, is it?'

I made a face at him. 'You're hilarious. Shall we watch the DVD?'

'Let's.'

James reached over me and switched off the bedside light as opening titles of *Snatch* flickered across the screen. He pulled me a little closer into his side and I lay my head half on his chest.

'Comfy?' he asked. I planted a little kiss on his chest by way of an answer and he kissed my forehead, his fingers twisting gently in my hair. 'Remind me later to tell you the story of my uncle Jim, the horse whisperer,' he murmured.

'I'm looking forward to that,' I smiled, as Brad Pitt said something incomprehensible and James pinched my shoulder for a translation. 'Hey, James, I've been thinking…'

'Mmm hmm?'

'About the end of season,' I began, 'and the summer. I haven't… I mean, what are we going to…'

'We haven't had a chance to talk about it properly yet, have we?' he said cheerfully. 'I've been thinking about it too. I really want to go to Biarritz and get a few weeks' surfing in. Or go mountain biking and climbing up in Chamonix. What do you think? Would you be up for some camper van adventures?'

'You and me in a camper van?' I laughed a little at the mental image, though I felt like hugging him tightly and never letting go. 'I thought you said you were terrified of Pikeys. Now you want to be one?'

'Well, you'd have to initiate me in their ways, obviously.'

'We'll have to work on your accent. And I can't surf.'

'Well then your main role will be stealing gates from locals and selling them back to them.'

'Or I could learn to surf.'

'Or you could learn to *fish*,' now he was getting really into the idea, 'and then you could cook my dinner every night.'

'What an honour,' I said. 'I also quite like the idea of Chamonix, though. Climbing and biking and all that. It sounds wicked. Which would you prefer?'

'Why don't we do both? But let's watch the movie first. Pipe down, young Connors. This part is hilarious.'

I could feel his hand on my back and hear his heartbeat through his chest, warm and comforting. *We've got plenty of time*, I smiled to myself. But somehow, when I closed my eyes later that night and tried to fall asleep it was still Jon's face I saw, intent and serious, pressing me to believe the very worst in James.

Jon's judgement of my relationship with James was nothing more than a projection of his own failure to see in his ex-girlfriend what was probably staggeringly obvious to everyone who knew them both. People always impose their own experiences on others and call it advice. *But I'm not Jon. And James is not Emilie.*

The more it swam around my head, the more it annoyed me. I swallowed hard, turning over again. Jon had no right to say what he said, to try to throw me like that. He had no right whatsoever.

Saturday 10 March

9.28pm

Rachel, Tom and I were just spreading out our collected spoils of dinner plates begged, borrowed and stolen from Tilly, Miranda, Mark and Joseph during chalet visits this evening, when there was an extremely loud banging noise from downstairs, a thunderous roar and the sound of a shelving unit tumbling over and crashing to the ground. (I say this retrospectively, because at the time it sounded like a stampeding rhino had just been felled by a bullet from a rifle.)

We looked at one another, alarmed, (although not so alarmed that we didn't continue to fight over Tilly's hoi-sin duck). The loud noises were replaced soon after by the staccato fire of Jan swearing profusely in German, punctuated by high-pitched noises that emanate from Gina in times of stress.

'A lovers' quarrel,' said Tom wisely, through a mouthful of noodles.

Gina's front door slammed shut minutes later and there was silence. We idly wondered for a moment or two whether we should go down and check that one of them wasn't lying in a pool of blood. Then we all got a group text message from Gina, and we realised that, logically, if anyone was lying in a pool of blood, it must be Jan. And *that*, we didn't give a rat's ass about.

The text message read:

'Sweeties!!! A meeting plz @ mine in 20 mins. Some v imprtnt news 4 u all!!! Gud news!!!'

'Oh, good,' Rachel clapped. 'Jan *is* dead.'

9.55pm

Oh. My. God.

I am speechless. I am without words.

There are no words.

None.

Not even one.

'I'm pregnant,' Gina repeated, still grinning, her eyes bulging with excitement and anticipation.

286

Rachel got it together a bit more quickly than I did. 'Gina! Wow, Gina! Congratulations! You must be so happy.'

'Yes, yes, congratulations,' said Tom, looking baffled.

'Oh, yes, sweetie,' she said, pulling Rachel and Tom to her chest and squeezing them hard. 'I am so, so happy. I am going to be a mother!'

'When?' I managed.

'Yes, how far along are you?'

'We think about nine weeks. Maybe eight. I saw the doctor today and he has given me a due date in early October. I'm going back in a few weeks for my first proper ultrasound scan and then I'll have a photo to show you. How exciting will that be? Ooheey!' she squealed again. 'I just can't believe how happy I am!'

It sounded like she was actually serious. This was all a little too focused and detailed to be another one of her notions.

'Have you told Jan?' asked Rachel carefully, though of course we all knew the answer.

'Yes, just a little while ago. It came as, well, a bit of a surprise to him,' she said, glancing inadvertently at the overturned bookcase of Snowglobe paperwork, manuals and records. 'But he'll get used to the idea. He's got to. He's going to be a father!'

Something in this sentence permeated through the general haze of my stupefied disbelief. He's going to be a father.

He's already a father. I looked at Rachel and Tom as Gina bounced up and down and chattered on about how she was already sure it was going to be a boy, and what a super aunt she had always been to her little nephew, and how she was going to raise the child right here in the mountains. Rachel caught my eye. She looked worried. Tom was looking sadly at Gina. She still had no idea whatsoever.

I felt a surge of the familiar murderous loathing toward Jan. But what to *do* about it?

Sunday 11 March

5.32pm.

'Do you think she'll name it after me?' asked Rachel. 'If it's a girl, obviously.'

'Do you think it's real?'

'Do you not?'

'I'm not sure,' I said, glancing at Gina basking in the glow of attention and excitement from the reps of other resorts as we all took our mid-morning coffee break between flights. 'I can't tell.'

James snorted. 'There's no way it's real, come on. This is Gina. Nothing ever happens to Gina, not in the real world at any rate. Except for mysterious and highly improbable thefts,' he added, bitterly.

'I don't know,' said Rachel dreamily, 'I think she will totally, you know, *be* a mother. I feel like there is this sort of *peace* coming from within her now.'

'Rachel, sober up,' said James, flicking a two-euro coin at her. 'Go get yourself a coffee.'

Rachel went to the doctor yesterday afternoon because her back had not been getting much better with simple stretching. It was time to go in search of something a little stronger. The regular doctor was away and in his place was a locum with a somewhat poorer-than-average command of the English language. The interview with him went something like this:

Doctor: 'Miss Scott, you need zeh pain medication and zeh muscle relaxant to stop zeh spasms so zat zeh stretching, he will work.'

Rachel: 'Go on.'

Doctor: 'Zer are sree levels of pain medication, *ja?*' He put three boxes on the table. 'Level one, he is no good for you. Not strong enough. Level two...' he made a shrugging movement and a noise like '*bof*' that Rachel said afterwards "makes me think he may have trained in France."

Rachel: 'OK, so level three then?'

Doctor: 'Ja.' He put the box on the table. Like the other two
     boxes, it had a brand name Rachel had never seen before.
Rachel: 'Right, what is this one?'
Doctor: (with a slightly maniacal grin, or was Rachel embellishing
     a touch?) 'He is Morphine.'

She opted for level two, or 'Bof.' This was on the grounds that
paracetamol was never going to make a dent in her pain, but a
full-on morphine addiction would be a whole other world of
problems for her. 'Bof,' by contrast, sounded like the perfect
middle ground. She is supposed to take one a day: always at night,
last thing before bed. The doctor told her that this would relax her
completely overnight and that 'mild effects' would keep her pain-
free during the day. She dutifully took one at eleven o'clock last
night. It almost instantly had the alarming effect of making her
stand out on the balcony, staring at the roadside and weeping at
the sheer beauty of the piles of days-old shovelled snow. And I'm
not sure how 'mild effects' translates idiomatically into his dialect
of German, but she is still as high as a kite and showing no signs
of coming down. I'm really not sure how she is going to get
through the rest of today. Lift pass sales targets? I'll be amazed if
she ends up in the right resort.

Gina is utterly oblivious to all this of course. Her main
preoccupation today was how she would break the news to James
of her impending motherhood. She decided last night that she
needed to tell him as early as she possibly could or she would lose
her nerve. I was gutted when she said that because, as always, she
was due to take the first coach down to Salzburg, which meant
that I wouldn't be there to watch his reaction (and there was no
way I was going to phone him last night and impart that morsel of
news in advance).

Naturally, then, I was thrilled when I arrived in Salzburg to
find her waiting in the Departures coach bay for me.

'I had to wait for you to be here. I need moral support,' she
said, gripping my arm and marching me toward Arrivals. She held
back for a moment at the door, paused, whispered, 'It's time,' and

walked in.

'James,' she said in a gentle voice. 'James, I have something I need to tell you.'

'Can it wait?' said the top of his head.

'No, I'm afraid not. Well, it can I suppose, but only for thirty-two more weeks, haw, haw, haw, ahem.'

'What?'

She took a deep breath. 'James, I am pregnant.'

He looked up, expressionless, from her to me and back to her. He said nothing, nor did he blink. I think he was waiting for the punchline.

'I'm going to be a mother,' she said eventually, with feeling.

'That is the usual end-result of being pregnant,' he said drily. I made a face at him and he looked back down at his laptop. 'Yeah, congratulations, Gina, that's great. Yeah, I thought you'd put on a few pounds lately. Nice one, well done.'

There was an awkward pause which I filled with a graceful 'right, eh, OK then, all done. Errm, coffee, Gina?'

She smiled beatifically. 'No caffeine for me, sweetie, but I will join you for an herbal tea.' She caught my arm and glided me in the direction of the exit doors.

James called after us, 'yeah, you can bring me back one too, Connors. Black, one and a half sugars, OK?' and he grinned at me and made a twisted face of horror at Gina's back.

'He took the news well, didn't he?' Gina smiled sadly once we were out of earshot. 'Oh, look, it's Sarah Datchet! I need to talk to her about a maternity uniform for the summer season.'

Jan is in the airport today too, and I am staying *well* out of his way, although it is a cheering sight to see his pointy white nose pink with rage. Rachel and I have thought long and hard (mainly when drunk and emotional) about how to exact revenge upon him for his evil slimy bastardness, and are both amazed that somehow Gina has unwittingly done a far better job than we ever could have. It's just a shame that a poor, innocent child will have to come of it.

'Do you think she will give birth in the normal way,' asked

James some time later, sitting behind his desk, staring at Gina, 'or will it burst straight out of her stomach, *Alien*-style?'

'I'm not going to think in any way about the concept of Gina giving birth, thank you very much. So now you think she *is* telling the truth?'

'No, not really,' said James, 'but I am intrigued by the thought of the spawn of Jan and Gina. What will it look like?'

We eyed up Jan at one end of the arrivals hall and Gina at the other. 'Probably blonde,' I said. 'Maybe it'll inherit her wide-ranging talents and his impeccable efficiency. Though hopefully not his personality.'

'Or maybe it will just get the ghastly combination of his nose and her voice. Imagine that.'

I tried not to. 'Just so long as it doesn't get his ears.'

'It probably will. And it will burst itself out of her abdomen during dinner some night and fly around the room like Dumbo.'

'James, that is a little dark, even for you.'

Just then, he frowned and stared down the arrivals hall to the passenger exit. 'What the fuck is *that*?'

I followed his gaze toward the passenger arrival doors, where there was a rather large clearing in the crowd of incoming guests off the Liverpool flight. In the midst of the clearing was a young man in dark sunglasses, a tight green t-shirt and ripped jeans, with the most improbably orange skintone I have ever seen (and I have lived in the vicinity of Gina, so I don't say that lightly). His hair was poker-straight, platinum blonde and streaked with heavy chunks of black and silvery-gray, and he standing very still and pouting, one foot placed at a calculated angle to the other.

I looked around for the paparazzi. The arriving guests were standing back, presumably expecting the same thing. Surely he must be some kind of Euro-pop icon?

James and I watched, transfixed, as he broke his pose and walked over to Kim. She looked around the room then and pointed to the last person in the world I thought he might have had anything to do with: me.

'Do you know him?' hissed James, incredulous, as the stranger strutted over towards where we were standing.

'Are you kidding?' I was still looking for the photographers.

'Hi*ya*,' he said, taking off his sunglasses as he approached me. 'I'm Robert. You're Poppy? From Reschengel?'

'Yes.'

'Great.' He shook my hand. 'I'm coming back with you to work in the hotel.'

I did an admirable job of concealing my disbelief that anyone so impossibly well groomed could possibly be en route to scrubbing a Snowglobe Club Hotel. James was less discreet. 'You're *shitting* me,' he blurted out.

'Robert, this is James Walker,' I cut in hastily. 'He's my boss, though not yours. Lucky you,' I added with a sideways look.

They shook hands, James still looking at him with an ill-concealed look of perplexed amusement. I took Robert by the arm.

'Right. Come this way.'

I was just steering him over toward Gina when I spotted a very confused-looking Rachel stuck in the middle of an out-of-service revolving door, bumping off the glass walls. 'Actually, Robert, I've had an idea,' I said, doing a U-turn and motioning at James to deal with Rachel while I steered the unwitting new rep recruit toward the coffee shop. 'I'm going to teach you about handling fees and exchange rates.'

Much later.

Pop Idol played a blinder charming Rachel's guests. He was rather less successful with actual lift pass sales, but he did confuse the guests enough on the subject for us to sweep in and secure the sales upon arrival under the guise of 'clarification' and so he earned himself a beer or two for that. By beer, of course I mean pitcher, and by pitcher, of course I mean Happy Bar.

Robert is the centre of attention. His is the first new face we have had in a while and, with his *Heat* magazine celebrity looks, he got more than the usual mildly interested questioning about where he was from and what he had been doing before this.

'I was on X-Factor,' he announced proudly. 'I got to the fourth round. Cheryl and Danii said I have what it takes, but that Simon Cowell was a right fookin' bastard.'

He explained that he is only here in Austria because he needed something to do between now and May, and Snowglobe is one arm of the same corporation that runs the cruise shipping line that have given him an entertainer's job for the summer season.

'Head Entertainer on the *Princess Starlight*, no less.'

'Do you do karaoke?' asked Tina, excitedly. 'My song is *It's Raining Men*. What's yours?'

'Stand back, lass.' He grabbed a handful of straws from the holder on the bar, held them up like a microphone and, putting on a voice it took me a moment to recognise (eventually identified it as Ronan Keating's), he closed his eyes and belted out Robbie Williams' *Angels*. It wasn't bad, actually (in so far as anything that sounds like Ronan Keating can be) and he got an encore. I thought that Tina was going to faint.

Three songs later (*Moondance*, *Brown Eyed Girl* and *Baby, One More Time*, for the record) Mikey raised a toast to our newest housemate.

'To Robert – welcome to Reschengel, mate. And here's to the month of March!' He raised his glass again. 'Let's keep the mid-season-blues casualties at only one, eh?' (Dick-the-chef, Weird Karl, Bastard Dylan, Isadora and Antonia all apparently don't count because they didn't even make it to New Year.) We all drank to that. 'Now, there's really only one other seasonaire pitfall to avoid,' added Mikey, 'and we are all home and dry.' He caught Eoghan's eye, and they both roared out in unison: 'CHALET-GIRL ASS!'

I hadn't heard that expression before, though I think from the pink headband-clad, pink snowboard-wielding female contingent of resort, I know just what they are referring to. Chalet hosts (and sometimes reps, though sadly not often) generally live off the same food that they serve the guests. The upsides to this are obvious; the downside is that after five months, all that butter, double cream and banoffee pie start to take their toll, and no matter what anyone thinks, no-one ever gets as much exercise on the mountain as they think they do.

Miranda and Tilly evidently hadn't heard the expression before either. They each let out a little gasp, glanced quickly at their own bottoms and exchanged a wide-eyed look of panic before they dived for the ladies room, presumably to confer.

Monday 12 March

10.55am

Rachel was Bof-ed off her face again this morning, so much so that she was unlikely to be anything but a liability if allowed to meet guests at ski school, so I left her lying in her bed, poking the diamond shaped lumps of mattress pushed out between the wire underlay of the bunk bed above her.

'They're like marshmallows. Squashy!'

I called in to Carol's apartment on the way back from ski school orientation to see if she was up for a spot of skiing. Over a cup of tea, I told her about Rachel's new druggie ways, which when you describe it aloud and when you know Rachel, really is not something you want to miss seeing. Carol followed me home.

'Bloody hell, Rachel. You're a state.'

'You're pretty,' smiled Rachel and poked her in the cheek. Carol grabbed her shoulder and spun her around. 'Wayyy-hayyyy-dizzy-*ouch*,' she said as Carol poked and prodded various parts of her back, bent her over one way and then the other.

'Show me the drugs they have put you on.' Rachel retrieved them from her handbag. Carol was incredulous. 'Are you seriously taking these? How much per day?'

'Just one tablet.'

'Rachel, this stuff is illegal in pretty much every other country in the world. And you're double-dosing. You should be taking half a tablet, you muppet.'

'Half a Bof? What's that? "Bo"? Or "Of"?' she giggled.

Carol gave me a pained look. 'Poppy, give me twenty minutes with,' she motioned at the still-giggling Rachel, '*this*. I think she might be relaxed enough to work some of the spasm out. Rachel! Shut up and go lie face-down on the kitchen table.'

'Shut up, I will not,' Rachel giggled on and tried to run away.

'I've got to go downstairs to Gina anyway,' I told Carol. 'I'll be back in a bit.'

She nodded as she steered Rachel into the kitchen. 'Brace yourself, Rachel,' I heard her say as the door swung shut.

'Come *in*, sweetie! What good timing!' trilled Gina, opening the door. 'Come, come, join us. Don't bother about any of that,' she said, taking the sales vouchers out of my hands, throwing them on the couch and leading me to where she and Tina were sitting cross-legged on the floor. Around them was arranged a sea of fabric swatches and colour cards, piles of books and five or six glossy magazines with names like *Pregnancy Today* and *Mother To Be*. Tina was leafing through a book of baby names and yelling out the ones that she liked.

'Cassiopeia!'

'Bit long.'

'But Cassie for short?'

'Yes, pretty! Something like "Cassiopeia Alexis Desireé" would work really well, wouldn't it?'

Tina nodded enthusiastically. 'Or Angel?'

'Oohey! "Angel Alexis," yes, I like that one for a girl, though I do think it is a boy. Don't ask me why. I have a feeling.'

'A boy…Calum?'

'Strong, manly, I like it. "Calum Tiger," because Tiger Woods is really quite inspirational, isn't he?'

'Ooh, yes, and fit. Or what about that Eagle Eye Cherry? "Eagle Eye" is a great name.'

'Oh yes, it is. I'm thinking, warrior. I'm thinking, *gladiator*. Ooh, "Maximus!" "Maximus Decimus Medirius!"'

Tina clapped her hands. 'So strong! So powerful! I hope he grows up to look like that Russell Crowe. *Phwoar.*'

Gina looked at me. 'What do you think, Poppy?'

'I think you're right,' I said, diplomatically. 'What's with all the interior design stuff?'

'Yes, that's the other thing. You're just in time to give your opinion on the nursery. We're thinking either "Springtime in Paris."' She held up a double page spread from one magazine. 'Or "Beachside Fun,"' she said, holding up another.

I tried to ignore the competing mini Eiffel Tower print curtains and the orange and blue beachball/umbrella motif, and focused instead on the broader picture.

'Where are you going to put the nursery?' I looked doubtfully around the small apartment, wondering if there was something I was missing.

'Oh, it won't be here. We'll be needing a new place when the little one arrives, won't we, Janny?' I jumped as I noticed Jan sitting in the shadows behind me. He scowled. 'Maybe down in Innsbruck,' Gina went on, 'where Jan is from. It would be so nice to be near the grandparents.'

'My parents are dead,' he barked suddenly, getting to his feet. He swiped at his jacket on the back of the couch and stormed out the door without another word.

Gina smiled patiently as the pictures wobbled on the walls. 'The poor thing. He's even more hormonal than I am these days! First-time fathers, eh?'

She and Tina shared a tinkly laugh.

First-time fathers indeed. For the millionth time, I wanted to say something, but was it my place? And what on earth could I say?

Saturday 17 March
11.10am

Still reflecting upon the above, days later, as I sit in the chalet kitchen, painting people's faces green in honour of St Patrick's Day. Mikey has managed to persuade all the hotel and chalet hosts to dress as leprechauns – including Miranda and Tilly, to my amazement – with the sole exception of Eoghan, who has insisted on dressing up as an enormous pint of Guinness. We're planning a day in Stüben, followed by an afternoon beer on the terrace outside Taps.

Rachel has headed off for the day with Nick and Jon to do some gentle cruising in the powder fields off the back of Schindler. She accepted without question my excuse that I wanted to celebrate St Patrick's Day with the hosts, but she gave me a rather odd look. 'OK. We'll come and meet you in Taps later, shall we?' she asked in a bright voice.

'Yeah, fine,' I said, tonelessly. 'Give me a call when you're

297

done and when Nick and Jon have gone home.'

I didn't really care how strange this sounded; I was not in the mood for seeing Jon, not until I had managed to pull my anger toward him under some kind of control. I was still surprised by how much it continued to prickle, even after so many days. She said nothing, just nodded and left.

I can hear Gina moving furniture around downstairs as I wait for everyone to get their gear together. *She might be alone now*, I realise. *Maybe now is the time to talk to her about Jan? Now, before we all leave to go skiing.*

I stand up, resolute. But then I'm hit by sudden doubt. *Can I really do it?* I ask myself. *Can I really break the news to her? Is it my responsibility? But equally, can I really stand back and let her believe in a man like Jan?*

'But I mean, how is one to know for sure?' Tilly breaks into my reverie. She is still fixated on the idea of 'chalet ass.'

'Try on your jeans. If they still fit, then there you go.'

'Jeans *stretch*, Mark.'

'Tilly, your ass is exactly the same size as it was two months ago. I think I would have noticed.'

'Would you?' says Odysseus, eyebrows raised. 'Well, well. He's been keeping a close eye. I wouldn't stand for that, Tilly.'

Tilly and Mark both blush scarlet, which is funny because Mark never gets flustered about anything. He recovers quickly though, and informs Tilly in a mock-posh voice that he 'will henceforth be your bottom monitor, m'lady, always on hand with a measuring tape, should your Ladyship require it.'

'Oh, shut up. I'll lace your dinners with secret injections of cream and lard and then you'll be laughing out of the other side of your face.'

'I actually do that to Suzanne's dinners,' confesses Odysseus guiltily. 'Adding extra butter and cream and stuff.' We all look at him, horrified and he gets defensive. 'Oh, come on! Look at her! Turn her sideways! She'd blow away with a light gust. I've probably saved her life, you know.'

Just then, we hear a crunching noise on the street outside and we all look out the window. A four-by-four has driven up over the curb and into the deep snow of the garden outside our chalet. We all watch as Fritz Spitzer climbs out, opens up the back door and begins unloading things. We sneak out onto the perilous balcony to get a better look. It is baby paraphernalia: first, a crib, then a bath, a wooden highchair and what looks like a folded-up pram.

'Oh, Fritz!' Gina's voice wafts up. 'You are such a peach for doing this! How wonderful! I love it, I love it all!'

We crawl out onto the perilous balcony to spy.

A girl I don't recognise gets out of Fritz's car and greets Gina with a warm hug.

'Who is *that?*' asks Odysseus in an awe-struck whisper. 'She is so beautiful.'

The mysterious girl is petite, pale and delicate-looking, with huge dark eyes and a bright, friendly smile.

'Do you think that could be Fritz's daughter?' I whisper to Odysseus.

'She can't be.'

We all watch her, mesmerised. She laughs as she unloads a basket of cuddly toys and then reaches in and pulls one out. '*Vati!*' she says, and admonishes him for trying to give away her favourite childhood toy.

'My God, that *is* his daughter,' I say, almost to myself.

'I should really go help them,' says Odysseus and, scrambling noisily to his feet, vanishes down the stairs like a shot.

'And they say arranged marriages can't work.' Tilly shakes her head, then thinks about it and adds, 'I'll bet it hasn't occurred to him that that might not even be Maria, but some other daughter. Like a married one.'

Arthur chuckles a low, evil laugh. 'And Maria is really a hideous beast who lives in the attic and survives on buckets of fish heads and liver-wurst leftovers.'

'And wears dungarees and plaits her armpit hair.'

They continue to speculate along these lines, but I am lost in thought. Something about all this is very odd.

Why is Fritz here? Why is he doing this now, so soon and so

299

enthusiastically? Fritz *knows* about Jan's wife and children. Wasn't he the one who told me? So why he is playing Happy Families here? And why has he not told Gina the truth?

Tuesday 20 March

3.25pm

Rachel had her physiotherapy assessment this morning and the verdict is in: she is fully back in action, hurrah! So it seems that Dr. Narcosis was spot on. All she really needed to do was to get utterly out of her mind on ridiculously strong drugs and then, in her overturned-woodlouse state of helplessness, be pummelled to a sobbing wreck by someone as merciless as Carol. This, followed by Pilates-like exercises for a week or so, has done the trick nicely.

The physiotherapist did warn her that big airs and aggressive rotations are off the cards for at least a few more weeks.

'*Dayymm*,' said Rachel, looking not the slightest bit upset.

In honour of her return, Jon, Rachel, Nick, Carol, Mikey and I are going to ski together tomorrow. It's been almost two weeks since I have seen Jon properly for more than a quick hello when I see him in the chalet or on the street, and it's probably time I let it go. He almost certainly knows he stepped out of line that day on Hinteres Ruhtai and he can't have meant to upset me; that's just not Jon's way. If I hadn't been so annoyed with James at the time and so vulnerable to unsettling thoughts, of course I would have seen it all more clearly. I'll smile at him and we'll ski together and quietly put things back to normal.

Tomorrow will be great. There's talk of Maienvasen and Kuhtälli, and Ristis trees and then maybe a little bit of Moose. We're going to meet the others there at four and introduce New Robert to the wonders of German aprés-ski music. *Jawohl!*

No crowd-surfing though. OK, maybe a bit. Hurrah!

Wednesday 21 March

10.42am. En route to Stüben.

Bugger. Slight change of plan for today's skiing. James just texted asking me to meet him for a ski. Or so I inferred from:

James: 'Rufigrat?'

Me: 'When?'

James: 'This morning.'

Me: 'No can do. I have a date with Maienvasen and the
         Reschengel posse. How about tomorrow? You can have
         me for the whole day. And if you're very good, I might
         even follow you home.'

He phoned me. 'No, Connors. I've got to drive to Thurlech
and back tomorrow and then off to Söll on Friday. If I don't see
you today I won't see you for the rest of the week.'

'Errr...' I could hear him frowning as I thought about it. 'I
could come over tomorrow night?'

'Only if you don't mind sharing the bed with two men. My
mate Danny's over from England. Got here last night.'

'Oh.' *Damn.* 'Is that why you sound so croaky?'

'Err. Yeah. There was a substantial quantity of alcohol
consumed. And not a lot of sleep.'

I sighed as I looked around the gondola at my friends, all deep
in conversation about the day ahead.

'I'd really like to see you, Poppy.'

Sigh. 'Right, OK, yeah, I'll see you at Stüben in half an hour.
How about that?'

'Wicked. We'll be there. The usual spot?'

'Yup. Albonalift.'

'See you in a bit.'

I felt massively guilty telling the others that I had to go, Rachel
particularly. I waited until we had got off the lift.

'*Mate.* I've just been resurrected from the dead,' she exclaimed.
'You can't leave me now.'

'I'm sorry, I'm sorry, it's just...'

'It's just Mr. Walker, that's what it is.'

I couldn't really argue with that. 'I'm sorry, Rach. Really, it's
just...I'm trying to get things...' I sighed again. 'Mate, I'm sorry,
really.'

She nodded, but didn't smile. 'I know you are, Pops. I know.
But I just wish you didn't have to be.' She saw the look on my

face then and gave me a hug. 'Hey, it's OK. Look, have a good one and I'll see you in Taps later. How about a proper Day of Fun tomorrow? Just us? I'll ditch the ball and chain.'

'I presume that is me,' said Nick drily.

She patted his shoulder, kissed him on the cheek and said, 'don't speak unless spoken to, dear,' then screeched as he picked her up, threw her into a snowdrift and jumped in after her. 'See you later, Poppy!' yelled the snowdrift, giggling.

I turned to say goodbye to the others and caught a look that passed between Jon and Carol. I opened my mouth to speak, but Jon just nodded at me, unsmiling, and skied off down onto the piste below.

'See you later, Poppy. Give James my love,' said Carol putting out her cigarette and turning to follow Jon's tracks in the snow.

12.01pm. Futterkar gondola.

James had been waiting in the usual spot outside the Albonalift when I got there. He looked tired but pleased to me. He did his usual exaggerated look to the left and right, pulled me a long kiss, then drew back then and said in a low growl, 'Hello, beautiful.'

I smiled, pleased to see him too. 'Where's your mate?' I asked.

'Gone to the jacks. He's not feeling the Mae West, as it were. Ah, look,' he nodded at someone behind me. 'Speak of the devil. Danny! Over here.'

He was tall and broad, with a chubby face that looked like it ought to have been pink and shiny, but was grey and waxy.

'Hi Danny, how are you doing?'

'Uhhh... dying.' He shook my hand limply. 'What the hell is in that Stroh 80 stuff, Jimmy, you fucking sadist? I think I am allergic to petrol.'

'The clue is in the name, Danny, my boy. The clue is in the name,' James grinned and remarked about the alcohol-intolerance of landlubbers and sea-level folk. 'We mountain men train hard to maintain our Stroh-fitness. It is the drink of champions.'

'Speak for yourself,' I said. 'Danny, Stroh 80 is not a drink. It is internationally classified as only suitable for embalming and high-

303

level political assassinations.'

'Come on, quit your bitching, ladies.' James clipped into his skis. 'Let's move.'

'James, are you sure we should be taking him up to Rufigrat like this?' I said doubtfully, nodding at Danny. He had just stood up from tying up his snowboard boots and looked like he might pass out. 'It's a hell of a hike at the best of times. He might bleed internally and die halfway up.'

'Indeed,' said James slowly, leaning on his ski poles. 'That thought did occur to me on the last lift when he nearly threw up on a kids' ski school class. I think Rufigrat is off the cards for today. Let's cruise the piste for a bit, yeah? Get our legs back.'

Great, I thought, three blue pistes later as I watched Danny extract himself from the orange padding around the base of a snow cannon. I gave up the Maienvasen gully for *this*.

We headed for the Nordhang lift after a while, having spotted on one of the piste boards that the Nordhang itinerary route had just opened in the past half hour. It was a route I had never done and James reckoned that with its northerly aspect the snow should still be in very good condition, so Danny might just survive the experience.

Something new to do! I was very excited arriving at the Nordhangbahn, until we realised that everyone else in the greater Reschengel area had come to exactly the same conclusion. The queue was out the door.

'Fuck it, let's do something else.' James turned his skis to push off in the other direction but I didn't move.

'No,' I said, 'I really want to do this. I've never done it.'

'We'll do it later. Come on.'

'No, it'll be completely tracked out then. I want to do it *now*.'

James' eyebrows shot up. It's not often that I push for my way, but for once I wasn't in the mood to be easygoing. I wanted to do this. Now.

'OK. Sure,' he said lightly.

Ten minutes later, we were wedged in the middle of a sea of people and even I was getting cranky. James had pulled out his phone five minutes before and was catching up on explaining icily to somebody somewhere the full extent of their incompetence. The crowd had pushed between us in the intervening time and he was then about twenty people across from Danny and me. I could see him speaking but could no longer hear the words he was saying. It was quite careless of him to let that happen, I can see in retrospect – quite careless and quite unlike him.

Danny made a noise and I looked around at him. It was something like 'gu-uurrrrgh.'

'Are you all right?'

'I hurt,' he said pitifully and then looked puzzled suddenly. 'Is there a fireman's pole in Club Fracas?'

'Yes.'

He looked relieved. 'That explains why my shoulder is so sore. I remember someone landing quite hard on me but I wasn't sure that my brain hadn't just made that up.'

'Hmm. Futterberg: Where memory cells go to die.'

'I am never drinking again,' he groaned and I laughed.

'Many's the time I have heard that said in lift queues, Danny. You just need time to acclimatise to the altitude.'

'I need time to acclimatise to the quantities you people can put away. You are machines.'

'It's true. Well-oiled machines. Work hard, play hard.'

'I need sleep.'

'Sleeping is for the flight home.' He groaned and I patted him on the arm. 'Hey, it's not so bad. At least you can nap. Imagine having to work out here too. Imagine getting up and cooking breakfast feeling like you felt this morning.'

'I was still drunk at eight o'clock.'

'So are most of the chalet hosts most days, actually,' I conceded. 'But hey, you can sleep this evening.'

'Yeah, I think I will. I'll send Jimmy to the pub and get a couple of hours' nap. I am not looking forward to sharing that little double bed with him tonight.'

I laughed again. 'You'd think that Snowglobe would give their senior management something better than a small room with a double bed, mini-kitchen and a shower. You two must have had a cosy night last night.'

'Nah, it was all right last night. Jimmy didn't come home with me. It's tonight I'm dreading.'

It was said so casually that I almost missed it. It took me a full second to rewind, replay and let the significance of those six words seep through the various levels of comprehension.

James didn't go home with him last night. He didn't go home.

I pictured his bed, and then the narrow old streets of Futterberg at four or five in the morning, empty and quiet after the clubs have closed and everybody has gone home. *Where did he go?* I asked myself, although my hands were already going numb and I could feel my lips drain of blood because I knew the answer.

No. He went to a party. Someone had an afterparty and he went there. He went there and fell asleep on the couch.

I swallowed hard. James didn't fall asleep on a couch last night and I knew it. I knew it and I was not sure why I knew it, but there was no doubt. There was just sick, sick finality.

I looked up, across the queue and saw James' eyes on mine. He was pushing through the crowd, pulling his skis behind him and ignoring the protests of the people he was shoving past. Danny was still chattering on, oblivious to the freefall that was going on inside my ribcage. James' face was hard, his eyes intent. *He has slipped up*, I thought distantly. He didn't think to warn Danny, and Danny hadn't seen him kiss me. He didn't know.

'Hey,' said James, panting slightly when he got to me. 'That was hard work. Must have got separated there.'

His voice was just a little too bright, his manner just a little bit twitchy and his eyes watching me just a little too closely. I said nothing as he snaked his arm between my rucksack and my jacket and let it rest on my lower back. The crowd pressed around us.

'Mate, rubbish queue,' said Danny. 'Are we ever going to get on this lift? Don't you own this resort or something? Do something.'

'No, I am only Lord of Futterberg unfortunately. Unfortunately we crossed the border back there somewhere and this is the slummy, nasty Reschengel side of town. Full of common folk, Pikeys and whatnot, eh, Ireland?'

Something perverse and strangely detached within me made me smile and say in a deadpan tone, 'Indeed. Though we draw the line at midgets and circus folk, of course.'

James chuckled at that. I knew that he would. I felt his arm slither the rest of the way around my waist, his fingers pressing closer against my side, drawing me to him. I looked up at his face as he continued to speak to Danny. I didn't hear what he said, I just watched the relief relax his face and his shoulders dropped slightly as he regained control.

A quiet, numb minute or two passed while I let the full significance settle upon me. I looked to my left. There were about ten people between me and the queue cordon. Beyond that was the scratched Perspex wall of the lift station, blurrily overlooking the piste outside. I closed my eyes for a minute. I kept them closed, because I knew that when I opened them, I would leave.

'You all right?'

'Mmm,' I nodded, half-opening my eyes but not looking at him. 'Slight headache.'

'Sorry, babe. Is it the queue or are our hangovers contagious?'

Babe'?? What the fuck? I snapped out of it then. This was all getting too weird. The blood was beginning to rush in my ears the way it does when I know I have to get far away and calm down immediately. I hesitated for a second and thought of my phone and in that moment, as though inspired, it beeped at me. I looked down at the screen, expecting it to say "Text Message Sender: Random Deity, doing you a favour."

It was Rachel. 'OMG, Pops. Funniest ever wipeout video of Mikey stacking it! Took us 10 mins to dig him out! Will show you at Taps – be there at four! Woop! Woop!'

'Oh,' I said, tonelessly to James and Danny, 'I've got to go.'

'What? You can't go.' James frowned. 'You just got here, fool.'

'I've got to.'

'Why?'

'Rachel needs me.'

307

'What for?'

'Something about her back. Sounds like she's in a bad way.'

'What are you going to do, operate on her?'

'She said that she needs me.'

'You two are bloody well joined at the hip,' he laughed. 'Should I be jealous?'

'On balance,' I said, 'probably not.'

Danny gave him a strange look then, and then looked at me. It was definitely time for me to get out of there before all the twos became four.

'All right. Take it easy, Connors.' James leaned down and kissed me softly on the lips. 'Tell Rachel I said, "sort yourself out, woman."'

When I smiled my lips felt sort of rubbery. I itched to get free of the airless claustrophobia of crushing bodies. Our eyes met for a long moment before I turned away and pushed free.

'Goodbye, James.'

Outside in the sunshine, the breeze was cool and pleasant. She answered her phone on the second ring.

'Anna? Are you busy at the moment?'

'No, not really,' she said brightly. 'I've been pretending to do my weekly report, but I've stopped kidding myself and I'm about to go skiing. What are you up to?'

'I'm up at the Nordhangbahn bottom station. Can I meet you somewhere?'

'Yes, of course. Top of the Futterkar gondola?'

'OK. I'll wait for you inside the restaurant.'

'What are you up for doing? Don't say moguls, please.'

'Actually, I mainly just want to grab a coffee if that's all right. I need to talk to you about something.'

'OK,' she said slowly. 'What's going on? You sound strange.'

'I just need to talk to you.'

'Are you OK, mate?'

'No, not really.'

'I'm on my way.' I noticed that she didn't sound even slightly confused as to what it might be about.

Thursday 22 March

8.30am

The others won't be awake for at least another hour, maybe two. The sun is already piercing through the gap where the curtains don't quite meet. Rachel's bed is empty; she must be at Nick's. Tina and Suzanne are snoring softly.

I am wide-awake. Not hungover, not tired or cold, but sick. So gut-twistingly sick that every time in the past eighteen hours I have had to think about getting out of bed, the idea of having to make cheerful conversation with anyone hits me with such a wave of anti-social nausea that I have just pulled up the duvet a little closer to my chin and closed my eyes again.

Her name is Elisa.

Friday 23 March

10.21pm. My bed.

Voices outside my room. Hushed. Whispering?

Please leave me alone. The front door closes. Quiet.

Her name is Elisa and it wasn't just one night. James has been sleeping with her for around two and a half months.

'Who first? Which one of us?' I had to ask although there was no answer I could imagine ever wishing to hear. My mouth was lined with cardboard and I could feel my pulse thudding dully in my fingertips. Anna frowned and sipped her tea.

'I'm not sure. I think you got with him first, but it was a matter of days, if I remember right.' She saw my face and went on hurriedly, 'Poppy, you have no idea how hard this has been. It has been *killing* me. I could see how happy you were with him and what a selfish little wanker he was being. I wanted to jump up and down and scream every time I saw you two together, but when it came to it, I just couldn't think what I could actually *do*.'

'It's OK,' I nodded dumbly.

'No, mate, it's not. At first I thought it would just be a one-night thing with you two, but then it went on and on, and there was that Anderau trip and Thurlech and all sorts of other running around, driving you over to Futterberg and back every week. By the time I was sure that it wasn't just a fling and you were really interested in him, it was too late to warn you off. I knew you wouldn't understand if I tried to tell you then.'

I tried to smile but it came out wobbly. 'I did wonder why you were so distant with me. I thought you might not approve of me being with him.'

She put her head in her hands. 'Oh, this is such a mess. I am so sorry. If I just told you before you got involved. If I had just…' She sighed. 'Ugh, I really hate this.'

We both looked at our drinks and neither of us spoke for a minute.

'Does Elisa,' and the effort to say her name with my cardboard-mouth was extreme, 'does Elisa know about me?'

Anna shook her head. 'No. She has no clue. She's still really happy with him.'

I felt my stomach give a long, horrified lurch. 'She lives in Futterberg?'

Anna nodded. 'She's a ski instructor. And a mate, which is the worst part. She is so lovely and so much fun. You'd love her, actually.'

I did not need to hear that. *Please stop talking.* I stared out the window at a flagpole outside. Horizontal icicles had formed a long ridge all down one side of it, the sharp ends pointing west. They were the icicles that form on fixed, upright things like poles and aerials when falling snow is blown by a strong wind. It must have been an easterly wind on this occasion, I thought to myself. I suddenly remembered sitting in the Keller Bar one afternoon way back at the start of the season at the seasonaires' avalanche safety workshop with the guy from the Powder Club explaining to us how important it was to take note of the phenomenon when you see it. 'Keep alert to this sign,' he had said, 'because it is a clear indication that very dangerous slabs of wind-blown snow have been formed on exposed slopes.'

'I wish you two could have known each other as friends,' Anna was saying. 'I wish none of this had happened and I could have introduced you. You would have got on so well with each other.'

'I've never met her, have I?'

'No, not through me, anyway, and I think you can be pretty sure that James kept you both apart.' Anna sighed again. 'James is a mate,' she said. 'He has been for years, but sometimes I just wonder how many more times I can turn a blind eye to this sort of shit. It was one thing when he was just whoring himself about the place every night, but now my friends are getting hurt. I used to joke with him that I could only be his mate because I stayed out of his complicated affairs and didn't think too deeply about his morals, but I'm starting to…just…' She shook her head and looked back down at her hands. 'I have been nagging him for weeks now to sort this out. He would promise me that he was fixing it, and then I would see you leaving his place in the morning and Elisa walking in that night.'

311

The numbness in my hands was like a cold-burning fire now, and was creeping up my sides and crawling over my scalp.

She shrugged sadly. 'I just don't know what to say. I wish I could make this better.'

'You can't.' I had stopped wanting to talk about it. It was time to get as far away from Anna and this cafeteria and Futterberg as possible. I pushed away my untouched coffee cup and gathered my things. 'It's my own fault. I should have known that it was all nothing to him. I should have realised sooner.'

She frowned. 'No, it's not like that, it's just that with him...'

'It is *exactly* like that.' I was standing up now, putting on my jacket. 'He didn't give a shit. Not ever, not even slightly.'

'Poppy...'

'I have wasted enough of my time thinking about him. And now that I know how little of his time was spent thinking about me, I think I will stop now.'

'Please, it's more...'

I smiled at her and gave her a quick hug. 'Please don't, Anna. Look, I really appreciate your telling me. Really, I do. And I don't blame you one bit. I only have my own stupid naivety to blame here.'

I left then, and I thought as I jumped on the lift and was carried blessedly far from that restaurant and the whole Futterberg area that I would ski forever, just keep moving and not thinking until I absolutely had to stop. But then every piste was a sea of faces, and all I could think was, 'which one is hers?' Was she instructing? Would she be in uniform? Or did she have a day off, and had James called her as soon as I left them at Nordhang so that she could come and take my place?

Were they skiing together? Would I see them? Would I run into them together, laughing and joking in a lift queue, or worse, get stuck beside them on a chairlift?

I couldn't bear it. I headed straight for Reschengel and came to my senses back in the warm, quiet undisturbed peace of my bed, which I am now maintaining a policy of leaving only for work-related reasons. After three months of pressing down my happy little secret, three months of keeping it tightly closed off from my daily life here in Reschengel, I don't know how to pretend it is not doing the opposite now, pulling me so far down and so quickly that I forget how to think of or say anything but the name 'Elisa.'

Elisa has been in my head ever since I heard her name for the first time two days ago. I should have asked Anna what she looks like, but I'm not sure I could have dealt with hearing how spectacularly beautiful she is. Still, the longer I obsess about it, the more beautiful she gets. She's taller than me, with long, blonde hair. No, raven-dark hair – shiny, straight and swishy, like a model's. Thinner than me of course, with a stunning smile and a perfect body. I can't think of James without picturing her beside him, his arm slung around her shoulder, his eyes on her and his voice saying her name, 'Elisa.' Then they are smiling, then laughing, and I have to screw up my eyes and try to summon any other image into my brain, but my imagination's only available stock footage of the sorry truth is rather persistent.

More than anything, I wish I could call my reaction disbelief, but it is now all too painfully easy to understand. I can see so clearly now how the time James and I spent together over the past few months could have been so different an experience for him to what it was for me. I can see now with the unforgiving obviousness of retrospect how every phone conversation and text message exchanged, every shared joke, affectionate moment and display of familiarity and trust, every afternoon skiing together, every night sleeping side by side and every covert little adventure had been combining gradually to form in my mind some sort of coherent emotional mass, every day deepening in tiny but important ways my perception of our growing closeness. Not so for James, of course. The difference was mathematical – I can see now that James was not giving anything he meant to be of any value; for him, the sum of all things was still zero, and when he was not with me, he had plenty of the same pleasurable nothings to give to and take from whomever he wanted. Of course there was no concrete reason why I should have assumed that his phonecalls and text messages implied anything more than that he happened to have thought of me in those specific moments; indeed there was absolutely nothing to guarantee that he wasn't with some girl at the same time, that he hadn't simply been amusing himself while she was out of the room. The enormous disparity between our two perceptions of the relationship we had had, such as it was, was entirely logical – disappointingly so. All it means now is that James is a very different quality of man to what I had let myself believe, which, in logical turn, demonstrates that the entire sorry mess is basically a fundamental and pretty unforgivable error in judgement on my own stupid part.

I have had rather too much time to obsess about all of this in the past two days, and although I have tried valiantly to sleep, work, smile at people and do all the other things required of a functional non-lunatic, my brain has just kept whirring and whirring through every single interaction I can recollect of the past five months and in every one, I see the same infuriating thing: how little I demanded of him and my own stupid naivety, taking everything I got at face value. I was so happy in such a simple way to have met him, to have shared some brilliant times with him (however terminally intermittent), and to have had the chance to feel the way I did about him, that I forgot to lock down any kind of certainty beyond the readily apparent signs that he felt the same way. *I let this happen*, I accept, exhaling cigarette smoke out the bedroom window with wild disregard for all my fear of death-by-rampant-chalet-fire, because I know now that the way I am feeling is, underneath it all, essentially my own fault.

The clarity doesn't help. James has been my centre of gravity out here for months, my friend and more, and he's gone now, vanished so completely it is as though he never existed. I know that I am going to need to accept that fact as quickly as possible, but I am feeling in the dark for anything at all and still I just cannot find my balance. He's gone, that man I cared so much for, whose hand I held, that man whose eyes sent lightning splinters through me with the intensity of his stare and the knowledge that he was looking at me – he's gone and I'll never see him again.

Since none of it was real, I have to learn how to not miss it.

His eyes used to rest on me, but he was never just looking at me. While I was nobody else's, he was just making room for me in a busy schedule and she was always, always somewhere nearby. She was Pete from Chamonix, she must have been. She was his buddy in Val, problems in Söll, the sick chalet host in Obergurgl, the panicking resort manager in St Anton, his constantly buzzing phone, the endless soft clicks of a text message in the quiet of the night while I was wrapped up warm and oblivious in his arms. She was everywhere when I thought I had him entirely.

I never had him at all.

11.33pm. Still in bed.

They're back, and noisy. And curious. 'You all right, Poppy? Still feeling rough?'

'Mmm hmm.' *Please fuck off.*

'Pops?'

Sorry, Rachel, even you.

'You OK, Pops? It's been two days, hon.'

'Yup.'

'Feeling any better?'

'I'll be better tomorrow.'

Rachel paused. 'OK. Do you want anything?'

'No thanks. See you later.'

The door clicked softly shut after a minute.

Rachel was not best pleased with me for failing to show up at Taps yesterday afternoon without any explanation and refusing to answer my phone, but she got over it when she saw that I stayed in bed all evening and didn't go out last night. She tried to bring me to the doctor this morning, but I told her it was a twenty-four hour thing and to leave me alone until tomorrow.

I will tell Rachel tomorrow. But only when the thought of saying it aloud doesn't make me want to curl up into a ball.

Elisa, Elisa. James has Elisa. And what do I have now? My duvet. That's all. But at some point soon I will have to leave it. Sunday. Airport day. When I will have to see James.

Ugh.

315

When I will have to speak to him.

Ack.

When I will have to stand there in my uniform and do as I am told.

Urrrgh…heuugghhh… In fact, I am not even going to bother with all the self-recrimination I am due on that front. There is no use in agonising over what an idiot I am for getting myself into this position.

Of course James has realised by now that I know. I don't know how or when he found out: it could have been Danny or Anna or maybe he worked it out with his own powers of deduction. A text message from him yesterday evening tested the waters:

'Hey, how's things over in RSL? How was the ski back?'

It was lazy. He might at least have made the effort to send me the kind of message we would normally exchange. I didn't respond. He called me an hour later and I didn't answer so he texted me again.

James: 'Why are you being so off with me?'
Me: 'You know why.'
James: 'No, what have I done? Tell me.'

I was seized by sudden doubt then, and it lifted me for a second. *What if I have got it all wrong?* The crash back down to reality a moment later was eight times worse. There was no chance I had got it wrong. There was no question at all.

I didn't respond to that last message. I couldn't, because, try as I might, I couldn't think of a single thing I could write that could adequately sum up what I was thinking, and how very, finally and terminally disappointed in him I was.

Three hours later, he texted me again. My phone beeped three times: a long message. I sighed, bracing myself as I unlocked the keypad to read it, thinking tiredly that there was nothing he could say that would surprise me, shock me or get my attention. But then I had to read the message twice, and not even on the second reading could I quantify my disbelief at his words. No, at his *audacity*, at his *unbelievable fucking audacity*. I froze, considered it for a brief second, blinking, and then threw my phone so hard out the window that I was not sure I would ever see it again.

James: 'Poppy, hey, look I wanted to actually say this to you but you're not speaking to me for whatever reason. Maybe you're busy or something but anyway. Look, I think Sarah Datchet might be starting to suspect that there's something going on with us. I'm sorry but it's just not a good time for me to have to deal with that. I need some time to myself now. Please don't be upset, but I have a lot going on and I need a bit of space. I'm sorry. You OK?'

I considered walking into the kitchen then and smashing at least half a dozen breakable objects. But then I thought about it again, and there were people in there and I knew that making a scene might be rather embarrassing in retrospect.

I stayed in my room instead and stared hard at the underside of the mattress of the top bunk, seeing only Elisa.

Saturday 24 March

11.44am

Hushed voices in the kitchen and the hallway again. I feel great sympathy for the little mountain creatures trying to hibernate around here, with all the skiers, boarders, lift installations, piste bashers and snow cannons getting in their way. I wonder if they spend most of their winter wanting us all to *just shut the fuck up and leave them in peace.*

A soft knock on the door. Again, why?

'Poppy?' Rachel's voice breaks through the duvet around my ears.

Please leave me alone.

'Come skiing, Pops?'

'No.'

'Oh, come on, lazybones, the snow is wicked up on...'

'I said no.' Silence. 'Close the door when you're going out.'

The door closes. Quiet.

Then opens again.

'I'm sorry, I'm not leaving you here again today. I'm worried about you.' Rachel walks to the head of my bed and leans over, pulling the duvet back and looking at me. 'I found your phone in the snow outside. It was ringing. Why was it out there?'

I make a vague noise but say nothing. She touches my face.

'You look like a ghost.'

'I'll be OK. It's just a bug.'

'Mate, it's not.' She sits down beside me on the bed. 'I've seen you sick. Remember that time you had haemorrhagic fever?'

'And you reckoned it was motor neuron disease.' I smile a little in spite of myself. 'But it wasn't either.'

'Amazing, eh? Yeah, well, I have seen you as sick as a dog with whatever that was – Ebola, maybe – so I know that if you were genuinely ill you'd be bored of your own company by now and at the very least you'd be moaning about it to anyone who would listen.'

'Rach, I don't want to talk about it now. Later, OK?'

'Has something happened at home?' I shake my head. She

318

frowns. 'Pops...'

'Rachel, I can't. Not now. Later.'

'Is there anyone you want to talk to? Shall I call Carol?'

'No,' I say and I half-laugh. Carol in this situation would not be the pillar of sympathy or compassion one would choose to lean on first. Though she would certainly pour neat spirits down my throat, probably straight from the bottle...which actually sounds rather tempting. But no.

'Jon, maybe?'

'No.'

'Mate, I've got to tell you, he's been really upset since you...'

'*No*,' I say, a little too forcefully and she looks a little taken aback. I don't care. Jon is the last fucking person I want to discuss this with. *He* knew. *He was my friend and yet he knew the whole time.*

'OK, but you should talk to someone. Shall I call James? Get him to come over? I'm sure he would drive over this afternoon if you need him.'

I smile mirthlessly at that, then laugh, but my face feels funny and Rachel is looking at me strangely. From nowhere, I'm crying so hard that it is difficult to catch a breath.

She strokes my hair and waits for it to pass. It does, of course, after a couple of minutes and I sit up, feeling a little foolish but vastly better. And then, in a calm voice, I tell her everything: Danny, Anna, James and Elisa, Elisa and James, and James' final, pre-emptive strike.

She explodes with rage, which of course I knew she would. It is pleasantly vicariously cathartic to watch.

'The fucker! That lying sack of shit *motherfucking wankfaced bastard*. By text message? How *dare* he? How fucking dare he allude to it by *text message?*' She is really seething now. 'Is he such a cowardly little piece of shit that he couldn't look you in the eye?' Her eyes flash (I have always wondered, up until this exact moment, what that looks like. Now I know) and she makes a ferocious noise. 'I am going to go chop down a fucking great tree the size of his *fucking* opinion of himself and go and flatten him with it. Oh, when I get my hands on that jumped up little...'

I have to laugh. I want to feel the same way Rachel does, I really do. It would be easier that way, to get sozzled on chardonnay while ranting about the fecklessness of men and plot some dramatic comeuppance-deliverance to That Bastard. But try as I might, I can't summon the necessary murderous loathing for James; rather I would just like to walk a very great distance in the opposite direction and quietly forget that I ever knew his name. I can't bear the idea of screaming abuse at him; I know that my pride will not let me so much as blink in a way that might hint toward the many rips and tears inside my chest for which he is responsible, and the immense struggle it will be to hold together an indifferent face for the airport audience all day tomorrow.

After a few thousand swear words, Rachel sits back down beside me on the bed and gives me a hug.

'I'm OK,' I tell her. 'Really.'

'Shut up,' she says gently, 'you categorically are not. Do you want me to hunt down the slutty little bitch too?'

'Elisa? No, it's not her fault. Apparently she has no idea about me. And apparently he makes her happy,' I add, trying not to sound too bitter and miserable.

Rachel's eyes are hard. 'You have to find her and tell her.'

'No.'

'Poppy! She has no idea about you. And now he thinks that he has got away with it. You have got to tell her. Ultimate revenge!'

'No. I have no interest in that. It's not going to make me feel any better and she doesn't deserve it.'

'She doesn't deserve him.'

'True, but I'm not going to be the one to tell her. If it's anyone's responsibility, it's Anna's, and she knows it.'

Rachel makes another strangled noise of frustrated wrath and punches the bed.

3.42pm

I tried to persuade Rachel to go skiing and let me retreat back under my duvet, but she was having none of it. She dragged some clothes onto me and hauled me down the street to the

320

Mondschein, where she has been filling me with glühwein for the past two hours.

I returned from the ladies' a moment ago to find that Rachel had phoned Carol after all, presumably with the order to get across the road urgently and assist with persuading me to let her put out a hit on James. Carol was already at the bar when I walked into the room. I braced myself for an earful, but Rachel must have warned her that now was the time to experiment with the strange notion of silent compassion, because when she saw me, she took off her coat, handed me a box of cigarettes and hugged me all in one movement, as Traudl passed us, carrying a tray of shot glasses and a bottle of sambuca to our table.

'Drink up,' Carol said gruffly, picking up a glass and handing it to me. 'Oh, and these are for you.' She held out a large bag of Galaxy Minstrels, her favourites and mine too. Many's the time we have bemoaned the difficulty of getting them out here. They could only have come by post from home and she must have been saving them. It was one of the kindest things any friend has ever done for me.

'Carol, I…'

'Yeah,' she nodded, 'OK.'

5.43pm
Shhhfine. Shhgonnabefine. Tomorrowssis another day, ha ha ha. Sshfine. Really.

Sunday 25 March
3.01am
Time to go. Gulp.

3.06am
Really shouldn't procrastinate any further. Really need to go.

3.07am

Argh, *no, no, NO*. Cannot face the ghastly prospect of today. Don't want to go to Salzburg. Don't want to see his face. Absolutely cannot bear the idea of hearing his voice. Want to lie down on the floor and have a tantrum about the unfairness of it all. Why must I go? Why? Why? Why? WHY?

3.09am

Sigh. *Fine.* Here we go.

3.32am

First coach is out. Gina's gone. I am very grateful for her pregnancy-induced self-involvement these days. I would have crumbled under an interrogation, but she is utterly oblivious.

Rachel gives my arm a squeeze as we walk down the hill toward the hotel. Then my phone rings. I look at the screen and see the words 'Club Hotel.' *Eh?*

'Hello?'

The sound of crying, broken by ragged gasps, and then 'Poppy? Is that you?'

'Suzanne?'

'Oh, thank God. Poppy, it's awful. He's…oh, there's blood everywhere. You need to come here quickly. You need to talk to the, to the, to the…' she sobbed, *'police.'*

'*What?* What's happened? Suzanne? *Suzanne?*'

She is crying again.

'Suzanne! Pull it together for a second. What is going on?' I have wild visions of crazed guests stalking around the dark corridors of the hotel, stabbing people, but I shake my head. This isn't *The Shining*. Someone's probably been hit by a car or trapped their fingers in a door or something.

Suzanne takes a shuddering breath. 'One of your guests has been shot.'

'Has been *what?*'

'Shot.'

'Shot?'

'Shot.'

'With a gun?'

'Yes.'

She sniffs. This is good. One-word answers, she can handle. The big question: 'Is he dead?'

'No.'

Phew.

'Where is he now?'

Evidently, the immediacy of the issue comes flooding back at that question, because so do the tears. 'Ah *huh, huh, huh.*'

'SUZANNE. For fuck's sake. Where is he?'

'In the foyer. Please come, pleeease, pleeease.' She dissolves into wracking sobs.

Rachel and I have already started jogging toward the hotel before I finish hanging up.

'Err, Pops?' she asks, 'Did Suzanne mention *who* shot him?' I hadn't thought to ask. We stop and look at each other. 'Do you think that maybe, errm, maybe there might be a crazed gunman on the loose somewhere?'

We freeze, and then both run really fast.

4.13am

I had counted two local police cars, three federal police cars and about thirty-eight Polizei wandering aimlessly about outside the hotel entrance when the same thought occurred to both Rachel and me.

'Where's the ambulance?'

We met Mikey and Eoghan just inside the front door. Guests were milling down the stairs, trying to see what the noise and sirens were about, and the boys were trying desperately to keep the foyer clear.

'No, no, nothing too serious, just a little accident.'

'But I heard noises, young man. Don't you tell me that I didn't.

323

There were gunshots!'

A ripple of alarm went through the amassed crowd on the stairs.

'We need to get out of here right now. My children...'

'No, madam, really there is nothing to be concerned about. Please make your way back up to your rooms and we will...'

'But my coach is leaving in forty minutes, I have to...'

'No, sir, it's all under control, we will call you when...'

'Well, I never....'

Rachel and I ducked our heads and sidled past it all, trying to look as little like company representatives as possible. Around the corner on the sofas we found the cause of all the drama. There was a very pale, clammy-looking man with dark circles under his eyes, propped up listlessly on a table with his trousers around his ankles, bleeding profusely all over the place. No-one seemed to be doing very much at all about this fact. One of his friends was on the couch across from him, supposedly mopping up blood with a towel, as far as I could tell, but actually just slumped, semi-conscious, his head lolling about. Had he been shot too? I wondered. No, he was just drunk. A third man was at the bar, slurring abuse and gesticulating belligerently at one of four impassive and unimpressed-looking police officers as a deputy took notes.

We stood there for a moment, taking all this in. Just them, Suzanne's head poked out from the office doorway. With a look of the most abject relief, she rushed over to Rachel and me, ignored Rachel completely and dragged me over to the four police officers.

'*Sie sprecht Deutsch, ja? Sehr gut, ja?*' she said to the group of police officers, elbowing the drunk man out of the way and gesturing frantically until one of them spoke to me, introducing himself and asking who I was. At that, Suzanne released my arm and, with a hugely relieved look of *auf wiedersehen,* she muttered something about a mop and vanished.

The police explained to me in German that the bleeding man had been shot while on the balcony of his second floor room.

'With a gun?' I had to ask again.

'Yes. We believe a shotgun.'

Holy shit. How does he still have a leg? 'Is an ambulance coming to help him?'

The Polizei looked bored. '*Ja.* Soon.'

They escorted me over to where Rachel was standing over the bleeding guest, looking more intrigued than concerned. 'Poppy, I'm no doctor,' she said as I approached, 'but that looks like eight different holes in his leg.'

'I've been shot,' he slurred weakly, his breath reeking of stale beer.

'Eight bullets?' I looked at Rachel, incredulous.

'Well, eight holes,' she replied, 'but only one of them is big. Do you think we should, I don't know, try to slow the bleeding or something?'

I hesitated – *ugh* – but in the absence of an ambulance, there was nothing for it, so I pulled off my jacket, shoved Head-Lolling Boy over on the couch and sat down in front of Bleeding Man to apply pressure to his groin area, thinking all the while that *this is so not in my job description.* 'Did I miss the briefing on street crime, Rachel?' I asked, making a face as his blood oozed through the gaps between my fingers, pushing under my fingernails and dripping onto the floor.

'It wasn't on the training course anyway.' She turned to the police officer again. 'Can we maybe call that ambulance again?'

He shrugged and waved dismissively. '*Kommt gleich.*'

He was far more interested in using me to translate the man's statement. He and his colleagues demanded, in increasingly fast provincial dialect, three repetitions of the precise details of the incident, specifically the exact sequence of events from early yesterday when he had four intact limbs, to this point, when he very much didn't.

Bleeding Man – whose name I discovered was Gary – explained woozily that he and his friends had gone into the village for a quiet drink or two and an innocent stroll ahead of an early transfer this morning. They were minding their own business on the walk back to the hotel when suddenly, three huge and very aggressive Germans appeared from nowhere and tried to beat them to a bloody pulp for no reason at all. The boys ran away (being lovers, not fighters) and the German ogres let them go. A lucky escape, thought our three hapless guests, as they arrived safely at their hotel room. They then went out onto their balcony to enjoy an innocent, calming cigarette when, out of nowhere, the peaceful tranquillity of the mountain night was shattered by gunshots. The ogres were evidently expert hunters and, with deadly skill, had stalked them back to the hotel to finish them off there. That was when Gary – let's call him Innocent Gary – was struck and fell to the floor, wounded, perhaps mortally.

The Polizei wrote down everything that was said, exchanging intermittent looks and making doubtful noises. Even I was a little sceptical, and suspected that he was skimming over certain parts of the story (like the truth) but I didn't really care. I just wanted them to sign it off and take Innocent Gary away to a hospital. By this point, I was wrist-deep in congealing blood and there was still no sign of the ambulance, which was of course worrying from a health point of view, but also because we had over a hundred guests to get out of resort in the next hour, including one coachload due to leave in ten minutes with me on it. I could hear Rachel on the phone to Tom, who was down at the coach stop, frantically trying to help him coordinate getting all the guests and their baggage onto the right coaches and promising that I would be down there as soon as possible.

Eventually, three minutes before my supposed departure time, with still no sign of the ambulance and the Polizei still bringing random witnesses over to me to translate one-line statements like 'I heard gunshots at three-fifteen this morning,' I conceded defeat and told Rachel to take my coach and that I would follow in hers as soon as they were finished with translations.

'OK,' she nodded. 'Shall we call Gina now?'

'No need to call her just yet: she'll just confuse the matter by trying to fix it from halfway down the mountain in a coach full of sleeping guests. Call her from the road.'

326

'Right. Good luck, mate.'

'Thanks,' said Gary, as though she had been speaking to him.

She picked up her jacket and bag and made for the door. And that is when things got complicated.

The head police officer spotted Rachel rounding up guests and making to leave, and he motioned to the thirty or so seemingly pointless Polizei floating about aimlessly outside the door. In seconds, they had formed themselves into an impenetrable barrier. Rachel stood there at the head of a rabble of suitcase-wielding guests, looking confused.

Head Polizei marched up to her, removed her clipboard from her hands and informed her in German that 'all your coaches are henceforth impounded until we get some answers from the three men responsible.'

'Responsible?' I leapt up from Bleeding Gary and turned toward the door, my blood-soaked hands dripping on the sofa as the watching guests variously gasped, swooned and took photos. 'I don't understand. Why are you treating them like suspects?' I asked. 'He didn't do this to himself. I mean, he didn't shoot himself in the leg.'

'I am not suggesting that he did,' Head Polizei responded calmly, 'but I am waiting to hear an explanation of why he and his friends were in possession of these.'

He held up a gloved hand, holding a small evidence bag containing what looked like bullet cartridges.

Oh.

4.50pm. Salzburg airport.

'What happened then?' asked Anna breathlessly. Around her, twenty curious faces blinked, waiting for one of us to speak.

'Well,' I said, 'it was time to call Sarah Datchet.'

They winced collectively, as did I, recalling the conversation.

Innocent Gary was still bleeding profusely, of course, so I had to ask Tina to pull my phone from my pocket and find Sarah Datchet's number in my contacts lists. I then had to pause, take a moment and confirm that this whole scene was in fact really, actually, seriously happening, and was not some sort of fondue-cheese-hallucination before pressing the green button with my nose.

'What kind of a delay?' Sarah Datchet sounded irritated when she answered.

'Well, one of our guests has been shot.'

'I'm sorry, this is a bad line. Could you repeat that, Poppy?'

'A guest has been shot.'

'Shot?'

'Shot.'

'Oh. Oh. I thought that's what you said.' She paused. 'With a gun?'

'Yes.'

'Is he dead?'

'Not yet,' I said looking down at the gloopy mess of blood under my hands.

'I can hear you, you know,' slurred Innocent Gary.

'Sorry. Err, Sarah, I can't really talk for long. He is bleeding rather a lot and there's no ambulance here yet and both of my hands are kind of stemming the flow of blood. I'm just calling to let you know that there is a question mark over how many coaches we will be able to get out of resort in time to catch their flights.'

'Oh. Right. OK, you carry on with that. Just tell me which coach will be delayed and I'll sort everything out at this end. How many guests we are talking about? Twenty? Thirty?'

I thought about Tom's panicked phone call from the coach stop five minutes ago: 'Poppy. Err, Poppy? We have just been surrounded by about twenty armed policemen. What exactly is going on at your end?' and I sighed and told her the truth, 'Umm...a hundred and seventy three.'

'*What?*'

'How did you get them to change their minds?' asked Simon, the rep from Söll.

'That was the best part,' beamed Rachel. 'We totally didn't even have to. As soon as the guests heard what was in the offing, they did it themselves. They marched up to every single police officer there and started to complain, over and over and over…'

'…at which point I grabbed the Head Polizei guy for a little chat and reminded him that if he didn't let the coaches go on time, almost two hundred deeply unhappy guests would be stranded in resort with no beds, and it would be his mobile number they'd be phoning, not mine. Which was so not true, for the record – they would have lynched us first, one way or another, but it was amazing to watch him put himself in our role for ten seconds. He went pale and gave in.'

'…which totally proves what I have always suspected: that we are more hardcore than the Austrian police, fact.'

'But what happened in the end with the crazed lone gunman?' Emma was biting her nail. 'Was he ever caught?'

'That's a good question,' I said, looking at Rachel. 'We'll find out when we get back to resort, I suspect.'

'Nothing exciting ever happens in Söll,' said Simon bitterly.

'Nothing exciting ever happens in the ski program, full stop,' said Sarah Datchet, who had been listening at the back of the crowd. 'I haven't received a phone call like that since I managed beach resorts.'

Gina was sitting in the corner, sulking that she had missed all the action (or attention, more specifically) and pretending not to listen. James was also pretending not to listen, sitting across the quiet room at his desk, stabbing at his computer. I still hadn't discussed the morning's events with him at all; it hadn't been necessary. Sarah Datchet is responsible for departures, and Gina is my manager. It was not for me to keep him in the loop as things progressed.

Regardless, he phoned me this morning about twenty minutes after my first phone conversation with Sarah Datchet. I considered not answering, and then remembered – *curse it!* – that I did actually have to speak to him if he phoned me about work-related issues.

'Yes?'

'Poppy, hi. It's James. Err, are you… Is it OK?'

I do have to talk to him, I thought, *but I don't have to chat.*

'Yeah, we're dealing with it, if that's what you're asking. I need both hands now though, so I'll call you if I need you, yeah?' and hung up.

11.55pm

Cynicism vindicated. Innocent Gary? Pah. The truth came out in the end, as it is wont to do.

A quick chat around town, and the Polizei had no difficulty discovering that Gary and Friends had been causing trouble all week. They had been thrown out of no fewer than eleven of Reschengel's finest establishments over the past six days, three of them on the night of the alleged murder attempt. (OK, last night. I can't help talking like this now. It's all about the 'perps' and the 'vic.' *CSI Miami* has a lot to answer for.) Eoghan confirmed that they had left the hotel bar at ten-thirty, already very much the worse for wear. They went on to pick a fight in Keller Bar, then got ejected from Rodeo by Marco for verbally abusing a barmaid who would not serve them and finally were asked to leave Damage after two of them vomited on the dancefloor. The security guard on the door at Damage said that it took about twenty minutes to move them along once they had been thrown out. He said that they only left the area when two large Austrian men walked past on the street, and our three idiot guests had the bright idea that it would be screamingly funny to follow them, making Neanderthal noises and trailing their knuckles along the ground.

Really, the incredible stupidity of the human race does give occasional pause for thought.

Anyway. No-one is quite sure what happened in the intervening time, but the first shots were heard at about two forty-five. It struck me as strange the first time I heard a witness give a statement to that effect, because I had not been phoned until forty-five minutes later, and I had been under the impression that I had been phoned within minutes of Idiot Gary hitting the deck. All became clear however when Inspector Frantz produced his evidence bag and explained that the cartridges they had recovered from the guests' bedroom were BB pellets, and that the most logical explanation for this whole sorry affair was that the Idiot Three staggered back from Damage to the hotel (presumably dragging their knuckles on the ground) to amuse themselves taking pot shots off their balcony at passing strangers. Someone, it would appear, was not quite so amused, and came back with a real gun about half an hour later. The mystery shooter fired one round and disappeared. It's not clear whether he (or indeed she) intended the bullet to be a warning shot or to actually hit one of the three idiots, but since we will never know who the shooter was, no-one is investing a lot of time in agonising about this (aside from Idiot Gary, I expect).

What is very clear is that Idiot Gary was very, very lucky. The bullet came extremely close, but actually missed him by about two centimetres. It ricocheted off the wooden railing just in front of where he was standing and disintegrated, which was a lucky thing for him, since he then ended up with eight bullet fragments in his leg rather than, well, a stump.

Post-dramatic sigh. Back at the staff chalet now and pretty bloody exhausted after the day that's been in it, though definitely on a bit of a high from the excitement and intrigue of it all. Now secretly fancy myself as a bit of a Jessica Fletcher, running around resort, solving all manner of complicated murder mysteries and grisly deaths.

00.12am

Though there are never really any murders or grisly deaths to speak of in Reschengel, not even this time.

00.14am

And, come to think of it, I didn't even solve this one.

00.15am

But I totally would have, if I hadn't had to be at the airport all day.

Rachel and I are now discussing over a little glass of wine in the kitchen the possibility of law enforcement in the Alps as a viable career plan. We resolve to investigate this further.

Monday 26 March
4.40pm
I fell asleep last night the instant my head touched the pillow. It was lovely to wake up feeling normal today, but then it all came crashing back as soon as I walked into the kitchen this morning.

Oh. I stood at the counter, facing the tiles, thinking about filling the kettle. Rachel walked in behind me in her fuzzy pyjamas just then and, without a word, wrapped her arms around my waist.

'One cup of tea at a time, sweet pea. It gets better.'

She was right. I already feel a bit better, now that I am getting used to the idea of regularly being punched in the stomach every time (approximately every fifteen minutes) I think of the name 'Elisa.'

Today would be easier if it weren't for the general mood of anti-climax after all the fun of yesterday (sorry, Gary, but it *was* fun). The blood on the floor and furniture of the Club Hotel has all been cleaned up and heavy throws acquired from Fritz Spitzer to cover up the stains on the sofas. Gary was patched up yesterday by the doctor, the shrapnel was removed and he and his vile friends were dispatched by taxi this morning to the nearest airport (at their own expense) and told in no uncertain terms by the Polizei that they are no longer welcome in the Austrian Alps. 'Take your thuggery elsewhere,' was the best translation I could come up with. Although this didn't quite capture the fullness of Inspector Frantz's contempt, I think they got the essence of it from his facial expression. I don't expect to see their names on a guest manifest any time soon.

I didn't speak to James even once at the airport yesterday. The day's work presented me with no pressing need to deal with him, and with Rachel determined to take her human-shield role very seriously, (I actually think she would have taken a bullet for me) I didn't even have to look at him. When evening rolled around, I just silently handed him my sign-out paperwork and left. He has not tried to contact me since that one phone call.

I should feel pleased to have had the last word and to have coolly retained my pride, but I just feel empty. I hate this. I don't want to score points; I want my friend back. I miss him. I miss him so bloody much.

But then I think about Elisa again.

On another note entirely, I still haven't seen Suzanne.

Tuesday 27 March

9.35am

Text message, oh. Stupidly, I always start a little when I hear my phone beep. *James?*

No, Poppy. Even if it's James, it doesn't matter.

Yes, but, James?

No, on this occasion, yet again. It's Jon:

'Please come skiing today, Poppy? Haven't seen you in so long. Almost three weeks! Are you OK? Are you alive?!'

I take a deep breath and try to suppress the urge to shout at him, or cry, or both. *How could you know and not tell me? How could you let me find out like that?*

I close my eyes.

I'm leaving here soon. It's going to be OK then.

Me: 'Hi. I'm fine. Can't come skiing today, really busy.'

Jon: 'Can I be honest, please? I am worried about you.'

Me: 'No need. I'm fine, just busy.'

Wednesday 28 March

12.04pm

It's been a week.

Anna came over to the Reschengel side of the tracks this morning to ski with Rachel and me. She hasn't said a word about any of it, but I appreciate the gesture although I do slightly resent that her being here has stopped me from bailing out and crawling back into bed after an hour.

There really are far too many female ski instructors on the slopes.

That's all I have to say about that.

Thursday 29 March
7.22pm

The chalet is quiet now. Everyone has gone across the road to Happy Bar, except Suzanne, who is still hiding over at the hotel. I have no idea why and don't care.

I'm sitting in the kitchen with a cup of tea and trying to read a book of Mikey's about a fishing trawler, but I'm not getting very far with it. It's been nine days since I last spoke to James and the silence is pressing down on me now. I need it be over. I need the whole sorry affair to end properly, not fade slowly into the confused and bitter memory of a person who was so much to me and then suddenly nothing; a friendship and a deep affection that vanished in the space of a few slipped words, a silence, and a goddamn text message.

I know that I should let myself be distracted by Reschengel and my friends, by Gina's drama and everything else that is going on over here, but I just want to hear his voice. I want him to fight to win me back. I want him to at least give me the opportunity to tell him quietly and calmly to fuck off and die. Most of all, I want it to not be as simple as it looks: that he never, ever felt a thing; that I'm gone from his life, and he doesn't even notice the difference.

Saturday 31 March
4.45pm

Ringing phone breaks through my nap.

'Poppy?'

'Tilly? Is that you?'

'Yes, errm, hi. Are you still ill, or are you up and about?' She sounds strange.

'I'm OK. What's up?'

'I need your help.'

'What with?'

'It's… I'm at the Elena and I've just found something of a

336

plumbing emergency.'

'A what?' I say sharply, sitting bolt upright and hitting my head on the wire underlay of Tina's bed.

'A plumbing emergency,' she repeats. 'Well, more of crisis, really. Can you come?'

'Of course, of course,' I say, with visions of water cascading down the beautiful stone walls and warping the wooden floors, with Tilly ankle-deep and sobbing in the midst of it all. 'I'll be there in five minutes.'

5.03pm

Plumbing crisis turns out to be a giant shit in the downstairs toilet. I look darkly at Tilly.

'Yes, yes, yes. I know that it is a shit. It won't flush away though, look.' She flushes the toilet. 'See?'

It is still there. I flush the toilet again. It doesn't budge. She is right. It is wedged firmly in there. To be fair, it is the largest shit I have ever seen. Could win an award, if such an award category existed.

We look at one another. She sighs a heavy sigh of despair, her porcelain brow wrinkled in consternation.

'What does one *do* in this situation?'

I can't help it. I really try to hold a serious face but I feel it slipping away. She looks at me, startled, and then her face crumples and she too loses control.

When we eventually calm down, my sides hurt and my face aches. 'Oh, Tilly. You have to laugh, eh?'

'Or else you'd cry,' she finishes, without thinking. I look at her for a long minute. 'What?' she says, looking confused.

'You're right,' I say simply. 'It's one or the other, isn't it?'

'Err, yes,' she looks sideways at me uncertainly, as though I might do something erratic at any moment.

'Come on,' I declare, exhaling properly for the first time in what feels like a long time. 'Let's get out of here. I need a drink.'

'I thought you were feeling poorly?'

'I was. But I have decided to feel awesome instead.'

337

'Just like that?'

'Just like that. Let's go to the Flying Hirsch. I think some of the others might be there already. And who knows? Maybe the Swedish boys have a large disposable plastic knife we can borrow.'

Tilly makes ill noises and follows me.

'I hope you realise that *I'm* not slicing it up.'

APRIL

The Melt

Wednesday 4 April
10.23pm. The Flying Hirsch.

April is here now and with it, undeniably, is spring. Up to now, it's been easy to ignore the change in the months. Yes, the days got a little longer, but the guest manifests were always chock-full, the ski schools heaving and the guest properties filled to capacity. And with so much crammed into each working day, it never felt like the time was slipping past; it was just full.

But this month is different. The ice-cold edge is suddenly gone from the air, replaced by the faintest hint of grass and sunshine as the spring thaw begins at village level. The tourist office announced three days ago that the lifts will shut in three weeks. Three weeks! The end of season is almost upon us.

This realisation is having a mixed effect on the seasonaire population. Some people, panicked by the imminent end of days, are scrambling to get out there while the snow is still skiable and wring the last out of all the secret spots they love so much, ticking off all the challenges they have waited all season to work up the courage for. Others, however, take the view that the snow is already 'gone to shit,' and spend their days lying out in the sunshine at Taps Bar terrace, the Moose or a handful of other spots in and above the village, occasionally going for a run on a slushy spring-snow piste or hauling themselves up to the park to spectate.

For my part, I have made a new month's resolution to pitch all the upset, pain, misery etc. of last month into the emotional void. I can't waste the last three weeks here. I have no idea what I will be doing in the next few months, but I do know where I have to be come September. I'll be damned if I waste my last months of pre-Mc-Intyre freedom on being furious with James Walker and with myself.

Instead I will be back to normal, beginning immediately. I will feel nothing but fun, think nothing but pleasant thoughts and will not let the anger creep up on me in moments alone. It's time to cheer the fuck up.

I'm not even going to be angry with Jon any more. He had his reasons, no doubt, for keeping the truth from me. So did Anna, and curiously, I'm not even particularly annoyed with her. Yes, I expected more from Jon, so it's taking an effort, sitting here in the Flying Hirsch across the table from him but, objectively speaking, he was in the same position and so I have resolved to feel the same toward him.

'Here's to the lovely Lady T,' said Mark, raising his glass as the final, enthusiastic chords of 'Happy Birthday' faded away.

'Happy birthday, beautiful,' he added with a gentle smile, clinking Tilly's glass.

Tilly blushed. 'Thanks, everyone,' she began. 'I have to say, I really was not…'

'Ho, ho, ho!' a voice broke in. 'What's this? A little party, *ja?*'

It was Jan, leering at the group and swaying slightly. Rachel, who was nearest to him, stood up. 'Did you want something Jan?'

He ignored her and pushed past, staring at the birthday cake on the table. 'A birthday, I see!' he exclaimed, still staring fixedly at the cake. 'Ho, ho! I am sorry my invitation got lost along the way!' He lurched forward and stuck a long, thin finger into the centre of the cake, pulled out a clump of sponge and icing and sucked it with a loud smacking noise. 'Good cake!'

My mouth opened in shock. At least five people went to stand up but before anyone could do anything, Tilly was on her feet.

'You are not welcome here, Jan,' she said in her clipped way. She placed her hands on her hips, towering over his short frame. Her voice was steady although she was flushed with anger. 'Please leave us in peace.'

Jan made a face at her, reached out and squeezed her shoulder. 'Relax! A little bit – how do you say it? – "PMT" are you now, Hilda? Or is it old age? Ho, ho!'

'My name is Tilly,' she said angrily, and swiped his hand off her shoulder. He went to replace it. It occurred to me then that he must have been drunk. That or he underestimated Tilly (which to be fair, we all did, because what she did next surprised us all). 'Don't touch me, you vile creature,' she spat and, quick as a flash, reached up and pinched his ear so hard he yelped. 'Now, quietly fuck off, please,' she said in a voice just loud enough that everyone in the small bar could hear her, steering him away from our table, 'and don't come back to this table unless invited.'

She let go of him, wiped her hand in disgust on her jeans and turned to sit back down. Jan hesitated for a moment, stunned and rubbing his ear as our table burst out laughing and Arthur high-fived everyone within reach.

'You little bitch,' hissed Jan, and lunged forward to pull her by the hair. Mark was too quick however. He stepped in, grabbed Jan's wrist and quietly escorted/manhandled him out the door.

Mark returned five anxious minutes later.

'Are you OK?' asked Tilly, jumping up as he walked in.

'I'm fine,' he smiled at her and squeezed her hand. 'Poor Jan isn't though.'

'Did you kill him?' asked Rachel, her eyes wide.

Mark laughed. 'No.'

'Oh.' Rachel was disappointed. 'Injure him? Knock him unconscious? Ooh,' she got really excited, 'did you break his beaky nose?'

'No, matey, sorry to disappoint. He started to get quite aggressive outside but then he just wandered off. I hope he finds his way home tonight.'

'I hope he doesn't,' said Tilly emphatically, taking a wobbly drink from her glass.

Mark put his arm around her shoulders and said something quietly in her ear. They both seemed to have forgotten that we were all there as she smiled a small smile, said, 'I know,' and laid her head gently on his shoulder as he kissed her forehead. A few seconds passed before they both realised at exactly the same moment what they had done and both looked up from their twined hands to see a table of stunned faces.

'Oh dear,' said Jon, beaming at them, 'now look what you have done.'

'Secret's out,' said Head, clapping his hands and punching Nick on the bicep. 'I win, buddy. Fifty euro, wasn't it?'

'Fifty kroner, I think you'll find,' said Nick mildly.

'You *knew?*' said Rachel incredulously, looking at Jon and Head, and then at Nick.

Nick shrugged. 'They made us promise.'

'How long ago did you find out?'

'A couple of months, I'm not sure.'

'*What?*'

'*I* knew,' said Miranda smugly.

'Tilly!' I said, still in disbelief. 'Mark! I can't believe you kept this a secret. I can't believe you never told me. I see you at the Elena *every day*. How could you keep this from me?'

'Poppy, mate, it's actually your fault we went on so long keeping it a secret. We absolutely could not believe that you didn't spot it,' said Mark grinning at me. 'It got quite funny after a while.'

'Yes,' smiled Tilly, 'we thought that you were just being incredibly discreet. It was only after about a month that we realised it that you just had absolutely no idea. Nick thought you'd get to the end of season without noticing.'

'Oh, come on,' I was indignant, 'you were *hiding* it from us. Of course I didn't spot the signals.'

'Pops, you walked in on us kissing in the kitchen.'

'I thought you really did have something in your eye.'

'Twice?'

'I thought you might be prone to eye problems.'

I genuinely had thought that. How gullible am I? Of *course* I should have spotted it months ago. Have I been walking around this resort with my eyes closed? What else have I been missing?

Thursday 5 April
10.12am. Bed.

Still reeling from Mark and Tilly's shock revelation. I really cannot believe that between Rachel and I there does not exist the investigative instinct to recognise a blatant cover-up right under our noses. We are now seriously concerned that we might not after all have what it takes to be great crime-fighting heroines like the great J. Fletcher.

I'm also growing increasingly disillusioned by the minute, as it has just occurred to me that said Jessica Fletcher would not still be in bed at this hour, but would be up and about, utilising every moment of her day off to go find corpses and clues and things, whereas we are still arguing over who should get up and make the first cup of tea.

'Shut up, it is categorically not my turn.'

'Yes, well I have temporarily lost the use of my legs and arms. Only tea will cure me, you know.'

'I'm bored of arguing about this. Let's get Tom up. He'll do it.'

Rachel gropes for her phone and a voice calls out from the next room, 'Rachel, don't even think about phoning me. I am not making you tea.'

'I'll buy you a Schinken-Käse toast later.'

'No, you won't.'

'I might.'

'Sod off. I'm sleeping.'

'No, you're not.'

'Nor is anybody else,' comes Harry's grumpy voice.

'Oh, goody, you're up, Harry,' says Rachel brightly. 'Fancy making us a cup of tea?' A long silence follows, and no tea appears to be forthcoming. 'Go in there, Pops, see if they're up.'

'Are you kidding? Into that biohazard?'

'Look anyway,' Rachel was still vexed about Mark and Tilly, 'what do we even call it? I mean, as a scandal? "M-illy"?'

'No, that's way too confusing. How about "Till-ark"?'

'No, that's rubbish. What about…hang on, what's Tilly short for?'

'Good question: Matilda, maybe?'

'Hmm. Then "Matild-ark"?'

'Err, no. No, no, no. That sounds like a prehistoric creature. We want something with a bit more of a ring to it, like "Brangelina" or "Bennifer."'

We think about it a little more, listening to the gentle snoring coming from Tina's bed.

'Mar-tilda? Is that a bit naff?' Rachel asks tentatively.

'Yes. It is.'

'I cannot believe how much mental energy we are committing to this,' says Rachel after a few minutes.

'I know. It seems almost wrong.'

'Particularly on our day off. At the very least such a casual waste of brain function should be done on Snowglobe's time.'

'True. Let's adjourn this conversation until visits tomorrow evening.'

'Agreed.'

'Make me tea.'

'No.'

'Curse you!'

My shoe makes the noise of an incoming text message. *Great, that solves that mystery.* Had no recollection of seeing my phone for most of last night and had been mildly, passively concerned that I had lost it in the Hirsch, a flushing toilet or similar.

'Who is it?' asks Rachel. 'Fuckwit?'

She isn't serious, but she is right. I fish my phone out of my shoe and there is a text message from James.

James? I stare in disbelief at the name in my inbox, the certainty that I would never hear from him again crumbling to dust. Suddenly, it's new again.

'What?' shrieks Rachel, sitting up in her bed, 'Really? Really? It's James?'

'Shuddup,' moans Tina.

'What does it say, Poppy?' whispers Rachel.

'He wants to meet me. He wants to talk.'

Rachel is out of her bed and over to mine like a shot. 'You're joking.' She grabs the phone and reads the message. 'Is he for real?'

James: 'Can we please talk? Can I come and see you?'

'Well?' says Rachel, watching me. 'Are you going to reply?'

'Hmm,' I murmur absently, still looking at my phone. What to say in response, I wonder, if anything? Many things flood to mind (all along the lines of 'have a chat with yourself.') Eventually, I shrug. 'I'm going to take a leaf out of your book, Rach, and tell him exactly what I think.'

'That he should crawl away and die of syphilis in a gutter somewhere?' asks Rachel hopefully.

'What *I* think, muppet.'

'How can you not think that?'

Me: 'No need. I haven't got anything to say to you.'

After a brief, herculean struggle with Rachel over the inclusion or exclusion of the suffix 'twat-face,' I press 'send.'

James responds almost immediately: 'Please, Poppy. Things are not as simple as you think. I've been having issues with another girl, but I think you have misunderstood what that's about. I would like to explain what's been going on.'

'He's got some bloody nerve, hasn't he?' Rachel whistles quietly in wonder. 'Does he not realise that you know?'

'Actually, no. I don't think so,' I say, and I can hear that my voice is still calm and level, though now it sounds strange and distant to me, like an annoying noise that's breaking my concentration on something else. I swallow hard as I stare at the words on the screen and think about Elisa. *Elisa and James.* 'Anna hasn't told him that she spoke to me. I suppose he thinks that I am under the vague impression that he has, or had, another girl in Futterberg at some point this winter, but that I probably don't know a lot more detail than that. He thinks that what I know, I know from what his mate Danny let slip.'

Rachel's eyes widen and she rubs her hands together. 'Oh, the potential for messing with him, Pops…'

I shake my head, barely listening now. *Another girl.* I can't believe James has used those words to me in a text message. Those words, after weeks of silence. What on earth is he trying to achieve?

I put my phone down and walk into the kitchen. *Do I want to see him?* I wonder as I pour water into the kettle and switch it on. *No, I want to ignore him.*

Bullshit, Poppy, you want to want *to ignore him. But you also want answers.*

Argh, though. No. Do I really want to understand? To hear him explain? Or perhaps even apologise? The stifling blanket of tingly anger is descending upon me again, blocking out everything else I had been thinking about and dragging my mood all the way back to the place it has been fighting to escape from for the past few weeks. *Damn you, James, for pushing your voice back inside my head. Why couldn't you just leave me alone?*

Rachel's voice cuts through the strange twisting mess of my rising fury and sinking heart. 'What would you to say to him if he came over?'

'I don't know. Can seeing him really make anything better?'

'Only if you use the opportunity to tell him what you think of him, and in no uncertain terms.' Her eyes are a mixture of concern and determination as she hands me my phone again. 'Make him tell you the truth. Make him take some fucking responsibility for himself.'

I pick up my phone again, not knowing what I am going to reply until the message is typed and sent.

Me: 'What's been going on, James, is very simple. You have slept with someone else. I'm not that interested in hearing all the details.'

Rachel frowns. 'That's a lot more vague than I'd... Ah.' She smiles as she reads it through again. 'Yes, very good, Connors.'

'Let's see what he does with that, eh?'

12.18pm

It took James a little longer to respond to that message. Eventually, I received a reply.

348

'Poppy, please believe me, it is more complicated than that. Can we meet? There are things you don't understand. Give me the chance to explain. I don't want you to hate me.'

I don't hate you, James, I thought, but I do understand. I understand you better than you would like me to.

I arranged to meet him in the Mondschein at five. It is the perfect location for a meeting I have such very mixed feelings about. It's low-key, discreet and empty of seasonaires. And, I think with a small smile, there is the added bonus that the regulars will run him through with that pitchfork if and when I give the nod.

Rachel is excited beyond all proportion by the prospect. '*Ohmygod* what I wouldn't give to be a fly on the wall when you catch him out. I would love to see his face. Please, please, please wear a headcam?'

'No.'

'Do you think Traudl would wear a wire?'

'No.'

'You're no fun. Wait…do you reckon we could get someone to shoot him in the leg on the way out?'

Friday 6 April
9.14pm. Staff chalet.

James was waiting outside the Mondschein when I arrived just after five. He was unfamiliar in pale, baggy denim jeans and a grey hoodie I didn't recognise.

'Hi.'

'Hi.'

Neither of us knew quite what to do. He almost went to hug me, but then thought better of it and made a joke instead about how he had waited for me outside because he was terrified of being alone in the bar after everything I had told him about it. I found an empty booth in the corner while he went to order us both a drink. He sat down across from me and another awkward minute passed as neither of us knew where to look nor what to

349

do. James' eyes wandered around the room and I studied my hands. We waited for Traudl to bring the drinks to the table so that we could concentrate on them. He cleared his throat nervously. 'Snow's still good, isn't it?'

I nodded. Traudl appeared. She looked questioningly from James to me as she unloaded the tray, but she said nothing and left us to it. I felt like telling her to sharpen the prongs as he sat there, sipping his beer and making small talk about Thurlech, Anna's latest fling and the snow conditions up on the mountain at the moment. This was harder than I had thought it would be. My left thigh was twitching with the effort of not letting my foot tap.

I interrupted him after a few minutes. 'What did you come here to say to me, James?'

He seemed thrown by this. 'Well, I...' he hesitated, groping for words, 'I suppose I just... well, I wanted us to talk again. It's been ages since I've heard from you. I've been worried about you,' he said, furrowing his brow. 'I wanted to check that you're all right.'

'I'm fine,' I said, though I hated the tightness in my voice and hoped that he couldn't hear it.

'Good. Good.' He nodded, unclasping his hands to take another gulp of his beer. 'So, how have things been over here? How is Gina's pregnancy going?'

'James, stop it,' I said. I didn't bother to conceal the irritation in my voice. I was not there for a passive reconciliation by small talk. 'Are you here to explain yourself or not?'

He blinked, opened his mouth and closed it again, but recovered quickly. 'Yes, well, sort of,' he started, sounding a little defensive, then clearly thought better of that strategy and went more for the offensive, 'I mean I'm not sure I like your turn of phrase, but I am here to clear up some misconceptions you seem to be labouring under.'

My eyebrows went up and I couldn't help but smile a little at his tone. 'Go ahead,' I said, sitting back, waiting, watching him.

He looked down at the table and then up at me again from under his brows as though wondering if I would hold him to it, then sighed deeply and ran his hands through his hair, his eyes darting across the faded old photographs and stuffed creatures mounted on the wall behind me as he gathered his thoughts.

'It's been really hard,' he began, hunching his shoulders and staring down at his beer.

I'll bet, I thought, and wanted to punch him, but then thought of Rachel and realised that it was about time I started saying these things aloud. 'I'll bet.'

'Poppy, please,' James said with the patient condescension of an adult to a child, 'relax.'

My fingernails dug into my palms as I battled to keep a neutral face. James shook his head and looked me in the eye. 'You obviously think that all of this has been very easy on me.'

'Has it not?'

'No. No, it hasn't, actually,' and he was getting increasingly agitated and self-righteous, 'It's been fucking hard work and not that much fun at all.'

'That's odd,' I replied, holding his eye, 'because I would have thought that sleeping around and getting away with it for so long would have been rather a lot of fun for you, though somewhat less for us girls. Or were the others all OK about me?'

'Others?' He gave a little laugh. 'What "others"?' he asked, half-smirking as though both amused and amazed at how utterly ridiculous I was being. I felt the colour rise in my cheeks. *Was it time to leave yet?*

'I'm assuming that there must have been more than one,' I said coldly. 'You've had months, haven't you? And all the way over there, with nothing to hold you back and no way of us ever finding out about each other. You knew what I expected from you, James – it wasn't a lot, and you should have respected it or you should have left me alone.'

'Poppy, what on earth are you on about?'

'Don't insult my intelligence, James. I wasn't in love with you, you know,' I said contemptuously, though aware that I was still not sure how true that statement was. 'You should have just been honest with me. You should have told me whenever it happened that I stopped holding your interest. In fact, maybe we should have just left it at a drunken one-night stand. God knows I wouldn't have missed out on much and it would have saved you from wasting so much mental energy thinking up convincing lies.'

'Poppy, seriously, what?' He shook his head as though baffled. 'Where on earth have you got the idea that I've been sleeping around?'

'Accumulated evidence, James,' I said breezily, watching for his reaction.

He blinked once and his eyes narrowed slightly. I waited for it, and it came. 'Did you not think to maybe to check your "accumulated evidence" with me first?' he asked. 'Did you not think that maybe there might be another explanation?'

'Is there?'

'Yes, actually, there is.' I sat back and took a sip from my drink. He cleared his throat. 'The "other girl" you've been getting so worked up about is my *ex*.'

'Your ex.'

'Yes,' he said patiently, 'my ex. Jenny. I had no plans to ever see her again, but then she showed up again last month with bad news.'

He looked at me pointedly.

Oh, come on. You cannot be serious.

'You mean she is pregnant,' I said flatly.

He nodded rapidly. 'Yes. Or so she told me,' he qualified.

'So is she not?' I was going along with this and I wasn't sure why.

'No, of course not. She was lying, but I didn't realise that for weeks.' His face was angry and his eyes hard. 'I honestly don't know what she thought was going to come of all of it. I certainly had no interest in being with her again but I didn't really know what to do.'

'And now?' I asked in a bored voice.

Irritation flickered across his face again. He was disappointed with how slight a reaction he was getting from me. I think he might have actually been expecting a hug.

'I only found out the truth two weeks ago. I caught her

smoking and drinking one night so I cornered her and asked her what the fuck she was playing at. That was when she told me that it had all been a lie. I could have killed her.'

'Two weeks ago?'

'Yes. That was when I… that is, when we….'

'Yeah, I get it.'

'I was just so furious at what a mess she had made of my head.' He lifted his gaze from his clenched fists, looked me in the eye and said earnestly and without blinking, 'I'm so sorry, Poppy. It had nothing at all to do with us, but I wasn't thinking straight at that point.' He ran his fingers through his hair again and exhaled sharply. 'I just needed some space, you know?' He continued to stare at me with the same earnest expression. I broke his gaze, feeling mildly nauseated. 'I'm sorry,' James said again, reaching across the table for my hand.

I reached for my drink. It was so weak, such an unbelievably poor story, that I didn't even know where to begin. I could have just said, 'Right, yes, I follow you so far. But where does Elisa fit into all this? You know, the ski instructor you have been sleeping with for the past three months?' It was also tempting to go with the time-honoured response in such situations: throw my drink in his face and leave without another word.

I didn't do either. My fingertips tingled but I didn't move. I could feel him watching me, waiting for my answer. The words were on my tongue – *I know the measure of what you are, fool. I'm watching you lie to me without blinking* – but I felt the desire to speak them wash away in a cold wave, leaving me numb of any wish to confront him. He had gambled on the chance that nobody had told me any specific details, and he had lost in the worst way a person can. I was back in the Nordhang lift station on that awful, sad day, watching the face of the friend I loved as it turned into the face of a stranger, someone I couldn't get angry with, or yell at, or cry for, because I didn't even know him.

'It's all over now, though,' he went on, taking my silence as encouraging. 'She's gone. The whole sorry mess is resolved and everything is back to normal.' I nodded vaguely, still looking at my drink. 'I'm sorry that in all of that I hurt you,' he said gently, 'but I would like to make it right.'

'How do you plan to do that?'

'Let's be friends. Can we be friends?'

'Friends?'

'I know that things won't be the same as they were with us. I'm not an idiot, but I don't want to lose your friendship over this.'

You mean my good opinion. After all this, he still just wanted me to think well of him. I looked at him and wondered for the millionth time what Elisa was doing at that moment.

I heard Rachel's voice in my head. She was telling me to tell him to fuck off and die, but those words deflated and died inside me too, and I sat there silent, just nodding in the same absent way, wanting suddenly for it to end quickly and with a minimum of conversation.

We left the Mondschein soon after. Traudl looked disappointed as the door closed behind us. I wondered idly if Rachel had told her what was going on, and whether she might have actually had some sort of implement to hand the entire time – certainly a substantial frying pan, at the least. Shame.

We walked down the steps to street level, blinking in the glare of the still-bright daylight after the gloom of the bar. James stopped. He was heading left toward the car park; I was going right, back up the road to the staff chalet.

'Goodbye, James,' I said, 'safe home.'

'"Safe home,"' he smiled. 'You and your funny provincial expressions.' He gazed at me, still smiling and said softly, 'I'm really glad you understand. Come here.' He pulled me into a tight hug. 'It would have been such a waste.'

I closed my eyes as he held me. He smelled exactly the same as always. He held me in his arms the same way he always had done. The stubble of his cheek felt exactly the same against the softer skin of mine and, as he pulled back slightly and turned his face toward mine to kiss me gently on the lips, it felt as it always had.

I kissed him back and in that moment, that close to him, I

354

could pretend for the length of a kiss that nothing had changed, that nothing had died.

I pulled myself out of his arms and walked away. I didn't look back, and I don't think for one second that James did either. I walked up the hill feeling empty, though in a rather different way to when I arrived.

*

'So?' Rachel bounced out of the kitchen and tackled me as soon as I walked in the door of the staff chalet. 'How did it go? Tell me everything. Leave nothing out. What did you *say*?'

I shook my head slightly and walked past her into our room. She followed me.

'Poppy?'

I took off my jacket, hung it up and began to rummage in the wardrobe for my uniform.

'Hey, look at me.' Rachel was frowning. 'What happened? What did he say?'

'Nothing I wasn't expecting.'

'Oh, OK. So you gave him hell then?' she smiled expectantly.

'No. Not really.'

'Eh? Why not?'

I shrugged and turned away again.

'Poppy?'

'It's done, Rachel.'

'Yes, but what did you say to him about Elisa?'

'It wasn't worth it.'

I felt her hand on my shoulder. She turned me around to look her in the face, still frowning.

'Please tell me what happened.'

I told her everything, leaving out the part where I kissed him back, because I thought she might slap me. (I might still slap me for that.) She was shocked enough by the abridged version, to the point of being almost angry with me.

'But...' she struggled to think of the question that might

355

deliver an answer from me that she could comprehend, 'but why did you not tell him that you know about Elisa? I don't understand.'

I walked back into the kitchen and put on the kettle. 'It would have achieved nothing,' I said after a few minutes.

'Nothing?' Rachel was sitting on the kitchen table, watching me through narrowed eyes. 'It would have shown him...'

'I mean for me. I don't know what I went there expecting him to say, but he couldn't say it, whatever it was. That much became obvious pretty quickly and I wasn't going to hang about and make him tell me all about her. I had to leave.'

'So he still doesn't...?'

'I don't care what he thinks or doesn't think. I don't even know him.'

'You should have made him apologise, Poppy.'

'Why? He wouldn't have meant it.'

I felt Rachel's eyes on me as I poured two cups of tea and handed one to her.

'So what happens next?'

'Nothing. It's done.'

'It's done,' she repeated incredulously. 'You do realise that you will have to see him in the airport for the next two weeks, don't you? What are you going to do, go for lunch? Talk about the weather? Did you really send him off on his merry way thinking that today's little show was enough to make it all OK?'

I made a face. 'No. I don't know. It's... I need to think about it more.' She made a sputtering noise. 'Don't, Rachel,' I waved it away. 'I'm not getting angry about this. I just want to erase it from my life.'

'But you *are* angry. You can't just decide it's time to switch that off. You should have let him have it when you had the...'

'You don't understand.' It was exhausting even just arguing with her.

'*I* don't understand? Poppy, you have lost your mind. First this thing with Jon that no-one understands, least of all you: you just cut him out completely to punish him for, as far as I can see, having absolutely nothing whatsoever to do with you getting hurt – and don't you bother denying it – and now, finally when you get the chance to let rip, you turn around and let James just walk all...'

'*Stop, Rachel*,' I snapped. 'Leave Jon out of this. It's got nothing to do with him. It's got nothing to do with anything anymore. It's done. This thing with James is finished now. It happened because I let it happen, and there's no taking it back. Yelling at him won't undo that. It won't make her disappear.'

'But he can't just...'

'Rachel, *shut up*. Please, please just shut up, OK? I know you want to help but just...*stop*.'

She hesitated, blinking, then nodded, placing a warm hand on my arm. I tried a small smile and left the room for the perilous balcony and a cigarette I didn't want.

Sunday 8 April

12.42pm

Oh, dear. Behave, Rachel. She was on fire this morning. I had to make her promise before I she left on her coach this morning that I wouldn't arrive in Salzburg to find the waxy-pale unconscious form of an area manager lying in a pool of blood on the floor of the arrivals hall.

'Fine. I won't *initiate* the violence, but if he slips and falls over – say on my knife or something – I can't promise anything.'

She did remarkably well until about eleven o'clock, when James called us all together for a briefing on the day's incoming flights. 'Right, you lot, listen up. The Manchester flight is delayed. It's still on the ground in the UK. Something about a passenger illness or something. Basically, it's caused a bit of a reshuffle of things, so it will be landing over at Main terminal instead of here.'

'So, the guests won't be coming through Charter Arrivals?' asked Emma, looking scared.

'No, Emma,' said James, with supercilious sarcasm that made

the other reps giggle, 'not Charter. Just Main. One terminal is all a plane needs, generally. Unless something very unfortunate happens on landing, of course.' He stared at her until she blushed scarlet, then cast his eyes to heaven. 'Otherwise everything's running pretty much OK from the UK end. In terms of coach allocations, who's on coach 151 to Reschengel? Rachel, that's yours, isn't it?'

'Yes.' Rachel's tone was ice, but James didn't appear to notice.

'Right. Jan has told me that it will be a fifty-seater, not a sixty-two. You only have fifty-three on that list anyway, right? So what we'll do is take three of them and move them to Tom's coach, right?'

'That would make sense,' she said frostily.

'Yeah. Right, so make sure that you pick the three lucky people from the arrivals off the *last* flight to land, yeah? The Bristol flight, and not an earlier one, yeah?'

'OK.'

Her face shouted, *you don't say, fuckwit,* but James was looking at his clipboard.

'And make sure that they find Tom and know to get on his coach. And that none of their bags end up on your coach.'

'OK, James. I think I can manage.'

He looked back up at her then and said slowly and deliberately, 'OK, when that's done I want you to make sure that you have crossed their names from *your* passenger list, so that you're not still head-counting for fifty-three. You'll only have fifty, yeah? Do you understand?'

'Yes, James.'

'Right. I don't want any fuck-ups on this,' said James curtly. 'Tom, make sure you remember to add three to your list. Write "plus three" at the end. Rachel, I want you to write "minus three on yours." Do it now.'

'James,' spat Rachel so icily that the amassed group of reps looked up simultaneously from their clipboards. 'You are speaking to me as though I am about half as intelligent as you. I think we both know that that is not the case.'

I thought Anna was going to fall over. She looked from Rachel to me and back again with barely-concealed delight. James' mouth opened slightly and his eyes were saucers as everybody giggled in that slightly nervous way when no-one is quite sure whether they are supposed to or not.

I willed him to shut up and take it. Fortunately he had the sense to realise that in this mood Rachel might say anything.

'That's it for now,' he said, calling over his shoulder as he turned his back on the group and walked back to his desk. 'Go on. Get lost, everyone. You've got twenty-five minutes before the next wave.'

I grabbed Rachel's arm and pulled her out the door towards the coffee shop.

'Sorry, sorry, sorry,' she said, 'I know, "behave." It just came out though.'

'Are you kidding? I love you.'

I hugged her tightly, grinning and feeling immensely better. The dignified silence of cool indifference is so much easier with mates like Rachel. I was very glad that next week is our last transfer day, all the same.

Gina glided into the coffee shop minutes later looking smug and sat down at our table. 'I don't know what has gotten into James,' she confided earnestly. 'He just had a go at me in front of Sarah Datchet about my skirt.' Gina has taken to wearing floaty gypsy skirts and Birkenstocks with her uniform jacket. She says that the elasticated waistbands take the pressure off her bump, though at barely eleven weeks, I suspect that she is being a little premature. 'I think he is really struggling with my pregnancy. I think it might be making him start to re-evaluate things, you know? Choices? Roads not taken, yah?'

'Mmm,' we all nodded.

'He needs peace,' she said, sipping her green tea. 'I think he would really benefit from a good programme of meditation. And of course the healing hand of friendship.'

'Or maybe a crystal?' Rachel suggested with a serious face. 'Maybe you should give him one of your healing crystals, Gina.'

Gina has been embracing the peace of Mamma Earth lately. Her apartment has been transformed into a feng shui-ed temple of organic chai teabags, panpipe music and dangling shiny, tinkly things. She has even started burning incense (though I have noticed that the incense smells remarkably like cigarette smoke at times).

'Maybe, maybe,' she mused. 'Anyway, Sarah Datchet told him that she had approved my skirt as temporary uniform until a maternity uniform can be found for me. James is not in the best mood now. I wouldn't rush back.'

'No plans to.'

Friday 13 April

4.56pm

Tonight, finally, I'm doing the Full Moon Ski. This is a long-running tradition in Reschengel and something Mikey has been pushing us to do since the start of season. Every full moon, provided the skies are clear, an intrepid group of season workers can usually be spotted making the taxi journey to Stüben after nightfall. Equipped with essential mountaineering equipment such as torches and bottles of prosecco, they wait until the piste groomers are finished and then set off for about an hour and a half's hike up the piste to the top of the Furggspitz lift. They arrive at midnight, pass around the bubbly and ski down into Reschengel by the light of the moon (hoping not to meet any kind of law enforcement officer along the way, since this is of course totally illegal).

Having not managed to get our act together to do this at any other full moon in the past four months, we have decided that tonight is our turn. When better than Friday the Thirteenth for executing a plan which brings together illegality and danger with such ingredients as high speed, darkness, invisible icy patches, snow cannons and other such immovable obstacles? Brilliant plan. Flawless. Inspired.

So far Mikey and I have recruited Carol, Eoghan and Harry, and Rachel has signed up the three Swedish boys. The taxis are booked for ten o'clock. We are due to set off on the long hike at ten-thirty. Which, when I think about it, sounds ridiculously energetic. A little nap first, I think.

A good deal later, under Furggspitz.

It's so beautiful, so strangely, unfamiliarly beautiful here. The night has made everything seem new and different, and so eerily quiet and peaceful. By day, the ridge is a bustling hive of activity, the lifts from Stüben and Reschengel meeting at this point and churning out hundreds of skiers and snowboarders every hour. But now the lifts are quiet, and the moonlight makes the wide expanse of the snowy ridge glow a blueish white against the

361

contrasting shadowy darkness of the forest on one side, and the stark rocky outcrops of the other. It feels like an undiscovered island. The sky above us is almost completely clear. The bright light from the moon catches the occasional small, dark puff of cloud and lights its edges with a glowing halo, and the rest of the sky flickers with the white light of an explosion of stars from horizon to horizon.

None of which I will fully appreciate until I manage to re-inflate my lungs. I totally underestimated the gruelling nature of climbing so far for so long, and am currently lying on the ground, heaving and gasping for blessed oxygen.

A shadowy shape looms above me, with a laugh and a voice I know so well, low and soft on the quiet midnight air.

'Are you still with us, Poppy? Do I need to start compressions?'

'No, it's too late.'

'Don't underestimate the healing power of prosecco,' says Jon, handing me a bottle. 'Or water,' he adds and hands me another. I sit up and drink gratefully from the water bottle. 'Better?'

'Thank you. You have reanimated me.'

'I'm glad you had not yet started to decompose. It's beautiful here, hey?' he says, surveying the valley.

'It's amazing,' I agree. 'I don't want to ski down. I could stay here all night.'

'Yes, but I don't recommend it. We tried that one year, camping up at the park, but we sort of misjudged how cold it can get here when you stay very still for a few hours, and...'

'And?'

'And that was how I lost three of my toes.'

'*Really?*' I ask, horrified.

'No, Poppy,' he laughs.

There is cigarette smoke on the air and the low hum of chat as everybody sits around enjoying the break after the long climb. There are about thirty of us here, a motley crew of season workers and ski bums, some of whom I don't recognise but others I know as staff from the Moose and Keller bars, the Diamond reps, a couple of chalet hosts from SuperSki and three ski technicians from Jürgen Sport 2000.

I lie back in the snow and stare up at the crisp night sky again, remembering my first night here in Reschengel so many months ago, how the stars seemed so impossibly many to me that night and how I thought I would never stop gazing at them in wonder. It really is incredible how quickly we stop actually seeing the things we see every day.

I can feel Jon's eyes on me. 'Poppy,' he says in his soft voice, 'I did something to upset you.'

I blink hard, staring up at the sky. 'Don't be daft, Jon,' I reply lightly, 'How many times have I seen your feet, for heaven's sake? I'm just looking at the stars.'

'No, no, not that,' he laughs, 'I mean...'

'No,' I say quietly, still staring at the sky, 'you haven't done anything wrong. I'm sorry I haven't been around so much recently. These past few weeks I've sort of just been staying afloat, to be honest.'

He waits for me to go on. There is a heavy pause as I struggle, wishing that he could just accept my apology and let us go back to the easy banter of friendship. I don't want to talk it through now, nor ever. I just want him to let it go.

'I believe you know about what happened with James?' I add eventually.

'Yes,' he says gently. 'Are you OK?'

'I'm fine now, yes. It's all sorted.'

He is still watching me, waiting to say something, or maybe waiting for me to speak. I don't know. I sit up again. This is getting awkward, so I mutter something about a paper cup and go to stand up.

'Poppy,' he says impatiently, 'where are you going?'

'Back over to the others. You coming?'

'Will you please stop this? Sit yourself down and be honest with me. Sit down now,' he waits for me to obey, and I do, surprised, 'and please explain to me exactly how I can make things right. I've hurt you, I know. But how can I know what to do to

363

help you when you won't even speak to me?'

'Jon, you haven't hurt me. We're fine. And I *am* speaking to you. I'm speaking to you right now, aren't I?'

'You know what I mean, Poppy. You know the difference.' He stares hard at me and I look away, back across the valley to where the moonlight catches the Silferhorn. 'Look, I'm sorry,' he says finally. 'Since that day on the mountain, I've been sorry for what I said. I had no right to offer you that judgement when you didn't ask for it and I have wanted to apologise for weeks, but you haven't let me say it. You've been avoiding me.'

'You have nothing to apologise for – not for offering an opinion, and not for what that opinion was. You were right, weren't you?' I laugh at little at that, a bitter, mirthless little laugh that makes my face feel strange. 'Spot on in fact. Perhaps too much so for me to handle. So like I say, it's me who should apologise, and I do.'

Jon tilts his head, still watching me closely. 'And we are OK?'

'We are,' I say, smiling at him as Carol calls to us to come over and prepare for the ski down.

'Good,' he says, standing up and offering me a hand to pull me to my feet. 'So you will come skiing with me tomorrow.'

It's not a question. I stand up and let go of his hand. 'The usual time?'

'I'll bring breakfast and the camera. You bring the chocolate bars.'

Saturday 14 April
1.42pm

The old familiar touring monster appeared on our doorstep after visits this morning equipped with croissants for breakfast and the news that conditions up on Schindlerspitz are really good at the moment, but that we need to get up and down before one o'clock, when the hot sun will begin to destabilise the snowpack.

I was ready to go when he arrived. We got up there in record

364

time and had a fantastic descent in perfect spring snow. Then for some odd reason (adrenaline? masochistic desire for self-harm?) I was feeling an excess of energy afterwards and suggested another run somewhere north-facing. Now we're on our merry way up Nordhang to the Rufigrat Ridge. And by 'merry way,' of course I mean that I am dying an exhausted death, while Jon has not even noticed that we are on a hill.

'Hey, Poppy?' Jon calls back to me excitedly.

'Yeah?' *Gasp, wheeze.*

'You know that couloir we saw the first time we came here? It might be in good shape to try out now, what do you think? Let's give it a look, eh?'

'The Couloir of Death?' *Wheeze, choke.*

'Oh, come now. Maybe The Couloir of Moderate Injury, but you're wearing a helmet. I promise I will let you go first. That way I can pick up the pieces if anything goes wrong, OK?'

I don't have the strength to argue. I'll save my best colourful language for when we get to the top.

Some time later.

I cannot believe what we have just done. What *I* have just done, rather, since it is all in a regular day for Jon. Holy crap. The nemesis. The terrifying nemesis. I have just skied the Couloir of Death.

And it was actually OK.

I can't stop grinning and turning to look back up at the white slice of snow in the black rock of the mountain face. I cannot believe I just came down through that. I cannot believe I was moving so *fast*. I need to do something. I need to tell someone. Haaa! This is so exciting. Here's Jon now.

'*OhmygodJon*, that was EPIC!'

He comes to a stop just below me on the slope, takes off his goggles and beams at me. 'Well done.' He squeezes my arm with his mitten. 'See, I knew that you would love it.'

'I can't believe it. I just…can't believe it. That was just such an incredible *rush*. The rock walls, the rock walls, Jon, they were like *three inches from my face.*' I shake my head, looking back up at it. 'I just don't know what to say.'

'That you want to do it again tomorrow?' he laughs, pulling out his water bottle and offering it to me.

'I'd love to,' I sigh, taking a drink. 'Maybe on Monday, if the snow is still good.'

'Of course, tomorrow is Sunday. Your last ever airport day, yes?'

'Yes,' I say, a little too forcefully, and then rush to explain myself. 'I mean, I'm not glad that the season is over. I'll just be happy never to darken the door of that arrivals hall ever again.' I could feel myself blushing. 'I'm just tired of…well, you know how guests can be, eh? And all that uniform-wearing, company flag-waving stuff. Did you know that Snowglobe's customer service motto is EXTRA MILE? You know what that stands for? "Everyday eXellence Takes Real Application. Make It Look Easy." I mean, come on. Personally, I would prefer "Customers Require All your Patience."'

I'm babbling. He is looking at me in that way he does, and I know that he can see through it. 'You'll have to see him there all day, won't you?' he says levelly.

'Yes.' I fumble for my transceiver, checking that it is still switched on and adjusting the straps slightly.

'That will be hard, with all those people around.'

'It's fine,' I say, looking past him at the slope. 'Shall we push on?'

Jon doesn't move. 'Are you ever going to talk to me about what happened with James? About why it ended?'

'Nope,' I say cheerily, 'no plans to.'

'Why not?'

'There's no need. It's done. It's over now.'

'Over?'

'Yes.'

'Poppy, it took me months to get over what happened with Emilie. It took months to even begin to get my head around it.'

'Yes, well, that was obviously different. You two had been

366

together for years.'

'It's not about how long you have been with someone. It's not even about the person in this sort of situation, is it?'

'Stop it, Jon, I don't want to...'

'What? Talk about it? Think about it? Deal with it in any way?'

'I don't want to let this waste any more of my time. It's done.'

He makes a face. 'Poppy, you can't just pretend...'

'I'm not pretending,' I interrupt calmly, 'but I'm also not going to wallow in it. "You have to laugh, eh?"'

He frowns as though this is the stupidest thing he has ever heard. 'No, you don't. You have to speak your mind.'

'*I* don't need to.'

'That is an idiotic thing to say. And you're lying, by the way.'

'How dare you judge me?'

'I'm not judging you,' he retorts impatiently, 'I'm just telling you that you need to stop being so ashamed of something that was not your fault.'

'I'm not ashamed,' I say automatically and, before I can stop myself, add, 'and it *was* my fault.'

He starts a little. I feel the colour fill my cheeks as he looks at me, his eyes soft. 'Poppy...'

I turn away. He reaches for my arm. 'Poppy, come here.'

'No!' I snarl, wrenching away from him. 'Stop it. Are you happy now? Just...fuck off, please, with your pity.'

'I don't pity you.' Jon pops out of his skis and marches over in front of me to where I can't ignore him. He takes me by the wrists and makes me look at him. 'I pity *him*. I *care* about you. I want to make it better, I just don't know how to if you won't even talk about it.'

'That *is* pity. And I don't need it. It's not your problem, Jon, and I don't need to be fixed by you. I'm managing just fine. Or at least I would be if you would just leave it the fuck alone.'

'Why are you so angry with me?'

'I'm not angry with you.'

He growls his frustration. 'You are. Why will you not say it?' He ducks his head to look me in the eye. 'Say it, Poppy.'

'OK, *FINE*,' I yell. 'So what?'

'So tell me why.'

'I can't. I don't...' and now my throat is hurting and my eyes are prickling with spikes of tears that I can't blink back. 'Because you *knew*,' I blurt out eventually. 'You saw it all along and you said it that day and you knew and I should have known. I should have known too.'

Damn it, my lip is wobbling now. Angrily, I scrub the tears from my eyes as his shadow falls over me and his hands are on my shoulders, gently taking the rucksack off my back and the helmet off my head and then he wraps me completely in his arms.

'It wasn't your fault,' he whispers in my ear.

'Yes, it was,' I say into his shoulder.

He pulls back from me and looks me in the eye, holding my cheek to wipe away a tear. 'You can't turn a good person into a liar and a coward by loving him too much,' he says gently.

'But I should have kept my eyes open. I should have known sooner.'

'It is not good to have a suspicious mind. You shouldn't need one.'

'It would have helped, though. It would have helped me to understand him and stopped me from bothering to care so much for someone so...'

'Weak?'

I nod miserably. 'And now he's over there with her, still getting exactly what he wants and what am I doing? Deleting half of my memories of the last few months. All the time spent away from here, running around with him, making up lies and excuses, annoying my friends and cancelling plans – and for what? Apparently nothing was happening after all.' I cough out a bitter little laugh. 'Just a whole lot of time wasted with a man who doesn't even exist. I'm such a fool. I'm a stupid, naive...'

'Shh,' he pulls me into his arms again as the tears return. This time I offer them no resistance. I just want relief from the worst part of all – to hear it said aloud, to hear why. 'Tell me,' and I am sobbing now, 'please just tell me. That day, when you said what

368

you said – you knew about *her*. Why didn't you tell me? Why did you let me find out like that?'

Jon pulls back again just enough that I can see his face. He looks horrified. 'Are you serious? *Fan!* No! Of course I didn't *know*. You're my Poppy; I would never have kept such a thing from you. I assumed that because of his reputation he would eventually disappoint you, but I didn't know if I was just being… *Jävlar,* if I had known that he was behaving like this already I would have tracked him down and killed him dead months ago. I might yet do it, you know. I get the camper van and go over there and…'

'…set the dinosaurs on him?'

I can't help but smile at the earnestness in his face as immense relief washes through me. *Jon would never have kept that from me.* I had no idea how much it had hurt me to have stopped trusting him until I finally could again. I pull him back to me and tell him that there is no need for righteous defence of my honour today, no need at all. He strokes my back gently and murmurs softly to me in his low, growly voice. I don't know what he is saying, but feel the warm comfort of his voice in my ear nonetheless. I relax in his arms and let the tears run slowly down my face, unashamed, for the first time since that sad afternoon last month when I told Rachel. Mostly, I know I'm crying for the disappointment, for how it felt at the beginning – for the man I thought I had in the fizzy, intoxicating excitement of those first weeks before the happiness was cut into by all the things I ignored and replaced by those slivers of reassurance I mistook for something else. Jon holds me close throughout, one hand on my back, the other slowly stroking my hair, and I feel with every ragged breath the big wall of sadness I have been building since that day cracking and crumbling a little more, the tension that held it together relaxing and dissipating in the gentleness of his embrace.

The tears subside surprisingly quickly. His hand is on my neck now and my whole body tingles with the gentle touch of his fingers on the little patch of soft skin under my hairline. His beard rubs gently against my cheek as he continues to speak softly in my ear, the same quiet words in Swedish I can't understand but I feel them soothe me. I take a deep, steady breath and smile into his shoulder as another wave of relief washes through me, a blissful lightness where the misery had been.

'Thank you, Jon.' He smiles back at me and cups my face with one hand as he wipes the last stray tear from under my eye with the pad of his thumb. 'You were right, for the record,' I add, 'in case that wasn't obvious. About everything you said that day.'

'I know. I'm sorry.'

'You have nothing to be sorry for.'

'Yes, I do,' he smiles and the sadness in his eyes makes me want to reach out and touch his face. 'You loved him,' he says softly, 'didn't you?'

'No,' I reply, and I know that it is true. 'I don't know what you would call it, but it wasn't love. Something a lot less honest and a good deal more selfish.'

'On his part?'

Jon seems to have forgotten that his hand is still on my cheek, held against my skin with the barest touch. The coolness of his palm and the slight touch of his little finger behind my earlobe send a tiny shiver down my spine.

'No. On both of our parts, just in rather different ways.'

Monday 16 April

10.15am. The Mondschein.

This last Monday dawned a little sadly for Rachel and me. In spite of all our complaining over the past five months, (and there really is no scale sufficient to quantify how much that has been) part of us will be a little nostalgic for the colourful, messy mayhem of Monday mornings: the hordes of confused newcomers, scared beginners, neon one-pieces, broken ski poles, lost vouchers, harassed instructors, panicking parents, tantrum-throwing toddlers and of course the giant foam-eared rabbit.

We found the ski school meeting point eerily empty this morning, devoid of noise, drama, confusion or indeed Snowli the Rabbit. We spotted Gav in his regular ski instructor's uniform, propping up the sidewall of Jürgen Sport 2000, hoovering up a Schinken-Käse Toast and a double espresso and looking rather grey. That much at least was a comforting reminder than not everything has changed. Still, we left the chalet dressed in our Snowglobe polo shirts this morning, and we walked down clean, cobblestoned roads and across grassy verges in bright sunshine to get here, where once we trudged bundled up through knee-deep snow in near-twilight. Spring is unavoidably here.

We're sitting in the Mondschein now having breakfast, discussing the end of season and trying not to feel sad. We are resolutely not thinking too much about the masses of paperwork and deep-cleaning shutdown of the chalets and Club Hotel which will begin on Monday, but rather what we are going to do after the last guests leave on Sunday to celebrate having the resort to ourselves (melty slush and all). The answer comes to me in a blinding flash of inspiration.

'A pool party in the Elena!'

'OH-*mygod*, that's inspired, Connors. Yes, a pool party. And a *barbeque*.'

'Brilliant. We can have venison burgers. Tilly will be chuffed to get rid of it all.'

'Did she not ever manage to shift any of that?'

Tilly accidentally ordered twenty-seven kilos of venison steak

371

back in January under pressure one morning when Adi the butcher showed up unexpectedly in the chalet to take her weekly order.

'Nope. She tried, but most of the guests she offered it to on the menu said they didn't eat deer that they hadn't personally shot. She gave up after about three weeks.'

'All the more for us.' Rachel rubs her hands together in anticipation. 'Venison steak, venison kebabs… Mmm, bambi-que.'

'Nice.'

'With homemade coleslaw and salads.'

'Mmm. Salads.' We both look down at our Schinken-Käse Toasts. However much I love Reschengel, I have to admit I am looking forward to a diet that consists of more than bread, cheese and meat. I think there is a reasonable possibility that I am in the initial stages of scurvy. Rachel thinks she may be too.

'You know, Rach, maybe going home – unappealing as it is in almost every way aside from the prospect of seeing friends and families – is rather a good thing, health-wise? We should embrace it as for our own good.'

'Hrrumph. If you say so, Pops, but I put it in the same category as cod-liver oil and wheatgrass shots.'

'Yes, but the glühwein lifestyle is unsustainable, really, when you think about it. The heating kills all the vitamin C, you know. And all that cinnamon, well…'

I swirl my cup sadly. *Drink it up, Poppy, and be grateful for what you had: drama and all, still the best five months of your life.*

'When do you have to be in London?' asks Rachel.

'Sometime before the fifth of September. That's when I start work, but I've got to find somewhere new to live beforehand. And get…well, back in the mindset.'

Rachel nods and says no more on the subject of the job, for which I am grateful. The choice is made; I don't need it to be made harder.

'But you'll be free for the summer, won't you?' she asks, suddenly excited as though seized by an idea.

'I don't really know. I haven't made any plans beyond staying at home for a month. I'll probably spend most of that time hiding from Kate and her insane plans to drive a Cadillac from Mexico to Colombia. Why? What's your plan? You leave here on the staff coach home on the twenty-eighth, right?'

'Errm, I've been meaning to talk to you about that. I'm not actually going on the coach. Nick and I have decided that, errm… I'm going north in the camper van with the boys.'

'For the summer? Or…?'

'We'll see,' she says, grinning as I squeal and dive over to her side of the booth to crush her in a bear hug.

'I knew it, I knew it, *I knew it*, you're going to marry him and go and live on a trawler and wear oilskins and fix bits of machinery with spanners and drills and things, and you'll have lots of ridiculously good-looking Scandinavian babies called Thor and Astrid and…'

'…Rex and Mats. Yes, we've discussed the babies' names already.'

'Really?'

'No, Poppy,' she says, laughing.

'But you are going to live on an oil rig, aren't you?'

'No, you muppet. I don't really know what we are going to do. Nick was going to take an offshore job, but he's had a change of heart and he's thinking of a land-based contract from July to December so that we can…'

'… build a log cabin in the forests and tame a pet bear and meet your future mother-in-law and learn Swedish and think about good schools for the kids.'

'I've actually been learning Swedish for the past two months,' she says, looking very pleased with herself. 'Nick says I'm a natural. With possible Viking ancestry.'

'Oh my god, you *are* getting married.'

'Shut up. We are planning to live in sin for at least the foreseeable future. And then, who knows? Hey, look,' she is suddenly serious, 'I'm going to see where this takes me. I'm not sure about a lot else, but I am sure about him. It's…I mean, with him, it's…'

'I know, Rach. It is. Anyone can see that.'

She blushes and squeezes my hand tightly for a moment until Traudl appears out of nowhere with another two glühweins and frowns at the display of emotion.

'So, you'll be shacked up in Sweden from July to December?' I ask, stirring in a sachet of sugar.

'Yup. And then the snow falls…'

'And you're coming back to Reschengel? Do come back next winter, please, please, please. I will make sure to spend whatever holidays I can here.'

'Yes, I reckon Reschengel will be where we'll base ourselves, but we'll be moving about quite a bit with this thing that Jon has… Oh.'

'What?'

'Nothing,' she smiles a cryptic smile. 'Actually, I just remembered that you don't know yet. It's Jon's news. You can hear it from him.'

'What? *What?*'

'Nothing.'

'Rachel.'

'Poppy.'

'*Rachel.*'

'No.'

'Tell me. Jon wouldn't mind. He always tells me stuff.'

'I know,' she smiles a little wider. 'He'll let you know in his own time.'

'Rachel, come on.'

'No.'

'*Rachel!* Seriously, I don't…'

My phone rings. The name Mikey flashes on the screen. I give Rachel a look of *I am not finished with you* and hit the green button.

'Poppy? Poppy??' comes a whispered voice.

'Mikey?'

'Shh! Come home. Come home *right now*. You will not *believe* what is happening in our front garden. You *will not believe what I am watching.*'

Later.

Oh. My. God.

My.

God.

Everything is just…well… Oh, my. I don't know what to say. Everything I know to be true is false. I keep looking around expecting water to flow uphill, gravity to be reversed and the sun to be tracking west to east across the sky.

Gina is a genius.

A *genius.*

Rachel and I rounded the last corner before the chalet, panting from the semi-sprint up the hill, utterly convinced that someone else had been shot and simply wondering who it was. And then we got past the high wall at Haus Eva and within view of the garden outside our chalet and only then, when we saw the scene with our own eyes, did we realise that it was far, far better than a shooting.

The soggy, waterlogged grass was a sea of black plastic sacks and strewn items of clothing. In the midst of it all was Spandex Boy, screeching with fury. He was tearing at the plastic of one of the stuffed sacks, ripping out what looked like Y-fronts and vests and, in his fit of rage, flinging them onto the grass and stamping them into the mud. Gina was sitting on the windowsill of her living room window, blithely smoking a cigarette and examining her fingernails as though this spectacle were not actually taking place before her eyes.

'How dare you? I'm going to kill you, you slut,' he shrieked, picking up a book from the ground and hurling it at her.

She dodged it easily. It bounced off the window behind her and fell harmlessly to the ground. 'Do be careful not to smash the window, won't you, Janny? I'd hate to have to bill you for that too.'

'Gina,' said Rachel, bravely drawing their attention in our direction, (I half hid behind her, afraid, frankly, of a barrage of Y-fronts) 'is, errm, everything all right?'

'Hello, sweeties. Yes,' she cooed, 'everything's just fine. How

375

was the ski school? Everything wrap up smoothly?'

'Grrr!'

We all turned to look at Jan. He swore again in German.

'Jan is just packing up,' said Gina, smiling serenely. 'Well, he's struggling a bit with it, obviously.'

'I'm not going anywhere without my money,' he roared, stamping his feet again. 'Give it back!'

'Can't,' she said lightly and smiled a smug smile. 'It's gone. Well,' she qualified that with a laugh, 'it's not *gone*. It's just in a nice, safe place where you can never touch it.'

He flushed a scarlet hue of such fury that his pointy features melted and slid off his face. (Well, almost. I was waiting with some hope for this to happen.)

'You are going to give me back my money right now or I swear I will...'

'Will what?' Tom's voice came from behind where Rachel and I were standing. He stepped forward, flexing his rugby-player's forearms by idly clenching and unclenching his fists with a pleasantly calm, interested look on his face. 'Will what, Jan?'

Jan reconsidered his position. At that moment, we all turned to look as a taxi drew up at the end of the garden path. The door opened and Fritz Spitzer stepped out. He left the door open and walked slowly toward Jan.

'You can get in, now,' he said in that voice he uses to make the Moose staff quake in their Uggs.

'I'm not going anywhere,' snarled Jan, 'without the money that thieving bitch stole from me.'

'Zero, six, five, five, three,' said Gina suddenly, 'four, zero, eight, two, nine, two.' Jan went pale. She held his eye for a long moment. 'I will do it,' she said softly to him. 'Don't think for one second that I won't. You should leave now, yeah?'

Jan opened his mouth and closed it again a few times, looking around him and then back at Gina. A small crowd of spectators had gathered on the street. No-one was quite sure what might happen next, though we all hoped it would be entertaining. I was gunning for Fritz to punch him, or maybe whip out a sawn-off shotgun.

Disappointingly, he didn't need to. After a protracted and rather constipated-looking struggle with himself, Jan eventually conceded defeat with a string of rather unimaginative expletives, grabbed an armful of clothes and flung them into the taxi's boot.

'You will not get away with this,' he spat, pointing a long finger at Gina as he swiped up the last of the bin bags.

'And yet somehow, I know that I already have,' said Gina, gleefully. 'Byee!'

The taxi sped off to a loud round of applause and a squeal of delight from Tina, Mikey and Eoghan, hiding on the balcony.

'Thank you, thank you,' Gina said, beaming at her audience and walking over to Fritz. 'Thank you,' she said and he hugged her.

'*Kein Problem, mein Fröschchen.*'

I looked from a baffled Rachel to Tom and then Gina. 'Errm, bravo of course, Gina, but can someone please explain what has just happened?'

'Basically,' Gina began, waving her cigarette in wide circles, safely back in her apartment, 'after the *Geldtasche* money "disappeared," and after I found out about his wife, I knew I couldn't just chuck him. I had to do better than that.'

And how she did. I had never credited Gina as the patient, meticulously calculating type – I didn't think she could even spell most of those words – but it turns out that she has an inner extortionist Mafia queen capable of planning and executing the perfect revenge plan.

She waited until the idea of her pregnancy had taken root with Jan and then threw a massive tantrum, claiming to have found out about his family in Innsbruck and to be distraught at what this would mean for her and the baby. She told him that she was a strict Catholic and that there was no way that she could bring the Child of Adultery into this world, that she had to have an abortion.

'Clearly he's not a practising Catholic.'

'No, he got kicked out of his local parish for stealing from the collection plate.'

'As a kid?'

'No, he was twenty-three. But obviously he was a bit rusty on the obligations of the faith. Anyway, he believed me.'

And last night, he finally handed over the four thousand euro Gina was demanding to fly home to England immediately for a discreet abortion. She took the cash, lodged it to her account first thing this morning and promptly threw him out on his ear.

'And the number you called out to him just now in the garden? The number that made him leave, what was that? Not a bank account number, I hope?'

'No, no, don't be ridiculous. His wife's phone number, obviously.'

'But you're still having the baby, right?' asked Tom dumbly.

'No,' Gina tittered, 'no, sweetie. There *is* no baby. Never was.'

'*Never?*'

Tom, Rachel and I were thunderstruck. Tina, Fritz and Gina laughed at our matching facial expressions.

'Oooh!' said Tina. 'You'll catch flies!'

'Sorry, sorry,' said Gina, 'but I had to make it convincing or I never would have got a penny out of him.'

'What are you going to tell everyone?' asked Tom. 'I mean, all the Snowglobe staff who think you're due in October?'

'Oh, yes, that.' Gina looked down at the floor, trying to hide a smile. 'I'll just say that I had a miscarriage. Very sad, eh? They won't mention it to me again after they hear that. "Poor Gina," yeah?'

'Are you going to at least tell James the truth?' asked Rachel.

'No, he doesn't really need to know, does he?' she said breezily. 'Let him think it was a miscarriage too. It's best all round. You know he'd just get upset and then he'd get very angry and I don't want him to compromise his working relationship with Jan over me.'

She looked very pleased with herself. I was back to being mildly-to-moderately disturbed by what Gina will do for sympathetic attention but decided for the sake of my own peace of mind not to think too much about it.

'Four thousand euro.' I shook my head in disbelief. 'Four thousand euro.'

'Four thousand three hundred and twelve, actually,' she smirked. 'I had to make that look real too.'

'What are you going to do with it all?' asked Rachel. 'Please buy a skidoo! Go on, buy a skidoo.'

'No, the money is to pay Sarah Datchet the balance of what we agreed I would cover from the theft.'

'But aren't you only liable for about three and a half thousand?'

'Yes, but, well,' Gina looked at Tina and they both giggled and clasped hands, 'I thought that I was entitled to a little bonus under the circumstances. Now G & T have a little something in mind as a treat for ourselves, don't we, Tina?'

'What is it?' I asked, intrigued.

'Oh, no, can't tell you 'til I show you,' she said. 'It's a surprise! Just wait 'til you see!'

'Oohey!' said Tina.

Tuesday 17 April

9.18am. Staff chalet.

Oohey, indeed.

Gina and Tina bounced into the welcome meeting yesterday evening and literally waved their 'surprise' in our faces: matching bum-length peroxide-blonde hair extensions.

'Oh, my,' said Rachel.

'Wow,' said Tom.

'Holy crap,' I said.

'I know!' Gina sighed. 'Aren't they fantastic? Oh, I've always dreamed of hair extensions. I feel like Posh Spice.'

'Ooh, get me!' squealed Tina, swinging her ponytail from side to side like a pendulum. Gina guffawed and joined in. They stood there for a good five minutes (it seemed) swinging their hair rhythmically at us while Rachel, Tom and I sat at the bar, literally speechless.

'That is...' Rachel searched for the appropriate expression, '...really special.'

'I know,' breathed Gina. 'And to think, all I had to do was hang onto Jan for a few extra weeks and now everything is great. Better than it was, even. It's like a dream come true,' she said, stroking her new mane.

'What's it made of?' asked Tom, and before he could stop himself, he reached out and picked up a golden lock.

'Horse hair,' beamed Gina and he dropped it and recoiled as though burned. 'Well, a very clever horse hair/acrylic mix actually.'

'Lovely.'

'How much did it set you back, Gina?'

'Three hundred euro.'

'Oh. One-fifty each, that's not so bad,' I said.

'No, no, no, three hundred each.'

Hmm. She spent six hundred euro having horse hair glued to her scalp. I might have to temper the 'genius' comment. She's still my hero, though. She made Jan's face melt before my eyes, and for the memory of that spectacle, I will forever be in her debt. It has made me smile all morning, and I'm still smiling now, walking up the chalet steps.

Brilliant, Jon's here already. We're going touring for the day. Not sure where. He said something about the Silferhorn. I know that he knows I know he has a secret – I can tell by the way he is smiling at me. Hmm. I'll extract whatever it is from him on the first chairlift. I have my ways.

12.42pm

Infuriating man! Grr! I must know!

1.32pm

Ha, HA! I found Jon's Achilles heel by taking his lunch hostage and dangling it off a chairlift. He finally caved in fear of losing his meatball baguette into the abyss, and the surprise, when I heard it, was infinitely more incredibly amazing than anything I could ever have guessed.

He sat me down in the snow, reached into his rucksack and told me to close my eyes. There was a shuffle and a rustle and something magazine-shaped was put into my hands.

'Open your eyes,' he said softly. It was a ski magazine, the front cover facing upwards. 'Anything about that look familiar?' he asked, nodding at the photo.

'It's you!' I said automatically. Then I looked more closely at it. 'Oh, oh, oh! It's the picture I took of you! The picture *I* took! That's you up on Ristis! Oh my God, on the *cover*!'

'I know,' he laughed. 'I sent it to them. And look,' he leafed through the magazine about ten pages, 'look at that!'

It was a six-page article in Swedish with pictures on every page: pictures I had taken.

'What's the article about?' I asked.

'A little bit about my sudden disappearance from the competition circuit and stuff, speculating about what I am up to and all that sort of thing, but they don't really know much, so it mostly talks about Emilie actually. I don't even know who wrote it. Doesn't really matter. What matters is the pictures. Are you happy?'

'Oh, Jon, of course I am. What an incredible surprise.' I hugged him tightly. 'I can't believe they printed my stuff. Wait until my dad sees this.' I shook my head, overwhelmed. 'I just don't know what to say. Thank you, of course; thank you for doing this.' I hugged him again.

'Thank *you*,' he said, 'for taking the pictures. Now wait until you hear what the result of them has been.' I looked at him, puzzled. 'You see, the magazine is not the full surprise,' he said, grinning broadly. 'Right, are you sitting comfortably? Good. Here it is: my master plan has come together in the past few weeks, and I want to hear what you think of it.' I nodded expectantly. 'Since this article came out,' he explained, 'my sponsors have agreed to support me in a big project.'

'What kind of a project?'

'Well, it has two parts. The first is a company I am setting up called "High Roads." The idea behind it is long expedition-style ski touring groups for people who want to tackle some of the big routes in the Alps, the US and Canada: everything from the Haute Route to snowkiting across Greenland. My sponsors have just signed up to provide all the skis and mountaineering equipment, which is a huge step. It's looking like we can begin our first tours at the start of next winter.'

'*Wicked.*'

'It will be.' He beamed with excitement. 'I can't wait to get it up and running. It's going to be a completely independent company, but we'll be working closely as a contractor with Karsten and Louisa at Element, you remember them?' I nodded. 'They already have all the administrative infrastructure and the local contacts in the locations we will use, and of course a very solid customer base to get started with. I've just seen the new brochure. It looks amazing.'

'That's absolutely brilliant. What a fantastic idea, and the name "Jon Berner" as tour leader will draw so much business.'

'And Nick Svedberg also. He is on board as the other expedition leader.'

'Awesome,' I said, thinking of Rachel too. 'So this is the project you were interested in having me build a website for?'

He nodded. 'Yes. And I'll be using the website to also distribute some of my sponsors' products. You know, skis, clothing, goggles, avalanche gear, that kind of thing.'

'OK. Yes, an online order service, secure server and all that. I can help you build that. Well done, Jon, that's some enterprise to take on.'

'Oh, that's not all.' He clapped his hands, his voice skipping with excitement. 'Next winter is going to be busy, busy. That's a big part of the reason I have asked Nick to work with me. I will only be taking about half of the High Roads tours. The rest of the time – and this is the second part,' he paused for dramatic effect and I caught myself leaning closer, 'my sponsors want to send me on a photo and DVD-shooting tour of the best backcountry skiing in the world, starting in Chile in July, and carrying on every few weeks through next winter.'

It took a second for this to sink in. 'Oh my *God.* They are going to pay you to ski all over the world for the next year?'

He nodded excitedly. 'Everywhere from Japan, Canada and Alaska to Iran, Kazakhstan, Georgia and Siberia. And guess what the best bit of all is?'

I shook my head, wide-eyed and totally swept up in his enthusiasm.

'They have said that they will pay for the photographer of my choice to accompany the expeditions. They're going to pay you to come too, Poppy!'

'Me?' I was stunned. 'Me?'

'Yes, you! Who else?'

I was still dumbfounded, and succeeded only in making strange, incoherent noises like 'buh' and 'ihh.' Eventually I managed, 'are you sure there isn't someone with more experience in the kind of...'

'Nonsense. You know what you're doing off-piste, and I can train you in anything else you need to know in the backcountry,' said Jon with a confident wave, 'everything. You will be *perfect* for

383

the job. And think how much fun we will have too, skiing in the Andes, the Caucasus, Japan!' He gripped my hand. 'Then the rest of the time, there is a job for you at High Roads. I mean, even aside from the website. We are going to market our tour packages as including the services of a professional photographer to record every step of the trip.'

'But I'm not a professional,' I said numbly, still blown away by all of this.

'You can do it, Poppy, look at the magazine for heaven's sake. You took that picture on the first shoot we ever did.'

'Beginner's luck,' I stammered.

'You know that you are well able to do it. Anyway, we will have so much time to practice over the summer. The first trip will be Chile, leaving on the twenty-ninth of July.' He looked at me, grinning his most infectious grin. 'It's yours if you want it. What do you say?'

'I can't... I don't know what to say,' I said and he frowned slightly at the uneasy tone in my voice.

'Take your time,' he said lightly. 'Think about it. I have a proper proposal done up for you with specifics about the work and the financial side of things.' *He has really thought this through.* 'But just think,' he said, grinning again, 'there's no need to go to London anymore! There's a job for you here doing exactly what you love!'

'But I have to go to London,' I said. 'I have to. I have to think of the future and my plan and...' I shook my head. 'I have a career plan, Jon. I can't... I don't... I mean, it sounds amazing, but I just can't throw away the security of that job, not now. Maybe in a few years, when I'm a bit more financially...' My voice trailed off into a helpless shrug. His grin slipped. He blinked and looked at me, deflated. I wanted to cry all of a sudden. 'I mean, I will certainly do the website for you,' I said, 'and I'll help you with whatever branding and things I can, but I can't stay out here. I have to get back to my life and my plans and...stuff.'

'Oh. OK. Well, the offer is there. Think about it. Maybe you will change your mind.'

'I would in a heartbeat, Jon, but unfortunately the decisions are already made. I have to see them through. It's not a choice anymore.'

'OK, if you think so.' He forced a watery half-smile as he kicked at the snow. 'It's a shame,' he said after a few moments' painful silence. 'It would have been really wonderful to have shared this with you.'

His words made my breath catch in my throat. I put my hand on his forearm. 'Hey,' I said softly and he looked at me, 'thank you for this. Thank you. You are the most incredible friend I have ever known.'

His eyes crinkled as he smiled and his chest filled a little.

Later, back down in the village and walking up the hill to our respective chalets with our skis over our shoulders, Jon stopped and reached into his jacket. He pulled out the magazine and handed it to me.

'Here, you keep this. My mother will have a few more copies, no doubt,' he said with a grin. 'Maybe it will remind you of me.'

'Like I could forget the person who made me ski into a pool within minutes of meeting me,' I sighed dramatically, 'and who spent the next three months introducing me repeatedly to my own mortality.'

'We have had some good times this winter, hey? Oh, there is one other small thing,' he said and reached into his jacket pocket again. He pulled out a piece of paper and handed it to me without another word. I gasped. It was a cheque from the magazine for twelve hundred euro, made out in my name.

'Jon! I can't accept this!'

'It's in your name.'

'But it was your camera, and you sent the pictures to them. And I was skiing on your bloody skis, for heaven's sake. I've been skiing on your skis for half the season.'

'Only because I asked you to show them a good time. You've been doing me a favour.'

'Don't be silly, Jon. The money is definitely yours.'

'No, it's yours. That's just how it is,' he said, with a sort of

385

calm stubbornness that invited no dissent.

'Then you will have to accept something for the skis at least.'

'I'll tell you what,' he said, slinging an arm over my shoulders as we carried on walking, 'I'll accept repayment in the form of you putting that money in the bank and using it to come and ski with me somewhere in the world next season. If that job of yours will give you a couple of weeks off, that is. Deal?'

'Deal,' I said, and instantly wondered how in my new job I would get as many as two weeks' consecutive holidays a year. Then I immediately resolved to fake kidney failure or similar to get the time off if necessary. *On this if nothing else, I will not let Jon down.*

Friday 20 April

2.28pm. Staff kitchen.

For once, the interruption of a Thursday night by a work-related text message from Gina was rather a welcome treat last night – well, for me anyway.

Gina: 'in da ktchn of staff accomm tmrrw @ 2pm plz!!! All staff 4 big meeting re SHUTDOWN!!! Poppy, cancl guidng, K? Tell em whateva. C u tmrrw sweeties!!! Dnt b late!!!'

'Two o'clock on a Friday?' asked Head incredulously. 'She really does not work on a skiers timetable, does she?'

'As if,' grumbled Rachel. 'She sings off her own hymn sheet in every conceivable way.'

I was delighted to have the morning free from guiding – well, until I realised that I was going to have to lie convincingly to a group of sceptical strangers. *The fear.*

'Sore throat?' offered Nick.

'No. It's been done. I'm thinking pulled muscle, maybe? Actually, no, I can't use any kind of an injury as a lie. Way too much bad karma.'

'Tell them that you can't take them to Futterberg because the linking piste over is closed,' suggested Head. 'Early melt, you know. The snow's all gone.'

'Global warming.' Jon shook his head sadly. 'It will be the end of us all.'

'Just tell them something has just come up and then run away before they ask too many questions,' was Rachel's sensible solution. 'Don't be specific. Specificity is your enemy, Poppy. Tell them that you've just got a phone call to say that one of your colleagues requires you urgently and that you have to dash. It'll be true: I'll be in the park with my game face on. And you know the pipe will be melty by two o'clock, so there is an amount of urgency to all this. We have to get snapping early, yeah?'

'Yes, but what if they don't let me go? What if they question me closely? What if they *see us in the park*?'

'Oh, you amateur. As long as you look suitably upset they'll assume that it's something life or death.'

'I don't know, Rachel, I'm very nervous of karma…'

'Karma, schmarma. It's all bullshit. Game face, Poppy. Game face.'

That was then, and this is now. Rachel is currently reconsidering such a cavalier attitude to the mystical retributive forces of the universe.

'Jesus, Rachel.' Tom looked up from his magazine as we walked in the kitchen door half an hour ago. 'What the hell happened?'

'Karma hates me,' she whispered and made her slow, painful way over to a chair in the corner and stood over it, examining its hard wooden seat.

'Do you want me to make you a ring cushion, Rachel?' I asked kindly.

She made a face of the most abject misery. 'I know you're taking the piss, Poppy,' she said in a pathetic voice, 'but would you please?'

Tom tried hard not to laugh as Rachel lowered herself onto a strategically arranged pile of hoodies and fleeces. She made a face at him and said nothing. I tried to distract myself by getting up to put on the kettle but I could feel my serious expression wobbling and trying to crack. He looked at me. 'Pops?

I couldn't help it. 'Rachel had a little…'

'POPPY!'

'But I…'

'Zip it!'

'Rach…'

'Zup!' She pressed her lips tightly together, her eyes wide as she stared daggers at me. '"Let's never speak of this again," remember?' she hissed.

'I know, I know, Rachel, but now you're walking like a cowboy. There will be questions.'

'A cowboy that's just been violated with a bar of saddle soap,' Tom snorted.

'And the saddle too, by the looks of it,' I added and earned a punch on the boob. 'Ouch!'

'Serves you right, Judas,' she hissed again and turned to Tom. 'I fell, Tom. I fell over in the park, OK? That's all.'

'She fell over a...'

'*Poppy!* The pact!'

Realisation dawned on Tom's face regardless. 'Oh my God, Rachel, did you nut yourself on a rail?' he exploded.

'No,' she said outraged, while I nodded and mimed the incident to Tom until he inhaled sharply and involuntarily shielded his crotch with his hand.

'Dude! Not good!'

Rachel gave me the death-stare. 'I did not "nut" myself, Tom,' she said with as much dignity as she could muster. 'I *winded* myself, actually.'

'Yeah, in the vagina,' I snorted.

'*POPPY!*'

A loud clatter on the stairs then and Gina bustled in. 'Right, right, right,' she bellowed, clapping her hands as she walked through the door, 'let's all get settled and...' her voice trailed away as she realised that we three were the only ones there so far. 'Where is everyone?' We shrugged. 'It's two o'clock.' We looked blank. 'Well don't just sit there. Go on, round them up!' We shuffled unenthusiastically out the door (some more slowly than others) as Gina shook her head, lit up a cigarette in the empty room and muttered loudly to herself. 'Can't get the staff, just *cannot* get the fucking staff.'

Much, much later.

'....and the key, the real *key*, will be efficiency. Efficiency and *time management*, yeah? So let's think about paths toward that goal. This is what the company manual calls 'yellow brick roads,' right? Are we all on page forty-two? Everyone? Good. Let's all look at the flow chart. We're going to use its structure to brainstorm exactly what needs to be done to achieve the goal of "shutting down..."'

If Gina doesn't stop making air quotation marks I am going to end her.

'...so we'll start by, yes, "strategising our timeframe," right?'
She looks around the room expectantly until everyone nods.
'Good, good. Let's begin with the chalets. I'm thinking LISTS.
And MIND MAPS. Let's have a show of hands: who prefers lists
to mind maps? Come on, hands high in the air, where I can see
them...'

5.23pm

'...which should all take about three days and is of course in
keeping with the three core principles of EXTRA MILE,' finished
Gina with a beaming smile as the smiley face logo on the final
frame of her PowerPoint presentation flickered a blue and orange
grin.

Tilly and Miranda looked despairing. There had been far too
much emphasis on bleach, powerhosing and heavy lifting for their
liking. Distractedly, Miranda untied and retied her hair into exactly
the same casual knot on top of her head, pulling out the same
accidental strands to frame her face. Tilly stared into the middle
distance and patted Mark's leg absently. *Ha, ha,* I thought; *she has
the right idea.* She was mentally delegating anything requiring rubber
gloves, I could tell.

Joseph, the host of the Chalet Gerda, was smiling a vague
smile and looking singularly unperturbed by the prospect of
scouring the entire chalet to within an inch of its life. *I guess he's
used to worse from his days in the army*, I thought. *I wonder if that's what
he's going back to at the end of season.* I realised that I had absolutely
no idea. All season, Joseph kept his distance and made it perfectly
clear that at forty-six years old, he was not at all interested in the
frivolous concerns of the youngsters of today. All we ever found
out about him was the fact of his military background (not exactly
a difficult thing to work out, seeing as he always sat bolt upright
and had the look about him of a man who was on the brink of
doing something extraordinarily dangerous). Even Rachel, who
repped the Chalet Gerda and saw him almost every day, said she
never succeeded in getting him to converse with her beyond the

390

necessary pleasantries.

'Right,' Gina clapped, 'any questions on that? No? Good. Now,' she said as she rummaged through her notes and produced a green plastic folder. 'Now for the Club Hotel.'

Everybody stiffened slightly and pretended not to look at Suzanne. Rachel passed me a note. 'Eight minutes before her eyes fill w/tears. Bets?' Tom gave her eleven. Carol snorted. 'Three, maximum,' she muttered.

'Well, obviously Suzanne is the final authority in the Club Hotel,' Gina began with a deferential smile that no-one believed for a second, 'but since I have had many years' experience of shutting down that particular property, if you don't mind, Suzanne, I will get the ball rolling with a to-do list?'

Suzanne nodded, the same pleasant half-smile on her face. 'Go ahead, Gina.'

'Right,' began Gina with undisguised relish, 'everybody, please take a Club Hotel Shutdown Checklist.' She passed a pile of A4 sheets to Tina to distribute. 'Now, as you can all see, the company's hotel shutdown procedure divides into five main sections: Bedrooms, Communal Areas, Storage and Refuse, Leisure Centre and Kitchen. Let's start with bedrooms. First things first, all the linen, curtains and rugs must be stripped and bagged for collection on Wednesday...'

I watched Suzanne's face throughout, waiting for a reaction as Gina explained everything from removing shower-grouting limescale build-up ('I find a good, stiff toothbrush works best') to scrubbing out five months' worth of crusty decomposition from the bio bins ('you just have to climb in and give it some elbow grease, yah?'), from disposing of fat from the drip trays in the kitchen to clearing the leisure centre drains ('use your fingers to scrape out the first layer of greasy gunk, and then you need to get your whole forearm right down those plugholes. After five months, you can expect a sizable hair plug in each one, OK?'). I waited for a twitch, a gasp, something, but Suzanne barely blinked. She sat there listening calmly, an unopened notebook on her lap, her hands clasped loosely together. I looked at her knuckles, expecting them to be the same anxious shade of stretched white as always, (even when asleep) but they were pink and normal. I wondered then if she had perhaps been medically sedated, but it didn't seem likely. She was paying attention, nodding intelligently every now and again and saying things like, 'Right, yes, absolutely.'

Gina, meanwhile, was getting close to the end of her list, and was openly perplexed at the lack of reaction she was getting. She seemed to be running out of steam. 'And... and, well,' she struggled, searching for something further to add to Point Nine about the pool area. 'Oh! The leisure centre toilets!' she beamed. 'I almost forgot. Someone will have to empty the sanitary bins. They haven't been done all season.' A collective groan of disgust went around. Gina waved it away. 'Yah, I know, I know, not nice, but try asking Fritz to pay for the crowd from Täsch to come up and sort it. So anyway, Suzanne, it will of course fall to you to, errm, *allocate* that task.'

'Do not even *look* at me,' said Tina with an emphatic click of her fingers.

A clamour of protest went up amongst the rest of the hotel staff as they each fought to get their word in first.

'That's fine, Gina,' Suzanne's voice cut through, cool, calm and steady. 'Is that everything for the hotel?'

'Errm...' Gina eyes darted in confusion from her list to Suzanne's face and back again a few times before she conceded defeat. 'Yes. Yes, that's everything. Of course if anything comes up that you can't handle, you know where to find me.'

'Of course,' said Suzanne.

Gina blinked. 'Right, well.' She shuffled some papers, trying to conceal her disappointment. 'Oh, did I mention that the pool in the Elena is being drained on Friday? Yah. And also, Tilly, Mark: I have a message for you from Fritz. He doesn't want you to clean out the wheelie bins anywhere near the swimming pool, OK? So Joseph, can you please go down to the Elena on Monday and help Mark and Tilly to wheel the bins up to the Gerda?'

'Well, actually, Gina...' Joseph began, 'there will be a problem with that plan.'

Gina frowned. 'What kind of a problem?' she enunciated slowly.

'I'm afraid I am not going to be here on Monday,' he said pleasantly, as though politely declining an invitation for afternoon tea.

Gina's eyes bulged. 'Where will you be on Monday, Joseph?'

'Bratislava.'

'Bratis-wherethefuck?' Gina's eyes narrowed. Tina giggled nervously. 'No, you can't have a day off on Monday. Forget it.'

'Bratislava,' said Joseph mildly, 'is in Slovakia. And I ought to clarify: I'm not going on Monday; I'm going on Sunday morning. And in case it wasn't clear, I'm not coming back.'

'But, but you can't leave on Sunday morning,' sputtered Gina. 'You've got a job to do. Chalet shutdown. There's still a week in your contract and you can't just…'

'Mmm. Yes, I'm sorry you're not happy about it but that is the way it is.' He shrugged. 'I have things to do, you see.'

'No,' said Gina suddenly. 'You can't. I won't have it.'

'Well, you can't really stop me,' said Joseph, with a slightly awkward laugh as he stood up. 'I'm sorry for the inconvenience but it didn't suit me to wait until the end of the week to move on.' He shrugged again. 'Relax. You'll manage.'

'But that's so *selfish*,' exclaimed Rachel.

Joseph turned to look at her, indifferent. 'Look, I don't owe Snowglobe anything,' he said in the same calm tone of voice. 'I'm sure that within the company there exist the resources to deal with whatever happens. They've paid me little enough all season; the money has to be *somewhere* in their bank account.'

'But Joseph, you know the company won't bat an eyelid or fork out a penny. *We'll* be the ones who'll have to take up the slack.'

'Yeah, well, that's life. We're not really friends, are we?' replied Joseph, looking around the room. 'Come on. We just happen to work for the same rubbish company, nothing more. Don't kid yourselves. You'll all get on your coach next week and go home from your little gap year and you'll never speak to each other again. Sorry to burst that bubble for you, but I'm not getting sentimental about this. You're nice people but I have things to do, OK?'

He walked to the door.

'Well, let me tell you,' said Gina, pointing a finger at him, 'you will never, ever work for Snowglobe again.' Joseph laughed at this idea. 'And you had better not take a single item of chalet stock or I will have you prosecuted for theft.' He waved back at her as he walked out the door. 'And don't expect to get your security deposit back,' she shrieked at his departing figure.

'Fuck,' said Carol, lighting a cigarette.

'*Wanker*,' spat Rachel.

'That little *shit*,' said Tilly miserably.

Everyone looked at Suzanne. She was staring at her fingernails, nodding slightly to herself as though bored. She said nothing. Gina paced up and down the kitchen tiles muttering furiously to herself and pulling heavily on one Camel Extra Strength after another.

No-one spoke for a few minutes until I broke the silence, speaking aloud, almost to myself.

'Well, it *could* be worse. At least there are plenty of us to…' I realised then the stupidity of what I had done. Everyone was staring at me. Gina looked delighted. Rachel threw a shoe in my direction.

'Well volunteered, numpty!' she hissed, shaking her head. 'Schoolboy error, Connors, schoolboy! Amateur! You're a ski rep; things can always get worse!'

Saturday 21 April

11.14am

The question of just exactly how much worse things could get moved from the realms of the abstract hypothetical to the starkly real at approximately six forty-five am this morning.

'Poppy? Poppy? Are you awake?'

Rachel's voice was far, far too brightly alert. I looked at my clock. 'No.'

'Pops, seriously, look at me. Does anything about this bedroom this morning seem odd to you?'

'That you're upright in it and it's not even seven o'clock?' I said bitterly, although I was already blinking and pushing myself into a sitting position.

'OK, anything else? I'll give you a clue. Look left.'

I looked left and saw that the wardrobe door was open. This struck me as odd for two reasons: first, Suzanne owns that wardrobe and Suzanne would never, ever leave the door open; she gets edgy about dust. But second, there wasn't a single stitch of clothing in it. Not so much as a pair of tights.

'That's weird. Why has she moved all her clothes?' asked Tina, pushing her *faux*-nytail out of her eyes. (Rachel was very proud of that one. Now I can't call it anything else.)

Why indeed? I turned towards Suzanne's bed to ask her that very question. It was empty.

'But she was in bed before us last night,' I stammered. 'She was fast asleep, remember?' Rachel nodded, looking baffled. My phone vibrated on the bedside table and began to ring. Caller ID flashed up as 'Club Hotel.' *Phew.* I pushed the green button, relieved. *It must be Suzanne,* I thought, *with some rational explanation for all this.*

'Pops? Hey,' said Odysseus at the other end of the line. 'Sorry, I know it's early but I think Suzanne's slept in. Can you possibly wake her up and ask her where the resort van is? It's not in its space.'

Oh, *bollocks.*

After an hour of espresso and denial in the Club Hotel office, ('Maybe she's been kidnapped. Maybe they've taken her hostage. Maybe they, err, stole all her clothes and things too...without waking anyone else up...') Rachel, Tom, Carol, Odysseus and I finally accepted the obvious conclusion and we phoned Gina to let her know that Suzanne had basically done a runner.

'I think this is a bad line, Poppy,' said Gina in her cranky-sleepy voice. 'Can you repeat that?'

'Suzanne stole the resort van and ran away during the night,' I said tonelessly.

'Oh. Oh, right. Yah. I thought that was what you said.' There was a long silence. 'Have you tried her phone?'

'Yes. About thirty-nine times. No answer.'

Another long silence.

'Fuck.'

In a flash of inspiration, Rachel suggested phoning the petrol company who supply our fuel cards and asked them to trace the last usage. She hung up the phone five minutes later looking resigned.

'Well?' asked Carol.

'Täsch this morning at five,' said Rachel. 'A full tank.'

'Oh,' I said. 'Oh.'

Täsch is on the road to Salzburg and the wider world. Suzanne could be anywhere by now. *Bugger.*

'So what do we do?' asked Tom.

We looked at Carol. She ground her cigarette into the nearest ashtray and swore. 'We have to report the van stolen now.'

'We can't call the police, Carol,' protested Odysseus. 'I mean, this is Suzanne we're talking about.'

Carol put up her hands. 'Look, I don't exactly enjoy the idea of putting the bloody Polizei on her, however much of a fucking idiot she is. But we haven't got a choice now: if we don't file an official report soon, somewhere down the line the insurance company will do what insurance companies do best, and suddenly you and I are left personally liable for this mess. We have to follow procedure or *we'll* get shafted.'

There was nothing to say to that. Carol was right. She sighed and picked up the phone.

5.22pm. The Mondschein.

We have waited the entire day for word from the Polizei, most of which time I have spent haunted by horrific mental images of Suzanne in a car chase on the Autobahn, being run off the road by

396

overzealous law enforcement officers a mere mile from the Swiss border, plummeting into a deep ravine and exploding in a fiery ball of flames.

And now that we have finally received news of what *actually* happened, we are sitting together in the Mondschein in no less stunned a silence. I cannot believe it. I just cannot believe it.

The van was found abandoned in the car park of Täsch train station this morning. There was no sign of Suzanne; presumably long since departed on a train to somewhere far, far away. Obsessed as she was with neatness and order, however, she had thoughtfully stashed the van keys and her company phone in the left wheel arch, presumably wrapped up in some kind of polite explanatory note no doubt asking the finder to return it at their convenience to the Snowglobe Club Hotel in Reschengel.

I say 'presumably' because no-one will ever get the chance to read it now. Suzanne hadn't thought to switch off her phone, you see, and nor had she anticipated the reaction that would be prompted by a van abandoned at dawn in a mostly empty car park with a repetitive high-pitched ringing noise emanating from somewhere around its engine area. The Austrian Federal Anti-Terrorism Unit swooped in at eight-thirty.

At that exact moment, I was slumped over Suzanne's desk in the hotel office, holding the telephone receiver to my ear, listening to call number fifty-three ring out to her voicemail. My desperate hope was dwindling only very slowly that she would answer on the next ring and explain that she was really just over in Futterberg and this whole thing was a big misunderstanding, but I was growing increasingly irritated at the probability that the whole stupid mess was going to make me miss my last opportunity to ski the Couloir of Mortality Defiance with Jon. Still, so long as the phone was ringing, she must still have it on her person, I reasoned, and so in the absence of anything else to do but annoy her until she responded, I just kept hitting redial.

At the other end of the line, bomb disposal experts assessing the situation established quickly that the ringing phone was certainly not within the body of the van, but was associated with the underside, and was therefore very likely to be some kind of remote detonation device. The threat level was set at Level Five (of five). The car park and a wide radius of surrounding buildings were evacuated, the whole area cordoned off and local hospitals put on high alert. Under the circumstances, and in the logical fear that there was a detonation fail-safe in place, officers were reluctant to approach the vehicle and force the doors to investigate further what sort of hazardous material it contained. The decision was taken at eleven twenty to proceed with a controlled explosion.

'How's Gina taking the news?' I ask with some trepidation, swirling the last of my glühwein as Traudl brings us over another three steaming mugs.

'Calmly,' says Carol with a wry smile.

'I gave her a Bof before I told her,' explains Rachel, staring down at her drink and we all lapse into another contemplative silence. 'I just cannot believe,' she says eventually, 'that they blew up our resort van.'

I am trying to focus on the gravity of it all, but I keep picturing the faces of the bomb disposal experts as they watched burning fragments of Snowglobe letterheaded notepaper, customer satisfaction questionnaires and the grotesquely melted remains of two hundred complimentary plastic snowglobes burst out of the back of the van in a fireball. The mental image is too much.

'Shotgun! Not phoning Sarah Datchet!' I gasp between convulsions of laughter.

'Ooh, me neither, me neither!' says Rachel, quick as a flash.

'It's not funny,' snaps Carol, taking a gulp of glühwein and trying not to smile. 'Suzanne is *definitely* not getting back her security deposit now.'

Sunday 22 April

3.30am. Reschengel coach park.

Ah, relief: the last Sunday of the season and the first departing coach is gone. Only two more to go. It should be the easiest transfer ever: we're not even bringing them down to Salzburg. We're just depositing them on their coaches and waving them off on their merry way, but still it's proving to be something of a challenging morning. No, not because we are missing Suzanne's absence keenly, (as if) but because Tom, Rachel and I have come directly from the Damage closing party and are all having some difficulty with the requirements of sobriety; Tom more so than us girls, so we've put him on luggage loading duty with the driver. Meanwhile we're struggling with the headcount and the passenger manifest for the second coachload.

'That's everyone!'

'No, I only have twenty-nine.'

'Did that woman get off to go to the toilet again?'

'No, but the baby in row eleven doesn't count.'

'You mean row eight. Shit, I counted him.'

'Him? I thought it was a girl. Yes, look, a girl in pink, row eleven.'

'Oh. I think there are two babies.'

'Oh. Right, yeah. Does that mean we could be missing two adults?'

'How many people are on the list?'

'I thought you had the list.'

Etc.

5.25am.

The last guests of the season are GONE! We're free! *Free!*

It's going to be a good day. The sun is up and already shining bright in a cloudless sky. Now for five or six hours' sleep to recharge the batteries, then skiing with Jon for a few hours and after that, *POOL PARTY!*

I'm resolutely *not* thinking about tomorrow and the beginning of resort shutdown. It will be fine. Naturally, Carol has everything in hand for the Club Hotel. It's already as though Suzanne had never even been here. I suppose in ways, she never had.

All that's left for us reps is for Rachel to close down the accounts with our suppliers while Tom and I get the Gerda done, and even that – however annoyingly NOT in our job description, for the record – will be OK with two of us to share it between us. We'll blitz it in two days. We'll be done by Tuesday evening.

And then I will have just one final day to enjoy Reschengel before I leave for home. The other Snowglobe staff members are being bussed back to London next Saturday, but since I'm heading back to Ireland to stay at my parents' place for a while, Snowglobe have agreed to fly me directly. I only found out yesterday what day that would be, when James texted me to that end: 'Hi Poppy. Hope you're well. Your flight home is booked. Thursday 26th, depart Klagenfurt at 1710.'

'Klagenfurt?' I frowned as I read the message. 'Isn't that...'

'Nowhere near here?' finished Rachel, casting her eyes to heaven. 'Yes, it's at least three hours away. Holy incredible inefficiency, Batman!'

Typical, I thought, typical bloody Snowglobe. They'll accommodate me by booking me a direct flight but naturally will manage to send me home from the wrong side of the country.

Me: 'OK, but how do I get to the airport?'

James: 'Yeah, I know... That is a slight issue. The train's pretty circuitous (ie 14 changes) and Snowglobe won't pay for a taxi so it looks like I'm going to have to drive you. I'll pick you up at 11.30am at your staff accomm.'

Wunderbar, I thought. Just fricking *wunderbar.* That'll be a fun three-hour drive.

Ugh. Whatever, it has to be done. This is what iPods were invented for.

Monday 23 April
9.47am. Chalet Gerda.

If I have gained anything from my time in this job, it is a deep, deep suspicion of ringing phones. Phones, in my experience, are harbingers of doom. They very rarely ring with good news. In fact, I have noticed a pattern (and I think there may be something, you know, actually scientific in this) that the unpleasantness, irritation and/or inconvenience of whatever I will have to do as a result increases in direct proportion to the lateness of the phonecall.

But it is not always so, apparently. I was just snapping on my pink Marigolds in the kitchen of the Chalet Gerda ten minutes ago when I heard the familiar ringing noise. All things considered (including Caller ID), I should have had some sense of what was about to happen, but was foolishly blindsided by the innocuously early hour and answered the phone with a cheery 'hello, Gina.'

'I need Tom,' she panted, 'please get Tom to come down here. I need him now. He has to help me sort it out, oh, oh, oh…'

It seems that Gina discovered an hour into her final accounts this morning that she somehow, mysteriously cannot account for ten or eleven lift passes sold during the season. OK, they're each worth a few hundred euro and if she has actually lost them she will be liable (and so she might have cause to regret that six hundred euro outlay on horse hair, perhaps?) but my sympathy has limits, particularly when her solution to the problem has direct implications for the number of toilets I will have to scrub today.

I said nothing, just made murderous, incredulous faces at the phone while Tom jumped up and down, cackling with glee.

'Fine,' I said through gritted teeth, staring at my rubber gloves, the Brillo pad in my hand and the caramelised remains of five months' worth of animal fat on the inside of the Gerda oven, and thinking about exactly what I would do with a Brillo pad if Joseph ever had the misfortune to cross my path again.

2.23pm

Ugh. I feel disgusting. I am disgusting. I decided to get the worst jobs out of the way first, the really smelly, gunky and horrible ones, so now I'm covered head to toe in dust and filth and grime from scrubbing every imaginable corner of the kitchen and the bathrooms. The kitchen is done and sealed off but I just ran out of toxic green squirty bathroom cleaner so I can't finish the bathrooms until I raid the Elena's cleaning store for another bottle. Ooh, maybe a cup of tea too.

I have to pick up their bins anyway. Ugh, bins. I've just opened the door of the Gerda bin room and it is in a *vile* state. I can't see that Joseph could ever have cleaned it out all season. I'm not even going to describe the smell. I think I will need some sort of a breathing mask. I wonder if Tilly has one. It seems likely, somehow.

7.43pm. The Elena poolside, soaked to the skin.

Oh. *Gulp*. An unexpected turn to the day. The day? The week. The *winter*. What to do? What to do now??

I went to the Elena for my break, where Mark, Tilly and I procrastinated successfully for about an hour and a half over tea and home-baked brownies on the sun terrace before I decided that it was time to get back to the Gerda for some actual work. I headed up the hill, manhandling the Elena's three wheelie bins very awkwardly and dreading the ghastly bin room with an intensity that simply cannot be described.

Out of nowhere came a voice calling out behind me in a loud cartoon-character voice, 'oh, oh, oh! Look out! It's the Wheelie Bin Bandit!'

I turned around. Head and Jon were ambling up the hill behind me, looking strangely out of place in ski boots amidst the grassy greenness of the village gardens and the summery colour of the chalet window-boxes.

'Stop, thief!' yelled Head, startling two old ladies on the street as he bounded full pelt at me in his ski boots, limbs flying everywhere.

'I surrender,' I said as he wrestled the bio bin from me. 'They're all yours. You're welcome to them. Especially that one.'

'Did you learn nothing from your last wheelie bin-thieving

experience?' asked Jon, taking the other two from my hands.

'I can't help it; it's a sickness.' I was suddenly very aware of how utterly vile I must have looked: grimy, sweaty and hair sticking up in unusual angles. 'How was it on the mountain?' I asked, trying to simultaneously scrape my hair into some kind of order and wipe my face surreptitiously on the sleeve of my t-shirt as we began to walk slowly up the hill.

'Warm and slushy,' said Jon, dropping his skis into one of the bins and pulling it behind him as he pushed the other one ahead. 'You didn't miss much.'

'Are you almost finished with the chalet, Poppy?' asked Head.

'I wish,' I groaned. 'I have a festering bin room to scrape, scour and disinfect this afternoon.'

They both made a face.

'Will that be as pleasant as it sounds?' asked Jon.

'You don't even want to know. I think Joseph might have been breeding lethal organisms for chemical weapons.'

'*Ach*, suck it up, it's good for the immune system,' said Head. 'Come to the Hirsch for one when you're done?'

'I can't. I have to go straight home and boil-wash myself as soon as possible. It's best for everyone, really.'

'That's OK, Head can't go to the Hirsch either,' said Jon. 'He has to work at four o'clock today, which is in,' he looked at his watch, 'seven minutes.'

Head froze, eyes wide. '*Shit*. Is it Monday already? Shit, shit, shit.' He dropped the bio bin without another word and we watched him tear off up the hill.

'Can you imagine him with a chainsaw in his hands?' asked Jon. 'Rural Sweden goes on high alert every April.'

We arrived at the gate of the Gerda. 'Thank you so much for helping with these,' I said. 'Might see you later on for a nice beer in the sun?'

'Well, I'm going to drop my skis home and get changed,' he replied, 'because I'm frying in these ski boots. However, I am free for the rest of the afternoon. Anything you would like some help with?'

'Don't worry, I wouldn't inflict the chemical warfare on you. I'll manage.'

'Are you sure? I used to do a bit of end of season cash-in-hand work and any chalet they ever made me shut down was lots of heavy lifting. Are you sure you can do everything alone?'

'Well,' I said, 'since you offer, there is one thing you could help with. I need to get all the bed linen, towels and curtains downstairs for the cleaners to pick up. If I go in now and bag it all up, will you help me lift it down? It'll only take five minutes between the two of us.'

'Sure. No problem. I'll be over soon.'

'You're a hero, Jon. Thanks a million.'

'Not a bother,' he said, 'see you soon. I won't be too long.'

An hour and a half later, there was still no sign of him. I had finished bagging up everything and had cleaned the last two bathrooms and I was puzzled that Jon had not shown up. I was tired and bored of cleaning and dreading the bloody bin room, and if it were anyone else I would have been grumpy and irritable, but I was confused because it wasn't like Jon to not be where he said he would be. And actually, when I realised just how late he was and I thought about it, I couldn't remember a single other time I knew of when he had made an arrangement that he did not keep. Very puzzling indeed.

I started rolling the enormous laundry bags down the stairs, but gave up on that strategy when the first one burst on the way down. It really was a job for two people. I left the remaining pile of bags in the bedrooms and walked down the stairs, thinking that he must have got distracted somewhere along the way, and must at least have tried to call me to let me know that he would be late. I went to look for my phone, glancing at the kitchen door for a second as I passed before I realised that of course he could not be sitting in there. I smiled to myself, looking through my jacket in the hall, as I thought of all the mornings when I could have set my clock by the sound of Jon clicking on the kettle in our staff kitchen and sitting there on the couch, happily reading random magazines to himself and waiting to see who would wander in for a coffee and a chat, and whether he could persuade them to come play on the mountain.

There will be a day soon, I realised suddenly and the shock of it made me stop still, holding my jacket and staring out the window, *that I will wake up and he won't be there anymore. I will be far away from here, and he won't be anywhere near me ever again. Oh*, I thought as my heart bounced off my shoes, *it's all really ending, isn't it?*

I looked down at my phone. There was no text message or missed call from Jon, but I wasn't really paying attention at that point, because I had been overtaken by another thought. *How I am going to say goodbye to him?* I wondered, and the wrench of misery was shocking in its intensity. *I have to go home and there is no friend like him waiting for me there. How do I say goodbye?* I sat down, feeling very cold and alone all of a sudden, looking straight ahead at the peeling paint of the wall in front of me as I searched the thoughts circling my brain for anything to make me feel better. I didn't move for a few minutes.

Eventually I steadied myself with a deep breath and a shaky laugh. *Well done, Poppy. About time it finally hit home that the season is over*, I thought, *now that you're here in the empty Gerda, stripping it of all traces of the winter. Of course it's a wrench, but you have to go home now. The snow is almost gone and your time here has run out; you have always known it was limited. Be grateful that the friendships you have made have been so special, and enjoy what time you have left.*

A muted bang somewhere behind the chalet stirred me just then. I went to investigate, opened the back door and almost walked right into Jon, wheeling bins into the bin room.

'Ah, you caught me.' He smiled guiltily. 'I was about to come and find you. Surprise!'

'Have you just...' I looked from him to the bins to the bin room. Everything was gleaming: windows, surfaces, previously crusty floor, everything. My jaw dropped. 'Oh my *God.*'

Jon laughed, delighted at my reaction. 'Godmother, I think,' he said. 'You can call me your fairy godmother. By magic, it is done and off your list. Now let's go move those laundry bags and then we can get out of here and spend the rest of the evening doing something fun, hey?'

'Thank you, thank you, thank you.' I threw my arms around him. 'Jon, I…oh.' I pulled back, remembering suddenly that I was a giant heap of kitchen grease, congealed dust and Cillit Bang. 'I smell vile, sorry about that.' I looked around the room, overwhelmed. 'You are my hero, my actual hero.' He grinned and shut the bin room door behind us. 'I need to buy you your bodyweight in beer for doing this for me.'

'That sounds like an excellent plan.' He steered me inside. 'Let's get to it, Cinderella.'

We left the chalet eighteen enormous laundry bags later, and Jon wheeled me down the hill in one of the Elena bins, making jokes about it turning into a magical carriage at midnight. (I really don't think he has ever actually read or seen *Cinderella*.) There was no sign of life in the Elena when we got there – Mark and Tilly were presumably at the Hirsch already – and as Jon put the bins away, I wandered over to the pool, picking up off the patio tiles a stray plastic cup from yesterday's 'Bam-beque' and gazing at the gentle ripples reflecting the flickering of the recessed lamps in the low, duskiness of approaching twilight. I thought about that first night I stood here, when the deep snow was banked up all around, and so close to the water's edge that we could jump into it with ease. (I still can't believe we did that. As a plan, it seems all the more insane, looking at it snow-free.) I smiled to myself as I remembered the three strangers I met here that night, the dark figures silhouetted against the twists of steam rising from the pool into the freezing night air, their voices low but clear, speaking to one another in a language I didn't understand.

Du har mig. The words popped unbidden into my head at that moment, the words he whispered that day not so long ago up on Rufigrat as I cried in his arms. *Du kommer alltid att ha mig.* I have often wondered what that means but have never asked Jon. I have never known quite know how to bring it up, and when I thought to ask Rachel if it's an expression she has come across, I couldn't quite remember the words.

I could still see Jon's face so clearly as it was that day; not

406

pitying – I could see that now – but sad, afraid and infinitely compassionate, and the words echoed in my mind, over and over, those words he spoke when his eyes and the touch of his hand on my cheek put me back together in a small but very important way. What was he saying? *I must find out before I go.*

And my chest went tight at the thought. *I am not sure I can bear the sadness of what is to come on Thursday.* I almost wanted it to come sooner, if only so that the dread of it would be less to endure. *I am going to miss him like nothing I have ever left behind,* I accepted in that moment, and the old familiar leaden plum rolled over and over in the pit of my stomach at the prospect of what lay ahead in the coming months. I looked from the light playing on the pool's surface to the dark shadow of the once-snowy bank where he squeezed my hand for the first time and told me that everything would be great, and I blinked back the beginnings of tears with a deep breath as I struggled to think straight.

You will meet him again, I told myself. *He will always be your friend if you both make the effort to stay in touch. Why are you so sad?*

Oh, I thought then, with a sudden start and I blinked once, twice. *Of course, Poppy, you plank. You...*

The thought froze in my brain, mid-realisation, as I was suddenly, unexpectedly and with absolutely no warning rammed into, lifted off my feet and launched into the air. *Ooof.* The missile had arms and a torso – I had time to realise before we hit the water – because they wrapped around me with a whoop of evil delight and we both went under with a splash. I fought my way to the surface a long six seconds later, splashing and cursing, with so much water up my nose, and with such a strong desire to launch myself at Jon's grinning face and separate it from his body that I almost forgot to finish my sentence.

...love him, don't you?

'I'm sorry, I'm sorry,' he cackled, looking the least apologetic I have ever seen him, 'but it was *so* tempting. And you did say you wanted a wash, eh?'

'Gfhuggghh...'

He dived out of reach of my flailing fists, chuckling to himself.

'Oh, come now, Poppy, don't deny it, you love an evening dip in the pool. It was the first thing I learned about you.'

'You're dead,' said my nose. 'All promises of beer are hereby rendered null and void.'

Jon gasped. 'Poppy, Poppy, no! Don't do anything rash.' He pulled himself up the ladder and reached for my arm to help me out of the water. 'We'll throw your clothes in the dryer and you can borrow something of mine to wear to the Hirsch. That rolled-up-sleeves look was a real hit the last time, remember? And your jacket's still dry on the gatepost, see?'

'That just proves that you premeditated this,' I said with a very convincing huff while my mind was somewhere else entirely.

He held up his hands. 'Maybe. Maybe, but don't let's do anything hasty now. The beer does not need to suffer. Think of the bin room, focus on the bin room.'

'True, OK,' I conceded as we turned to walk out the gate, and then I stiffened slightly as he slung his arm over my shoulders in the way he does.

Oh, oh, oh. I can feel the tension crackling like static between us as we wander up the hill to his chalet, but he seems oblivious. *Will he realise? Or does he already know? Haaarrrghh… What to think? What to say? What to do now??*

Much later.

The twitchy paralysed shock phase didn't last excessively long, fortunately. I dived into the shower as soon as we got to Jon's place and was rescued from a massive wave of crippling self-conscious indecision by the useful combination of surprisingly hot water and one very sensible thought: 'what would Rachel do?'

After that, things were rather straightforward. Jon found me standing in the kitchen waiting for the kettle to boil for tea (tea was just the fortification necessary) and as he stood before me, warm from the shower, rolling the sleeves of his hoodie up my wrists and chuckling about something to do with the Swedish dubbing on *Honey, I Shrunk the Kids* (I didn't catch any of the detail), I looked at his eyes, crinkled with laughter, and I knew

408

exactly what I was going to do. I didn't even think about it. Well, I did, but only for the brief moment or two between catching his hand, turning it over slowly between mine, and looking from it to his startled face. That was when I thought 'Am I really going to do this?' and then 'Yes, I am,' and I placed one hand very gently on his cheek, stood up on my toes and kissed him.

His hands closed on the small of my back, and that's all the detail I remember. The rest was a blur of happiness, proper actual happiness, a perfect kind of honesty and nothing to confuse or distract it. The whole world was in that kiss, everything that mattered.

He pulled back just enough to rub his nose gently against mine. 'Poppy-flower,' he said in a low voice and my heart thudded once. I felt him smile as his arms wrapped tighter around me, and he tilted his head back to kiss my forehead. My fingers explored the ridges and hollows of his shoulders and back, and his eyes were on me then, searching my face as though for some new feature, some strange difference or sign that this was not happening. It was happening, so I kissed his nose to prove it.

'You know, I was going to wait until I put the trainer on your foot,' he said with a broad smile, 'to see if it fit.'

'You were thinking about kissing me tonight?'

'I've been thinking about kissing you for three months, Poppy,' he said, as his fingertips traced lightly across my hairline and down to my collarbone. I shivered slightly at the touch, at the low growl of his voice and the shock of his eyes on mine. 'But no, I don't think I would have worked up the courage tonight.' His fingers were tangled in my hair then and I pulled him closer.

'Damn it,' I groaned as we heard keys scratching around the lock of the front door and Nick's voice on the other side of the door, loudly recounting some incident with passport control in Liechtenstein.

'The ugly sisters,' whispered Jon, and we pulled apart as Rachel walked in the door.

'Now, children, what do we have here?' said Rachel, instantly suspicious of how close we were standing to one another.

'Jon is dressing me,' I replied as he reached for my sleeve again and she raised an eyebrow. 'I got wet accidentally.'

'Behave, Poppy, have you been skiing into people's swimming pools again?' She seemed mildly disappointed.

'No, unfortunately not,' Jon answered her. 'It would be a long jump from the nearest patch of snow to the Elena pool these days. No, no, she smelled really bad, so I threw her in. You should all thank me,' he added, dodging my fists.

'Ugh, yes, I can imagine.' Rachel made a face. 'How was the Gerda, Pops? All you dreamed of and more?'

'Don't.' I shuddered. 'I still have a whole day of it tomorrow, oh, joy.'

'But in the meantime,' Jon interjected, 'Poppy is taking me to the Hirsch for lots and lots of beer to thank me for putting her out of her smelly misery.' He looked sideways at me. 'In a way of speaking.'

I pretended to scowl at him. 'You really are determined to test the limits of my gratitude, aren't you?'

'Gratitude for what?' asked Rachel.

'Jon is my hero,' I explained. 'Yes, Jon, you are still my hero for now, but don't push it. He cleaned out the Gerda bin room this afternoon, you see. It was grim and now it's sparkling. Like magic.'

Rachel looked at him in awe. '*Jon*,' she breathed, '*big* respect,' just as her phone started to ring. 'Bollocks,' she muttered, expecting Gina, then brightened up when she saw the Caller ID on her screen. 'Oh, it's Mikey. Hello, Pumpkin.'

I looked at Jon. He was watching me, his face inscrutable. I wanted more than anything to take his hand and vanish into some convenient shadow and make the rest of the world disappear for a while. Much as I love Rachel and Nick, I really wanted them to be anywhere else in that moment so that I could be lying on his pillow, everything else forgotten. There was so little time, and suddenly a whole world of ways I needed to know him better.

'Can we get away from here?' murmured Jon in a low voice.

His little finger touched against mine and sent a rippling shock

410

through my body. I nodded quickly, urgently.

'Yes, let's go. We...'

'Hey, Pops?' Rachel cut in. 'What do you know – hypothetically – about chlorine gas?'

'Err...' I searched my brain, '...that it's fairly poisonous? Killed lots of people in the Great War?'

'I mean, more practically... you know, *descriptively*.'

'It's green?'

She turned back to her phone. 'Yes, yes, it's green. Uh, huh. OK, do that. And quickly, I should think.' She hung up. 'Poppy, I think we should go to the staff chalet now.'

She marched out the door. Nick, Jon and I stared after her.

'Is she serious? Do you think she's serious?' I asked no-one in particular as I began to follow her.

Jon snorted in response. 'Gina probably swallowed some pool water or something,' he said resignedly, handing me a trainer as he followed me out to the hall.

'Or accidentally melted her *faux*-nytail on a candle and has been poisoned by the fumes, perhaps?' I suggested, crouching down to tie the shoelaces. Jon smiled, but when I stood up to say goodbye, he was staring out the open door with a frown in his eyes, preoccupied. I touched his arm and he looked back down at me. 'You OK?' I smiled, hopeful.

He nodded quickly, his hands on my shoulders. 'Yes,' he said and kissed me briefly on the lips, but his eyes were still lost in the same thought and his gaze was intense. 'Poppy, can we...'

'Poppy, are you *inventing* the shoe?' Rachel's voice drifted impatiently in the door.

'Hey, you'd better go,' said Jon, lightly, kissing me again. 'You've been summoned.'

'Never a quiet moment, eh?'

He smiled back, but the smile was one of disappointment. 'Let me know how it goes.'

'I will. And I'll come back as soon as I can,' I promised, squeezing his hand.

Rachel took me by the arm and we marched down the hill. I

tried to listen as she explained about the latest drama to hit the Club Hotel, but I was really just thinking about Jon's hands and eyes, his chest and lips warm and pressed against mine, and I was holding the sleeve of his hoodie to my face to hide from her a smile that I could not suppress.

But really, chlorine gas, Poppy. Very serious. Focus…

Actually it was pretty serious.

It turned out that New Robert had been in a bit of a hurry to clean the leisure centre this evening (it was a Seventies-themed closing party in town and he was going as an ABBA member) and so he didn't really pay attention to what chemicals he poured into what buckets. Somehow the chlorine mix for the pool ended up in the same bucket as the toxic acid stuff for unblocking the drains. I wouldn't pretend to be an expert on the chemical composition of any of the stuff involved, but when the bucket basically exploded with green gas, I don't think I would have done what New Robert did, which was try to soldier on with the mopping regardless. After about four minutes, he said his eyes were 'stinging a bit,' so he opened a window. After about six minutes, he began to think that perhaps this room-filling-with-smelly-gas business might be a very, very bad thing, and started to get scared that might get in trouble so, in a panic, he tipped the whole bucketful into the pool (cue massive green toxic gaseous explosion) and ran out, locking the door behind him and hoping that by the time anyone went back in there, the whole sorry mess would have dissipated.

Unfortunately he was feeling rather unwell at this point, which was a bit of a giveaway. He made it back to the staff chalet bathroom and locked himself in, but three minutes later he was coughing and retching uncontrollably. The rest of the staff became understandably alarmed, and phoned the first person they thought of – Rachel, inexplicably – to check whether New Robert might maybe need to go to the doctor's or something.

'The hospital! The hospital!' shrieked Carol, arriving on the scene at the same time as us. 'Not the local ambulance, he needs a bloody helicopter, *argh!*'

She was on hold to the emergency services at this point and

was staring daggers at her mobile phone. New Robert looked up from his prostrate position on the bathroom tiles and had the stupidity (or maybe he was delirious) to moan a little about not being sure if his health insurance covered this.

'Health insurance?' Carol roared at him. 'You're going to die, you little twat. Shut up this instant!'

The local ambulance arrived at that moment. Carol practically threw New Robert onto the stretcher and informed the two paramedics in swift, no-nonsense German that not only were they going to drive to Täsch Hospital immediately, and not the local surgery, but that she was coming in the ambulance too. They didn't attempt to argue, which was wise.

Rachel volunteered the pair of us to follow the ambulance down to the hospital in the resort's bright orange rental van.

'And of course we'll nip into the McDrive on the way for a choccy milkshake. Result!' Rachel whispered gleefully to me, totally oblivious to my utter lack of enthusiasm and strong desire to be somewhere else entirely at that exact moment. She clapped her hands, then looked at me and mistook my expression for something it probably should have been, and she qualified her words. 'Well, not for New Robert, ahem. Yes, of course I do hope he is OK.'

5.37am. Reschengel.

New Robert is OK. The staff on call at Täsch Hospital last night had never actually had to treat a case of chlorine gas poisoning (another victory for Brits abroad everywhere) but they got him onto a nebuliser quickly and he is doing well. They estimated that his exposure was not enough to do permanent lung damage, but they are keeping him there under observation for a couple of days.

All of that got sorted out in the first hour or so, but we got stuck in Täsch hospital for a further four hours because Robert was right: apparently someone at Snowglobe Recruitment in the UK forgot to sign him onto the company health insurance. This caused a tangle of bureaucratic wrangling, the details of which I

413

would rather forget (except to note with some bewilderment that there are in fact people who think it wise to persevere in an argument with Carol. Amazing).

We only just got back to Reschengel. Obviously it's too late to meet up with Jon now. I sent him a text message at about midnight to keep him posted on the endlessness of the waiting-room tedium. His reply was brief and to the point: 'Heading in to town for a little while. Call if you get back soon, or see you tomorrow.' I replied an hour ago to let him know that we wouldn't make it, and I've heard nothing since.

Trying not to imagine what he might be doing or not doing at this moment. I blame James for my newfound loathing of text message conversations, (or more specifically, the silence between them and its unpleasantly wide spectrum of possible interpretations). Can't get to sleep.

Tuesday 24 April
10.42am

The absolute worst thing that can happen just after the sudden dawning realisation that you are hopelessly in love with your best male friend (and, more specifically, after you have just taken the initiative to…well, *jump* him) is that circumstance separates you from each other for an extended period of time. This is because of all the creatures in the animal kingdom, humans have the most phenomenally highly-tuned sense of unnecessary drama, and the unique ability to take the most straightforward of situations – including the most rational of other people's behaviour patterns – and work themselves up into a state of panicked conviction of imminent doom.

Or maybe that's just a female thing. I'm not sure.

In any case, I woke up this morning with the niggling feeling that something was very wrong. First, I was utterly convinced that the events of last night had been a dream (of the vivid, cheese-before-bed kind), but then New Robert's empty bed did away with

414

that idea. Then, playing it over frame by frame, I realised that I couldn't swear to the fact that Jon had actually kissed me back by choice, and not (oh, horror) as some kind of shocked reaction. Because, after all, the absence of any more than that one irritatingly functional text message from him could mean that he was having very serious second thoughts about it all, couldn't it? What had he actually said? And his body language as I was leaving – had he seemed happy? Perplexed? Perhaps something even worse, e.g. alarmed, panicked, repulsed or horror-struck? It took perhaps eight minutes of over-thinking along this vein to come up with a very definite conclusion: *What the ghastly hell have I done??*

I stared at my silent phone, willing it to beep at me, suddenly very, very afraid that I had made a big mistake last night, that I had misread him and that he might then, at that exact moment, be lying in his bed wondering how best to extricate himself from this situation and/or find the best hiding places in Reschengel to avoid me for the next two days.

My cheeks flushed with anger – not with him, but with myself. *Jon would never let me down, I know that. He would never hurt me, but would he have chosen this? Did I give him the choice?*

I held my breath as I walked from my bedroom into the kitchen, wondering if he would be there. He wasn't. I procrastinated over breakfast, wondering if he would arrive, but he didn't. I took this as a very bad sign, swallowed a cup of tea to suppress my nerves (it didn't work) and resolved to go and wash the Gerda skirting boards to distract myself until I heard from him.

I resolutely did not waver as I walked past his door on the way up the hill. I didn't even look at it, but reassured myself with every empty step that it would all be OK. *I'm going home in two days. It's fine. It will be fine. I shouldn't have...but whatever. It doesn't matter. It won't matter, soon enough.*

And then I rounded the last bend and he was there on the steps of the Gerda, engrossed in an Italian newspaper, wearing an expression of profound confusion (largely, I imagine, because he doesn't read Italian) with the familiar coffee cup and paper bag from the *Bäckerei* by his side and a bread roll of some description in his hand. I hesitated a moment, watching him, smiling as relief flooded through me and I accepted at last, finally, the happy simplicity of justified faith in a man that I knew without question I would always love.

'That's not a *pain au chocolat*,' I said and he looked up from his newspaper to me. 'And you're not in your ski gear.'

'You're right,' he smiled back, 'it's not. And I'm not. The times, they are a-changing, you see. Venison sandwich.' He waved it at me, very proud. 'Want a bite?'

'I try not to before midday, generally.'

'Very sensible. They say it's a slippery slope.' He was on his feet and gathering me up in his arms. 'And anyway, I have plenty more of it to feed you later. Tilly gave us five kilos of the stuff. How about venison stew for dinner tonight? Would you like that? Or, if not,' he hesitated, and suggested, looking doubtful, 'venison salad?' I made a face. 'OK, good, I thought that would be weird but I am thinking of your scurvy, Miss Poppy-flower. How about venison fajitas?'

'Venison sushi?'

'Do you think that would work?'

'No, Jon. Not in any way. But venison stew gets a resounding "yes please."'

'Good answer,' he smiled and kissed me again. 'It's the only one I have any idea how to make.'

'Does it have potatoes in it?'

'Yes, it does.'

'Mmm, now you're talking. I haven't had a stew in years, and I think I'll need it after today.'

'There's still a lot to do in there, isn't there?' he said, nodding in the direction of the chalet.

'Nothing difficult, just washing windows, skirting boards, light fittings, that sort of thing. Then a bit of final sign-off paperwork with the various property owners and a meeting with Gina at five, where I sign over the Gerda and try to avoid being press-ganged into ghost-writing her end of season report. Rachel has been working on her excuse for about a week. I might have to resort to drastic measures, like crying.'

'No, you won't, said Jon with sudden firmness, frowning his determination. 'You have no business writing anything of the sort. You're leaving on Thursday, remember?'

Like I could forget.

'So just hand over the keys and tell her that you have finished your job and that you're very sorry but there is no time left to do hers for her. Tomorrow is yours to enjoy with your friends, and tonight you're having dinner with me, and that is that. No further discussion necessary.' His serious face invited no dissent, but his voice was soft. 'I'll tell her myself if necessary.'

'No need,' I said, my hand on his cheek and he smiled again, 'no need. I'm yours tonight, and that's a promise. I'll tell her that she will have an angry Viking to answer to if she tries any funny business; that should do the trick. Now, off you go, up the mountain. What time will I come over to yours later?'

'Actually,' he said, releasing me from his arms to pull a piece of brightly-coloured cloth from his pocket and tie it around his head, 'I'm trying something new today. It's called "Extreme Window Washing."'

'No,' I laughed but shook my head. 'You're not.'

'Yes, I am.'

'No, you're not. It's so good of you to offer, but you've helped me loads already. I'll manage the rest really quickly on my own.'

'And so with two of us, it will be done in a matter of minutes, leaving most of the afternoon to sunbathe on the terrace. I hope you brought a bikini.'

'No, Jon.'

'Even better.'

'No, I mean, *no*. Go up the mountain with Nick and Head. It's a beautiful day, go skiing. There's so little time left.'

'Exactly my point,' he said lightly, but his lips against my forehead were hard and urgent, 'exactly my point. Let's get started.'

'You got that headscarf from Tilly, didn't you?' I said as the

417

door swung shut behind us.

'Yes, it's her lucky cleaning scarf. How did you know?'

'An educated guess, Jon. It's a Nicole Farhi.'

'A what?'

'Never mind.'

Wednesday 25 April

11.38pm. Happy Bar.

Happy Bar closing party is in full swing. It's strange to see this normally quiet, out of the way little place crammed full of non-Snowglobe season workers (and especially strange to see people actually swinging from the rafters. Apparently that's not just an idle turn of phrase). A vague rumour of "one-euro shots of anything" went around resort in the past few days (Rachel thinks she might have inadvertently started it) and it was that which lured everybody here tonight. However, in a victory for wishful thinking everywhere, Pieter is honouring the promise and enthusiastically dispensing triples and quadruples. The speakers are thumping out another one of his endless Nineties grunge playlists, and all the non-regulars are wondering why on earth they haven't been coming here all season.

By rights, I should be utterly beyond repair by now too. Today was my last full day in Austria, and since nobody else from Snowglobe leaves until Sunday, they have been happily concentrating their full energies on drowning me in alcohol as punishment for my early departure, safe in the knowledge that they will get to sleep off their hangovers all day tomorrow and will not, for example, be expected to endure a car journey for three hours to bloody Klagenfurt with bloody James.

Sadly, though, their best efforts all day haven't had much effect. That knot that has been twisting and twisting in my stomach at the prospect of tomorrow and everything it means has somehow turned into an alcohol-siphoning gremlin, and no matter how much Stroh 80, Jägermeister and toffee vodka they try to pour down my throat (and it is measurable by the litre at this point), it's just not quite managing to get through to me. I've been trying all day – from pootling on the sugary slush of the melting piste to dancing on tables on the empty sun terrace of the Moose – to spend my last day completely here, in mind and body, and not there, in the too-easily imagined future of suits and BlackBerrys and waiting for the Tube in uncomfortable shoes. Yet although the party is raging around me, somehow I am already on

419

the aeroplane.

'*Swing low, swayyyyt CHA-ri-OHHT…*' Another paper cup lands on Arthur's head, sitting across from me. 'Alright, Scotland? Sco*t*L*AND?*' Gav's voice booms from the next booth and the paper cup is followed by a handful of beermats. Arthur casts his long-suffering eyes to heaven. Scotland lost to England in a recent Six Nations match, and, by gum, Gav is making sure that we all know about it. 'Domination, mate, just embrace it. God *save the Queen! THE EMPIRE!*'

Arthur is impervious. 'I don't even like rugby,' he says, shrugging and taking a sip from his beer.

Almost everybody is here tonight, a rare turnout of the Snowglobe staff, wedged into, onto and around the booth, excitedly exchanging plans for the coming months as the pitchers and shakers of shots flow. Tilly and Mark are sitting with Odysseus and Maria, Fritz's daughter, talking about Vienna in the summertime. Against all odds (and to everyone's amazement, including theirs) Maria and Odysseus hit it off on their arranged date and are now planning to spend most of the summer together. Tilly and Mark are going to visit them in Vienna for a couple of days on their one-month rail trip around Europe before Tilly begins at Durham University.

Mikey, meanwhile, is deep in conversation with Tom, Arthur and Eoghan, laying plans for Glastonbury in a couple of months' time. I haven't overheard much detail, but from what I gather there is some sort of a business proposition at work involving a vintage VW camper van and a very large quantity of nitrous oxide balloons. I'm not sure I want to know.

Gina and Tina are sitting up on the seat backs behind them, arms linked, with one eye on the passing talent as they chatter excitedly about next winter and how Tina is going to come back as a rep next time.

'A rep! Get me, a ski rep!' she giggles.

'Oohey!' says Gina, clasping her hand. 'I'm so excited, T, finally, someone I can rely on. We're going to have such a good time, eh?'

'Grr! You better believe it, G! It'll be just like my Ayia days! Just you wait for my bar crawl. Hello, boys!' They both cackle.

Miranda is here somewhere too; I have just seen her pass by. She stopped for a moment on the way through the crowd to introduce me to a boy with improbably voluminous wavy hair in snowboard pants so baggy the crotch was scraping the floor.

'Yah, hi, I'm Max,' he said, shaking my hand.

'You're a ski instructor?' I asked, nodding at the jacket he was still wearing in the sweltering bar.

'Yah, yah, fully. Just got my BASI Level one today, actually.'

'Congratulations, that's fantastic.'

'Yah, thanks. Feeling good, yah, big relief. Massively celebrating now, of course.'

'So anyway, Pops, Max was just buying me a drink, I believe?' Miranda cut in, raising her eyebrows at him. 'Want one?' she asked me.

'No, thanks, I'm OK,' I said. 'You two go ahead.'

She hauled him to the bar without further ado.

A flash of glittery yellow sparkle catches my eye and I spot New Robert and Harry in the DJ box behind the bar. Robert is back from death's door, I can report with some relief. He arrived in Happy Bar with Mikey and Arthur at about ten o'clock this evening, straight from Täsch Hospital and already in his bright blue, red and yellow bare-chested Spandex ABBA costume. He knew it wasn't a theme night tonight, but he was 'cheated, robbed, I tell you' of the prize for Best Costume on the night of his chlorine gas incident, and he said that he'd be damned if all those sequins were going to waste. Robert won't commit to which of the two ABBA men, Benny or Björn, he is meant to be, and nor will he let Rachel draw a moustache and beard on his face in permanent marker, but he has promised me that if his voice is OK and can persuade Pieter to turn down Nirvana for a few minutes, he'll do a rendition of *Super Trouper* on the karaoke mike in my honour that will 'knock your flippin' socks off.' Then Harry suggested that he do it *against* the Nirvana backing track and Robert seemed pretty taken with this idea. I can't wait.

But first things first: it's my round now. It was agreed that a nice refreshing Jäger-bomb is just the thing, but as I meander to the bar through an almost impenetrable sea of swaying but otherwise immovable Diamond and SuperSki chalet hosts, mentally counting up how many cans of Red Bull I will need, I am suddenly reminded of the one person who isn't here, the biggest Jäger-fiend of them all: Carol. I had hoped that she would show up eventually, but it's almost midnight and there is still no sign of her.

I suppose I shouldn't be surprised, not after the conversation we had earlier this afternoon on the chairlift up to Ristis, but I am disappointed in her stubbornness.

'So,' Carol began as we pulled the bar down. The tone of her voice put me immediately on edge. Her eyes were narrowed in that way that makes Tina babble nervously and drop things in her haste to get away.

'So?'

'You're really going tomorrow, aren't you?' she said levelly.

'Yes. I fly out in the evening,' I said lightly. 'James is driving me to Klagenfurt. Ghastly prospect, no?'

She ignored me. 'And your last day in Reschengel,' she said, 'how has it been so far?'

I smiled a little and looked away. 'Bittersweet, I think.'

'Bittersweet,' she repeated, still staring at me.

'Yes.'

'And why's that?'

'Oh, you know,' I said, fixing my gaze across the valley at the opposite peaks, the south-facing snowcaps glistening with meltwater in the hot April sun. 'It's going to be a hard place to leave. It's been a great time here. I'm really going to miss everyone. But, you know, "all good things," eh?'

'"All good things" what?'

'You know, end.'

'End?'

'Yes, end. Cease to be. Change. Come to a conclusion. We move on.'

She regarded me coolly for a long moment. 'So what you're saying is that, by definition, everything and everyone that makes you happy is temporary, and that only the mediocre or downright miserable has got staying power?'

'No, that's not what I…'

'Actually, Poppy, that is exactly what you are saying.' She looked away from me to the chairlift ahead of us and silence fell between us. 'You're a coward,' she said suddenly, 'and a fool.'

'I beg your pardon?' It took a moment for my irritation to catch up with her audacity. 'How dare you judge me?' I felt my anger rise with every word. 'My plans for *my* future are absolutely no concern of yours.'

'I'm not judging you, I'm just saying that you're being weak.'

'Weak? *Weak?*'

'Yes.'

'Weak,' I sputtered, tumbling over myself in furious indignation. 'You don't have the slightest idea what you're talking about, Carol. Weak is the last thing you could accuse me of being. I have made a commitment to this job and I am seeing it through.'

'That's what I mean.'

I shook my head, baffled at her logic.

'You have never once spoken to me about your life in London, Poppy, did you know that? Not once.'

'Yeah, well, out here it's pretty far removed from…'

'You have talked to me about everything else in your life that matters. I know you, Poppy. And I know that with the exception of the unfortunate James Walker, you don't actually have an off-switch on any other subject. This led me to conclude quite some time ago that the reason behind it is one of two things. Either you're dreading going back, or you're ashamed. But it's both, isn't it?' She watched me open and close my mouth, saying nothing. 'And all the more since you threw Jon's offer back at him. They really own you, don't they? You've made your bed; now you're afraid to get out of it.'

'How can you say that makes me weak? Do you not realise that it's taking every ounce of my strength to do that, to leave him?'

423

'I do realise that.'

'I know exactly what the next few years is going to be like: bloody hard work and no play, that's what. How can you say that makes me a coward? Do you not think it would be infinitely easier and less miserably lonely to just stay here?'

'No, actually I don't,' she said calmly, holding my eye. 'It is evidently easier for you to hide behind the unavoidability of some imaginary obligation to yourself than it is to accept that there could actually be a different kind of life for you. You'd rather rush home and sign a contract to bury yourself in mindless work for the next three years than have the imagination to work out what other path there might be. And *that* is weak.' She shook her head with an exasperated sigh. 'You're running away, Poppy. And you know the stupidest part of it all? You're not running away because you're miserable, but because you aren't, and you seem to think you should be. If you can think of a way to explain the fucked-up-ness of that logic to me, go right ahead.' The chairlift was coming into the top station and we lifted the bar. 'Until then,' she threw over her shoulder, 'forgive me for just being straightforward disappointed in you. And for thinking that you have absolutely no courage whatsoever.'

I had no opportunity to answer her, skiing down the off-ramp of the chairlift to where the others were waiting and babbling excitedly about the helicopters circling over the Schaufelspitz, where it looked like an enormous wet-snow avalanche had just come down. Nor did I get the chance to catch her later and finish the conversation. She didn't stay long after that, just told us that she was going to give the Moose a miss because she had some things to take care of in the village and that she would see us later, but she is not here, and I have had to accept that she is not coming.

Pieter spots me standing at the bar and, without a word, slams a bottle of whiskey and two shot glasses down in front of me.

'So! Your last night, eh? Let's drink to the end of an era, what do you say?' He pours us both a large shot and looks around the bar. 'Or should we say "to freedom, at last"?'

'You're glad to be leaving?'

'You're not?'

'Not really, no. So you're not coming back next season, then?'

'To this shithole? Ha. Are you kidding? No, there's no point.'
He slumps across the bar, pretending not to look over my
shoulder to the packed booth where Rachel is perched on Nick's
knee. 'There's nothing for me here but this shitty job, and I'm
done with it now. I'm going home for good.' He shrugs and
looked at me. 'This isn't real life here, is it? It's just time off. I'm
going back to Amsterdam to get a real job. And you're doing the
same in London, yeah?' He raises his whiskey glass. 'Here's to
growing up, eh? We all have to do it someday!'

I drink the shot with him and he wanders off without another
word to find eighteen large tumblers and pour seventeen
Jägermeisters.

'To absent friends!' toasts Arthur, back at our table, reaching
forward to nudge the line of shot glasses into a domino slide into
the Red Bull. Everybody cheers, reaches for a glass and sinks the
frothy mess of sugar, caffeine and alcohol in one, shouting out the
names of fallen comrades, Karl, Dylan, Isadora, Antonia, Dick the
Chef, Joseph and Suzanne, as they slam the empty glasses back
onto the sticky table.

'And the resort van!' yells Rachel and everybody but Gina
makes explosive noises.

Jon squeezes my hand. 'How are you doing?' He looks at me
closely and frowns a little.

'Not so well.' The whiskey was a bad idea. I hate whiskey. I
was only drinking it to be polite, and now I feel slightly ill. I need
to get out of this bar, into the fresh air. I need to think straight.
'Take me home,' I say in a low voice that only he can hear. 'Please
take me home, Jon.'

Thursday 26 April

12.17pm

My eyes were closed as we sat on the steps of the staff chalet, my head on Jon's shoulder. We said nothing. His fingertips trailed lazily up and down my back, as we listened to the distant sound of a lawnmower. The sun was getting high in the sky as midday approached, but the air was still cool in the shade. It smelled of cut grass, and the smell confused my senses: a sudden flash of a thousand summer days as a child, yet strange, unfamiliar and out of place here in this context, where until so recently the air smelled only of ice and diesel smoke.

The stone steps underneath us were cold. I shifted slightly, uncomfortable. They would warm up quickly once the sun moved past the gables and shone directly on them, I knew, but I also knew that by then, I would be gone.

We weren't talking about that, of course. We were studiously not mentioning the obvious elephant in the corner (or elephant-sized pile of belongings, more specifically) but were sitting there for all the world like today was just another lazy day in a sleepy village, with no expectation of change nor desire for it.

'Will it snow again, do you think?' I asked idly, opening my eyes and looking at the blue sky with some doubt.

'Hard to say, really,' replied Jon. 'Up high, yes, probably. There's usually a late-season dump in May. But in the village it will just rain.'

'Will it be good snow up high?'

'It can be. Gets better the higher you go. But the lifts are usually shut by then, so it's all walking the whole way up.'

'Oh. Hard work.'

'Yes. Very. You'd have to really want it.'

'Hmm.'

We fell silent again and in that moment I longed more than anything for him to get to his feet then and say, 'right, Poppy, come on, time to get going, it's getting late,' and for it suddenly to be just another of those mornings when we would head off up the mountain, Jon making purposeful plans and my ears ringing with the names of the mysterious and dangerous-sounding places he was taking us to, my scalp tingling in anticipation of turning these place-names into experiences and memories: 'Rufigrat,' 'Nordhang,' 'Schindler Couloirs,' 'Kuhtälli' and all the others.

But not today. There was too much missing: the snow on the street, for starters, and our ski gear, the paper bag from the bakery, the bitter taste of strong coffee, the feeling of excited expectation, the thrill of possibility and the simple, endlessly wonderful awareness that this (*this!!*) was our normal life.

All that was over now. In its place, there was nothing but the clock to watch, because my bags were packed and eleven-thirty was coming and that would bring James to take me away. I turned my face into Jon's shoulder and breathed deeply, as I had done over and over in the restless hours last night as I tried and tried to quieten the thoughts that were chasing sleep from the room, until Jon's hand tilted my face to his and with one look cut away all the accumulated layers of words, leaving behind only the simple fact that tomorrow would be goodbye, proper goodbye. There was a depth of sadness in that moment that I could have lost myself in. More than sadness, actually, because once everything else had been stripped away in that unsettling silence of night-time, I found that at essence, my sadness was not the simple negativity of regret but a horrible stab of sudden uncertainty about all of the basic assumptions upon which I had built my picture of the future, all the protective explanation and sensible rationality, and I found myself wondering for the first time, properly, finally, if I was making a mistake.

'I'm sorry,' I whispered without thinking, and wondered if he could hear my voice fray a little at the edges.

'I know you are,' murmured Jon. 'I just wish so much that you didn't have to be.'

My eyes filled with tears and he pulled me close, stroking my hair as I clung to him. He held me like that until I drifted off to sleep.

Fortunately, there was no time for more tears this morning. I had left my packing until the last minute (naturally, and in spite of all experience to the contrary, assuming that the process could only require an hour or so, tops) and in a panic, had no time to contemplate any deeper mystery than the physics of matching volume of stuff with capacity of luggage. On the positive side, this made the many goodbyes I had to say a good deal easier than they might have been. Instead of the long, drawn-out, emotional series of farewells and promises to stay in touch that I had been dreading, everybody just stood around drinking tea and laughing at me sitting there on my bed, looking despairingly at one suddenly very compact-looking suitcase. I shooed the lot of them out the door with orders to go up to the park and enjoy it before it melted into afternoon slush.

I have no illusions about just how far we will all scatter now, all around the world and across every conceivable walk of life. One of the beauties of this season lifestyle is the incredible variety of people it attracts, but the flipside of this is that most of us share very little common ground outside of a love for the mountains. From living in each other's pockets to the lives of distant strangers, soon we'll be united only by shared memories of a brief time in a little Austrian village, high in the mountains. I can only hope there will be the occasional chance to meet up again, although with only a few exceptions, I can scarcely imagine where or when.

So then, finally, there on the steps, with the zips of my bags straining but intact and my poor, neglected old snowboard propped listlessly inside the front door, sacrificed for space and abandoned – I mean, *donated* – to lucky discovery by some future seasonaire, the clock crept noiselessly up to half past the hour. There were only three goodbyes left to say. One of them was sitting beside me, holding my hand, while the second lurked in the chalet kitchen wooing her hangover with tea and HobNobs and pretending as resolutely as we were that this was just another morning. And then there was Gina, who nobody had seen nor heard from so far that morning, but I wasn't worried about missing the chance to see her one last time. I had a sneaking feeling she was saving her appearance for when James got here, when she would come hurtling through time and space like an iron filing to a magnet to deluge me with an effusion of kisses and promises to be friends *forever.*

Three more goodbyes to say, just three, but two of them would be the hardest of all. I knew that I still had some reserves of panic to focus my attention on if I needed some convenient distraction to get me through (I mean, I still had Ryanair's baggage weight restrictions to contend with at Klagenfurt – oh, financial pain) but for the moment I waved that and all other considerations of goodbye to the side of my brain and just sat there by Jon's side, looking at the windowboxes of the opposite chalets and the slivers of still-snow-capped mountains between them, feeling blank although not in a contented-silence sort of way. The choice was made and I was exhausted with it. I laid my head back down on Jon's shoulder again. He squeezed my arm.

A familiar figure appeared on the road then, striding up the hill in the sunshine, shoulders hunched against an imaginary cold wind. He turned down the garden path toward the chalet. 'Alright,' said James, starting up the steps.

There was a slightly awkward pause as I took in the at once familiar and unfamiliar face, and tried to remember what I was supposed to do then. 'Yes, err, James, this is Jon,' I said, gesturing between them, somewhat pointlessly.

James nodded quickly. 'Yeah, I think we've met before, actually. Jon Berner, isn't it? How are you doing, mate?'

Jon nodded at him.

James looked at me. 'So. You all set then, Connors?' he asked lightly, shifting his weight from foot to foot.

I watched him for a long moment, taking in everything about him – his clothes, his facial expression and his body language, wondering with detached amazement (and even some amusement) how this stranger could be the same as the James I had once thought of as mine. I turned to Jon. He half-smiled and raised his eyebrows. *Time to go, then.*

We both stood. James went to pick up my ski bag. 'Jesus, Poppy, is there a corpse in here?'

'Not yet,' said Rachel darkly.

I turned around. She was standing behind me.

'Right, right,' she said, crisp and businesslike, taking me by the shoulders, 'come on then, let's make this quick, OK?' I nodded obediently. 'You're really going, aren't you?' she said suddenly, and I blinked a couple of times, surprised – of everyone, Rachel had never pushed this question with me. I hesitated, thrown, and she sighed. 'Right, I'll take that as a "yes." I thought so, but I figured I might as well check.' She glanced over my shoulder at Jon, then back at me. 'So, anyway, the way I see it…well, here's the thing: this isn't really goodbye, not really, because when I phone you from Sweden in a few weeks, you'll definitely be in Anti-Climax Central, what with the Irish weather and the whole *the-rest-of-the-world-went-on-without-me-all-this-time* shock, and so according to my calculations, you'll be ripe pickings for persuasion to come to Sweden for a little Scandinavian holiday in June, *ja?* I nodded, lifted by the idea. 'Good. Hopefully by then, Nick and I will have found a place to live with lots of couch space so everyone can come and stay at the same time. Otherwise we'll be staying at Nick's mum's, and a big reunion in her place may not go down so well.'

'I'll learn the Swedish for "campsite" just in case, shall I? Best not to offend Mamma Svedberg. I've heard she's terrifying.'

'Don't I know it. She has ordered us to come and stay with her as soon as we get to Sweden. You'd better believe I'll be swotting up on my Swedish table manners before that. I've already got Nick to write down every swear word he knows so that I can make sure not to sneeze the wrong way and accidentally call her a prostitute's arse or something.'

James cleared his throat at the bottom of the steps and we all turned around. He looked up at me from under his brow, his head bowed over the mobile phone in his hand, and tapped his watch. I turned back to Rachel and she smiled resignedly. 'Right, enough chat. We'll talk on the phone soon enough anyway. Come here. Take care of yourself.' She hugged me tightly. '*Nu säger jag adjö*, right? I will see you very soon. And you can call me any time,

OK? Don't forget, Poppet, *du har mig,* so don't go getting all depressed when they work you to the bone and you start fantasizing about freewheeling your Boris Bike into the River Tha…'

I had stopped listening. *Du har mig.* I could see his face again; feel his hands in my hair and the cold, crisp air on my tear-stained cheek. '*Du kommer alltid att ha mig,* Rachel,' I heard myself whisper before I had time to think. 'That's it, that's what I was trying to remember. What does it mean?'

Rachel opened her mouth and closed it again. Her eyes flicked over my shoulder to Jon and she looked like her heart was breaking. She gripped my arm, harder than I was expecting. 'Pops, look, I know you know what you're doing,' she said urgently, and I wasn't sure if it was a question, or if there was more coming, so I waited, watching her, and she looked back at me, then Jon, then me. She released my arm and pulled me into a brief hug. 'Goodbye,' she whispered, squeezing my hand very tight. 'I'm going to miss you.' She dived into the chalet without another word.

Jon picked up my suitcase and we walked toward the top of the steps. 'Are you sure you have everything?' he asked. I looked around and nodded. 'OK, I'll carry this to the car park for you.'

I knew that it would be easier to say goodbye there, at the chalet. I had just started to tell him that when, sure enough, Gina appeared in a burst of pink exuberance with a loud call of 'Ooh! I thought I might have missed you!'

I turned to reply to her, but she wasn't talking to me. She was descending upon James with a blue plastic crate of paperwork and mobile phone boxes, yapping excitedly about her end of season report and her return of inventory.

'Yeah, alright Gina,' James answered her tonelessly. 'Look, my hands are full now with Poppy's gear, so it'll have to wait.'

'Oh, don't worry, James,' she cooed, 'I'll carry it all down to the car for you. So! What's new with you? Anything exciting?'

'I'm driving to Klagenfurt. That's about the extent of it.'

'*Klagenfurt!*' she gasped, as though this were news to her. 'That's

431

a long drive, isn't it?'

'Yes.'

'Mmm. Yah. I drove to Venice from here once, you know. That was really far.'

'It would be.'

'Mmm. It was. Have you ever been to Venice, James?' He shook his head. 'Oh, James, but Venice is so beautiful, so *beautiful*,' she gripped his arm, her eyes bulging with sudden eagerness. 'Why don't I take you there sometime? Road trip! What fun! Remember our trip to Innsbruck?'

'How could I forget?' he said, drily.

'Haw, haw, Poppy, you should have been there! Poor James didn't know what hit him!'

I believed her.

'Oh, you,' she swiped playfully at his chest, 'you know you love my iPod really. You try to deny it, but you *lurrrved* it. I'm your guilty pleasure, aren't I?'

'Hardly,' he muttered, staring studiously at his phone.

'I saw your fingers tapping the steering wheel to that Britney track! Haw, haw, haw,' she guffawed. 'I did, Poppy, I did, you know.'

'Right then, Connors, it really *is* time to be off, I think,' James called up to me, slightly desperately. 'You all set?'

'Yes, I…' I looked around yet again, '…I guess so. Yeah. That's it, isn't it?'

I looked at Jon and he nodded, but I hesitated another moment, unsure. It was only when James cleared his throat for the second time that I realised they were all waiting for me to move.

Is this really it, though? I wondered. The street was silent, empty like the chalets that lined it. I glanced over Jon's shoulder at the perilous balcony and the kitchen window but the staff chalet was silent too. There was nothing left to happen, I realised, but that didn't seem true; it didn't seem *possible* that Rachel would not come bounding out with something *amazing* to report, that Mikey would not appear and take me by the arm to show me the latest development of the boys' extreme bumboarding track, or that my phone would not ring with some new disaster or other to sort out.

And then I looked back at the faces watching me and I knew that there would be no phonecall; I didn't have a company phone anymore, nor a uniform. I had given it all back. And all my goodbyes had already been said. All that was left to do was say the last and hardest one of all.

Jon's hands were on my waist then, and against my forehead I felt the warmth of his chest through the soft cotton of his battered old t-shirt. I closed my eyes, knowing that when I opened them it would be time to go.

'Call me when you land in Ireland,' he said softly in my ear. 'I just want to know that you made it home safely, OK?'

'I'm going to miss you,' I whispered into his shoulder, and I held him tightly as my imagination leapt upon the words I had just spoken and began to pull me through all the lonely places where they would be true and, with a lurch, showed me how it would feel there, starting with James' car, then the airport, the plane, the baggage belt on the other side, and then the drive home, and the months ahead, and the telephone conversations where I would hear Rachel's news from Sweden and all the plans for the approaching winter, and a whole mental picture of a life going on without me. 'Jon, I'm...'

'Don't be sorry, Poppy. You shouldn't be.' He smiled down at me. 'Be excited about your new start instead, hey?'

I nodded, but all my imagination had to offer on that front was the inevitable greyness of a London winter, of being alone again in the unbearable crowds of the morning commute, of finding a new place to rent for a few years, yet all the while knowing not to get either too attached or too disillusioned with any of it because of the get-out-clause I constantly reminded myself of; that McIntyre, London and my whole life there was only a stepping-stone. But a stepping-stone to what? Some imagined future happiness whose shape I could not make out in the shadowy haze of possibility but whose fulfilment I hoped would taste a little like this feeling I was just beginning to understand.

And in that moment I finally grasped what it was that I was

doing: I was setting off on a long, long road, all alone, hoping to some day get back to essentially the moment I was leaving. In a sudden flash, the possibility that I might never make it back filled me with horror. *I may never see this face again.*

'You're right, Jon, I shouldn't be sorry,' I said, 'and I wouldn't be if it was the right decision.' The threads of uncertainty began to weave together, tighter and tighter. I was back on that snowy bank above the Elena swimming pool and I was afraid to look down, except the difference was that this time I was holding Jon's hand and I didn't want to let it go. 'If it was the right thing to do, I wouldn't be so scared, would I?'

'Scared?' He blinked, unsure.

'Scared,' I nodded.

'Good scared or bad scared?' His eyes were suddenly intense, almost afraid; his fingers pressed a little into my back.

'Bad scared,' I whispered.

Jon didn't move, not even a twitch, just regarded me for the longest moment. 'Are you sure, Poppy-flower?'

James did not take kindly to the news that he had driven all the way to Reschengel for no reason. I did try to point out that my change of heart had a net benefit, in that it saved him the much longer round-trip to southern Austria, but he wasn't inclined to appreciate the half-fullness of the glass just at that moment.

'You're joking.' He stared at me for a full twenty seconds, his face a mixture of disbelief, impatience and irritation. 'You do realise that the company has paid for your flight and that it will not be paying for another one?' I did. 'I don't fucking believe this,' he spat, looking around him, incredulous.

I didn't know what to say. I felt a little bad about it, but not as bad as I might have, all things considered.

'Poppy!' cried Gina, laying a gentle hand on James' arm. 'What you are suggesting would be an enormous waste of James' time. I'm sorry, but that is just not on. He is a *senior member of Snowglobe management.* Now you will just have to…'

'Oh, fuck this,' snapped James, throwing off Gina's hand with a violent jerk. He dropped my ski bag to the ground, turned on his heel and strode off down the garden path, onto the road and out of sight. I had the distinct feeling that I would never see his face again, and I was surprised to find that the thought made me a little sad.

Surprised, because I had vaguely expected that some day my feelings on the subject of James would catch up with Rachel's anger and that I would eventually have that same desire to Show Him! (Waving fist etc.) Rachel never could understand why I had not unleashed a world of abuse at James that afternoon in the Mondschein, and why I had shown absolutely no interest in trying to punish him thereafter. Eventually, she stopped suggesting dastardly schemes. This morning, I finally understood it myself, watching him stalk away. It had never been worth the effort because it hadn't been one single thing he had done that had caused me pain; it was the person he was and would probably always be. It would have satisfied nothing to watch him put on a show of remorse that he did not have the emotional generosity to feel. It was better to just draw a line under the whole sorry affair.

The drawing of said line I completed finally without actually noticing. When Anna dropped into conversation on the phone the other day that Elisa and James had parted company rather permanently and would not be remaining friends, I didn't ask for details. I was rather pleased to find that I didn't really care to know.

I realised then, watching him leave this morning, that long after I have forgotten what his hand once felt like in mine and why I ever wanted to hold it, long after I have forgotten the sting of losing him and the shock of seeing the insignificance of the time we shared through his eyes, he would still be that same man, inflicting greater or lesser pain on those who came next. I didn't hate him and I knew that I never would; instead I felt horribly sad about it all, because short of something personality-altering, he would always be that same rock of selfishness that people broke themselves against, trying to hold on to. I wanted in that moment to run after him, to catch his arm and pull him back from that future, tell him *it's not yet too late* and show him some kind of mirror in which he might see himself as I had once seen him – a person with so much going for him; a man about whom there was so much to love and care for, if only he could realise that all he had to do was understand how to deserve it.

But it was not a lesson he could ever learn from me. The friendship we had had would never outgrow his months of thoughtless, indifferent disrespect and my profound disappointment in him. It was gone, stamped underfoot, and the waste, such as it was, was all his. I let him go.

'James! Wait!' squealed Gina, picking up the blue plastic crate and scurrying after him. She vanished around the corner, her voice trailing behind her. 'Wait, James! Wait for me!'

We stared after her in a slightly dazed way, then at each other. I opened my mouth to say something – I have no idea what – but a voice behind us made us both jump.

'Oh my *actual* God.' Rachel bounded across the porch towards me. 'SHUT UP to the power of fifty-three, *you-did-not-just-do-that.*' She gasped and threw her arms around me and spun me around, squealing, 'I love you, I love you, I love you, *I love you*,' then gripped my face between her hands and turned to Jon, squeezing my cheeks between her palms so hard that I struggled to breathe. 'I love this girl,' she said, matter-of-factly. 'I love her.'

'Well, you're not the only one,' he said sternly, removing her hands from my face and replacing them with his. I smiled up at him, startled once again by the warmth in those crinkled, ice-blue eyes. I felt my heart thud once, hard against my ribcage, amazed to realise that I never had to leave this man, and even more amazed to think that until moments before I had actually thought I could.

'I love you too, too,' I whispered.

'EPIC!' Rachel roared, squeezing us both into a vice-like hug and then running back inside the chalet to grab her phone from the kitchen. '*EPIC!* I have to tell someone. Carol? Carol, hi. You most emphatically *will not* believe what Poppy has just done.' She paused and burst out an incredulous 'how did you know?' and looked down onto the street and at the balconies of the nearby chalets as though Carol had us all under surveillance. 'Yes, yes, he's here with her now. I know, but...' She turned to me. 'Poppy, Carol says that you have no follow-through whatsoever. She's very proud of you. *Oh my God*, though, Carol,' she went on, 'you should have seen it, it was just...' and wandered off into the chalet.

Jon's hands were on my waist, my shoulders, my face, my waist again. He didn't know what to say, but kept looking at me and holding me as if to be sure that this whole scene and the promise of everything I had just said was real and really happening. I kissed his nose once, twice, until his serious face broke into a broad grin. He was still holding me very tight. I think he knew that the choice was made, but he couldn't quite believe it and he wasn't taking any chances.

Sunday 29 April

1.14pm. Reschengel Bus Terminal.

'No, Rachel. Just no. I'm putting my foot down.'

'Why? What have you got against ice-skating?' Rachel folded her arms and pouted, but Head was not caving.

'Nothing,' he said, 'except that it is of course a completely crap sport, but my real objection is that those ice-skates cost you and Poppy less in the supermarket than the weight of carrying them in the van all the way to Sweden is going to cost in diesel. And look at the van.' We all looked at it, its belly scraping on the gravel. He did have a point. 'Do you really think that there is room in there for any unnecessary crap?'

Head had taken the news of the addition of two girls to the camper crew surprisingly well, even enthusiastically, (and even more enthusiastically when he was told that we four would be sleeping out in tents) but that was before he saw how much extra stuff two girls would bring to the equation, and now he was in something of a grump.

'Head, I hardly think one little pair of ice-skates is going to make that big a difference.'

'They are non-essential.'

'Non-essential! To you, maybe. I'm very attached to them.'

'How many essential ice-skating experiences do you think we will have between here and Sweden?'

'How many essential sombrero experiences do you anticipate?' she retorted.

'Rachel!' gasped Nick, taking the sombreros from her. 'You can't be serious. I can think of at least four situations where these sombreros may well save our lives.'

'And who's to say the ice-skates won't?'

'How?'

'Think like MacGyver,' she said mysteriously. 'The ice-skates stay. They won't get in your way, I promise. Here,' she reached for a door handle, 'I'll chuck them in this...'

'No! That's the...'

'...bathroom,' finished Jon, diving in at the last second to

438

steady a tower of cardboard boxes before they fell on a hapless Rachel. 'Head, what is all this?'

'What?'

'Head…'

'Err, schnapps.'

'All of it? How many bottles are here?'

'Forty, I think. Possibly more. Don't look at me like that, Rachel. It was a gift. I had to accept it or Fritz would have been offended.'

'So instead of a bathroom, we have forty bottles of schnapps.' She raised an eyebrow. 'Do not even talk to me about the weight implication of a pair of ice-skates.'

'Come on, come on, let's leave it for now,' interrupted Jon, shooing us all out the door. 'The coach is about to leave.'

The driver had closed the luggage doors of the staff coach and was wiping his hands on a rag as he walked around the bonnet. Moments later, the engine shuddered to life.

Gina was flapping around the front of the coach, trying to simultaneously talk on her phone, do a head count and gather everybody into a group at the bottom of the steps. 'Yes, yes, Anna, we're on the way,' she barked into her phone, grabbing Arthur by the arm and pulling him back down the coach steps, 'come on, come on, everyone…seven, eight, no, *nine*, no, eight…or… Shit! One, two, three…'

'Do you think if we went and got lunch, they'd still be here when we got back?' said Carol.

'Are you not going on the coach with them?' asked Jon.

'Are you joking? Twenty-nine hours of *that*?' Carol jerked her chin in the direction of Gina, who was at that moment reading out her list of Coach Journey Dos and Don'ts while various staff members made bids for freedom: 'Do remember to keep your seat-belt fastened at all times and your armrest down. Do not…Mark!'

'I'm just going to the vending machine for…'

'Get back here now! Where was I? Do not smoke in the toilets. In fact, Gunther has said that you are not to use the toilets at all unless it's for, you know,' she paused and said in a loud whisper, *"'Number Ones...'"*

Carol smirked and ground her cigarette into the asphalt. 'No, not a chance. I'm driving the rental van back down to Täsch and then taking a train to Chamonix.'

'Chamonix? Are you not going back to the UK?'

'No, I'm meeting someone in Cham. My...well, my ex-husband, actually.'

'What?'

'It's a long story. Anyway, best be off. See you all in the winter. Be here by first lifts in November, OK?'

And just like that, she was gone.

'Not even a hug,' said Rachel wistfully to the back of the orange van as it screeched off down the valley road.

I gave her a look. We both gave in to a fit of the snorting giggles at the idea.

'Goodbye, Rachel, Poppy, boys!' called Miranda, waving as she struggled up the coach steps with the most enormous handbag I have ever seen.

'Goodbye, Pops,' said Tilly, blinking back tears as she hugged me. 'I do so hope we shall meet again. You absolutely *must* write and tell me how Chile goes, and the season next winter. Oh, I envy you so!'

'I envy *you*. Have a wicked time on your travels. Take lots of pictures. And you, Mark, let me know how the job search goes.'

'Will do. Fingers crossed I get an interview for the one in Durham. But, hey, there's always Snowglobe if I'm stuck for something, eh?' Tilly gave him a dark look. 'Or not,' he added hurriedly with a grin at Rachel and me. 'Well, we'll be out to Reschengel to visit anyway,' he promised. 'New Year's maybe? Depends on work, but we'll be in touch before then.'

'What is this?' came Gina's screeching voice, and everybody looked up. She stomped down the coach steps, holding something large, round, fuzzy and white: Snowli the Rabbit's head. 'Who is responsible for this?' Mikey, Arthur and Eoghan ducked their heads low. She scowled at them, then at her watch and made a high-pitched noise. '*Ohmygod* we are going to be so late if we don't leave this *instant*. Come on! All of you, in, NOW. I will not have Anna and her staff thinking that we can't keep to a timetable. Get on the coach, Harry, Mikey, Robert, come on. Tina! Where's Tina? T, I saved the front seat for you. Arthur! Get back here now and onto the coach. Now, let me see. Where is...? Ah, yes.' She spotted us and strode over, gripping Snowli's head by the ears. 'Here, will one of you be a dear and get this back to Kerstin at the ski school office?'

'Sure, Gina, no problem, absolutely,' said Head diving forward and taking it from her with a happy grin.

'Oh, thanks, Björny, you're a star,' she said in a honeyed voice and turned to us. 'Sweeties, have a safe trip, mwah, mwah,' she air-kissed us all as a group. 'See you next winter!'

And before we knew it, the coach was off. Its doors hissed to a close as it started to roll forwards, and with a puff of exhaust fumes and a flash of two pairs of buttocks on the back window (Eoghan's and Mikey's, I'd put money on it) the coach disappeared around the corner and out of sight.

And with that, we were alone in an empty coach park. The sleepy village of Reschengel lay nestled in the valley up to our left. Green meadows, broken only by a few brave slivers of brownish white snow where pistes were being maintained, rose into grey-black mountain peaks, many of them still capped with patchy snow. The glacier at the distant end of the valley glistened in the afternoon sun and nearby we heard the rushing torrent of the river swollen with meltwater. Flowers were pushing through the grass and the birds were singing. Spring was here. It was time to go.

Jon's hand in mine pulled me gently towards the van but my feet were heavy with a sudden wave of déjà vu. I had never before been in the Alps at this time of year, but the green meadows and the muffled harmony of cowbells and church bells were all strangely familiar, somehow. 'Hey, Rachel, you know what I like?'

'What, Poppy?'

'Raindrops on roses.'

'Oh, no,' she said, following me up the van's steps as Jon shut the door behind us, 'no, you don't.'

'No, really, I do. And whiskers on kittens.'

'How do you feel about bright copper kettles? And warm woollen mittens?'

I shrugged. 'Ah, you know. But brown paper packages tied up with string… You know, I feel the strongest urge to tell you all about it.'

'Through the medium of song, perhaps?'

'Is there any better way?'

I cleared my throat and Head slammed on the brakes. He turned to look at us.

'Poppy, Rachel, if you sing one line of that song between here and Sweden, I will eject you and your ice-skates from this van without hesitation.'

'*Fine*,' I sighed, picking myself up off the floor of the van. 'You're the driver. Anyway, that's not even the song they sing at the end, is it Rachel? Hey, what is that song? Does anyone know? You know, when they're going up the mountains to cross into Switzerland and it's all sunny and summery?'

'I don't know,' said Jon distractedly, 'but I do know that *we're* not supposed to be going up the mountains. We're supposed to be going down the valley, Head. So why are you taking us up the road toward the pass? Is it because you are having difficulty driving in that rabbit head?'

'No, it's surprisingly light, actually, although it does smell of sausage. No, this is the right way. Nick, did you not tell them?'

'I thought you were telling them.'

'Telling us what?' asked Rachel, looking at me. I was as baffled as she.

'Well, you see Nick and I had an idea this morning,' explained Head, his rabbit ears bobbing earnestly in the rear-view mirror. 'It's sort of last minute, I know, but have any of you ever been to the Black Sea?' We all shook our heads. 'Well…?'

Jon looked at me. 'What do you think, Poppy?'

'Why not?'

'Err, Head,' said Rachel in a small voice, 'is the Black Sea Russian? I mean, do we absolutely have to cross any, err, Russian borders?'

'No,' said Head slowly and with great suspicion. 'But we might have to if we decide to take an overland route to Sweden. Why?'

'Well, I doubt it'll still be an issue…'

'Rachel?'

She sighed. 'OK, well, there was this time a few years back when I was on a train from Moscow to St Petersburg with my mate Lindsay, and we thought – as a joke right – that we would pretend to be in a Bond movie and…well, it's a long story, and the plastic-cup-and-string thing would take ages to explain, but, well…basically we got deported.'

'What?'

'And told never to return.'

'*What?*'

'Yeah I know, no flippin' sense of humour, those guys. Though actually Linds did make jokes about us being MI5 when they were questioning us, which, to be fair, was not the best idea. It took us about five hours to convince them that we were not really British Intelligence. Intelligence! Imagine!'

'It's certainly not a word I would apply to this story,' I said drily.

'So you're *persona non grata* in Russia?' asked Nick.

'Yeah, I suppose so,' said Rachel. 'Well, they might have forgotten. But we'll have the ice-skates to defend ourselves with just in case, eh, Pops?'

She nudged me with her elbow. I leaned into the cab. 'Head, please do not take us further east than Romania.'

'Right. Romania it is.'

I kissed the top of Jon's head and he turned around to look at me. 'Hey, Jon? Is Bratislava on the way to the Black Sea?'

'It can be, why?'

'I have a Brillo pad with Joseph's name on it.'

'Poppy, let it go.'

THE END

Wish there were more?

There is! Visit www.warandpiste.com or find us on Facebook at
www.facebook.com/WarAndPiste where you can do all sorts of
fun things like read deleted scenes, share photos and stories from
your own mountain adventures, leave a
glowing/scathing/hilarious review or just say hi to the author,
who would love to hear from you.

ACKNOWLEDGMENTS

I've got two pages for this. Get comfortable.

Big love to my wonderful parents who have supported this project so enthusiastically from the very beginning. Thank you. You are both seriously brilliant. To my sisters, Liz, Sarah and Laura, thank you for lending a hefty dose of your collective awesomeness to the making of this book. From plot continuity to design advice, typo-spotting, general encouragement and…I'm going to stop now before you send me a bill. Suffice to say, legen…wait for it… Tomster, you are also a legend. So is your face. (Yeah! I did! I went there!) Max, your eyebrows are a source of inspiration to me.

Maura R, thank you for your common sense, foresight and belief in me. I have never forgotten you. I hope that some day I will get to share this and many more stories with you.

To my fantastic friends who read early (i.e. horrific) drafts of *War & Piste*, thank you for being so brave. And to the many more who offered support and encouragement along the way – thank you, thank you. I really hope you have enjoyed the outcome as much as I enjoyed writing it. In particular, thank you to Ryan, whose immense kindness, patience and spearfishing talent I will never forget, and to Mitch, for some very brilliant suggestions. Thanks also to Trine Bregstein for sustained enthusiasm and those really helpful final edits.

To Hannes at Tom Dooley's in St Anton, I'm pretty sure the idea for this book was born in your pub. It is definitely where Poppy prevailed upon me to use her name for our heroine, something I suspect she has lived to regret several times over. Thank you on behalf of all Nasserein seasonaires past and present for those memorable Jäger Nights.

If I had known that evening years ago what I now know, would I have just ordered another Jäger and laughed off the idea? Probably. I'm very glad I did not know. Agent Lucy, thanks for believing in this book at exactly the time such faith was required. And thanks for all your hard work.

Huge thanks also to Anna Lewis and the team at Completely Novel for really useful guidance and for providing a brilliant community space for all writers to share ideas and feedback at www.completelynovel.com.

To the inspirational team at TRAUDL, your energy, enthusiasm and friendship has meant the world to me. 'Thank you' doesn't really begin to cover it, but let's not get gooey. Let's go skiing.

To the artists whose work I am honoured to have as part of my book: Christina Hägerfors, your brilliant cover artwork brought the book and website to life – thank you so much. www.christinahagerfors.com. Grace Chao, you saved the day! I heart you! You are a good friend and a great talent. I am forever in your debt. Thank you. www.gracechao.co.uk. Fabulous Freya Harrison, thanks for adding your brilliant piste map illustration to this book. No-one will ever get lost in Reschengel again! www.freyaharrison.com. Jon Smith, thanks for designing a wicked website and for being very cool throughout the process. www.studiosmith.co.uk. And to Rachel Alexander, our cover girl from sunny Zermatt – thanks for your deckchair chillin' skills, pretty lady. Thanks also to Tom Bainton for turning the random bits of film into something so very cool.

To our design reviewers, thank you for sending us down the right track: Seb Brown, Chris at the Big Kick, Dominique Broomfield, Irena 'Tick' Péchon, Judy King, Gaby Appleton, Arzu Rezvani Webb, Nell Boase, Philip Stevens, Debbie Daldry, Audrey Cook, Shazanna Karim, Rebekah Billingsley, Jana Bakunina, Oliver Walter (who almost doesn't deserve this acknowledgment but in the interests of equality is getting one nevertheless), Jeff Binder, Tara Moore, Michelle Blake, Alice Courtney and the lovely Lindsay Haig. Thanks also to Janicke Svedberg for her Swedish language expertise.

Very many thanks to Ben Blane, Alice Aldridge, Libby Finch, Sarah Curtis, Georgie Dart, Geraint Jones, Helen Lascelles, Dave Hanney, Dan Raven-Ellison, Menah Raven-Ellison, Will Henley, Jonny Milligan, Tom Bury, Andy Loble, Leza O'Flaherty and Ed Taylor for promo advice and invaluable help with spreading of the *War & Piste* love generally. Thanks also to Zoe Symington, St Anton's weathergirl and *Chalet Girl* celebrity, and to Tom Davies, our man in Havana (Chamonix). Special shout out to Liz Adams to whom I'm especially grateful, not just only her enthusiasm for *War & Piste*, but also for introducing me to one of the great loves of my life (baked camembert) and alongside Al, helping me work through the 'Bof' haze with about eleven flavours of Risoul's finest rum. Good flippin' times.

To Zack and the team at Natives, who do an outstanding job of looking after season workers and to whom I owe my first job – cheers! www.natives.co.uk.

To the many brilliant friends across the Alps with whom I have worked, hiked, skied, aprésed and partied until dawn, whose backcountry lunacy I have photographed and whose stories of adventure and misadventure I am very glad I was there to share – it is the literal truth that this book would not exist without all of you. Thanks for lots and lots of great times (and for the occasional floor/sofa/vacant luxury chalet – much obliged). To the resorts of St Anton, Lech, Zürs, Saas Fee, Zermatt, Verbier, Grimentz, Zinal, Grindelwald, Engelberg, Andermatt, Tignes, Val d'Isere, Meribel, Courchevel, Chamonix, Morzine, Les Gets, Risoul-Vars, Alpe d'Huez, Serre Chevalier and Montgenèvre – thank you for facilitating said great times. Please remain as wonderful forever: www.respectthemountains.com.

To Matt, for his remarkable tolerance of a fixation with snowclouds that borders on the unhinged. And for lots more besides.

And finally, to the four badass schnee and Jäger fiends who refused point blank to let this go. Pops, Al, Blue and Polly – this one is for you.

Lightning Source UK Ltd.
Milton Keynes UK
UKOW032026131212

203648UK00014B/485/P